HEAVEN IN HIS ARMS

LISA ANN VERGE

ZEBRA BOOKS
KENSINGTON PUBLISHING CORP.

ZEBRA BOOKS are published by

Kensington Publishing Corp.
850 Third Avenue
New York, NY 10022

First Printing: April, 1995

Printed in the United States of America

MORE THAN DESIRE

"André . . ."

"Be quiet and let me kiss you."

He kissed her. Ah, the kissing. She'd never get enough of this, never in a hundred years. The sweet, hard merging of lips and bodies and souls into one— so pure, so powerful, overwhelming her senses so she could not think—*this* was lovemaking, *this* was the meaning of the feelings that had surged in her from the moment they'd met. When the kiss was done, she clung to him as if the earth had fallen away beneath her feet.

She pressed her cheek against the warm curve of his neck. Her heart pounded hard in her chest. She wrapped her arms around his wide shoulders and waited for her body to stop trembling. His breath, fast and hot, warmed her hair just behind her ear. "It's useless, isn't it?" he said.

"What is?"

"Fighting you." Hungrily, he kissed the line of her jaw. "I'm damned tired of trying to swim upstream against the rapids."

She arched her neck, giving him access to the tender skin of her throat, but he wanted something else. He kissed her again, nudging her lips apart, tracing the line of her teeth, seeking the warm, honeyed recesses of her mouth. She surrendered herself to him, tilting her head at his urging, opening her lips wider. His caresses were magic, pure and heady, swirling a fog in her head until all she could think about was lying with this man under the open sky and giving him anything—anything—he demanded. . . .

TODAY'S HOTTEST READS
ARE TOMORROW'S SUPERSTARS

VICTORY'S WOMAN   (4484, $4.50)
by Gretchen Genet
Andrew — the carefree soldier who sought glory on the battlefield, and returned a shattered man . . . Niall — the legendary frontiersman and a former Shawnee captive, tormented by his past . . . Roger — the troubled youth, who would rise up to claim a shocking legacy . . . and Clarice — the passionate beauty bound by one man, and hopelessly in love with another. Set against the backdrop of the American revolution, three men fight for their heritage — and one woman is destined to change all their lives forever!

FORBIDDEN   (4488, $4.99)
by Jo Beverley
While fleeing from her brothers, who are attempting to sell her into a loveless marriage, Serena Riverton accepts a carriage ride from a stranger — who is the handsomest man she has ever seen. Lord Middlethorpe, himself, is actually contemplating marriage to a dull daughter of the aristocracy, when he encounters the breathtaking Serena. She arouses him as no woman ever has. And after a night of thrilling intimacy — a forbidden liaison — Serena must choose between a lady's place and a woman's passion!

WINDS OF DESTINY   (4489, $4.99)
by Victoria Thompson
Becky Tate is a half-breed outcast — branded by her Comanche heritage. Then she meets a rugged stranger who awakens her heart to the magic and mystery of passion. Hiding a desperate past, Texas Ranger Clint Masterson has ridden into cattle country to bring peace to a divided land. But a greater battle rages inside him when he dares to desire the beautiful Becky!

WILDEST HEART   (4456, $4.99)
by Virginia Brown
Maggie Malone had come to cattle country to forge her future as a healer. Now she was faced by Devon Conrad, an outlaw wounded body and soul by his shadowy past . . . whose eyes blazed with fury even as his burning caress sent her spiraling with desire. They came together in a Texas town about to explode in sin and scandal. Danger was their destiny — and there was nothing they wouldn't dare for love!

Available wherever paperbacks are sold, or order direct from the Publisher. Send cover price plus 50¢ per copy for mailing and handling to Penguin USA, P.O. Box 999, c/o Dept. 17109, Bergenfield, NJ 07621. Residents of New York and Tennessee must include sales tax. DO NOT SEND CASH.

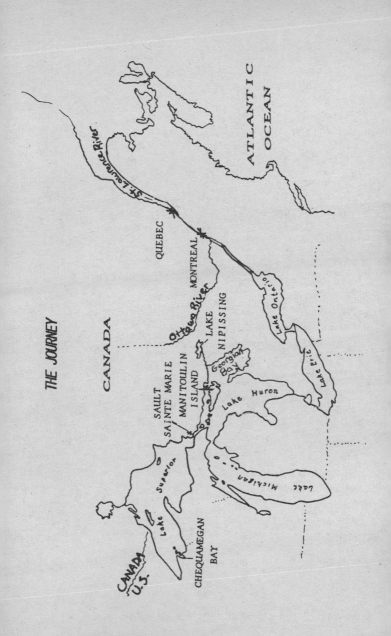

THE JOURNEY

You asked me for seeds and bulbs of the flowers of this country. . . . [There are] none here that are very rare or very beautiful. Everything is savage here, the flowers as well as the men.

—Marie de L'Incarnation
Québec, 1653

Prologue

Paris, July 1670

This was her only chance.

Genevieve Lalande clutched a bundle close to her chest. She straightened against the wall and merged her silhouette with the shadows. The dampness of the stone seeped through her thin woolen dress and chilled her skin, already clammy from fear and anticipation. She dug her fingers into the bundle. She had come this far. All that was left was to pass the guard at the end of the hallway, and she would be *free*.

The distraction had already begun. A slip of a girl emerged from one of the doorways that pocked the hall. With a flash of white legs, the sylph raced toward the dozing female guard and seized her arm. The guard started from her nap, staring at the wild-haired creature with glazed eyes. The young girl, a deaf-mute, pointed frantically toward her room. Cursing, the stocky woman hefted herself out of her seat, grasped a sputtering candle, and lumbered after the thin wraith.

As the guard disappeared into the chamber, Genevieve launched herself through the hall, her bare feet swift and soundless, her gaze fixed on the dull gleam of the high oak doors, one of the last remaining barriers to freedom. She would have only a few moments before the guard realized that the young woman's unspoken fears were imaginary—the crazed ravings of a simpleton, the sleep-befogged guard would think—and then the old laywoman would shrug them off and return to her dozing.

The brass handle chilled Genevieve's hand. She eased the door open to prevent the hinges from squeaking. When it was cracked enough, she slipped through and edged it closed behind her.

She leaned for a moment against the outside wall, sucking in the humid night air as she waited for her heart to stop pounding in her ears. As the soft breeze filtered around the building and cooled her skin, Genevieve listened for pursuers. Shifting her bundle, she murmured a prayer of eternal gratitude to the deaf-mute who had aided her in her plans. Then she put it behind her. She had no time to waste—she was already late. If she didn't hurry, her second accomplice would lose courage and destroy all their well-made plans.

Peering around the corner of the building, she scanned the enormous courtyard of the Salpêtrière. The night was clear but moonless. Bits of smooth, flat gravel scattered the meager starlight, making the courtyard glitter as if it were covered with frost. There was no sign of her accomplice, but she didn't expect to find her waiting like a lost child in the middle of the open courtyard. She glanced at the debris scattered at the opposite end, where the church of Saint Louis was being built between the two long buildings of the Salpêtrière. There was no better place to hide and wait but among the hewn stones, the piled earth, and the skeletal wooden scaffolding on the site. She was certain she'd find her accomplice there.

Genevieve turned the corner and clung to the walls as she worked her way toward the site. Sharp chips of gravel bit into the callused pads of her feet. A night breeze swept through the open courtyard, heavy with the ripe stench of rotting refuse that rose from the nearby Seine River. She glanced up at the rows of windows in the opposite building, winking at her like a thousand eyes, then stumbled and bit back a curse as she kicked an abandoned pick. The tool clattered loudly on the gravel. Her bare toe smarted. She squeezed her eyes shut until the pain passed. Then she limped on until she reached the shadows of the scaffolding.

She shifted the weight of the bundle to her other arm, tensely awaiting the appearance of someone from the darkness. Her accomplice must have heard her stumbling in the dark—the clatter of the pick against the gravel had been loud enough to wake the dead. As the minutes passed and no one emerged, Genevieve worked her way through the debris and began to search. She followed the curve of the church, its wooden dome just beginning to take shape high above the masonry, then circled each pile of stones and peered around the tumbled stacks of wood and earth.

Marie Suzanne Duplessis was not there.

Genevieve clutched a support of the wooden scaffolding. A splinter pierced her skin. Marie should have been here by now. The last note Genevieve had sent her was specific: Tonight was the night they were to meet in this courtyard to complete the plans they had made over the last three weeks. She and Marie had been passing notes back and forth through the same system without fail for too long for there to be a sudden mix-up.

Somewhere in Paris, beyond the walls of the institution, churchbells rang. Genevieve counted each discordant resonance and scanned the courtyard. *Come, Marie. Come.* She hugged her bundle more tightly, stepped over a pile of wood, and edged along the shadows of the construction. She startled a bevy of sleeping birds into an anxious fluttering of wings. A slow stream of silt filtered down from the higher scaffolding, dusting her shoulder. The sleeping birds settled, and she continued her careful course to the other side of the unfinished church.

Amid the fading clangor of the churchbells, a figure emerged from one of the buildings. Genevieve pressed back against the masonry. If one of the guards saw her, all would be lost. But as she watched the figure enter the courtyard, she knew it was no guard. It was a woman, a young woman by the quick pace of her walk, an anxious woman by the way her head pivoted back and forth, by the way her hands darted out of her cloak and curled into its neckline. As the woman headed toward the debris around the church, Genevieve knew it could be no other than Marie.

Genevieve intercepted her near a pile of bricks.

"Marie?"

The young woman stopped short and pulled back the edge of her scarf, revealing a pale, drawn face. She peered in Genevieve's direction as she stepped into the starlight.

"You are Genevieve?"

"Oui. Come into the shadows."

Genevieve scrutinized the woman as she approached. She had never seen her as close before today. She noticed with relief that they were of the same height. Of all characteristics, height would have been the most difficult to disguise.

"Thank God you are here . . . I feared you would leave." Marie loosened her headrail and pulled the scarf off her hair. "The *gouvernante* on my floor would not fall asleep, and I was forced to check three doors before I found one unlocked."

Refined speech, Genevieve thought, shifting her bundle under one arm. Well, she could mimic that well enough. "You need not have feared. I would have stayed until dawn."

Marie peered at her face in the darkness. "I have never seen you before."

"Nor I you." Genevieve didn't bother to explain that she was housed in a separate building, isolated from women like Marie. Marie was a *bijoux*, a jewel of the Salpêtrière, an orphaned daughter of the petty nobility, pampered and educated and protected from those like herself. "There are hundreds of other women in the Salpêtrière."

"You write with such a fine hand," Marie murmured, glancing at Genevieve's common russet wool skirts, "that I thought you might be one of the noblewomen."

Genevieve's lips tightened. In another time, in another world, she might have been worthy of being called a *bijoux*. But that was long ago and best left forgotten. She gestured to Marie's skirts. "Is that what you planned to wear tomorrow?"

"Yes." Marie parted her cloak to show a glimpse of a dark blue traveling dress. "I've packed a small case and left it by my bed. In it, you'll find what you need to disguise yourself, several other dresses, and

Lisa Ann Verge

a few gold *louis*. This is all I can give you for what you are doing for me.''

''You should have kept the money,'' Genevieve argued. Such foolish, innocent generosity. ''You'll need it more than I will.''

''I couldn't. I owe you a debt greater than gold.'' Marie twisted her headrail in her hands. ''You do know what you're doing, don't you? I couldn't live with myself—no matter how happy I'd be to escape my fate—if I misled you.''

Genevieve dumped her bundle on a pile of bricks. ''*I'm* the one who suggested this plan.''

''I'm going to be sent away,'' Marie continued, ignoring Genevieve's words. ''King Louis XIV himself has dowered me. He has paid my passage to some horrible place called Québec''—her breath hitched in her throat—''and he intends to marry me off to some coarse, rough-handed settler . . .''

''I know you're a king's girl.'' Genevieve snatched the mangled headrail from the other girl's hands, then shook it out to judge its fit. Every year since Genevieve had arrived in the Salpêtrière, dozens of girls of all social classes had been dowered by the king and sent off to the Caribbean islands or to the northern settlements of New France, to marry and settle in the colonies. ''I chose you *because* you're being sent away from this place.''

''Haven't you heard the rumors? Don't you know anything about . . . Québec?'' Marie's smooth white hands, bereft of the headrail, knotted and twisted and pulled at each other. ''The forests are filled with red-skinned savages. The winters are long and frigid, and there's so much snow that it tops the rooftops.'' Her voice wavered. ''And the voyage—over the sea— halfway across the world, in storms and sickness . . .''

Genevieve expertly snapped the headrail smooth. "Have you changed your mind?"

"Oh, no, no!" Marie clutched her hands to her breast. "It's just . . . why are you doing this? Why would you take my place and go to that dreadful colony and leave all this behind?"

Genevieve glared at the two long buildings of the Salpêtrière and thought, *I'd rather sell my soul to Lucifer than spend another year in this wretched place.*

She bit her tongue to repress the retort. Marie wouldn't understand. She and Marie both lived in this "charity house," but they lived in entirely different worlds. Marie lived in the Salpêtrière of King Louis XIV; the charity house that succored aging servants with no pensions, old married couples of good birth, and the younger daughters of impoverished petty nobility; the charity house staffed with religious women and headed by a benign Mother Superior. Genevieve lived in a place ruled by brutal guards, a place peopled by orphans and waifs and beggars and whores taken forcefully off the streets of Paris. Since the day she herself had been captured, three years ago, she'd found no charity in this house—only an eternity of hunger and drudgery.

A hundred times, as she scrubbed and rung and batted linens by the Seine, she had considered escaping by racing toward the nearby gates of Paris and losing her pursuers in the maze of streets she knew so well. But she was also aware of what awaited her in those streets . . . those streets she knew too well. Nothing had changed. She was the same girl the police had seized from the courtyards of Paris all those years ago, except that she was three years older and wise enough to know the fate of a nineteen-year-old left alone without means in the streets of Paris.

And now, this Marie Suzanne Duplessis offered an escape far, far better. Marie offered her a new life— *her* life. But Genevieve knew that trying to explain her reasons to this *bijoux* would be like trying to teach a blind man to see. Marie had never tasted a stolen apple. She had never raced through the streets of Paris after cutting a nobleman's purse, fearing hunger more than the threat of capture and punishment by whipping. Marie would never understand the forces of utter desperation.

"I'm . . . I'm surprised Mother Superior didn't recommend you to the king himself," Marie continued when Genevieve did not answer. "I've been told she's having difficulty finding enough girls of . . . of modest birth to fill the king's ship to Québec."

"I'll make a better marriage disguised as a Duplessis than as a Lalande," Genevieve argued, folding the headrail and laying it upon her bundle. "Because of your birth, you'll be put aside for the wealthiest men in the colony."

"I see." Marie cast her gaze down. "I didn't think of that."

You wouldn't, would you? You with your good birth and your sheltered upbringing and your ignorance of the harshness of the world. Genevieve wondered whether she'd have grown up with the same wide-eyed innocence, if the world had been kinder, all those years ago.

"But of course, it makes perfect sense. How very sage of you." Marie's hands fluttered white in the starlight and she released a nervous laugh. "I almost didn't dare believe. . . . When I found your first note among my laundered shifts, I was sure someone was playing a trick on me. *None* of the girls want to go to this dreadful place. The halls echo with their sobbing, as if tomorrow they'll all be executed in the square."

Fools. Fools who don't know their own good fortune. "You will do this, then?"

"Yes. *Yes.*" Her face lit with joy. "I received a note this morning. François is waiting for me, just inside the gates of Paris."

So that was his name, Genevieve thought, the name of the French Musketeer Marie loved enough to risk everything to marry—even the displeasure of the king. For this woman's sake, Genevieve dearly hoped he wasn't like the other strutting, shifty-eyed Musketeers she had known in her younger days. In their blue coats and gold or silver braid, they had terrorized the city, taking whatever women pleased them and pulling their swords at the slightest provocation.

"Then we mustn't delay any longer." Genevieve nodded to Marie's cloak. "Take off your clothes."

The young woman started. "Here?"

"Quickly."

Marie glanced up at the skeletal scaffolding of the church and crossed herself. "What am I to wear? I can't escape in your clothing."

Genevieve waved at her bundle. "You'll wear the clothing of a *gouvernante*—a black wool skirt, a white coif, and a black mantle. Dressed as a governess, you can leave the Salpêtrière without being stopped."

"Where did you get it?"

"Hurry."

Genevieve unlaced her bodice, tugged it off, then slipped out of her coarse russet wool skirt. The night was warm and balmy, and the breeze toyed with her tattered shift as she stuffed her old clothes beneath a pile of bricks. She scrutinized the girl more closely as Marie fumbled with her laces. Marie's tresses were long and chestnut-colored. Genevieve's own hair was a mass of copper, a gift, her mother had once told her, from the father she had never known. Marie's skin was smooth, while Genevieve had a sprinkling of freckles across her nose. Problems, she thought, but nothing that couldn't be overcome by brushing the roots of her hair with a lead comb, covering the rest of it with an ample headrail, and patting her face thick with powder.

"Tell me about your family." Genevieve snatched Marie's bodice and thrust her arms through the sleeves. "I'll need to know their names, ages, and everything about them that's important."

As Marie struggled out of her skirt and petticoat and reached for the bundle of clothing, she told Genevieve about her past. Her mother had died in childbirth when Marie was only a few years old. Later, impoverished by the civil wars of the Fronde, which had flared through France, she and her father had lived on the charity of distant relatives until her father died, leaving Marie to the mercy of an unscrupulous second cousin. He refused to dower her or pay to put her in a convent, so she was sent to the Salpêtrière. Genevieve dispassionately noted all the names and dates as she slipped on Marie's discarded petticoat and skirt. She would need to know as much as she could remember; the rest she would have to make up as she went along.

But her mind wandered from Marie's hushed, trembling monologue as Genevieve ran her hands over the brushed broadcloth of the blue traveling dress. It had been a long time since she had worn clothes so fine, and the feel of the soft cloth against her skin brought a rush of memories of a better time. . . . She blocked them out. The past was the past—it was the future that mattered now.

Genevieve set her mind to fitting into Marie's bodice. Marie was small-boned, but despite the meager rations of the Salpêtrière, Genevieve was generously formed. It took both of their efforts to lace the tightly boned bodice closed over Genevieve's bosom.

"There's another girl in the building who will be going with you tomorrow," Marie said as she secured the last knot. "Her name is Cecile."

"She knows, yes?"

"Yes. She will await you tonight and take you to my bed."

"Good." Genevieve smoothed her fingers down her boned form, then arranged the crumpled head-rail over her hair. She twirled before Marie. "Well?"

"You've the carriage of a noblewoman." Marie plucked at her plain black robes, hesitating. Her voice quivered with hushed bewilderment. "Perhaps . . . perhaps this shall all work out as you planned."

It will, Marie Suzanne Duplessis. I swear on all that you hold holy, it will.

"You'll be leaving at dawn tomorrow for Le Havre," Marie continued. "Cecile will help shield you from Mother Superior as you board the carriage."

"Mother Superior will never notice. I'll be crying like an onion seller into my—your—handkerchief. Will we be traveling in a public carriage?"

"Oh, no!" A fluttering white hand emerged from the black sleeve to rest on her throat. "It will be sent by the king, of course."

"Who else will be in it?"

"Some guards will ride outside to see that we are protected until we reach the ship. You know there will be other girls following from the Salpêtrière?"

"Yes."

"What if someone recognizes you?"

Genevieve leaned over to force her feet into Marie's boots. "None of the women who live in my section of the Salpêtrière were chosen. Once I'm out of Paris, I don't have to worry about being recognized."

Marie hesitated. She slipped her foot nervously in and out of Genevieve's common wooden shoes.

"There's no need for you to wait any longer." Genevieve glanced up from where she struggled to lace Marie's tiny boots over her much larger feet. "Go. Your Musketeer is waiting."

Marie turned on one heel, then as Genevieve straightened, she suddenly whirled and embraced her, swift and hard. "If I could give you a bag of gold, I would," Marie said fervently, seizing Genevieve's hand. "I will never forget you for the sacrifice you've made for me. . . . Oh!"

Genevieve pulled her hand from Marie's grasp— but it was too late.

Marie stumbled back and covered her mouth. Genevieve met her shocked gaze squarely. What did the girl expect? Did she really expect another *bijoux*? Or one of the poor orphans who crowded the halls of the Salpêtrière? Would any of those women be so bold as to switch places with a king's girl?

No.

"So now you understand how I could send notes back and forth to you, and how I stole the clothing you wear, and why no other king's girl would recognize me." Genevieve watched Marie's face in the darkness. "Obviously, I'll need gloves. Even in Québec, I imagine, no one will believe that a *bijoux* has the hands of a washerwoman."

Marie backed away, then whirled and raced swiftly toward the arched entrance that led out of the Salpêtrière. Genevieve tilted her chin and stared sightlessly at the place where she had been. These last three weeks, Genevieve had been right to hide her true identity from that daughter of the petty nobility. Marie would never have agreed to this desperate scheme if she had known the truth.

In the Salpêtrière, it was common knowledge that the only women who washed the linens lived in *La Correction*, the section of the institution reserved for wayward women . . . and common whores.

Genevieve pulled her headrail over her hair and strode toward Marie's building. *Let her believe what she will.* God willing, Genevieve would never lay eyes on the real Marie Suzanne Duplessis again.

Chapter One

Québec, August 1670

"I'm here."

André Lefebvre slammed open the door to his agent's office and entered, splattering wet moccasin prints on the polished floorboards. He tossed his balled linen shirt on the imported rosewood desk, spraying Philippe Martineau with grit and river water.

André glared at his old friend. Philippe leaned back in the creaking wooden chair and blindly wiped the grime from his blue silk coat and silver buttons. His gaze swept over André's nudity, broken only by the flap of a breechcloth, and rested with distaste on the water sluicing down his legs and darkening the rug.

"For a week I've been trying to get you in here." A froth of lace spilled over Philippe's hand as he rolled his fingers toward a chair on the other side of his desk. "I'm pleased you finally saw fit to grace me with your presence."

"I'm not staying long enough to sit," André argued as he paced across the rare Turkish carpet. "What the hell do you want from me, summoning me like a lackey in the middle of the day?"

"That's when most men conduct business," Philippe mused wryly. "In the middle of the day."

"I was doing well enough," André growled, slamming his hands on Philippe's desk, "conducting my *own* business before your boy interrupted—"

"Business?" Philippe's cold blue eyes remained level under the slow arch of one brow. "Splashing at the river's edge like a boy is that what you call business?"

"It was a canoe race . . . and it's a hundred times better than *this*." André swiped his shirt off the desk, sweeping some papers to the floor with it. "Because of that race, Tiny has agreed to sign on with me."

"Tiny Griffin?" Philippe cocked a brow higher. "That burly woods-runner?"

"*Oui.* The best steersman in Québec, joining me on this crazed voyage of mine. Not a bad day's work, eh, partner?" André tossed his shirt to the floor and waved a hand over his agent's strewn desk. "Now just collect the papers and tell me where to sign, so I can get back to my work."

André turned and strode toward the window. He banged open the shutters, flooding the room with bright July sunlight. Philippe's warehouse wedged up against the sheer rock face of the cliff of Québec, gazing strategically over the cul-de-sac where the boats unloaded goods from the French ships anchored in the St. Lawrence River. The crowd that had watched the race still lingered on the shore, a motley clutch of Ottawa Indians, bearded woods-runners, and a few Frenchmen pecking around like tamed peacocks set out in the wild.

André shook his head, like a great shaggy dog, spewing river water across the room, not giving a damn that he was splattering Philippe's precious gleaming furniture and exotic Turkish rug with river-bottom silt. Serves the peacock right for sending a boy to drag him away from the river. André had explained the division of labor from the moment he and Philippe had become partners in this upcoming fur-trading voyage: They would do what they both did best—Philippe would take care of paper and politics; André would hire the men, outfit the canoes, and make the voyage.

Make the voyage . . . yes, make the voyage. André raked his fingers through his shaggy hair and shook it wild. His heart still pumped wildly from the race. His arms ached, and the burn between his shoulder blades had only just begun to cool. He flexed his arms in circles to unravel the kinks from his muscles. Damn reckless fool he had been, daring Tiny to a race when Tiny was only a month back from a season in the woods—work-hardened and strong—while André had just returned from France, having done nothing more arduous than pace in the antechambers of courtrooms. And the race had been but from one side of the Saint Lawrence to the other—easy currents, open water. Three years away from Québec had made him soft; he only had a few weeks to toughen up before the voyage began. For then, he would lead an expedition fifteen hundred miles into the interior—over mountainous portages, through the most ferocious of whitewater . . . into uncharted territory.

He'd had three years to dream of *that*.

"My dear André, we could more easily discuss this matter if you weren't gazing out the window like a schoolboy dreaming over his lessons."

"I'm paying you to take care of things, not to discuss them with me." In the midst of the St. Lawrence, a ship unfurled its limp, salt-stained sails like a portly priest undressing, setting anchor in the midst of the river. "Another ship is in." André cocked an elbow on the sill. "Shouldn't you be out there, cataloging your wealth or whatever you do when you're not suffocating on your own perfume?"

"It can wait." A drawer squealed as Philippe pulled it open. He thumped a wrapped package onto the desk. "Unfortunately, this conversation of ours can be avoided no longer."

André sucked in the clean river air, then snorted out the stench of cleanliness and order. *Hell and damnation.* Business, always business. Would he ever be free of it?

He leaned back against the sill, his hands dangling on either side of him. Philippe had removed his blond wig, and his sweaty, close-cropped hair stuck up awkwardly all over his head. André watched as his friend sliced off an end from a carrot of tobacco. Then, with all the stoic majesty of an Indian chief presiding over a circle of his men, Philippe tapped the tightly packed leaves into his pipe and lit them with a spark of flint against steel, hollowing his cheeks as he drew in the first smoke.

It was an old ritual, an Indian ritual, anachronistic in this low-raftered room with all its oiled and gleaming French furniture. It was a peek at the old Philippe, whom André remembered with fondness. But the sight made him edgy, as did the smile Philippe cast his way. The movement pulled the skin around the mottled scar that ran jagged from Philippe's temple, through the edge of his thin wax-tipped mustache, and faded into the tuft of blond beard in the center of his chin. It gave him a rakish, devil-may-care air, in sharp contrast to his fripperies.

But André knew the man too well to be fooled by that easy grin. He'd fought too many Iroquois skirmishes with Philippe, spent too much time in the woods hunting and fighting and struggling to survive. André noticed the tense crimp of muscles that edged one of Philippe's cool blue eyes as he sucked on the pipe, and he knew his old friend was bracing himself for something.

What could it be now? André wondered, striding across the room to snatch up his damp shirt and rub it across his stubbled face. What the hell could it be now? Hadn't he had enough trouble wheedling his own inheritance from the courts in France? Hadn't he spent three years fighting for what was his by right, all the while itching . . . *itching* to be back home, here, in Québec?

Philippe extended the pipe. André frowned at the face of the fox carved in the bowl—Philippe's totem, from the old days, before his marriage. André considered refusing it. He belonged on the shore right now, seeking out the fur traders just in from the west, plying them with good French brandy and sucking dry the last bit of their knowledge: the lay of the western land, the fierceness of the rivers, the distribution of the Indian tribes. It was *Philippe's* duty to make arrangements with the fur trading company, to get a trading license, to take care of all the minutia André wanted nothing to do with. And he suspected he didn't want to hear whatever it was that Philippe had to say.

"No brandy for me?" André flipped his shirt over his shoulder and seized the pipe. "You have a look upon you as if I'll need it."

"Brandy? *Moi?* In the middle of the day?" His petticoat breeches rustled as he rose from his chair and opened a small cabinet in the corner. He clinked a bottle of amber liquid on the marble top. "I'm a married man with three children," Philippe said, setting out two glasses. "A respected member of the community."

André seized the back of the chair, jerked it around, and straddled it as he exhaled a blue stream of smoke. "And Marietta would have your head."

Marietta was Philippe's hot-blooded Italian wife who, even five months gone with child, brooked no nonsense from the husband she'd only half tamed. Philippe's grin turned rakish again as he poured. "*Oui,* she probably will." He handed one glass to André and raised his own. "To old friends, *mon vieux ami.*"

"*Salut.*"

The amber fire burned the back of his throat and lit his belly with warmth. André clinked down the empty glass, savoring the hot taste. He would miss only two things when he finally left civilization: brandy and a Frenchwoman's scent.

"Three years in France did you no good, my old friend." Philippe nodded at André's smoke-ripened deerskin breechcloth, at the damp moccasins, and finally at the Indian medicine bag slung around his neck. "Already, the old ways creep up on you."

"Thank Christ." André snorted at Philippe, in his blue silk coat, shiny silver buttons, and froths of lace at neck and wrists. "One more day in waistcoat and petticoat breeches, and I would have sprouted breasts."

"*Oui*, well . . ." Philippe gave a purely Gallic shrug. His chair squeaked as he settled back into it, cradling his half-empty cup of brandy. "One must change with the times. Life is not the same as it was three years ago."

"*You're* the one wearing a skirt, not I. And this"— André scowled and gestured to Philippe's desk— "how can you stand this vomit of paper?" He'd lose his mind scribbling over a desk all day. Already, the sickly perfume of wood oil and soap permeating this room threatened to make him sneeze. But Philippe seemed to thrive in it. When the two of them had left the local militia to go their separate ways after the war with the Iroquois, Philippe had just begun his business in a makeshift siding-and-rubble hut, and had a wife, a child, and another on the way. He'd done well in such a risky business, as an agent for small fur traders; it showed in the office's carved paneling, the tinkling of the chandelier above the desk, the rich smell of oil and leather emanating from a shelf full of books. Philippe had always had a good sense of the blowing of the political winds, whether they be Indian or French.

Which was why, André reminded himself as the brandy essence rushed through his blood, he had hired his old friend to tackle that labyrinth *for* him.

André narrowed his gaze on his agent. Philippe twisted the glass in his hand, around and around, spilling drops of brandy on his pale fingers.

Something was wrong. Very, very wrong.

André clattered the pipe into its clay holder, splattering red embers out of the bowl. "Out with it, Philippe."

"Really, André, carrying on a civil conversation with you these days is like teasing a hungry bear." Philippe finished his brandy in one gulp and placed the glass on the table with two fingers, then tapped at the embers until they sizzled out. "I was getting to it. I spoke of great changes these past years, but I didn't mean in us; I meant here, in Québec."

André rolled his eyes and snapped his shirt off his shoulder. "Spare me one of your speeches."

Philippe managed a tilted smile that looked more like a grimace. "You were never very interested in politics."

"Politics." André rubbed his hair vigorously with his shirt. "If it's the peace with the Iroquois or the English fur-trading in Hudson Bay you want to discuss, then I'll stay and have another brandy."

"It's not politics, really. It's more a matter of philosophy. . . ."

André snapped his shirt out with a *whack* and stood up, banging his chair out of the way. He leaned over Philippe's desk, close enough to smell his perfume over the curling tobacco smoke. "What the *hell* is going on? Have you lost your edge, Philippe, in this black-aired room? Why did you drag me here?"

Philippe tugged a piece of parchment from under André's hand, then laid it on the edge of the table as he took the pipe. "I had hoped you'd discover this yourself this past week and spare me the unpleasantness."

André looked at the thing as if it were a piece of rotten meat. "I hired you so I would never have to look at another piece of paper again."

"You've had your head buried in too many warehouses and ships' holds since you returned. If you had taken a moment out of spending that inheritance of yours, you'd have seen this notice posted all over the city . . . and I wouldn't have had to send four shopboys to summon you."

André knocked the paper off the table and sent it

skimming to the floor. "I've got better things to do than read petty ordinances."

"It contains strict orders from the king's minister." Philippe hooked his lip over the end of the pipe. "And it concerns restrictions placed upon men seeking trading licenses."

"Of course it does." A breeze flooded the room, rattling the other papers on Philippe's desk like autumn leaves and sending the crystal drops on the chandelier chiming. "When in the history of this damned settlement *hasn't* the government tried to suck the life out of the fur trade? Jesus, Philippe, just take care of it. I've had a bellyful of bureaucracy in France. . . ."

"It's not that simple."

"Anything is simple with money." He wrestled into his shirt and yanked the hem over his rippled belly. "Do whatever you have to do. Offer the king's minister a percentage of the furs. . . ."

"The king's minister won't be bribed."

"Then bribe his administrators," André growled, frustration thickening his words.

"Don't you think that was the first thing I tried?" He raised the pipe to halt André's words. "I'm not one of the best agents in Québec for nothing. But you see, this is not a matter of money. As I started to tell you, it's a matter of philosophy."

André kicked the chair, though it was not in his way. He crossed the width of the room in four wide strides, to glare out the window at the bustling street. The first *barque* had landed on the shore, and the crowd buzzed like a hive of bees around the bounty unloaded from the new French ship.

He should be there, haggling over provisions for his trip into the interior. Instead, he was suffocating in this low-raftered room . . . he was suffocating under

Philippe's gloom. Philippe didn't understand. André would have *no more trouble* with this voyage; he'd waited too long to see it done. He'd traveled the familiar route to the west a thousand times in his mind during his self-imposed exile in France. Right now, he wanted nothing more than to be waist-deep in the rapids of the Ottawa River, portaging around a violent set of falls or paddling across silvery Lake Nipissing, closer and closer to Georgian Bay. It had been three years since he last journeyed into the wilderness, and the soles of his feet itched for his well-worn moccasins and the feel of the rocky path. To live with the roof as his sky, to live forever roaming, to live with a commitment to no one but himself. He was so close he could taste gritty Indian *sagamité* in the scent of woodsmoke.

Nothing . . . *nothing* more could prevent him from fulfilling the dream he had harbored since he had first set foot as a boy in the North American wilderness: a dream of traveling farther west into the unexplored forest than any white man had ever gone.

Certainly no petty government ordinance.

"When you lived here last, André," Philippe began, despite his friend's rigid back, despite his attention to the goings-on outside the window, "the philosophy was to suck the lifeblood from this country—take the beaver pelts from the west, search for minerals and whatever. And so every autumn the strongest men flooded into the woods, and every spring we returned as wild and disruptive as brandy-soaked Indians. But now the king doesn't want us leaving every winter. He wants to settle Québec. As the English and the Dutch have settled their lands in this New World— with farmers, blacksmiths, tanners . . ."

"What has this got to do with me? With the voyage?"

"You must fulfill the requirements of the ordinance

to trade furs. It's that simple." Philippe tugged on
the edge of his lace cravat and took sudden interest
in the brass edging of his inkwell. "The requirement
is simple, really, and won't cost you much. . . . You
must"—he cleared his throat—"marry."

André's knees loosened, abruptly and instinctively,
for it seemed as if the floor bucked beneath him, like
a birch bark canoe riding the swells of whitewater. It
kept bucking and rolling and the room rocked
around him, and only his latent skill in riding the
swells kept him upright, glaring steadily at Philippe
like the only steady point on the twisting horizon.

"More king's girls are coming to Québec." Philippe raised a finger from its delicate brushing of the
inkwell to point toward the window. "There's
undoubtedly a whole new batch in that ship just coming in. The ordinance requires all single men in the
colony to marry within a fortnight of their arrival, or
else . . ." He rolled one shoulder. "Else they'll refuse
you a hunting, fishing, or more relevantly, a trading
license."

"The bureaucrats of Québec can't enforce that,
and you know it. It's like condemning all of the settlement to starve."

"They *can* enforce it—and they will. I told you this
place has changed."

"Not that much."

The skin of his palms cracked as he curled his
hands into fists. *Not here, not here.* He'd just returned
from Louis XIV's France. The monarchy was like a
great, choking parasitic vine; it could not have found
a way to reach across the Atlantic to strangle this New
World.

"If you refuse, I can do nothing for you."

"Is this *you* talking, Philippe, the man who fought
the Iroquois with me in '66? You've been behind that

desk too long. The stale air of civilization is curdling your brain. They want money, as all greedy bureaucrats do.'' André speared the air westward, pointing toward someplace well beyond the walls. ''There's a bay out there, a bay where a dozen Indian tribes travel to fish and trade each spring; you and I have both heard the talk. You know there's no better place to build a permanent fur trading post.''

''You don't have to convince me.'' He shifted in his seat. ''I've a hefty bag of gold invested in you.''

Yes, in that, and in more than that, Philippe . . . In the dream. For this single trading post will only be a base for further exploration into the uncharted western forests. It would be the first of many posts, stretching farther and farther west until I reached the elusive China Sea.

But best of all, I will live like a Caesar of the wilderness, a king of my own domain, and there would be no one to tell me otherwise—no commitments, no obligations, no ties, no one left behind . . . definitely no wife.

''He's going to fill Québec with abandoned wives and the forest with cuckolded husbands.'' André crossed the room and planted his hands flat on the desk. ''Get me out of this.''

Philippe tapped the pipe onto the desk, loosening the last blackened coals. Then he looked up, and memory passed between them.

''It's not the same world.'' Philippe set the pipe down, leaned back, and folded his hands across his swelling middle. ''We are at peace with the Iroquois now.''

A cloud passed across the face of the sun, casting the room in darkness. Shadows dripped from the corners of the room, and the rafters loomed low and dark. Christ, he was in a box, suffocating in here. He tugged the neck of his wide-opened shirt until the sound of a tear filled the room. *It makes no difference.* André knew that now. Peace or no peace, he'd not have a wife in the settlements.

Then a thought came to him. He laughed—a dark, humorless sound. A twisted grin stretched tight over his teeth.

"By God, the last time I saw a look like that," Philippe murmured warily, "you were facing two Iroquois warriors who took a liking to the color of your hair."

"We *are* at peace with the Iroquois, aren't we?" He slapped his hands on the desk. "I can go into their country now. I can trade furs with the English at Fort Orange. They'll give me twice the price that the French will, and they won't charge me tax."

"That's smuggling." Philippe's fingers stilled on the bowl of the pipe. "That's *treason.*"

André snorted. "Is this the same man who traded brandy with the Ottawas despite the threat of excommunication?"

"Treason can get you *hanged.*"

"Only if I'm caught."

"Think, André. For once use your head and not your impulses." Philippe tapped the ash out of his pipe on the side of the desk, already pocked with dents. "Smuggling to the English the amount of furs you intended to collect is unreasonable . . . impossible. And what of the string of trading posts, hmm? If you refuse this edict, that dream of yours will crumble before the foundation has even been set. . . . By God, where are you going?"

André slammed open the door without a pause. He had to get away from these walls, this roof; he needed a good long suck of brandy. "Find a way out, Philippe. I won't marry."

No, no *no*, he thought as he plunged out into the muddy street. He wouldn't marry.

Never, ever again.

Genevieve gripped the weathered railing of the ship's prow as the vessel sailed deeper into the channel of the St. Lawrence River. On the northern coast, a pewter wall of rock heaved up from the lip of the river, its rough surface pitted with gnarled spruce trees and streaked with scrawny tufts of grass that clung along the sheltered clefts of the naked stone. On the southern shore, luxuriant blue-green forests bristled to the very edge of the horizon, seeping the fragrance of pine sap and moist, mulchy earth into the air.

Genevieve tightened her one-handed grip on her mantle as the chill September wind whistled through her bones. Out of the corner of her eye she glimpsed a flap of a gray habit—one of the Ursulines who'd accompanied them across the sea. Lurking in the shadows and watching me, no doubt, Genevieve thought, suppressing a shiver. Eager to drag me down to that death-hold with the other girls, stuff noxious ointments in me, and make me cough my life into a dirty linen.

No, no. Not me. She pressed her belly against the railing—for support, she told herself. The river rocked differently than the open sea, but her legs had not yet learned the movement; that's why her head was swimming so much, that's why nausea heaved in her throat. But she couldn't show one flicker of weakness now, not when the fulfillment of her dreams loomed just beyond the next shimmering curve. Genevieve had suffered the long, hard voyage, not succumbing to the shipboard fever that had claimed a dozen girls' lives and lingered, even now, in the stinking ship's hold below. She'd survived, yes, again she'd survived.

Hot exhilaration rushed through her blood, ebbing away the wind's chill. A hoarse giggle escaped her raw throat. It was over; she had *won*. With stiff, shaking fingers, she tore off the headrail that enveloped her head and let a gust send the cloth to the sky. The wind yanked at her loosely bound hair, tugging it free to rise weightless in a cloud around her face, sweeping clear the black clouds of memory.

Genevieve Lalande did not perch here, watching the cold blue sky of this New World melt into an evening gold. The shadow called Genevieve had died at Le Havre. Now she was Marie Suzanne Duplessis. Now she would have a roof above her head instead of the sky, a house to call her own, a fertile place in which to settle and set down deep roots. A shaky laugh rippled out as no more than a breath. *Oui*, a husband, too, something she'd never imagined in her lifetime. And a family. Someone to love who'd be all her own, children to raise in a civilized place.

Oui, civilized. Her gaze drank in the whole of the country, the endless forests not yet tamed by plow or sickle, the deep silence broken only by the caws of the cliff swallows wheeling above the ship. She had dreamed it would be like this, but she never allowed herself to believe her fantasies. In Paris, even in Normandy, she had never seen so much uninhabited, uncultivated land.

A woman could hide in such a place forever.

Oh, the girls were so full of children's bedtime stories. Savages ruled these woods, they told her, men of bronze skin and painted faces, men of unimagined cruelty. And the winters grew so cold, they said, that the trees exploded from it. She'd already known a place like that, in the heart of the civilized world. A curl twisted her lips, cracking the skin. No place, no matter how raw, could be worse than the streets of Paris.

It was over now, Genevieve thought, letting the past fade like the brightness of the sky. She had won. Now nothing—nothing and no one—could ever thwart her dreams again.

Then she crumpled into a heap on the deck.

Chapter Two

André stepped out of the inn and collided with a cartful of eels. Limp black fish lolled over the edge and licked his wide skirts, streaking them with slime. Waving the profuse apologies of the fisherman away, he absently scoured the stain with one gloved hand and stomped sullenly through the mud.

Good, he thought as he noticed the black streak marring his clothing. He was wearing his best French outfit, an ensemble he had bought in Paris for the sole purpose of appearing in front of the officials responsible for holding back his inheritance. But the damned green coat fitted too tightly, the silver buttons were nothing but nuisances, and the seams dug into his skin and itched. The matching breeches strangled his legs at the knees, where they were gathered and gartered with a frivolous spray of emerald ribbons—the least feminine of his options at the time. He wanted nothing more than to toss his tight shoes, his wretched coat, and his damned breeches in the St. Lawrence River. Now, he thought, as he slid a slime-coated, gloved finger between his neck and the linen edge of his cravat, he would have an excuse to do it after today's deed was done.

He splattered out into the middle of the street, his red-heeled boots sucking deep into the mud, and headed toward Madame Jean Bourdon's house. A tepid breeze wove through the buildings clustered in the lower town of Québec, carrying the tart scent of a recent rain. The sun glittered off the towering granite mass of the *Cap aux Diamants*, the cliff that thrust abruptly from the earth to form a backdrop to the town at its foot. Several warehouses nestled close to its base, and in and out of these flowed a line of settlers with the local currency—beaver skins—strapped across their backs. High above, in the upper town, the churchbells gonged for the first Mass of the day.

André clutched the bulge straining out between the second and third buttons of his coat, pulling on it so the ties dug into his neck. Damn Indian magic. *Where's the rain? The thunder? The lightning?* A good Ojibwa shaman could read signs of a man's future in the wind and the weather, but André didn't need Indian wisdom to know what a blue sky and bright sun portended. A fool he was to believe in such things. The sun had no reason to shine on this black day.

He knew which house belonged to Madame Bourdon the moment he turned the corner onto her street. A crowd of men swarmed around the door like bees scenting nectar. Several officers milled on the outskirts. One Frenchman, dressed in a brilliant silk doublet and breeches festooned with ribbons and lace, stood apart from the swarm.

"André!"

André lifted his plumed, wide-brimmed hat to shade his eyes from the glare of the morning. The sunlight glinted off Philippe's fair corkscrew curls. "Christ, look at this, will you?" André said as Philippe stopped at his side. "Rutting season in Québec."

"Last batch of the king's girls for the season." Philippe tucked his hat under his arm and snapped a familiar slip of paper out of his pocket. "Though I'm pleased you finally came to your senses, André, you could have decided earlier in the season to send me this message and saved my heart the strain. I was sure I'd see you swinging by the neck before year's end."

André slid his gloved fingers under his cravat and yanked. "Can't you see the noose?"

Andre glowered at the crowd, at the closed door to Madame Bourdon's house, then he looked up the black cliff of Québec toward the palisades of the upper city. Nearly two months he'd prepared for this voyage, and too frequently he'd come up against something: *voyageurs* unwilling to sign on with him; merchants unwilling to accept his credit; provisions held in warehouses for "inspection," to search for secreted brandy; bureaucrats turning away from the sight of gold gleaming beneath his hand. And all the while time slipped away. Now the first breath of autumn cooled the evenings, and every day another flotilla of canoes headed west as he watched on the shore, grinding his teeth, thrashing inside like a mountain cat trying to find a way out of this trap.

"You've done the right thing," Philippe murmured, stuffing the paper into his pocket. "Marriage, even a reluctant one, has its benefits, hmm?"

"Not *this* marriage."

"Come, come, old friend." Philippe tapped his wrought-wooden cane into the mud, clinking on a block of stone beneath. "A warm bed, a willing woman. . . . Such things I've never known you to turn away."

"This will be a marriage of convenience." André slapped his hat over his dark wig, snapping one of the delicate ostrich plumes in the process. "When I come back in the spring, I'm getting an annulment."

"André . . ."

"I'm in no mood to hear you rhapsodize about the wonders of the conjugal bed." André rubbed his elbow against his side, trying to scratch an itch where a seam was rubbing his skin. "I'm marrying because I was given no choice: marry or give up the trip. So here I am. But there's no requirement that I *stay* married."

Philippe's smile faltered. He twisted away and gazed over the black waters of the St. Lawrence, watching a small boat navigate the currents to the opposite shore. A team of oxen lumbered by, strapped to a cart laden with ribbed green watermelons, fresh from the farm. One fell off and splattered into the mud, spewing its sweet rosy fruit over the ground.

"I suppose," Philippe began on a sigh, "that you won't consider a relationship with this woman."

"No consummation, no marriage."

"I suppose not." He reached into his pocket and pulled out a circular gold case, which he snapped open with a click. The river breeze careened a whirlwind of dust off the contents. "To think, after I received your message last night, that I entertained the notion you might actually be coming around. . . . My own folly. Old ghosts are rarely buried so abruptly, eh, *mon vieux ami?*"

Philippe pinched out a puff of powder and pressed it against a nostril, snorting it deeply.

As expressionless as an Iroquois chief, the bastard,

André thought, and all while he speared an old wound with a red-hot poker.

"So what are you to do with her?" Philippe sniffed delicately, brushing his nose with the back of his hand. "I know you won't winter in Québec with her, and I know you won't leave her here alone."

A murmuring began among the crowd of men as the door to Madame Bourdon's house cracked open. André turned away and shouldered into the crowd, blocking out the flare of memory Philippe was doing his damnedest to ignite.

But the crowd jostled and did not move, and soon they were all herded into a ragged line. The orange scent of Philippe's strong perfume wafted over his shoulder.

"In rather a hurry, André, for a man so sullen about marriage."

"The sooner this is done, the sooner you'll get me my trading license." His nostrils flared as he glanced easily over the heads of the other men, toward the river. "The sooner I can be out there."

"Marietta will be doubly disappointed." Philippe used his cane as a barrier, eyeing anyone who dared consider crossing it and cutting in on them in line. "She was looking forward to a female companion over the long winter months."

"She'll get her heart's desire. Did you think I summoned you here just to be a witness?"

Philippe's blue eyes narrowed, and not against the glare.

"I'm giving you a governess for the winter, old friend."

"Governess." Philippe swung his cane in an arc and gripped its middle. "You wretched dog. I should have known you'd be up to something."

"A dozen times, you said you needed someone.

Marietta is heavy with child. She'll need help with your three young ones when the babe is born."

"You wouldn't think of asking me or Marietta first, hmm?"

"I'm asking you now." André leaned closer. "You do want some return on your investment? You *do* want me to go west and bring back a harvest of beaver like you've never seen before?"

Philippe tapped his cane up the stairs as they came to the head of the line. "It's the beaver that you're leaving in my house that I'm concerned about."

Madame Bourdon, an imposing woman dressed in severe black, met them just inside the door. She reminded André of a pursed-lip nun who'd tormented him as a schoolboy in Aix-en-Provence.

"Your name, monsieur?"

"André Lefebvre." He gestured to Philippe. "My friend only came to leer."

"It has been some time, Monsieur Martineau," she said, ignoring André's comment and nodding to Philippe. "It doesn't seem that long ago when your wife was housed here as a king's girl. How is she?"

"She's well and expecting another child."

André swallowed his growl. Philippe puffed out his chest whenever he uttered those words, as if he had succeeded at some feat never before accomplished, when to André, it was the prevention of conception that was the more difficult task.

"Send her my regards." Madame Bourdon turned her attention back to André and raised a quill over a yellowed book. "Monsieur Lefebvre, what is your means of livelihood?"

André told her he was a fur trader, and that he owned some land outside of Montreal that had once belonged to his father but had been neglected for several years. He told her that during the course of the next year his wife would be housed with the Martineau family. Madame Bourdon's nod was noncommittal. Philippe then interrupted to inform her that André's father had been a Parliamentarian in Aix-en-Provence and that André had just returned to France after collecting his inheritance.

Her demeanor changed entirely.

"If I had known, monsieur, that you came from such a good family, I would have made sure you did not have to wait among the others." With a flutter of hands, she motioned for one of her domestics. "We have an exclusive group of women set aside especially for men like you. Well-bred women. Women of good family, who will grace your home with their charm and education."

André frowned. The last thing he wanted for a wife was some cold, high-strung, inbred bitch. Before he could say anything, Philippe nudged him to follow the domestic down the hall. They passed a large room milling with young women in common dress, then continued on up a narrow flight of stairs. Midway, André turned to Philippe and muttered, "You left a few things out of my biography."

"Nothing of note, I'm sure."

"You forgot to tell the good Madame that I've already spent my inheritance."

"You'll be a rich man soon enough."

"You also neglected to tell her that my father was a rebel Parliamentarian, exiled here during the wars of the Fronde."

"That was decades ago," Philippe argued, waving it away like a gnat. "Besides, it wasn't your father's money you were claiming, it was your brother Leonard's."

"You know damned well that Leonard's money was my father's money. He hid it amid Leonard's affairs before we left France."

"Details."

"Those *details* kept me tied up in the royal courts for three years."

"I don't think it's necessary for Madame Bourdon to know that you came from a family full of rebels. Leonard appeared to be a good royalist, and it is all ancient history now." Philippe frowned. "It seems I must take charge of this issue of choosing you a wife. All you need is a trading license, but I'm getting a governess for my children. I want one with some intelligence, not some broad-beamed dullard." Philippe bowed mockingly before the open door, allowing André to proceed him inside. "Of course, if she has any intelligence, she won't marry you, so obviously we'll have to settle for breeding."

The domestic ushered them into a bright room facing the St. Lawrence, on the second floor of the three-story house. As he and Philippe entered, a dozen women turned and peered at them expectantly, fans fluttering like butterfly wings. André could guess their ranking by the richness of the ribbon edging their dresses.

"What am I supposed to do now?" he muttered, rolling his shoulders uncomfortably in the binding clothes. "Choose one as a butcher chooses his sheep for slaughter?"

"You have an open field, soldier." Philippe nodded a greeting to the one other man in the room, an aging officer of the Carignan-Salière regiment, which had fought in the Iroquois wars. "Any woman in this room would rather marry a fine buck like you than that aging stag."

He felt like a buck—like a buck facing a pack of hunting dogs. "They'd be better off with the aging stag. At least he'll be home to rut."

"Don't choose the prettiest one." Philippe swept off his hat and bowed to the room. "Marietta will positively skewer me if I bring home a beauty."

"You sound as sour as an old whore." André extended one stiff leg in what he hoped was a courtly bow. "You and Marietta need a girl in the house. I need a wife to get a trading license. It's the perfect solution."

"Why then," Philippe said, through a frozen smile, as one woman approached them, "does it feel like extortion?"

André pulled on his cravat as the scent of sweet, light Parisian perfume wafted from the petticoats of a woman who stopped boldly before them. She snapped her fan closed to reveal a tightly boned bodice and wide, shoulder-to-shoulder *décolletage*. His fingers itched to pinch one of those fleshy mounds to test it for firmness. Certainly such an act would be allowed in this market. After all, one wouldn't take home a soft melon, would one?

"I am Renée Affillé," she breathed, bouncing in a pert curtsy, "recently from La Rochelle."

He bowed and felt his coat strain dangerously across his shoulders. "Monsieur Lefebvre."

"What sort of position do you have here in Québec, Monsieur Lefebvre?"

Currently, an extremely uncomfortable one. "I'm a fur trader."

"*A coureur de bois!*" A second woman swept to his side and slid her hand up his forearm. She smiled at him like a doxy at the Marseilles harbor, all wet lips and shining eyes, the melons rolling agreeably beneath a strip of yellow satin, firm and fleshy. "How romantic! Why, I've heard so much about men like you. Do you bring home many furs? Marten, mink?"

"Beaver."

"Yes," Philippe murmured, flexing a brow, "today he will surprise us with a live one, I think."

"Oh, I so much love mink. I had a muff of mink when I was in Rouen—"

"I understand that fur traders spend a great deal of time in the wilderness," Renée interrupted, her dark eyes flashing at the other woman. "The whole winter sometimes. Is that true of you, Monsieur Lefebvre?"

He met a half-dozen pairs of eyes, all awaiting his answer, all staring at him with various degrees of invitation. Such *white* creatures, these Frenchwomen, all perfume and narrow shoulders, all pinched nostrils and fair curls and delicate satins; they looked like exotic butterflies trapped in a jar, imported here and totally ignorant of the harshness of the environment outside the glass.

It would be a wonder if half of them survived the Québec winter.

Renée tapped her fan against her open hand. "Well, Monsieur Lefebvre?"

"I'm in Québec so seldom," he said suddenly, "that my house is a ramshackle bit of timber and moss, hardly worthy of a . . . of a beaver."

Philippe snorted into his sleeve as the circle of women around them raised a collective, muffled sigh of disappointment, dispersing into random clusters around the room. Philippe elbowed him in the ribs. "You're supposed to be encouraging them."

"I'm not going to lie."

The woman with the gleaming smile was unmoved by his admission. She brazenly pressed her breast against his side. *Yes, yes, quite ripe.* She was not a pretty woman, but she had an earthiness about her that in another situation André would have willingly exploited to their mutual satisfaction. He made his first decision. This woman was too aggressive. He needed a quiet woman, a shy one . . . a *meek* one. He scanned the room. Several girls stood on the periphery of his small circle, avoiding his gaze. Farther away, in a corner, he saw three women huddled together, ignoring his presence entirely.

Excusing himself with as much grace as possible, André extricated himself from the grip of the smiling woman and approached the threesome. They talked quietly among themselves until he cleared his throat.

"Oh!" The three turned at the same time. One, a blonde with a spray of curls pinned fashionably on either side of her head, flushed as her gaze met his. She lowered her lashes. *Not her,* he thought. *Too young, too green. Needs more time on the vine.* Besides, Marietta would unman him with her sharp Italian knife if he sent this fair young beauty into her home.

A pitiful, retching string of coughs erupted from behind the ladies' skirts.

"What in God's name—"

"She's ailing, monsieur." The blonde twisted her fingers together and glanced over her shoulder. "We only arrived in Québec hours ago and there's been no time to take her to the Hôtel-Dieu."

The bright skirts parted with a rustle to reveal a tiny woman curled up on a chair. Lank hair dripped from beneath a ragged linen headrail, darkened with perspiration. She blindly took the dry handkerchief André held out for her, dropping the sodden one to the floor. She yanked a blanket more closely around her as she collapsed into a new fit of coughing.

The runt of the litter. He stepped back and scowled.

Every year about this time, the ships from France unloaded a whole new crop of diseases into the colony. Only God knew the cause of this poor woman's suffering. Her forehead gleamed with fever, and dark circles dug gray caverns beneath her eyes and cheekbones. Above the drooping edge of the blanket the frail line of her collarbone jutted beneath her translucent skin. She was hacking out her life in his linen handkerchief, and the effort sent shivers through the body swathed beneath the rough woolen blanket.

"She shouldn't be here." *Risking the spread of the illness.* "Why isn't she abed?"

"There are no more beds, monsieur. So many girls are more ill than she that they've claimed all the beds upstairs." The blonde shrugged prettily. "Marie will recover soon, I'm sure. She is strong. She tended me when I was sick aboard ship."

What had the officials in Paris been thinking when they sent such girls here? Simpering, frail Frenchwomen had no place in this new country, none. New France was a country only for the hardiest stock, and this chit looked as fragile and limp as a Provençal flower. He'd wager a barrel of brandy she'd be the first butterfly to die in New France. She'd never survive the autumn.

His eyes widened on the creature as an idea dawned.

She'd never survive . . . never survive . . .

"Philippe?"

Philippe disengaged himself from a crowd of women and tapped his way to André's side. "What is it?"

"There's been a change of plans. You haven't got your heart set on a governess, have you?"

"Scarcely." Philippe glanced at the three women standing before them. The blonde flushed prettily, and a spark of surprise lit Philippe's eyes. "What the devil are you up to, André?"

"Later." He waved vaguely toward the door. "Get Madame Bourdon."

"Then you've chosen?"

"I have." He pointed to the woman curled up on the chair. Her coughs stopped abruptly and she stared at him with red-rimmed, watery eyes. "Tell Madame Bourdon that I will marry Marie . . ." He glanced at the blonde for help.

"Duplessis, monsieur." Disappointment sank a pout into the blonde's lip. "Her name is Marie Duplessis."

"There you are!"

Genevieve woke abruptly from her doze. She blinked her eyes open and stared blindly up at the bare branches of an apple tree, starting as a yellow-throated warbler flew from its perch with a flurry of wings. All vestiges of sleep fled. She straightened on the wooden bench and swiftly scanned the orchard. Through the fence of knotted tree trunks came a flutter of gray robes.

"Merde!"

Her hiding place had been discovered. One of the hospital sisters barreled toward her through the trees, and by the nun's determined stride, Genevieve knew the nun would try to take her back into the hospital. She cursed beneath her breath in a way that would make a Parisian boatman blush, then grasped the edge of the bench and searched for escape. Behind her, the tall, straight logs of a cedar palisade blocked her retreat. In front of her, the nun strode closer. She grasped the red woolen shawl that lay twisted about her hips and stood up. It was too late to get away. She'd have to face the sister and the battle she knew would ensue.

For four days she had lain in the crowded hall of the Hôtel-Dieu while the sisters tended her in her illness. Although fresh food, cool water, and sleep proved strong enough medicine to break her fever, the sisters insisted she remain in the hospital until she fully regained her strength. Genevieve wanted only to leave. She didn't trust her long stretch of luck, and she didn't want to tempt fate any longer by lingering in the Hôtel-Dieu. This hospital reminded her of the dreaded Hôtel-Dieu in Paris, where once she had been forced to spend several weeks recovering from smallpox. It was a place of death, and now that she had made it to Québec, she wanted to *live.*

The nun halted in front of her. She planted her hands on her formidable hips. "We've been looking for you all morning."

"I needed the air, Sister Ignatia." Genevieve defiantly inhaled the early autumn scent of moist earth and resinous pines. "It's the first breath of fresh air I've had since I left Le Havre."

"Do you have any idea what diseases come with the autumn winds in Québec? And you out here in nothing but a shift!"

"There's no one here to see me."

"I'm not concerned about your modesty, I'm worried about your health."

"There are more diseases in that wretched hall," she said, nodding toward the Hôtel-Dieu. "I don't want to catch whatever my five bedmates are suffering from."

"Then listen to the woman who changed your bedding and fed you broth and wiped you down during your fever. Come inside."

Genevieve dug the heels of her bare feet into the brown grass. "The sunshine is reviving me."

"A sharp tongue and a stubborn disposition is no measure of health. The color of your cheeks says you've still got a fever."

"The color of my cheeks is from the sun. I've been dozing here all morning."

Sister Ignatia folded her arms in front of her. The hem of her gray gown shook as she tapped one foot. "I wouldn't have bothered looking for you, you insolent girl, if our Reverend Mother hadn't summoned you."

Genevieve took an anxious step toward the nun. For two days she'd been insisting on seeing Mother Superior, ever since her fever broke and she became conscious enough to understand what kind of place she was in. Only the Reverend Mother would have the power to release her over the protestations of the sisters. "Mother Superior has agreed to see me?"

"She's been waiting all this time while you 'revived' in the sun."

Genevieve brushed past the nun and raced down a row of trees toward the side entrance of the Hôtel-Dieu. She grasped the handle and pulled the door open, holding her breath as she was assaulted by a wave of humid, fetid air. She plunged into the room. The door slammed closed behind her and the sound echoed off the stone walls, mingling with the endless wails of the ailing and the calls for mercy. Genevieve walked swiftly through the two rows of straw-filled mattresses, crossing herself as she passed a priest in black robes administering last rites to one of the dying. The smoky scent of incense lingered in the air, not quite strong enough to overwhelm the acrid odor of urine and human excrement that reeked from the floorboards.

At the end of her pallet lay the battered woven case

and the blanket given to her as part of the king's dowry. She tossed her red shawl over the forest of bare, dirty limbs poking out beneath the woolen coverlet of her bed, fell to her knees, and untied the rope that held her case closed. She yanked out the best of Marie's clothing—a pale pink bodice and matching broadcloth skirt. With swift fingers she slipped the skirt on over her shift and thrust her arms through the sleeves of the boned bodice. She'd lost weight, yes, more than she'd expected, for the dress fit her far better than it ever had. She laced up the straight front and tucked the ends beneath the beribboned edge of her bodice. With the help of Sister Ignatia, who hovered behind her, Genevieve tied the wide linen sleeves of her shift around her arms with pink ribbons, creating three soft folds. She shook out a headrail of fine linen and draped it over her bare shoulders, tying it just above the edge of her bodice in front. Then, searching through a smaller woven basket, she found a few precious hairpins. She brushed her hair and coiled it into a heavy roll at the base of her neck.

"Come, come. Enough of vanity," Sister Ignatia scowled. "Our Reverend Mother is waiting."

Genevieve tossed her brush back into her woven case and searched for a pair of stockings. Her hand fell upon a wadded ball of linen. She picked up the material and smoothed it out, fingering the fine embroidery that lined the scalloped edge. It was not part of Marie's belongings, nor had it been given to her as part of her dowry from the king. She had almost forgotten about this memento. It was the handkerchief given to her on the wedding day she could barely remember, by a husband she didn't know.

She dug her fingers into the fabric. *André Lefebvre.*

His name was all she knew of him, and that only because the *hospitalière* sisters kept referring to her as "Madame Lefebvre." The fine linen of his handkerchief proved that he was a man of means. She wondered why, in four days, no one had brought her word of him or delivered any of his messages.

"Madame Lefebvre."

Genevieve tossed the handkerchief back into the case. There would be a lifetime to find out all about her husband—as soon as she was released from this hellish place. She swiftly picked out a pair of stockings and slipped them on, gartering them with ribbons just above her knees. She stepped into her boots, then followed an impatient Sister Ignatia through the hall.

Mother Marie de Saint-Bonaventure-de-Jésus squinted up from her task of writing as Genevieve was ushered into her office. The Reverend Mother's gaze rested on her for a moment, then returned to the paper. Genevieve stood just inside the doorway and waited for her to speak. Moments passed. She shifted her weight impatiently and looked around the room, remembering enough of the nuns at the Salpêtrière to keep quiet until spoken to. A row of cushionless, high-backed chairs lined the wall. Lace draped the edge of a small window, which afforded a view of the orchards, and sunlight splashed over Mother Superior's polished and paper-cluttered desk. A fire raged high and hot in the grate. A mountain of cut wood lay next to the hearth.

"You are late."

Genevieve straightened to find the nun's colorless eyes fixed on her. The elderly woman's face was as pasty white as the cap of her order. "Forgive me, Mother Superior. I was walking in the orchards and didn't know you summoned me."

"Come closer."

She approached the desk. She felt the nun's perusal as her gaze swept from the slight dishevelment of her hair to the dark leather boots peeping out, unlaced, from beneath her skirt.

"You are healthier than Sister Ignatia led me to believe."

"I am fully recovered."

"So the patient has become the nurse, has she?" A smile softened the dour lines of her face. "You gave the sisters a fright by disappearing from your pallet."

"Forgive me, Mother, but there's hardly enough room for me in it anymore."

"I know, child." The nun shook her head. "The ships have brought much disease this year. Soon we're going to have to house the sick in the church."

"Which is why I wanted to see you." Genevieve stilled her hands by clutching the cloth of her skirts. "I would like to offer my pallet to someone who needs it more."

The nun's eyes flickered over her. "Sister Ignatia told me you should stay three or four more days to regain your strength."

"I can regain my strength just as well in my husband's house."

"Child, a sickly wife is useless to a man."

Genevieve spread her arms. "Do I look sickly, Reverend Mother?"

"Sister Ignatia has been a sister in this hospital for years and she knows what is best for you." Mother Superior leaned back in her chair and folded her hands over her belly. "You're a king's girl, aren't you?"

"Yes, from Paris."

"Ah." The nun nodded in understanding. "Now

I agree with Sister Ignatia's hesitation. You don't know the rigors of setting up a household in this settlement, child.''

"There can't be much rigor in setting up my household.'' Genevieve remembered the fine embroidery that edged the handkerchief her husband had given her. "My husband, André Lefebvre, is a man of means.''

The Reverend Mother puckered her forehead in thought. "His name is unfamiliar to me.''

"But you must know him. . . . He must have sent several inquiries by now.''

"I've received no messages for any of the girls.'' At the sight of Genevieve's stunned expression, the nun added, "It's harvest time, dear. The men of the colony are working their fields or catching the season's eels. Your husband is undoubtedly too busy preparing for winter to send a message.''

"My husband is not a farmer or a fisherman.''

"Wealthy men must prepare for winter as well. The last ships are leaving for France, and accounts must be settled, letters must be written. There is much for all of us to do this time of year.''

"If he is busy, then that is all the more reason why I should let him know I am well.'' She walked to the desk and stopped across from the nun. Four days had passed since her marriage, *four days* and not a word? "Let me send a message to him.''

"Sister Ignatia warned me that you were stubborn.'' Mother Superior pursed her lips. "But, I suppose if he is a wealthy man, he should be able to see to your care himself, and we need every bed we can get. . . .''

Genevieve sensed victory, but she took care not to let it show on her face.

"You must remember not to exert yourself, child. I don't want to see you back here within a week.''

Hell will freeze over first.

"I'm sure I have his instructions somewhere." The nun riffled through a pile of papers stacked on one side of her desk. She removed one, then placed a pair of spectacles on her nose and began to read.

Genevieve tried to peer over the edge of the paper. Her heart quivered in elation. Her husband had a bold, slanted script, but she couldn't read his words from where she stood. A shiver traveled up her spine as she realized that soon she would meet the man who had penned these instructions, the man with whom she would spend the rest of her life—the man whose home she would tend, whose bed she would share, whose children she would bear. There would be no more hunger, no more fear. The past was over and the future was about to begin.

She took a deep, shuddering breath and tried, for the hundredth time, to remember something about him. The day she had married, her illness had been at its peak. She'd had no strength or inclination to scrutinize the man who had so swiftly chosen her as his life's mate. Genevieve vaguely recalled the strength of his arm as she'd clutched it during the ceremony, for the floor seemed to buck and roll beneath her feet. She remembered leaning her cheek against the fine wool of his green coat, for the room in which they married had been as stifling and hot as her cramped berth on the ship, and she had been faint from hunger and fatigue. She also remembered the pleasant feeling of being buoyed up in his strong embrace and placed on the cart that brought her to the Hôtel-Dieu. But she couldn't remember his face, his expression. She wished she had a clearer picture of him to prepare her for what lay ahead.

Oh, frippery and folly! Perhaps she still did have a touch of fever, to be thinking such silly romantic thoughts. What difference did it make what he looked like? As long as he could provide a roof over her head and roots under her feet.

"Your husband is a *coureur de bois*." Mother Superior's face sank into dour folds. "My dear child, I didn't realize you were married to a fur trader."

"I didn't, either." She wondered why the nun said the words *coureur de bois* with such contempt. "I remember nothing of the day."

"Oh, dear."

Genevieve started as the nun continued reading and pressed her hand to her chest. "What is it, Mother Superior?"

"You were ill the day you married, weren't you, child?"

"Yes."

"Oh, vile, vile man!" Mother Superior set the paper away from her as if it were full of blasphemy. She pulled off her spectacles, clattered them on the desk, then curled her gnarled fingers around the polished head of her cane. She rose from her chair and tried to regain her composure. "It is . . . unfortunate that such a man chose to marry you, my dear child. I fear he took advantage of your illness and the fact that you are so fresh from France."

"I don't understand."

"You wouldn't, would you, my sweet, innocent Marie?" The nun patted her chest with a trembling hand. "Oh, this wretched place! To send such a gentle soul here, to the untamed wilderness . . . Men like your husband *feast* on such innocence."

Genevieve stilled a scowl. What was the old biddy babbling about? What was in that letter that made the holy sister so agitated? "Reverend Mother, you said you didn't know my husband."

"I know his kind all too well." The nun stumbled

as she tried to walk around the corner of the desk. Genevieve hurried to her side and clamped her hand beneath her elbow. Mother Superior wrapped her fingers tightly around Genevieve's arm and stared at her with piercing, fervent eyes. "You should be warned, child, as much as the news shall pain you. This is a savage place, little Marie, and the men who come here grow savage as well. It's better that you enter marriage knowing the true nature of your husband's soul than to walk in ignorance." The nun's eyes clouded with tears. "Oh, I shouldn't tell you. I should let you walk in innocence a little longer. . . ."

"Tell me."

"It's the brandy!" The words burst from the nun's lips. "It's that wretched devil's brew. For every one heathen soul the Jesuits save, two more are lost to brandy. The savages have no tolerance for it; it opens their soul to the demon. Every spring, this hospital is full of men with hatchet wounds, and nearly all of them inflicted by drunken Indians."

Genevieve controlled the urge to shake the truth from the trembling, aged sister. "What does brandy have to do with my husband?"

"It is the *coureurs de bois* who sell the brandy to the Indians, in defiance of all the laws against it. No matter how many of the traders the bishop excommunicates, they continue to sell it to the savages." Mother Superior's fingers tightened on Genevieve's arm. "Your husband is one of them, child, one of those men. . . ."

"Is he excommunicated?!"

"No, but he is one of the *coureurs de bois*, and they all traffic in that devil's brew."

Genevieve closed her eyes so the nun would not see them roll. She didn't care a fig if her husband sold brandy to the savages. She had broken enough commandments in her lifetime to forgive a graveyard full of sinners—enough to send this nun reeling away making the sign of the cross, if she knew the truth. The Reverend Mother was working herself into a lather over nothing, and she didn't even know André. All the holy sister knew was that he was a fur trader, and she was condemning him on that alone.

He *was* a good man, she told herself. The fact that he had married her, sickly and feverish, when a dozen eager and healthy women were available to him, proved that he was a man of great compassion.

"Now I know why he hasn't contacted you, child. He's undoubtedly roaming in the woods at this time of the year, committing un*speakable* sins." The nun released Genevieve and patted her arm. "It's best you stay here for a few more days and then—"

"Oh, no!" She would rather drink the putrid waters of the Seine than stay another day in this hospital. "I must see him as soon as possible. How can I contact him?"

"Dear, I'm sure he's gone by now, at least halfway to Montréal." Mother Superior fingered the paper and squinted over it. "Yes, yes, see? He was instructed that we contact a Monsieur Martineau in the lower city. You are to stay with Monsieur Martineau's family." The nun patted her chest and nodded vigorously. "A good man, Monsieur Martineau, and a fine wife. Three children they have, and she's due to deliver another—"

"Can't I just send a message to my husband?"

"Dear, this is not Paris. We have few horses, no roads, and no men to spare for such a frivolous task."

Genevieve clamped her jaw tight against a curse. She was tired of delay, tired of waiting, but she supposed she could swallow her impatience for a little while longer. "Very well, then. How long must I stay with them . . . with the Martineaus?"

The nun rounded the desk and avoided her eye. "Why, until he comes back, of course."

Something fluttered in her stomach. "When will *that* be?"

"It depends." The nun shrugged. "May, June . . . whenever the ice breaks on the river."

Her breath caught in her throat. *May, June* . . . Eight, nine months. A lifetime. A burn worked its way up her chest, over her neck, choking her with anger.

The paper fluttered on the desk, buoyed by a draft. Genevieve pushed off the nun's spectacles, snatched the paper, and raised it to the light.

"Oh, Marie!" Mother Superior lunged for her and stopped as Genevieve whirled away. "Your stubbornness will bring you nothing but pain."

Genevieve read the instructions swiftly, then, stunned, she read the paper again. "I don't understand this." She glanced up into the nun's teary face. "My husband leaves instructions for my . . . burial."

"I'm sure he was just thinking of all possibilities. . . ."

"I wasn't that ill."

Surely, Genevieve thought, he could tell that she would recover from her illness as soon as she had a few days' rest on solid ground. She was no frail flower, not Genevieve Lalande. Did he know that in this Hôtel-Dieu, just like the one in Paris, death was more probable than life? And if he was so convinced she would die, why had he chosen to marry her at all?

Mother Superior was babbling about brandy and savages and fur traders, twisting the knob of her cane with her gnarled hand. Genevieve tried to make sense of it all, of this unexpected broadside.

". . . the number of annulments in this parish already is disgraceful—utterly disgraceful—and all because of the Intendant's new ruling. It has brought nothing but grief and sin—"

"What ruling?"

The nun started as Genevieve interrupted her. "My dear child, you don't know about that, either, do you? Such a cruel, vile man! May God show him the face of His anger!"

"What ruling?"

"All single men in the colony must marry within a fortnight of the arrival of the king's girls." Tears glimmered in Mother Superior's eyes. "If they don't, they'll be denied trading, fishing, and hunting licenses."

Genevieve pierced the paper with her thumbnail. The truth slapped her like a frigid wave of seawater crashing over the bow of a ship.

"Now you know, my dear Marie." The nun's tears flowed, but her eyes shone with righteousness. "These men are devils, all of them, preferring the profligate life of the savages than taking a good, honest wife. I'm surprised this hasn't happened more often. I'm surprised they're not here in this hospital right now, fighting over the pallets of the dying girls, demanding the priest perform the sacrament of marriage before the sacrament of the last rites. Oh, wretched, vile men!"

Ramrod-straight, Genevieve swiveled away. She snatched one of the plums lying in a bowl on the Reverend Mother's desk and sank her teeth into the reddish-purple flesh. Her mouth puckered from the sour taste but she didn't spit it out. The sourness fueled her anger. It reminded her that the men who lived on these shores came from the same seed as the men who lived in France. André Lefebvre was a rich man, the cruelest of the breed. She should have known that here in Québec she would find the same cruelty as she had known in France.

She chewed the flesh of the plum while the sticky juice ran down her chin. What an idiot she had been to believe that a man would marry for any reason other than his personal gain. The fever must have made her daft. Apparently, André Lefebvre wanted a trading license, not a wife, and could only get one with the other. Because of her illness, she'd been swept into the union, and now she was married to the sort of man who freely abandoned his newlywed wife in the hellish halls of the Hôtel-Dieu, hoping for her death rather than for her life.

Well, she was back from the grave, Genevieve mused bitterly, sucking another bite of the sour, fleshy fruit. She had come clear across the Atlantic, nearly losing her life in the process, for the chance at a home, land, a family. She had waited too long, worked too hard, and risked too much to let a single man ruin everything.

She would not wait eight months for a resolution. She would not wait another day.

Tossing the plum pit in the bowl, Genevieve clutched a handful of her skirts and hiked them over one shoulder.

". . . vile, wretched men. . . . My dear girl! What are you *doing*?"

Genevieve tugged free the ties of a lumpy bag slung around her waist, emerging from beneath the froth of her skirts hefting it in her hand. She clanked the bag onto the table. "I have some money, Mother."

"Dear child, there's more gold in your hand than in all of Québec."

"My dowry from the king," she lied. Genevieve

scowled at the worn leather sack of gold. *The price of a woman's honor—the price of my honor.*

"I will hire a guide with it." Genevieve yanked her skirts straight and met the nun's astonished gaze. There was no better way to spend this long-hoarded fortune than by buying the illusion of an honorable future. "I will find my wayward husband and help him see the error of his ways." A humorless smile slipped across her face. "Surely you must help me in this holy cause, mustn't you, Reverend Mother?"

Chapter Three

André gathered the last of his papers and tossed them on the bed. He rose from the chair and strode to the window of his sparsely furnished room, peering between the ill-fitting slats of the shutters toward the Montréal shore. Pulled up on the bank, several birch bark canoes lay belly up in anticipation of the morning's departure, the last caulking with pine pitch drying in the air. A half-dozen *voyageurs* hunkered around a campfire nearby, smoking pipes and passing around a bottle of brandy.

The fire cast a rosy glow upon the faces of his hired men, illuminating out of the shroud of darkness a twinkling eye, a flash of laughter, a companionable grin. He would give a dozen beaver furs to be out there, breathing in the scent of the pinewood fire, drawing the stinging tobacco smoke deep into his lungs, feeling the river breeze on his face. This tiny room stifled him with its odorless silence, with its low roof, soft mattress, and smothering woolen covers. He had stayed out of the room all day long, but come evening he had no choice but to sleep in this coffin. As leader of this voyage, there were limits to how companionable he could be with the men he had hired.

André pushed away from the window. He yanked his sweat-stained brown silk doublet off his shoulders and tossed it on the floor, where it joined the wig, shoes, and cravat he had discarded the moment he had entered the room. He paced at the foot of the bed in shirttails and breeches, forcing himself to think of the details, anything to take his mind off the walls closing in on him, the flickering of the candlelight off the solid log walls. The cornmeal and peas had been bought and bagged; the hatchets, glass beads, knives, brandy, blankets, and other trading goods had already been packed in tight ninety-pound packages. He had hired and paid out one-third wages to two dozen *voyageurs*, most of them work-hardened, tough, dependable men. The canoes were pitched and ready to be loaded. All he awaited was the dawn.

Finally. All the bargaining, all the delays, all the unexpected new rules in the colony—they were over now. This was his last night in the settlements. Tomorrow he would put on his well-worn leggings and moccasins and return home to a hard, earthen bed and an open sky.

A knock on the door interrupted his musings. André glared at the portal. He had finished his business for the day. The last thing he wanted to do was haggle with a merchant over last-minute prices or argue with the authorities over the behavior of his drunken *voyageurs*.

The knock came again, more persistent.

"It's open." André swept his wig off the floor and

jammed it on his head. "And you'd best have a damn good reason for disturbing my peace."

The door swung open. A blur of pink swept in like a gust of wind. The creature suddenly stilled and fixed him with a fiery, green-eyed glare. With a start, he realized that the guest was a woman.

A *beautiful* woman.

"André Lefebvre?"

Surprised into silence, he stared at her. He had expected Tiny with some problem concerning the canoes or the men, or, worse, a merchant with bad news about promised cargo . . . not a woman with green eyes and pouty red lips and copper-colored hair that gleamed in the candlelight, falling in windblown curls over her shoulders and . . . *Dieu*! Though she was corseted tightly, no amount of boning could crush those curves. His shock abated; his thoughts whirred. He wondered if the innkeeper had sent her up to him, but one look at the fine rose-colored ribbon trimming her pink bodice told him that this was no public woman. Courtesans of this caliber didn't live in New France.

"You must be André." She slammed the door behind her. "No other man would be so shocked to see me." She clattered a woven case upon the floor between them, like a nobleman tossing a gauntlet in challenge. "I'm not a ghost, monsieur, but I have come to haunt you."

Haunt, little firebrand. He'd never exorcise such a vision from his bedroom. Who the hell was she? She seemed to think he knew her. André peered at her features in the darkness, frantically trying to place a name to a face. When he was last in Montréal, he had spent a few passionate evenings with a young widow before he returned to France. What was her name? . . . Charlotte? Colette? It didn't matter. This couldn't be the widow of Montréal. The woman tapping her foot before him couldn't be more than nineteen or twenty years of age, which meant when he was last in Montréal, she couldn't have been more than sixteen—and he avoided sixteen-year-olds as religiously as he avoided Indian stews.

"Well?" She crossed her arms. Her mass of reddish curls quivered about her face, and the point of her booted foot tapped, lifting the soggy hem of her skirts. "Are you going to stand there and stare all night, or are you going to congratulate me for recovering from my illness?"

His gaze fell to the provocative swelling of her bosom above the straight edge of her bodice, and he decided in an instant to play along. "Congratulations. You appear to be in the full bloom of health."

"How unfortunate for you."

"On the contrary . . ."

"Don't you dare deny it!"

"Deny what?"

"You wanted me dead!"

He held up his hand. "I don't think—"

"It's true! You got what you wanted, then you abandoned me to my fate."

Fool of a man, whoever it was that this woman searched for. No man with red blood pumping in his veins would take this woman and then abandon her without a final taste; there were few enough women in the settlements, and fewer of such generous bounty. She definitely had the wrong person, though she knew him by name. André had a policy about Frenchwomen that he made clear before a love affair: no promises, no commitment, no complications.

He approached so she could get a better look at his face, for the candlelight in the room was dim. "I think you judge me too harshly, *chérie.*"

"Don't you *dare* call me darling."

"You don't understand—"

"Oh, I understand better than you think." Her bosom heaved dangerously against the restriction of her clothing. "You chose the wrong woman to take advantage of, monsieur. I was sick, not a fool."

There was still no doubt in those green eyes, only anger and accusation and a growing impatience. It was on the tip of his tongue to tell her she had made a mistake, but the words stuck like glue to his lips. If he told her, she would leave, and this was the most intriguing visitor he'd had since he returned to New France.

It was his last night. One final sniff of French perfume would be a fine way to say goodbye to civilization.

"Speechless with shame, are you? I should think so. How does it feel to be caught slipping away like a thief in the night?"

His gaze wandered over her pale pink dress, lingering on the creamy swell of her breasts, then slipped down to her narrow waist and over the flair of her skirts. "I find myself . . . pleased to be captured."

Her lips parted in a gasp. Desire rushed hot through his blood. Not since Aix-en-Provence, where he had made the mistake of taking a mistress who expected more out of him than money, had he enjoyed a woman. It had taken weeks to disentangle himself from that relationship. Frenchwomen always complicated a good night's worth of lusty lovemaking with so much baggage—vows of eternal devotion, fidelity, paroxysms of guilt about their own sensuality. André was looking forward to the simple, honest passion of an Indian woman.

He met her eyes. They sparkled with a strange mixture of fury and surprise. He wondered if she were playing some sort of vixen's game. Perhaps she had seen him in Montréal, had wanted him, but now that she had dared to join him in the confines of his room, she'd lost the courage to tell him precisely why she was here. He glanced down at the woven basket she'd tossed between them. There was no doubt; she had come to spend the night. It wouldn't be the first time a woman had played an elaborate role in order to justify her own infidelity. The lengths civilized women went to hide their own passion. . . . Well, he was more than willing to go along with the charade if it meant an evening rolling in the linens with this lovely creature.

He pressed closer . . . close enough to cast his shadow over her. "I think there's been a misunderstanding between us."

"You call abandonment a *misunderstanding*!"

"I was a fool to abandon you," he murmured, playing along with the game. Her lower lip was plump and wet, fuller than her upper one. As juicy as a ripe peach it was, all pouty and centered with the faintest dimple. He wound his fingers around her shoulders and pulled her against him. "Come, love. Forgive me my wrongs."

She jerked in his embrace. "You must be jesting."

"At least let me make it up to you."

Her mouth parted, but before she could speak, he met those inviting lips with his own. Her breath caught and held. Her heart thumped hard beneath her breasts, hesitated, and stopped, then thumped harder still. He pressed his nose against her cheek as he deepened the kiss, smelling river mist and rain, along with fresh pine-scented air, clinging like dew to soft, soft skin.

Dieu! It had been too long. Pure passion in his arms she was, all quivering, curvy, and warm. He slid his hands off her shoulders and wound them around her back. She fit against him, the fullness of her bosom giving against his chest, swelling soft, soft, even as she stiffened. He slid his hands down farther, to her narrow waist, digging his fingers into her side . . . only to come against the hard whalebone rib of her corset. Damn the Frenchwoman's clothing, all those laces and knots and rigid seams and layers—for man's benefit, they said, all these locks and keys. He wanted to feel bare, hot flesh, not seams and satin. He buried his free hand in the silk of her curls, pulling her head back to fix his lips more firmly on her own. His blood coursed hot and fast through his veins.

The tips of her nails dug into his linen shirt, her only movement other than the give of her body and lips. Pleasure or resistance? He couldn't tell, and as long as her lips lay open beneath his, André refused to retreat. She parted those lips still further to gasp, and he took brazen advantage of the breach. He tasted the juice of her mouth, sweet, and delicious, vaguely naughty, forbidden fruit. But before he could drink fully of the nectar, she began to struggle.

No, no . . . don't. Dammit, why must Frenchwomen always fight the rush of their blood, the fury of their own passion? He wouldn't hurt her. He'd show her all the pleasure there could be between a man and a woman in lovemaking—and he would see that she would not grow big with child after he left. He held her tighter, trying to squeeze the fight out of her, to see if this struggle were nothing but another parlay in the elaborate French game of refusal and surrender. Her heart raced in her chest. He spread his hand over her lower back. Boldly, he ran his tongue over the silky swell of her lower lip. She started as if she had been struck with fire.

He didn't like the feel of her shock. André released her lips and raised his head only enough to see into her eyes. They were misty and bright, like the color of a shallow lake in the summer sunshine. She no longer looked like the fiery woman who had burst into his room, so full of rage and self-righteousness. She looked young, confused, and thoroughly, thoroughly kissed.

"What is it, *chérie?* What troubles you?"

"You're kissing me."

He grinned. "Obviously."

"Does this mean you'll start treating me . . . like a wife?"

He had been planning to treat her like a wife—in his bed. By the serious expression in her eyes, he knew she meant something more. Her pink tongue darted out and lingered on her lower lip. With an inward groan, he followed the journey of that pink tongue as it swished back and forth across her lower lip. She looked like a child tasting licorice for the first time.

André started. Christ, she'd never been kissed before. He released her abruptly. This was no wayward wife looking for an infidelity. He examined her clothing and his suspicions grew. She dressed too well to be without family or husband. Frenchwomen arriving in the settlements were married almost as soon as they set foot upon Canadian soil, he knew that well enough. His gaze fell to the battered woven case on the floor, which was large enough to hold enough clothes for several days. Perhaps she had run away from her family. Perhaps she was looking for someone to take care of her. For the first time since she'd walked in, André began to wonder if there were more to this than he suspected—like a musket-wielding father downstairs, waiting for his daughter to emerge ruined from the stranger's room so he could force him into marriage.

Ironically, he already *was* married. Temporary or not, he still had a wife in Québec. As much as he wanted to lay this woman down on his bed, spread her coppery curls over the pillow, and merge with her supple, young body, he knew he couldn't let this charade continue any further. She probably was— *God forbid!*—a virgin.

André took one step away from her. "I think we should have a talk, you and I."

Her fingers had replaced her tongue on her lips, but at the sound of his voice, she dropped her hand. "Long overdue, that."

"Is it?"

"I want to know your plans." Her gold-tipped lashes curled up as she met his gaze. "For us."

She sounded so sure of herself, so sure of him— as sure as he was that he had never before laid eyes on her. "Do you know who I am?"

Her brows twitched with sudden uncertainty. "You are André Lefebvre?"

"Yes. Do you know that I already have a wife?"

She looked at him as if he were crazed.

He spread his hands and sighed. "I married only recently."

The girl's bosom heaved. A fiery flush infused her cheeks. Her eyes glowed with new flames, reducing to ashes any hopes he had of spending the night with her. When she finally spoke, her voice was full of incredulous fury. "You don't know who I am, do you?"

If she could shoot venom through her eyes, he'd be dead a hundred times over. He shrugged help- lessly. "It's been a few years since I've been in Mon- tréal. . . ."

"You wretch!" She wiped the back of her hand

against her lips. "All this time, you thought I was just some whore throwing herself upon you—"

"Would that all women be so passionate," he interrupted. "I wish I were the man you're seeking . . . but you've mistaken my identity."

"Mistaken!" She planted her fists on her hips. "You didn't mind pretending you were the man you thought I mistook you for!"

"You're too tempting a morsel not to bite."

"Oh!" She sucked in her breath through clenched teeth, then swirled in a swish of skirts. "I shouldn't be surprised at all!"

"You shouldn't, not when you enter a strange man's bedroom after dark."

"You're *married*!"

"I'm not dead."

"You've got the morals of a stray cat!"

"You dropped into my lap like manna from heaven, *chérie*." He glanced with appreciation at her body. "And you're a creature that would test a Jesuit's own chastity."

"Am I?" Her fists slipped off her hips and she leaned forward, tantalizing him with a glimpse of deep cleavage. "That's good to know. You'll be easy to cuckold."

"I told you, I'm already married—"

"I'm your *wife*, you fool!"

André choked on the word.

"Yes. *Wife*."

Impossible. *Impossible*. This couldn't be his wife. His wife was a pitiful little thing with red-rimmed eyes and dark freckles against gray-tinted skin. She didn't have hair like burnished copper . . . but then again, she had been wearing a linen headrail when he'd married her, and her hair had been soaked with perspiration. He struggled against the fog of memory. She had been half dead that day in Madame Bourdon's house, a weak, tiny thing clinging to his arm for support and slurring her vows. Undoubtedly, she was still at the Hôtel-Dieu, recovering from her illness . . . if she weren't already dead.

Illness. What had this woman said about illness when she first arrived?

"Has your memory returned yet?" She swayed closer to him, emboldened by his silence, clutching the edges of her cloak. "Let me refresh it for you. My name is—was—Marie Duplessis. We married in Madame Bourdon's home in Québec, in the presence of Philippe Martineau and about a dozen other couples. Then you abandoned me at the Hôtel-Dieu."

He stared at her. With a start, he noticed a spattering of freckles across her nose, paler now against skin that had flushed an angry rose.

His blood ran cold when he realized how close he had come to consummating his own marriage.

"That's more of the reaction I expected from a man caught cheating on his wife *with* his wife."

"Last time I saw you," he argued, stepping back and meeting those sparkling green eyes with a new wariness, "you were retching at my side."

"It was nothing more than shipboard fever, my *husband*."

"You're supposed to be at Marietta's."

"I didn't come across the ocean to be the governess to another woman's children. Yes, yes, I went to Marietta and she told me you'd planned to keep me there until you returned. But I did not come to Québec only to be abandoned by my husband. . . ."

"I didn't abandon you." He snapped the words and turned away from her. The candle sputtered in the corner on the desk. A sheaf of papers balancing precariously on the edge of the bed slipped off the pile and swept over the floor. "I left for a voyage already long delayed. I made arrangements—"

"For my burial."

Guilt twinged at him. *Damn it.* His gaze swept over her, from the jiggle of her curls to the hem of her skirts, and anger started at a slow burn, sizzling away from the guilt. All Frenchwoman . . . worse, all aristocrat. The breeding showed in her long, white neck, her delicate skin, her pointed chin and cheekbones. He'd noticed the signs in her sickness, and now, in the full of health, she stood before him the embodiment of the one kind of creature to whom he wanted no commitment.

A woman like this didn't belong in his world. He couldn't protect her, he couldn't keep her safe.

"You didn't look like this when I last saw you," André argued, raking his hand under his wig. "I made arrangements for you to stay in a safe place in a warm house with people I trusted, in the closest thing to civilization you'll find in this country."

"For how long? Forever?"

"Didn't Philippe tell you my plans?"

"Which ones? Burial or slavery?"

He frowned. She'd been too sick to remember her own name at their wedding, let alone understand his plans; and he had been too busy making arrangements for his voyage to check on her at the Hôtel-Dieu. He'd told Philippe to take care of everything— including explaining his intentions to his new wife. Philippe, with his usual distaste of unpleasant tasks, had delayed this one too late. Marietta had probably flown into a rage when this woman appeared on her doorstep, most likely seeing to it that she was on a boat to Montréal within minutes of her arrival.

He crossed his arms in front of him, steeling himself

for the inevitable confrontation. "You've come a long way to hear what Marietta could have told you."

"I wanted to hear it from the coward's own lips." She looked him up and down, her nose wrinkling in an aristocratic sneer. "I also wanted to know what kind of swine would abandon his wife so quickly."

"You won't be my wife for long."

Something murderous in his eyes must have given her pause. She stepped back, stumbling over one of his abandoned shoes. "If you touch me, I'll scream so loud that every man in this inn will come running—"

He cut her short with a jerk of his hand. "I'm a fur trader, not a murderer."

"How comforting," she snapped, kicking away the offending shoe and giving him a view of a slim, booted ankle beneath a muddied froth of skirts. "Fur traders don't kill their wives. They only abandon them after they get their trading licenses."

"Then you know about Talon's ruling."

"You're not even going to deny it!" she sputtered. "How noble! A brigand who's honest about his treachery."

"This marriage is a convenient one for both of us."

"It isn't convenient for *me* to care for someone else's children, in someone else's house, or wait nine months for my husband to return from God knows where to tell me what he plans—"

"If I hadn't married you, someone else would, and you'd have very little choice in the matter."

"I had no choice in the matter when a ruthless lecher plucked me off my deathbed."

"I'm giving you a second chance. Come summer, when I return to Québec, I'll have our marriage annulled. Then you'll be free to marry again. . . ."

"So you *will* get rid of me." She tossed her head

of curls and crossed her arms snug under her breasts. "I thought as much. What do I do between now and summer . . . other than give you horns?"

His jaw tightened. He had no doubt she'd find a dozen willing men to quench her desire in his absence, and briefly he wondered how a daughter of the *petite noblesse* had managed to cultivate such passion, such spirit. "Philippe and Marietta will see to it that you behave like my wife."

"So while you're roaming in the woods, I must sit in a stranger's house for nine months, waiting for you to return so you can toss me off like an old wig?"

"Come summer, you'll have a choice of men, unlike the other girls who have to decide on a husband within fifteen days."

"I came clear across the world to start a new life in this colony. I didn't do it so I could be abandoned by my husband within days and divorced within months." She uncrossed her arms and wagged a finger at him. "You married me, Monsieur Lefebvre. You're going to treat me like a wife."

"Am I?" He let his gaze roam insolently over her lovely body. "You don't even know what that means, *chérie*."

"It means," she said, ignoring his look, "that you put me in *your* house and not leave me with utter strangers."

"I don't have a home here."

"None?"

"I've nothing but an abandoned old hut on a piece of land I inherited from my father, land that has long returned to forest."

"You're supposed to be a rich man," she countered, brows as sweeping as sparrow's wings tugging together. "You must have a house bigger than Marietta's. . . ."

"I don't, not a habitable one, which is why you're staying with her."

"Oh, but I'm *not* staying with her." She glanced around the room and saw his small bag packed in the corner. "Wherever you are going, I am going."

Amid the swirling currents of anger, André felt an urge to laugh. She was a stubborn creature, a willful woman-child, and the thought of her sleeping on the hard ground under the open sky or perched upon all the merchandise stuffed into a birch bark canoe was too ludicrous for him to ignore. "You have no idea where I'm going. You belong with Marietta, in civilization or what passes for it here, not in the forests."

"I've been in forests before."

He had an image of her strolling calmly through the well-tended woods of some country estate, with exotic peacocks calmly pecking in the courtyards. "Not forests like these. These are full of savages."

"So are the settlements, I've noticed." She shuffled through his scattered clothing, peering at him through narrowed eyes. "You have to spend the winter in those forests. Where are you going to live?"

A fur trader named Nicholas Perrot had built some crude buildings in Chequamegon Bay when he was last there, but André doubted this woman would consider them worthy of the name "home."

"You *do* have a home," she said, clapping her hands twice. "I'll stay there with you."

"This isn't a pleasure voyage," he argued, kicking aside a pair of his breeches and planting his hands on his hips. "Until we get to that place, we'll be sleeping on the ground with nothing above our heads but an overturned canoe. We'll be eating cornmeal mush and boiled peas for most of the trip. We'll be crossing rapids like you've never seen in Paris, and we'll be walking hundreds of miles to get around them. There's danger from bears, from wolves, from savages who for one reason or another no longer like the French and would do almost anything to have such a pretty scalp as yours."

She rolled her eyes. "I outgrew such gruesome tales when I was given my first corset."

"You're still delirious." He clutched her upper arm. "You're going back to Marietta's, and you're going back now."

"Am I?"

The fire flared in those eyes—unusual eyes, a pure jade flame. She dug her heels into the floor. She was more child than woman if she thought she could impose her will on him. André tightened his grip on her upper arm. She tried to wrench away but failed. He thought it was a pity that she was his wife; he would have enjoyed kissing the fight out of her.

He headed toward the door, dragging her with him. "This will be easier if you don't make a scene on the way out."

"I have no intention of making this easy for you." She yanked on his arm as he pulled her out into the hallway. "I'm not going to let you just abandon me, your own wife, in a strange country. . . ."

"Then I'll have to tie you up and make sure you stay tied up until you're back with Marietta."

"The governor will love to hear of that," she snapped, pink skirts flying as she struggled, tiny pointed boot tips nicking his shins. "I'll go to his house trussed up like a sack of flour, then he'll know how badly I've been mistreated."

"Don't threaten me, woman."

"I'm Marie Duplessis, your *wife*, not some common fishmonger! The governor will arrange for an immediate annulment when he hears about this. . . . If you're not going to keep me, then I'm not waiting until next summer to get rid of *you*."

André froze in the middle of the hallway. He knew with deadly certainty that she would do exactly what she said she would. The girl was nothing if not resourceful, having made it this far and finding him. The governor would be none too pleased to be confronted with the abandoned wife of a fur trader. André knew exactly what the official would do when he heard this woman's story. The governor would see to it that the marriage was annulled and this woman remarried. In punishment, he would revoke André's trading license, when it was too late for the fur trader to do anything about it.

A door cracked on the far end of the hall. André whirled and dragged her back into the room. He kicked the door closed behind him.

She faced him squarely, wiping a lock of hair out of her eyes. "So, you are going to discuss this now."

"There's nothing to discuss." He tugged her arm and thrust her back against the door. "Unless you want to be a great source of entertainment to the guests of this fair inn, I suggest you shut up while I tie you up and carry you back to your boat."

"Don't bother tying me up. I'll go willingly." She leaned her head back against the door and blew the errant lock of hair from her eyes again. "What difference does it make to you if I get an annulment now or later? You've got your license. You don't need me anymore."

The wench didn't even know the power of her own words. She didn't know that if she went to the governor, everything that he had worked three years to obtain would be destroyed. His grip tightened on her arm. Why had she come? And why now, on the eve of his departure? He should never have answered the door; after all, good news never comes at night. Some evil *manitou* was at work here, determined to crush his dreams, and it took the form of this stubborn, beautiful, willful woman who threatened everything and didn't even know it.

He should just escape the settlements tonight, André thought, before she ever had a chance to go to the governor. He could do it. He knew where all his *voyageurs* were sleeping. He could go deep into the interior and roam the wilderness and forget all that had happened here. But when he returned there would be hell to pay—and it was a hell he could not afford. They'd hanged the last men who'd tried to smuggle illegal furs into Québec, confiscating everything for which they'd worked. He had struggled so hard to keep everything legal—Christ, he had even *married* to keep everything legal. Short of imprisoning this woman in Marietta's house, once he left the settlements, there was nothing he could do to stop her from ruining him and all his dreams.

She was staring at him steadily, waiting for him to say something. If he were a different type of man, he would wrap his fingers around her frail white throat and choke the life from her. André saw a flicker of fear in her eyes as she tried to jerk away from him, but he held her fast. He was trapped ... trapped more firmly than she was in his embrace. He couldn't free her from this marriage, nor could he leave her here in the settlements to wreak havoc. He had made a mistake in marrying this woman. He had mistaken illness for docility.

He had to take her with him. Damn it, he had no other choice. She'd slow him down, and any more delays on this voyage could be disastrous. It would take at least four or five weeks just to reach Sault Sainte Marie, the falls that marked the entrance to

Lake Superior. Hundreds of uncharted miles separated Sault Ste. Marie from Chequamegon Bay—his destination—and only a few white men had ever traveled that far. The weeks wasted before he'd gotten his trading license had cut his time short. If this trip was delayed or slowed any more, he'd never make it to Chequamegon Bay before the winter freeze.

It would be a hard, long drive to the west, he thought, made a thousand times more difficult by the presence of this woman. He tried to imagine her negotiating the treacherous hills and narrow ledges of the long portages around the waterfalls, teetering on her heeled leather boots. She'd be battered and bruised in the birch bark canoes as they were poled upstream against the raging currents. She'd be useless weight, unable to carry any of the goods during the portages or paddle the canoes over calm water. She'd cry when mosquitoes feasted on her pale, exposed skin; she'd complain about sleeping on the cold earth; she'd cause endless delays. She was a noblewoman, for God's sake! Weak and pampered and utterly new to this country. He wanted to leave civilization behind, not carry it with him in the form of a well-bred wife. He'd give her two, maybe three days on the voyage before she screamed to come back to civilization. Then what would he do with her? He'd be too far away from Montréal to spare anyone to escort her back to the settlements. She'd be dead weight, a hundred pounds of whining, crying, complaining Frenchwoman.

Then an idea came to him, as swift and straight as an arrow and just as lethal. His body flinched when it came, for the arrowhead was poisoned with guilt.

He couldn't. *He couldn't.*

Damn it, he'd left her in Québec, with Marietta and Philippe, in the one part of New France that had become civilized over the past few years. She'd been as safe there as any woman could be in the new world, especially now that the Iroquois were at peace with the French. And so he'd rationalized that he wasn't abandoning her, as he'd left another Frenchwoman behind once before, not so long ago. . . .

He squeezed his eyes shut. By God, why did they come here? Why would these women, these frail swan-necked creatures, leave the security and ease of France to hang themselves about the necks of the men of Québec? What did the new world give them but danger, the threat of starvation, of cold, of a hard, rude life of labor? For men there was the freedom of the uncharted forests, the challenge of the unknown; for women there was nothing but grief and drudgery.

He blinked open his eyes and glared at her, the tilted, defiant chin, the level gaze. She'd thrust it upon herself, the willful aristocrat, for not staying in Québec. He'd warned her . . . he'd warned her of the dangers, yet still she wanted to go. He could not let her stay and wreak havoc on his plans, so he'd let her join him—for as long as she lasted.

Then God save them both.

"Whatever you're planning," she said, "I don't like it."

"Yes, you will." He released her abruptly. "I've changed my mind. You'll come with me."

She rubbed her forearm where he had grasped her. "After all that fuss?"

"It's in your best interests to stay, but you're a stubborn woman." His gaze traveled over her intimately. This, at least, wasn't a lie. "Stubborn and beautiful. Far too beautiful to be left alone in Québec while I'm wandering in the interior."

"Ah. So you're taking me just so I won't give you horns."

"You underrate your own charm."

"And next spring?" she asked boldly, ignoring the compliment. "Are you still planning to annul this marriage when we return to the settlements?"

He lifted a brow. She was far too smart, far too sharp for an innocent daughter of the *petite noblesse.* He could lie outright, but he sensed she would suspect such an abrupt about-face.

But that kiss . . . that kiss had unnerved her. He would use it to his advantage.

So he planted his hand above her head and leaned closer to her, covering her with his shadow while the candlelight flickered gold on the rough-hewn log walls. Her pupils constricted, her nostrils thinned as she inhaled deeply. He felt his own blood surge at the aroma of her perfume, rising from her skin, her hair—French scent and woman-scent. "Nine months is a long time for a husband and wife to be alone in the wilderness, *chérie.*"

She pressed back against the door, suddenly breathless.

"Spring is hundreds of nights away. Anything could happen between now and then. You may decide I'm a terrible husband."

"I'm convinced . . . already."

"Then *you'll* be the one screaming for an annulment next spring, not I." Her lips pouted so invitingly that he had to restrain himself from kissing her. "You took me by surprise this evening." He forced the lie between his lips. "I want to think about this annulment."

Her eyes flickered, narrowing. "What caused this sudden change of heart?"

By God, it was too bad she was his wife. Beneath all these prickles was a passionate woman, and he would love to clip off the thorns and make the rose bloom, just for him. His gaze swept from the cascade of her copper curls to the toes of her booted feet. He lowered his voice to a whisper and told her another truth. "You, my wildcat, are not what I expected."

She blinked at him. He saw surprise, hesitation, and suspicion reflected in her lucid green eyes. Her will was wavering. She was swallowing the bait. He pushed one step further, hating himself even as he did it.

"Have you ever gambled, my wife?"

She frowned, confused by the sudden change in topic. "Charity houses don't allow gambling."

"You're gambling now, as am I. I hadn't considered taking you with me, not only because you were ill, but because Frenchwomen never travel into the interior." He leaned closer, so his mouth was only a breath away from hers. "It can get lonely out in the wilderness, with no one but the Indians and my men for company. A Frenchwoman would be a welcome companion . . . if she could withstand the rigors of the journey." He couldn't resist any longer. His lips brushed her tip-tilted nose, then, with the softness of a bird's wing, brushed her lips. They seemed to blossom beneath his touch. He forced himself to pull away. "That's where you must gamble. It's a long, difficult journey. I can't make the decision for you. You alone must decide whether you are willing to face the risks." *And the consequences.*

"I came here to be your wife, to live in your home," she argued. "I'll go."

He smiled into her sparkling eyes, a smile that he knew was more of a grimace. She was a bold, willful creature, a fool. André wondered how long she would last through the rigors of the great North American forest, how long it would take to break her spirit. He stifled the guilt he felt for having gone to such lengths to have his way. But she'd brought it upon herself; the consequences would be her own.

He pushed away from the wall and watched the golden candlelight flicker over her features. "We're leaving at dawn. I'll make arrangements with the innkeeper to get you another room."

"Oh, no." She wrapped her fingers around his arm. "I'm staying right here with you."

He felt a heavy rush of warmth to his loins. "Such an eager bride."

"Did you think I was going to let you escape in the middle of the night and leave me here alone?"

The room was stifling again, but it was a different sort of closeness, the kind that urged him to draw nearer to her, to reduce the world to two warm, willing bodies in one soft bed. He needed a woman. He wanted *this* woman, he was honest enough to admit. André forcefully reined in his desire. He had to get away from her now, before he made a very serious mistake.

"Trust me, my lusty wife." He slipped her hand off his arm and kissed her fingertips, one at a time. Then he bowed, sweeping his hand out as if it held a feathered hat. "I wouldn't leave you behind for all the beaver in Québec."

Chapter Four

He was too damn handsome.

Genevieve paced in her room, rubbing her clammy hands up and down the linen sleeves of her shift. She was alone in this tiny room in the back of the inn, alone in the dim indigo light of predawn, but she felt as if she stood in the midst of a Parisian marketplace, knife tight in hand, limbs tense, waiting for a victim with a heavy purse to slice, her body poised to race away like the wind.

She had spent the night pacing this room, trying to calm herself enough to sleep. Her instincts roared like thunder. Long ago, she had learned never to ignore the prickling at the back of her neck, the tight knots of her belly, the silent screams inside her head, yet now, when the prickling had turned to needlelike stabs, when the knots of her belly had solidified to stone, and when the screams grew so loud that her ears rang, she knew she *must* do exactly what every sinew of her body warned against.

She must trust a man who grinned like one of the gargoyles carved into the stone of Notre Dame.

Falling to her knees, she groped along the floor of her room and searched for her scattered clothing. She told herself she was just dressing in preparation for another confrontation with her husband. She told herself that morning was nearly here, because she had heard the first birds peeping outside the walls of the inn, and there was no reason to tarry. She told herself that if she stayed in this room any longer, she'd wear the floorboards down to dust.

Genevieve sat back on her shins and clutched her bundle of clothing tight to her chest, closing her eyes against the voices warring inside her head. The icy cold of the floorboards seeped through her thin shift and chilled her legs. It took every last dram of her will to stifle the urge to run away from this inn, to run like the devil away from *that man*. But she had come too far to escape like a coward. She reminded herself that nothing awaited her in Québec except the battle for an annulment ... an annulment she wasn't even sure she could win without his presence, and if she failed, she'd be forced to wait nine long winter months in another woman's house with another woman's children until he decided to return to Québec to set her free—and thus risk the vague but terrifying possibility of discovery. *That* would get her a quick enough annulment, she thought with a fresh shiver, and a swift and brutal return to Paris as well.

But if she stayed here with this man with eyes like a lion's, if she stifled all her screaming instincts, then she would have what she had crossed an ocean to obtain: a home. A *home*. A place of her own where she could be safe, warm, and protected from the world. All she had to do to make it hers was to follow this sly-smiling, heart-stopping rogue of a husband into the wilderness.

She stood up and draped her clothing over the room's single chair, taking a deep breath as the fury of her fear ebbed. There was no question what she would do, but still, someone should have warned her. Someone should have told her that he was young, tall, broad-shouldered; that his chest was muscular and golden; that he had no qualms about brazenly displaying it beneath his open, billowing white shirt. Someone should have warned her about his lazy smile, his roving eyes, his strong, hard hands; someone should have warned her that he was not the gentleman she'd expected.

Genevieve fumbled with her rose-colored bodice, slipping her arms into the sleeves as her instincts threatened to overwhelm her anew. When he had drawn near to her last night, with that smoky look in his eyes, everything she had planned to say during the trip from Québec to Montréal had melted like butter on her tongue. She had had no time to fight— no will to fight—when he engulfed her in his arms and *kissed* her.

She jerked the laces of the bodice closed tightly across her chest, then dragged her skirt off the chair and stepped into the folds. A bubble of humorless laughter slipped through her lips at the irony of it all. It had been her first kiss. He'd sensed her surprise, and he'd probably mistaken it as innocence.

Her cheeks burned for the hundredth time since she'd entered this tiny room. She should be thankful. She knew the price she had to pay for the protection of a husband: She'd have to submit to the man's fumbling lusts. She'd long steeled herself for that.

But André hadn't grasped her greedily, he hadn't pawed her with rough hands or scratched her with ragged nails. And when his arms had tightened around her and his lips had suddenly parted, her entire body had jolted with a shock of something she'd never felt before, and her heart had raced and tumbled as if she had been running away from the royal orchards with a skirt full of ripe apples. It had scared her to death. She wanted no part of that feeling; she didn't understand it, she didn't trust it.

Genevieve whirled and paced back and forth across the room, the wooden floor icy beneath her bare feet. She reminded herself that the kiss had taken place *before* he'd realized she was his wife, when he'd thought she was nothing more than a whore looking for a companion for the evening. After he'd discovered the truth, he had looked at her as a well-dressed bourgeois might look at manure caught on the heel of his boot: He had spent the rest of the night trying to kick it off.

Until he bared his teeth in some semblance of a smile and agreed to take her along with him.

She pulled her stockings off the back of the chair, plopped down on the edge of the bed, and thrust her toes into the worn wool. She didn't have to be the most perceptive woman in the world to know that he didn't want this marriage. If he did, she wouldn't be sleeping in a windowless room on the other end of the inn. Rather, she'd be tight between the sheets with him, in the midst of the "marital duties." Genevieve stifled the strange feeling rising in her belly. Better for her that he didn't demand those favors yet, but it simply meant that he didn't want a wife, for she knew better than most women that all men craved the lifting of a woman's skirts with blind, mindless heat. There had to be another reason why he

had agreed to take her with him into the wilderness.
A dark, deceptive reason.

Have you ever gambled, my wife?

She tied the garter at her thigh with a jerk. Genevieve remembered the gambling halls of the *Cour des
Miracles* in Paris, the hot, dark rooms where men
risked their money and their lives, and women bet
their faded charms on the turn of a single card. She
remembered the drunkards who risked the bounty
of a day's begging on the clatter of the bones on the
paving stones.

Oh, yes, she thought, her eyes narrowing with
secrets, *I've gambled, my husband.* She had gambled
enough to recognize André as a dangerous man. She
imagined that Marie Duplessis's Musketeer would be
of the same ilk—roguish, charming, devil-may-care,
full of promises but empty of conscience. Men like
that had abounded in the books that were hidden in
Maman's library, the books Genevieve had spent many
a night reading by the flickering light of a fragrant
candle. And now she faced one in the flesh. During
the course of a single evening, André had manipulated her like a puppet at the fair of Saint-Germain.

She should know better. Genevieve vowed not to
let him surprise her again. Her stomach curdled like
overheated milk as she pulled on her leather boots
and laced them up. She was acting like a weak-kneed
little fool, letting her emotions and her fears overrule
her common sense. She didn't know what André was
planning for her, but she knew the dice were weighted
in her favor. She was gambling that once she reached
their new home, this silver-tongued fur trader could
be manipulated into giving her what she wanted most:
the protection of his name and his wealth, the security
of his house, and most of all, the knowledge that she
would never—*ever*—be set out on her own again.

Nine months was a long time in the wilderness, a long time for a husband and wife to live like celibates in close quarters. If their unlikely marriage was consummated, then her future would be secure.

The past would be gone . . . forever.

Genevieve stood up and smoothed unsteady hands over her skirts. She clutched the handle of her case. The sooner they started on this voyage, the sooner they would reach their new home and the less time she would have to falter like a coward. Straightening her bodice, she strode out of the room. The door swung shut loudly behind her, echoing in the silent hall.

The darkness reeked of brandy and stale sweat. She headed blindly down the hall, trailing her hand along the wall as a guide. She stumbled twice over prone bodies, then continued ahead. It took a few minutes for her to find André's door, and when she did, she rapped on the wood and waited.

No answer. No shuffle of linens, no grunts of sleepiness, not even the patter of footsteps.

She knocked again, this time more insistently. The door gave way under her fist. Startled, she stared at it for a moment, then pushed it wide open.

The room was empty. An inky blue light spilled through the cracks of the wooden shutters, splashing stripes of color across the twisted linens. The covers lay half on the bed, half on the floor. André's pack was missing from the corner.

The stinking son of a poxed whore.

Genevieve strode in and searched the room for a note, a message of any kind, tearing the linens off the mattress. He had sounded so sincere when he said he wouldn't leave her behind! Short of sleeping in the hall outside his room or throwing herself upon him, she'd had no choice but to take him by his word.

She whirled and raced down the stairs to the common room. Ignoring the sleeping innkeeper slouched behind a small counter, she stormed across the room and barreled through the door.

A diffuse bluish light bathed the shore. A breeze ruffled the inky black expanse of the St. Lawrence River, rippling the pale light gleaming on the waves. The bank swarmed with activity. Most of the long, narrow boats that had littered the shore the evening before were gone. A long line of men, hefting sundry kegs and bales, trudged westward, parallel to the row of compact wooden houses that formed the settlement of Montréal. Their laughter drifted over the breeze and broke the heavy silence of the early morning. Genevieve searched for André's silhouette, but she couldn't see a feathered hat or a wide-skirted coat among the men on the banks. She watched them disappear into the darkness. Beyond, the great western forest loomed, the spiky peaks of the pines stark and black against the indigo sky.

He was gone. She suddenly saw herself, standing in the mud outside this Montréal inn, clutching all her worldly possessions in her arms and staring out toward the wilderness. *Abandoned again.* She had no idea where he planned to go after Montréal. She'd been told that this was the last settlement in this country, huddled against the enormous expanse of wilderness. Beyond these well-fortified stores and warehouses were nothing but forests and savages, and no roads but those forged by men like André. Her fury grew. *Coward.* Why didn't he grant her the annulment and end this marriage before it had ever begun?

She straightened her shoulders. She would get her annulment. If she had her way, she would get her annulment before the week was out.

"Madame Lefebvre?"

She started and turned around. The driver of a cart that had pulled up in front of the inn leapt agilely off the wooden seat and strode toward her. Only one person could have told this man her name.

She lifted her skirts from the mud and marched to meet him. "I suppose he sent you to. . . . Oh!"

Her case fell with a thump to the mud. She recognized the deep lines that fanned out from his brandy-colored eyes, the only similarity between the Frenchman she had faced last night and the savage apparition now standing before her. André's shaggy mane of fair hair—which last night had been covered by a curled periwig—was now tossed back haphazardly from his wide forehead, falling straight and unencumbered to his shoulders. Fringe hung from the sleeves of his form-fitting deerskin shirt, belted low and reaching mid-thigh. His hand rested easily on the butt of a pistol, which jutted from a beaded sash, accompanied by the hilt of a dagger. Below the hem of his shirt his thighs were naked.

Naked.

Her breath caught on a gasp. All the restless virility, all the repressed animal grace she had sensed last night, lay raw and exposed before her. She had the distinct feeling that she was staring at her husband— her *real* husband—and that last night she had been fooled by a wolf in sheep's clothing.

And there was a dimple in his buttocks.

"Having a change of heart, my wife?" He glanced at the case at her feet. "Last night you were screaming like a brandy-crazed squaw to come with me."

He was clever, very clever, trying to make her look as if she were the one escaping. "So the pot calls the kettle black! I went to your room to find you and you were gone, slipped away like a thief, leaving no note, no message."

"I wish I had been there to reassure you." A sly, dangerous smile slipped over his lips. "But I had business to take care of, and I didn't expect you to wake so early."

"Are you sure you didn't just forget me?" Her glance dropped to his bare, sinewy thighs. "As you forgot your breeches?"

He bent one knee to show her the fringed tube of deerskin that covered his leg from his knee to his ankle, held up by thongs that gartered somewhere below the hem of his shirt. "They're called leggings. You'd best get used to them. All my men wear them." His smoky gaze slipped lazily over her. "And you're not an easy woman to forget."

"Flatterer." She curled her hands into fists. "I've just taken you by surprise."

"Faithless, aren't you?"

"Faith is for God. I trust no man who has a grin as toothy as a wolf's and morals as loose as a cat's."

His teeth gleamed in the predawn light. "I see a night's sleep hasn't dimmed your spirit."

"I've been awake all night thinking about what you were scheming. . . ."

"You'll regret that by sundown. We've got a lot of distance to travel." He gestured to the men working along the shore. Three of them heaved the last narrow boat upon their shoulders and headed down the muddy bank toward the edge of the encroaching forest. "We'll be taking those canoes into the interior. We can't launch here because there are rapids just upstream of Montréal. We're going to cross the island and launch at Lachine to avoid them."

Lachine. She frowned. He was toying with her, as if she knew nothing about geography. She'd had enough lessons forced upon her by that wart-faced old priest Maman had hired as her tutor. "China," she said pointedly, "is rather far for these oxen to walk."

"Lachine is the name of the launching point. It's only a few leagues away." A wildness lit his eyes. "We're going much, much farther than Lachine. We're going to places you've never heard of before, places that aren't even mapped. Are you afraid?"

"No." Genevieve winced as soon as she said the word. This man believed she was a pampered daughter of the petty nobility, who should be frightened by the unknown. She tilted her chin. "Why should I be? You're escorting me, and we have a home somewhere out there, don't we?"

"Mmm. In a place called Chequamegon Bay." He nodded to the empty cart behind him. "I spent the morning looking for a cart and oxen to borrow. You can ride with me to the launching point. It's no carriage, but it's better than walking."

Genevieve glared at the cart. She felt like a ship at full speed whose wind had been sucked out of its sails. He hadn't escaped without her but rather had made arrangements for her comfort, which only confused her more.

"You won't be needing that." He reached for her case. "I'll make arrangements to store it in the inn."

She tightened her grip on the handle and pressed it close to her side. "I'm taking it."

"Sacré!" He curled his fingers over hers and pulled the woven case, rattling the contents. "What do you have in there?"

"My dowry from the king. Pins and needles and scissors and a comb and two knives—"

"You won't need all that frippery. All you'll need is a blanket to sleep in."

Her fingers tightened around the handle. "I'll need it to set up a household."

"There's no room for it in the canoes," he argued. "We're packed to the gunwales."

"If there's room for me, there's room for it." Genevieve wrenched it from his grip. "It is all I have in the world."

She hated herself for sounding like a poor waif clutching her last crust of bread, but she had already left more than half of Marie's clothing at Marietta's, and she had no intention of parting with what remained of her meager possessions. "I gave up many things when I decided to come to Québec," she explained, her chin lifting. "These few comforts are too important to me to leave behind, and I'll need them to set up a household."

André opened his mouth to argue, paused, then shrugged his shoulders, the fringe of his shirt fluttering with the gesture. "You'll have to carry it. My men have more than they can carry as it is."

"Fine."

He reached for her case. This time she gave it to him, making sure her fingers didn't come into contact with his rough, callused hands. He slung the case in the back of the cart with a clatter. "Are you always this garrulous in the mornings? Or is it just the lack of sleep?"

"It's a lack of trust."

"That's no way to start a marriage."

"Neither is making funeral arrangements for your wife."

He grimaced, then rubbed his stubbled chin. "It looks like I've got some explaining to do."

"The only thing I want to hear," she said as she picked her way toward the cart, lifting her skirts from the mud, "is about this chewywagon place."

"Chey-way-megon. I'll tell you all about it on the way." He climbed on the cart and held out his hand to her. "Come. I want to be on the water before sunup."

A lock of his hair, more golden than the rest, fell over his forehead. He confused her, this handsome man. He looked half savage in those smoke-ripened, well-worn deerskin clothes—what there was of them. He switched faces like an actor switches roles, and she wondered which face was really his. Then she remembered last night's devilish grin.

Suddenly, from the marrow of her bones came the scream *Run! Run!* so strong, so compelling, that every muscle, every sinew in her body, vibrated with the plea.

"Second thoughts, wife?"

She stared up at him, the primal fear whirling in her gut. She felt the softness of the mud beneath her boots, the cool river breeze on her cheeks, and realized she was staring into the golden eyes of a lion, the eyes of a predator . . . the eyes of the only man who could fulfill her dreams.

Or destroy them.

Her fingers found their way into his outstretched hand. André smiled that slow, wolfish grin as she settled beside him in the cart. He picked up the reins and snapped them over the oxens' backs. To Genevieve, the oxens' hooves against the earth sounded eerily like the clattering of rolled dice.

The morning light cast lacy shadows upon the forest floor when André first glimpsed the water of Lake St. Louis through the dense forest growth. As he urged the oxen on, the cart reeled over the deeply rutted earth, its wheels sinking into the mud and plowing new furrows among the older tracks. The rickety boards squealed in complaint, creaking against one another as the vehicle plodded its way beneath the feathery pines.

"I trust you can handle a boat better than you handle these oxen," his wife snapped as the cart nearly keeled over, only to right itself as it found even ground. "If this cart were a boat, we'd have drowned by now."

André suppressed the grin of triumph that tugged at his lips. He had discovered, several leagues back, that the only way to stop this woman from barraging him with questions was to make the cart sway dangerously over the rocky, uneven ground. As it stood, she had already wheedled too much information out of him. She knew the voyage was going to take six or seven weeks—and it should, if weather permitted and there were no injuries, wolves, bears, or Indian attacks en route, all of which he didn't mention. But she was dangerously close to discovering that neither he nor anyone else on this voyage had ever been to Chequamegon Bay, and he knew nothing about the "home" she asked so much about . . . even if it did exist. He was close enough to the launching point to smell the spruce wood fires.

Nothing—not even a stubborn, willful French wife—was going to come between him and this expedition now.

Genevieve clutched the edge of the seat, the bones of her hands standing out against the soft kid of her gloves. Her green eyes were fixed forward, on the uneven road. He had wondered last night, as he tossed and turned in his empty bed, if this woman would be as beautiful in the bright of day as she was by candlelight. Now he could see the freckles speckled over her tiny, tip-tilted nose; he could see the full, luscious curve of her lower lip. The dawn light reflected off her hair, and the tendrils, escaping her chignon and struck by the golden rays, shone like fine, clear brandy. Too brassy to be considered lovely, too unruly to be considered elegant. She was not a beauty by the standards of many—his Provençal mistress would have called this woman *gamine*, a little chit of a country girl—but he found an irresistible allure in her freshness, in the sensuous disorder of her hair.

She straightened and pointed to a large stretch of sparkling water that came into view as they rounded a copse of pines. "Is that it? Are we at the launching point?"

André saw his three largest gaily painted canoes floating in the placid water of a small bay, low and heavy with merchandise. His chest filled with anticipation. "Welcome to Lachine."

The spicy scent of the camp fires grew stronger as they entered the clearing. A bluish smoke hung heavy beneath the boughs of the sheltering pines. A few small piles of kegs and barrels littered the shore, marked in black letters with their contents: saltpeter, shot, arrowheads, kettles, glass beads. His two dozen men milled about in the clearing, heaving the bales upon their straining shoulders, sloshing through the water to deposit them in the canoes.

Tiny had done well in his absence, André thought as he scanned the shore. The men were ready to launch.

"Strange name for such a place." His wife eased her grip on the boards of the seat as he pulled the cart to a halt at the edge of the clearing. "Why is it called China?"

"The man who used to own this land was named La Salle," André answered absently, counting his men. "For years, he stopped everyone returning from the interior and asked if they had heard anything about the route to the China Sea. The *voyageurs* called this place *La Chine*, after him.''

''Is he here now?''

''No. He sold the land so he could go and look for the sea himself.''

She raised both brows. '' 'Those whom God wishes to destroy, he first makes mad.' ''

From the faded memories of his schoolboy days in France, André remembered the quote as coming from some classic poem. Greek poetry and philosophy were common enough subjects to study as a boy but were exceptional in a woman, even a well-bred noblewoman. '' 'There is no great genius without a touch of madness,' '' he countered, quoting from what he remembered of Aristotle. André gestured to the great expanse of water before them. ''It's a big country, but somewhere it has to end.''

He leapt off the cart and sauntered around to help her down. When he rounded the oxen, he saw his wife jump off the cart of her own volition, sending up a spray of mud in the process and exposing a well-turned pair of booted ankles. She glanced at him, startled, then brushed past him to stare at the scene on the shore.

''Are all the boats yours?''

''Canoes. Everything you see here is mine.'' He pulled her case out of the back of the cart, realizing the sooner he got her into the canoe, the better his chances would be of actually getting her into the interior before she got a good look at his men and had second thoughts. ''It's all going with us.''

She scanned the bags of cornmeal, the pots, the rolls of birch bark, the oilcloths. Her eyes narrowed as she turned to him. ''There's enough here to take to that mythical China Sea of yours.''

''So the *Onontio* has finally come!''

The voice bellowed in the clearing. André glanced over his shoulder. Tiny emerged from the water, his meaty thighs bare above his leggings. André smiled at the timely interruption and strode to meet him.

"After yesterday," the giant roared, "I thought you'd be rousing us from our beds before the first birds awakened."

André tilted his head toward his wife, who followed in his wake. "I ran into a delay at the inn."

"*Jésus*! André!" Tiny pulled off his red cap and bowed to her as she reached their side. "Not three weeks since you've stepped foot on Canadian soil and you've captured the finest filly in the settlement. By the passion of Sainte Thérèse, where'd you find such a sweet morsel?"

"Certainly not in the brandy-house you spent the night in," he retorted, backing away from the path of the giant's breath. "Are all the men here?"

"All but the Roissier brothers. I sent Siméon to drag them out of the widow Toureau's house." Tiny gestured to her with his cap.

"Are you going to be a boor, old man, or are you going to introduce me to this heavenly vision?"

"Madame, I'd like you to meet my most experienced *voyageur*, Tiny."

He saw the surprise on her face. There was nothing tiny about Tiny. His shirt alone was the product of the skin of three stags, stretching across his shoulders and belly and barely covering his privates.

"The real name's Bernard Griffon," Tiny corrected as he reached for her hand. She gave it, belatedly, then tugged it away as Tiny leaned over and kissed it. "He forget to mention that I'm as strong as a black bear and can carry four hundred pounds of cargo without breaking a sweat. . . ."

"He's also a shameless liar," André added.

"I've never said a lie in my life!"

"Ah, yes," André mused, "as saintly as the blessed Virgin . . ."

"Let's not be committing blasphemy, not with a lady about." Tiny turned his attention back to her. "Tell me, sweet creature, where have you been hiding from me, and where did this ruffian find you?"

She tilted her head. "So I'm not the only one who thinks he's a ruffian."

Tiny roared. "The woman knows to call a rat a rat when she sees one!"

"I wouldn't insult the rodent."

Tiny's bushy blond brows raised high on his forehead. "Tell me there are a dozen others just like you! Where can I find them?"

"The same place where this ruffian found me— in front of a priest."

His yellow teeth gleaming, Tiny glanced sideways at André. "Going to Mass, now, are we? Praying we'll make it to Chequamegon Bay before the first frost?"

André shook his head. "Making marriage vows."

"Making vows? Well, there's a fine way to—" Tiny stopped mid-sentence. His blue eyes bulged above the high, ragged edge of his bushy blond beard.

"I hope the canoe isn't fully loaded." André thrust her case into Tiny's belly, then released it and slipped his arms around his startled wife. He heaved her high in his arms. "We've got a bit of unexpected cargo."

Tiny opened his mouth but no sound came out. He grew blue around the lips, as if he had swallowed his tongue, then he emitted a faint croak.

André laughed aloud and splashed into the water, leaving the giant sputtering soundlessly behind him. His wife's arms slipped around his neck, warm and soft.

He felt her breath on his cheek when she spoke.

"You took great pleasure making a fool of him, monsieur."

"I've waited twelve years for an opportunity to make that blowhard speechless."

"Your men are gaping like visitors to a menagerie," she murmured. "Did I mention that they look like they belong in cages, dressed as they are in nothing but feathers and beads and skins?"

"Shocked?"

"Surprised. I didn't expect so many." Her eyes narrowed. "Is there something you've neglected to tell me, *husband*? Are we off to find the China Sea like that madman La Salle?"

"So full of suspicions." His grin widened, for he was knee-deep in water and this woman in all her skirts was tight in his arms. Success smelled good and he was close enough to taste it, even with the bitter edge of guilt. "I wouldn't mind having my name bandied about after I'm rotting in the grave, so if I happen to stumble upon the China Sea during my travels . . ."

"Now you're making me think you're mad."

" 'I am not mad, most noble wife, but speak forth the words of truth and soberness.' "

"Quoting the Scriptures won't convince me otherwise," she argued. "You didn't tell me this was such a large expedition. There must be thirty men here."

"You sound disappointed." He leaned over and toppled her onto the oilskin, toward the rear of the canoe, where the French flag in white with gold *fleur-de-lys* snapped in the wind. "Did you think we'd be alone?"

She tilted her head so her hair slipped off the column of her white throat. "I suppose there are always ways," she said, her voice dry and husky, "for two people to be alone in a crowd."

He released her abruptly. The canoe wobbled as she searched for a steady seat atop the uneven floor of boxes, bales, and kegs.

"For a lady," he said hoarsely, while she settled her bottom in the center of a keg and curled her legs to one side, "you have a disconcerting habit of speaking your mind."

"You, my *husband*, are as slippery as an eel." She lifted her hands to her hips, then thought better of it as the canoe wiggled beneath her. "Now, convince me again that we're going to this chewywagon place."

"Chey-way-megon," he corrected. "We'll have little time to go any farther west." He nodded woodenly toward a young man clutching the end of the canoe. "Julien, make sure she doesn't drift away. I'll be right back."

He walked away from her, still reeling from the effects of a few whispered words. André couldn't remember a time when he'd ever turned away from a willing woman—least of all a beautiful one. Now he was faced with five or six days in the wilderness with this bold creature—a wife who offered herself willingly—and he hadn't touched a woman in months. She was a dangerous temptation. He'd best get himself a willing squaw, he thought, for his sake and his wife's, for she had no idea that she was tempting her own ruin.

"Married, my ass!" Tiny, fully recovered from the shock, thrust Genevieve's case into her husband's belly as André reached the shore. "By all the flaming martyrs, you almost fooled me! How long are you going to leave her bobbing out there?"

"It's no trick."

"By sweet Saint Anne . . ."

"The Intendant's ruling, remember? I married her right after the last ship arrived."

"What did you do, pluck her off the ship before it even warped into its moorings?" Tiny squinted against the sun to get a better look at her. "The fops at Québec would never let such a fine piece slip out of their net."

"I'll have time enough to tell you the story after we're far away from this place. She's running over with questions and I can't keep her still."

"Shouldn't have left her out there with that boy."

André turned around and saw his wife, dressed in her rose-colored, beribboned, boned dress atop a savage-looking canoe in the middle of the wilderness. Her bright hair was close to Julien's dark head. André splashed quickly back into the water. As he neared the canoe, he heard Julien's words.

". . . it's made out of bark from a birch tree. The bark is stretched over some cedar beams, and it's all sewn tight with spruce root and caulked with pine resin so it's watertight. There's not a nail in the whole damn—excuse me, ma'am. It can hold almost two thousand pounds of weight without cracking the gum or sinking, and it's light enough to be carried—"

"You'd better hold the canoe tighter than that, pork-eater," André interrupted, using the common term of derision for men on their maiden voyage into the wilderness. He turned to Tiny, who followed behind him, and whispered, "Shut that boy up until we're out of here."

"Eh, pork-eater," Tiny bellowed. "Are you ready to start your first voyage?" A gleam lit his eyes as he approached the young man. "Are you ready to live hard, lie hard, sleep hard, and eat dogs?" Tiny placed one meaty hand firmly over Julien's head, the other on the gunwale of the canoe. He dunked the boy in the cold lake water and smiled at André's wife. "Didn't mean to frighten you, ma'am." Julien sputtered and struggled beneath the giant's grip. "You see, the boy needs to be baptized, it being his first trip and all."

She lifted a brow and asked, "Will I be baptized as well?"

"Oh, no . . ."

"But it is my first trip."

"But you aren't a *voyageur*, madame," Tiny explained. "You're a guest."

Julien surged up from the water and shook his head. His long brown hair flattened against his forehead and cheeks. He wiped it out of his eyes and glared at his attacker, then glanced at the woman perched upon the canoe. Julien's cheeks exploded with color.

Hip-deep in lake water, André waved for his men to join him. He glanced sideways at his wife as he took his position near the stern and the other men approached to take their positions around the canoe.

"Men, this is my wife. She'll be joining us on our journey." Her eyes widened as she perused his crew. "Madame, let me introduce you to the men who will be our companions in this canoe for the next six weeks." He held out his hand to them, one by one, and they bowed in the water. "This black-bearded rogue is Siméon, our resident religious who has recently recanted his vows. Those bleary-eyed men are the Roissier brothers, Anselme and Gaspard, looking worse for wear from a night at the widow Toureau's house. You know Tiny and Julien already." He watched his wife carefully as he gestured to the knotty-armed Negro standing across from Tiny. "Wapishka is an old friend of mine, an adopted member of an Algonquin tribe. The man at the bow is The Duke, a Huron Indian. He'll be guiding the canoe."

Genevieve nodded at each of them, then looked down at André from her perch upon the canoe. "If

you expected me to be frightened of heathens and
fallen angels," she said, "you'll be sorely disappointed. I've already met you."

The men smothered their laughter. André smiled
wickedly, then gave the signal. He and the seven men
surged up the side of the canoe and tumbled in.
Julien, exhausted and inexperienced, tumbled in late.
The vessel rocked wildly, but within minutes, as the
men took their positions, the canoe balanced itself,
and all that was left of the wild motion were the waves
radiating out on the surface of the lake. Genevieve
clutched the thin rim of the canoe with white fingers.

Immediately, the vessel began drifting backward.
André stood up behind his wife and picked up the
cedar paddle. He heard her gasp. As he steadied the
canoe, he noticed that she was staring at The Duke,
who stood at the prow wearing nothing but a
breechcloth.

His grin widened. "If you keep staring at him, wife,
I'll have to call him out."

"What will you duel with? Stones? Wooden sticks?
The bones of long-dead ancestors?"

"He might be a savage, but he can guide this canoe
better than any Frenchman."

"I'm not surprised," she retorted, "since it's held
together by spit, bark, and heathen magic."

"You shouldn't be deceived by appearances."

Genevieve stared at The Duke's skimpy breechcloth
dripping water onto the oilcloth. "That savage isn't
concerned about hiding *anything.*"

"I mean the boat," he explained. "The boat is
stronger than it looks."

"Twigs and sap do not a seaworthy vessel make,"
she retorted. "Someday you'll have to explain—"

"Later," he murmured as he guided the vessel
toward the opening of the lake. "Later."

André felt the familiar rocking of the canoe beneath his feet, the open air brushing his body, the current tugging against the red-painted end of his paddle. Six of his men clutched their paddles and began rowing, three on one side, three on the other. A volley of shots cracked the silence. Upon the shore, blue puffs of smoke rose in the air. The two men remaining on the bank raised their arms in farewell. Suddenly, Tiny's voice filled the air with song.

> *"I've braved the tempests and the floods*
> *of the Saint Lawrence.*
> *In my bark canoe laden with Indian riches*
> *and paddled by good men . . ."*

The men in the other canoes joined in. A golden glow shimmered off the trees that clung to the edge of the banks. André watched the receding shoreline, and he felt as if his bonds were being stretched to the limits, until finally, joyously, they snapped and he knew he was free.

The voyage was beginning; the dream had begun.

He crouched down behind his wife and pointed toward the bank. "Take one last look." His voice whispered softly in her ear, causing a curl to flutter against her earlobe. He couldn't prevent the grin of triumph from spreading across his face. "Take a good look . . . then say goodbye to civilization."

Chapter Five

"A terre!"

Genevieve sighed in relief as André cried out the order to land. The naked savage who stood in the front of the canoe twisted his long paddle and aimed the painted prow toward a rock-faced clearing on an island in the middle of the Ottawa River. She was sorely tempted to lean over the edge of the canoe, dip both hands into the water, and paddle—anything to hasten their arrival on dry land—but she knew if she felt the cold, clear water flowing through her fingers, she'd lose what little control she wielded over her aching bladder.

She shifted her weight and winced. Her legs lay cramped beneath her, but she didn't dare adjust her position atop the wobbly keg. The sound of the river water sloshing against the sides of the canoe, the endless bobbing of the vessel in the current, all conspired to torment her. The men had stopped

on dry land only once since they departed from
Lachine this morning, and then only to eat a bowl
of gritty cornmeal and to pay homage at a rough-
hewn church dedicated to Saint Anne. Groaning,
she thought about the skin full of clear mountain
water she had drunk to wash down the gritty *sagamité*. She wouldn't do that again, and by the sight
of the squirming men, neither would they. Several
times during the trip through the Lake of Two
Mountains and up the mouth of the Ottawa River,
she had gazed beyond the naked, widespread legs
of André, standing behind her in the canoe, and
glimpsed one of the *voyageurs* from another canoe
passing water over the gunwales. Her presence
alone prevented the men on this canoe from standing up, pulling up the hems of their shirts, pushing
aside their loincloths, and relieving themselves in
the wide, flowing river.

A cool evening breeze kicked up, ruffling the surface of the river, bringing with it the scent of damp
earth, pine resin, and mist. They neared the clear
stretch of shore, nothing but a bare, flat rock jutting
out from a dense growth of scraggly pines. André
gave the signal and the men made one last stroke.
Their paddles clattered in the boat, and before the
momentum faded, they gripped the lashed edges of
the vessel and sprung out of the canoe into the water.
Genevieve gripped her uneven seat as frigid water
sprayed over her, soaking into her linen headrail and
bodice and running in tortuous rivulets into her
cleavage.

By the muffled, collective sighs of relief, she knew
the men, waist-deep in the river, weren't waiting to
reach dry land to ease their discomfort.

Genevieve glared at André, who was paying no
attention to her. He was grinning and watching the

rest of his colorful flotilla slice its way through the water to the shore. The golden light of the sunset gleamed on the dark blond lock that streaked his hair from his forehead to his shoulders. Soon the men were pushing aside the tarpaulin atop the merchandise and starting to carry the cargo, piece by piece, through the water to the island.

"Well?" she said loudly when her seat became loose enough to wobble dangerously beneath her. "Are you going to leave me here all night, or do you expect me to swim to shore?"

His grin widened as he sloshed through the water to the side of the canoe. "How did you find your first day afloat?"

"Long," she retorted, wondering if he'd chosen the word *afloat* on purpose. Carefully, she straightened out her legs and tugged her wrinkled skirts from beneath her. "I'm tired enough to sleep on bare rock."

"We'll do better than that." He slid his arms beneath her thighs and back and pulled her against him. She groaned as her hip bumped into his chest, dangerously jostling her innards. "Tomorrow we won't spend as much time on the canoes. There are rapids upstream and we have to portage around them."

Genevieve wished he would stop using words like *rapids* and *upstream*. She stared at the dense forest beyond the clearing with a sort of lust and steered her thoughts in another direction. "What's the name of this place?"

"It has an Indian name . . . a name your tongue couldn't hold. It means 'Island Surrounded by Flowing Water.'"

She closed her eyes, then opened them again, for

the swaying motion of being carried in his arms was dangerous.

"No," he mused, "that's not right. I think it means 'Place in Center of Raging River.'"

She glared at him. He was grinning.

"Or maybe it's 'Where Stream Passes—'"

"It'll be called 'Place Where Frenchwoman Murders Insufferable Husband,'" she interrupted, "if you don't get me to the bank soon."

André threw back his head and laughed, his Adam's apple standing out in the thick column of his throat. He clambered onto the slick, rocky bank and released her legs. Genevieve stumbled as her feet touched the solid ground. They hadn't held her weight for hours and were stiff and cramped from the ride, but as soon as she regained her equilibrium, she broke away from his embrace.

Julien handed her her case, which he had carried from the canoe. She gripped the handle in one hand, walking toward the forest that rimmed the tiny clearing.

"You'll need an escort—"

"*You* stay right where you are."

"It's a big island and you have no idea what creatures inhabit it. If you can't abide me, then take one of my men."

She whirled and peered past him, at the men who labored to empty the canoe. "If I must choose between two philanderers, an ex-Jesuit, a giant, an acknowledged heathen, a naked savage, and *you*," she retorted, "I'll take my chances with the wolves."

As if to prove her point, he smiled like a wolf. "Then you'd better stretch your legs over there," he said, indicating an area to the right of the clearing, just as The Duke emerged from the woods. "Else you'll end up frightening more than the wildlife."

"The only thing I want to do right now," she muttered, "is water it."

She forged into the woods, her heavy case bruising her knees with every step. Despite the urge to crouch behind the nearest tree trunk, Genevieve walked through the thick underbrush, pushing aside branches of saplings and stumbling over upraised roots until she could no longer hear André's laughter, until she reached the western bank of the island. She tossed her case upon a stone outcropping and burrowed in the privacy of the bushes.

Moments later she emerged, feeling much lighter and far more comfortable than she had all day. She rolled her head to stretch the tendons of her neck and watched as the sun cast its last golden rays through the straight tree trunks, laying stripes of sunlight upon the rocky ground. She tugged on the knot of the linen headrail draped across her shoulders and let the scarf drift to the earth, then pulled on the laces of her bodice to ease the constriction around her chest. She took a deep breath, smelling the scent of the cool, damp forest, the fertile scent of wet, mulchy vegetation, and the more distant odor of camp fires, probably from the *voyageurs*, judging by the distant thwack of axes upon wood and the bawdy laughter of the men.

Removing the pins that held her chignon at the nape of her neck, she let her hair tumble down her back. Genevieve opened her case and felt around inside until her hand curled about the smooth handle of her brush. She pulled it through her knotted, wind-blown tresses until they fell soft and shiny to her shoulders. For the first time since she'd left Lachine, she relaxed. It was so quiet here, beneath the shade of the great, swaying pine boughs. The trees towered above her, like tall, straight sentinels, stiff and unyielding, guarding the wild forests. All was silent but for the sighing of the wind in the boughs, the occasional crackle of leaves falling into the litter, the swoosh and gurgle of the river, the splash of a jumping fish. Though during the voyage the men in the canoes had laughed and sang and raced one another over the lakes and rivers, beyond the circle of their flotilla all was calm and peaceful now. Even the canoes slid soundlessly through the water, creaking only when she shifted her weight or the men's paddles clattered against the rims.

Genevieve bent at the waist and shook her hair so it flowed over her head and the ends brushed the ground. The ache in her lower back eased and she felt the pleasant stretch along the cramped muscles of her legs. She hoped her wretched husband had been telling the truth when he'd said that tomorrow they wouldn't be on the canoe all day. She didn't know if she could stand another moment motionless atop that bumpy seat without her legs cramping permanently in a sitting position. He'd said they would be walking, but she didn't dare believe him; André lied as smoothly as he told the truth.

She flipped her hair over her head and shook it so it fell over her shoulders. Tossing her brush in her case, she walked to the edge of the river. In Paris, she never would have dared let the muddy, turbid waters of the Seine anywhere near her person, for it was always thick with raw sewage and runoff from the Parisian streets. But this river flowed so swift and clean that she could see the pebbles rolling on the bottom. She knelt and dipped her hands in the frigid water, splashing a handful of the clear, sweet-smelling liquid on her face and drinking the rest out of her palms.

Not since her youth in Normandy had she tasted such fresh, clean water.

As the cool liquid iced her throat, Genevieve stiffened, for she heard the sound of a woman's laughter, as clear as a bell on a crisp winter's day.

But the forest was silent. She sat back on her heels, letting the water drip down her neck. She thought she had buried those memories so deeply that they would never again surface, yet here in the silence of the woods—woods so much more savage, so different from those of her youth—the memory assaulted her, so vividly that her ears still rang with her mother's laughter.

It's the river, she thought, splaying her glistening fingers. The taste of the river water reminded her of the tiny creek that twisted and turned down the rocky mountainside behind her mother's manor house. It reminded her of a hot summer day when she and Maman had decided to walk through the forest, and they had come upon the creek, peeled off their silk stockings, tucked their satin skirts between their knees, and dipped their bare feet into the icy stream. She had done a little courtly dance for her mother along the smooth, flat stones in the creek, and Maman had laughed at her antics.

Maman had laughed so seldom during those few happy days before their world was destroyed.

Genevieve stood up and pushed the memories aside. She wondered why now, after all these years, after all that had happened, she still could remember Maman's voice and laughter as clearly as if they still lived in that ivy-covered manor house in the hills of Normandy.

A thousand lifetimes ago.

She turned around and walked back onto the outcropping, deafened by the memories. Not until she was within footsteps of her open case did she realize she was not alone.

"Hell and damnation!" Genevieve stumbled back. André stood in front of her, a tall, brooding figure whose deerskin clothing and bronzed skin merged naturally with the dark, knotted trunks and the fading night-green of the forest.

"I took you by surprise."

She grasped her chest to still herself from instinctively reaching for the dagger wedged in her boot. "How long have you been standing there like a ghost?"

"Long enough to have stolen all that glorious hair from your head, if I were Iroquois."

"What in God's name is an Iroquois?"

"The name of the Indian tribe that claims this territory."

She tried to still her racing heart as she stared at him, dressed in his fringed buckskins, his leggings, and his beaded moccasins. "The only savage in these forests is the one dressed in animal skins, carrying a dagger, sneaking up on me like a thief."

"If you come upon the other kind, you won't live to tell the tale. The French have been warring with the Iroquois for decades."

"What do I have to fear from a tribe of wigmakers?"

"Wigmakers?"

"If they want my hair, they can have it," she retorted. "It's always in my eyes, anyway."

His lips twitched. "The Iroquois take scalps as war trophies."

"Please, not the savage stories again." She sighed as her heart began to beat at a normal level. "The least you could do is not insult my intelligence by telling me those ridiculous tales. And any decent man would have let a lady know he was near while she was in the middle of her toilette.''

"A lady doesn't curse.''

"You scared the wits out of me,'' Genevieve argued. She'd slipped; Marie Duplessis would never curse, but it had been so long since she'd acted like a lady. "Sneaking up on me in the darkness and then just standing there, staring at me.''

"It's a pretty site to come upon a Frenchwoman in the middle of the woods, all clean and . . . undone.''

His gaze wandered to where the golden light illuminated the softly brushed mass of her unbound hair, then slipped lower to her damp, loosened bodice and her bare shoulders rising from the ribboned edge. Genevieve became acutely aware of the sagging of the sleeves over her arms and of the cool, damp cloth that covered her suddenly sensitive breasts.

She toyed with the hanging ends of her bodice laces as her heart began to race for a new and different reason. "Why were you prowling around in the darkness, anyway?''

"Looking for you. You shouldn't have wandered so far from the campsite.''

"I'm not allowed a toilette in privacy?''

"This isn't Paris.'' He reached out and took a tress of her hair between his fingers. Her heart leapt at the briefest brush of his callused fingers against her bare skin. "There are no walls to keep out the dangers.''

"Obviously.''

"I can't watch you always, though looking at you now . . .'' He released the tress upon her bosom, letting his fingers graze the swell of her breast. "I can think of only one thing I'd want to do more.''

Genevieve drew in a deep, ragged breath. She saw

something, bold and unguarded, in his tawny eyes. She'd seen that look a hundred times before. The knowledge came to her, swift and sure, as undeniable as the sound of the wind soughing in the pines above their heads.

He wants me.

She hadn't expected this, not yet. She'd expected him to avoid her until he was sure she would make it to that chewywagon place; she'd expected him to watch her like a hawk during the trials and tribulations of the journey, to test her, to judge if she were worthy to be his wife. That's why he'd brought her out here, she'd concluded after a day of thought. Yet here he was, on the first day of the voyage, alone with her in the woods, staring at her as if she were some sort of succulent dessert.

I'm supposed to want this, to submit to this. The voices she had heard earlier this morning clamored in her head, but they were dull now, muffled by some other, stronger sound, something new, something that she had never heard before. It was a primitive music, unfamiliar and yet familiar, strange and potent, full of sensation and emotion, rising from a primal source, deeper than any instinct. It had no words, no voice, no reason, and it surged in her from a place far too distant and far too deep for her to control. She stared at the tall man before her, watching the stripes of light illuminate his hair, the fire grow in his eyes, and Genevieve knew that somehow he was the source of this new feeling.

She smelled the damp, smoke-ripened skin of his shirt, saw the sudden gleam of his eyes as she dropped her hand from where it lay protectively against the laces of her bodice. Words rushed to her lips, words she knew she shouldn't say. But she found herself thinking that it was right to encourage him, that once their marriage was consummated all would be secure, all would be right, and her battle would be finished, even though she sensed in her heart that there was more to this than she could yet understand.

She dared to reach for him, to finger the frayed fringe of his sleeve. "We could stay here for a while," she whispered. "The men wouldn't interrupt us."

A muscle moved in his cheek. His nostrils flared. He reached out and buried his hand in her hair, lifting it so it was lit by the last ray of the sun. Then he let it slip, tress by tress, through his fingers. "Such a brazen bride." His voice was tight, controlled. "You're supposed to be frightened, little Marie, not staring at me like this."

She slid her hand from his shirt. "Don't call me that."

"You are a bold wife," he murmured. "Too damned bold for your own good."

"No. Not . . . not that."

Genevieve dropped her gaze. Perhaps she was being too bold. She had to be careful . . . careful. In her veins ran the blood of her mother—that had become clear enough in Paris. But that was not what bothered her. This was the first time he had called her by her false name, and it jarred against her ears.

She had prepared for this long ago, but she didn't expect to have to lie now, when her tongue was thick in her throat and her senses whirled in confusion. This was too important to her. If she were to be his wife, she couldn't stand to hear another woman's name on his lips until her dying day.

"No one ever calls me Marie," she said with a shrug. "There were a thousand Maries in the Salpêtrière."

"What should I call you, then?"

"Genevieve."

"Ah, yes." He traced her cheek. "You nearly wrote that name on the parish register."

She started. "I did?"

"You were so delirious that one of the other girls had to remind you of your name." His finger slipped to her mouth and rubbed her lower lip. "It fits you somehow. Marie is such a common name for such an uncommon woman. Genevieve. . . ."

Time stopped. The whole world condensed to this one place, to this one moment in time. The last ray of light died, bathing them in a dusky blue glow. She heard the river lapping gently against the stones. She heard his slow, ragged breathing; she felt the warmth of his body; she watched a hundred emotions pass through his eyes. Genevieve waited, interminably, for him to lean just that one inch closer and take what was already his.

Instead, he passed his hand over her breast, then cupped its fullness in his palm.

She flinched at first but did not move away. His touch was gentle, not what she'd expected. Shadows swathed his face, and she could see nothing but the glitter in his eyes. He squeezed her breast tenderly. Her nipple hardened against his palm. Her knees felt ridiculously weak and her heart pounded in her chest, though she stood as still as a doe sensing danger. *Come, Genevieve, you're no shrinking innocent. Come, come, you know something of the lusts of men.* She knew he could feel her heartbeat through the layers of chemise and boned bodice. His hands were so warm on her body, the skin of his callused fingers scraping where he touched the bare skin above the sagging edge of her bodice.

And he touched her gently . . . gently. No roughness, no harshness here. He kept touching her, making *her* feel something . . . something strange. Perhaps a taste of what a man feels when he wants a woman.

She was swimming, swimming . . . and these were unfamiliar waters.

The silence stretched on. She grasped his upper arms and swayed slightly, as if the solid rock beneath her feet had suddenly broken off from the shore and floated into the river. She wanted to understand these strange feelings. She wanted him to kiss her, as he had once before, and show her how it *could* be between a man and a woman.

"I thought you would be like this," he said, his voice strangely ragged. He brushed his thumb against the rigid peak of her breast. "All needles and sparks on the outside, but on the inside, pure molten fire."

Of course . . . She should have known that her mother's blood would flow true through her, that she could never escape it. She pressed her hand against his own, forcing his fingers hard on her breast, reacting by instinct again, even as some secret part of her bucked against the truth. "André . . ."

He swooped down upon her. She welcomed his lips, closing her eyes as they moved over hers, demanding, greedy, hungry. His arms wound around her and crushed her against his solid frame. His unshaven cheeks prickled her skin. He tasted of tobacco and heat and passion, and as he forcefully bent her head back and parted her lips, she went limp in his strong arms. Genevieve felt as weightless as an autumn leaf being buffeted about in a tempest, but before she could lose herself completely, before the winds of passion swept her away, he released her and left her standing, swaying, alone.

"I didn't come out here for this." His breath was

uncertain as he ran a hand through his long hair. "I came out here to bring you back."

"Stay."

"Sacrebleu." He stepped away as if she had struck him. "Do you want to lose your virginity within shouting distance of the men," he asked hoarsely, "with your skirts bunched around your waist and your back hard against the forest floor?"

She didn't answer. She couldn't. She couldn't tell him that the thought of his strong body poised above hers had robbed her of the power of speech, that it had brought with it a rush of other memories, cold, hard, and ugly, rusted daggers from a past she had determined to forget.

"Jésus!" He turned and strode into the forest. "Come now, back to the campsite . . . before I fulfill my own damned prophecy."

Genevieve gripped the gunwale of the canoe, her fingers raw and stiff from clamping the lashed edge. All around her the river seethed in fury, whipping up a froth as thick and white as milk as it tumbled down a bed of worn stones. Here and there, jagged edges of bare rock thrust from the boiling cauldron, stopping slick tongues of current and transforming them into torrents of foam. Sudden eruptions of spray thrust high from the roiling surface of the river, then slapped down like thunder. Powerful whirlpools eddied in secluded bays along the steep banks, churning fallen branches and slender tree trunks into slivers of splintered wood.

In the midst of the froth and the spray, in the mouth of the current, stood André. The water pounded against his bare chest as he clung to one side of the canoe. He steered the vessel upstream, keeping the fragile birch bark away from the bank and maneuvering it around the boulders hidden beneath the churning surface of the river. His hair, dripping with water, clung to his head and neck, and periodically he would shake it and send the glittering spray whirling around him.

A rope tied to the canoe's curved bow led to the shore, where Tiny and Wapishka pulled the canoe forward as they stumbled over rocks and stumps and climbed over trees growing out of the solid stone. The other *voyageurs* traveled a steep path farther inland, carting over land most of the merchandise that had cluttered the vessel, to protect it from damage and to make the boat lighter and easier to maneuver. André had suggested, with a wicked smile, that she ride in the canoe while he pulled it upstream. *It will give you a taste,* he said, *of the voyage to come.* Now she clung to her bumpy, uncertain seat on one of the cedar ribs in the canoe's half-empty belly, watching him battle the powerful currents that vibrated the canoe's thin rind. Despite the weathered wooden crosses that dotted the shore, evidence of the loss of life along this stretch of white water, she felt no fear. The roar and tumble of the rapids filled her with breathless awe, as did the sight of her bare-chested husband, waist-deep in the wild fury, his arm muscles bulging and his ripple of ribs pressing against his gleaming sides.

Tiny stopped and waved from his perch atop a bare elevated clump of rock, yelling something to her that was lost in the noise and tumult but was understood by André. André loosened his grip on the side of the canoe and guided it forward, letting the gummed edge graze his rippled abdomen. She wanted to ask how much longer they must fight through these rapids, but her tongue lay thick and unresponsive in her mouth. Talk was a waste of energy, anyway, for the current roared and dispersed all sound, and his efforts were concentrated on directing the canoe farther upstream to a place where the men could pole or paddle again. André took a position near her, at the widest part of the canoe. His smoldering golden gaze alit on her briefly, as it had a dozen times since they'd left the campsite.

Her cheeks burned as he pushed the canoe into deeper water to avoid an outcropping of stone and earth. They had exchanged no more than a few words since last night. After their kiss, she had followed him back to the campsite and lain down on a fragrant, springy bed of spruce boughs the *voyageurs* had made for her, but sleep had eluded her. During the night, her thoughts had tormented her worse than the little gnats the men called mosquitoes. She told herself she must encourage him, she must *seduce* him. Once their marriage was consummated, she'd have a name, a wealthy husband, and a home in truth, not just in name.

Still, there was something more to her boldness than cold-blooded utility, something she was afraid to name. On a practical level, she must seduce him. What bothered her was the part of her heart that *yearned* for . . . something. If she admitted to those feelings, then she would be admitting to a nature she'd been determined to suppress; she'd be admitting that her enemies had been right.

Genevieve clutched the cedar rib behind her as a contrary current surged around the outcropping and jerked the canoe to one side, bringing her attention back to the dangers of the moment. André's knuckles whitened on the gunwale as he stopped and searched for safe footing on the cold, slick rocks beneath the surface. He took another step forward. The water reached his chest. A stinging spray spattered endlessly over the edge of the canoe.

It seemed to take hours to inch past the outcropping, for the current pounded down upon them, harder with each of André's steps. The rope attached to the bow of the canoe hung heavy with water, though Tiny and Wapishka tried their best to keep it taut and firm. Slowly, carefully, André eased the canoe past the outcropping and into a small bay. Genevieve felt the lessening of the current through the thin bark. Her ears rang as the roar of the water eased, and she dared to dry her soaking face as fewer and fewer waves crashed against the bow and soaked her with the frigid spray. She sat straighter in the vessel as she smelled burning tobacco, evidence that the *voyageurs* had stopped their work to smoke one of their frequent pipes. On the shore, she saw Julien fighting yet another baptism in the frigid waters of the Ottawa River.

Genevieve glanced at her husband. His chest heaved and his breath was audible now, out of the thunder of the white water. Red welts rose on his skin at the level of his dark nipples, evidence of the force of the current. Veins bulged like bluish lead wires over his biceps and along his knotted forearms. As the water level fell to his hips, some of his men splashed into the bay to help unload the canoe.

André draped his arms over the rim of the canoe as the men approached. Water dripped from his chin and ran in rivulets over his chest, sprinkled with whorls of golden hair. Genevieve rose from the belly of the canoe and sat on the middle lath, arching her back and pressing a hand against the soreness caused by the cedar rib bumping into her spine. She was intensely aware of her husband's eyes on her body.

"Well, wife, how did you like your ride?"

She winced and glanced sideways at him. "I feel like a bean in a baby's rattle."

"It's going to get worse." He wiped his dripping chin with his forearm. "There's twelve more miles of this before we hit calm water."

Genevieve ignored his lopsided grin. She wasn't worried about the journey taking its heavy toll of her. She had been through worse . . . much, much worse. She was worried that there were twelve more miles of watching him in action, and she was wondering how long she would have to pretend to ignore his fascinating, powerful, half-naked body, like the lady she was supposed to be, before she was caught staring at him as no gentlewoman should.

She nodded toward the banks, where the men gathered among piles of merchandise. "Why are we unloading the canoes here?"

"There's a waterfall less than a mile ahead." He reached into the canoe and slid his bulging arms beneath her back and knees. "We've got to portage around it."

She wound her arms around his neck, feeling the cordons still taut and hard from the exertion. His bare chest was slick and as cold as the river water. He smelled clean and wet . . . and felt very naked.

Suddenly, she felt very hot.

As soon as he reached dry land, André released her onto the shore, turned around, and returned to the canoe. Genevieve stood upon the banks and watched the back of his lean thighs flex as he splashed into the water, but her leisurely perusal was interrupted as the men swiftly brushed by her, running from the bank to the canoe, unloading what remained in the vessels and piling the merchandise in some sort of mysterious order upon the shore. She scattered

away from the activity, finding an elevated post to
arch her aching back and watch the preparations.
Another canoe rounded the outcropping and eased
its way into the bay, and soon the men were hard at
work unloading its wares. The *voyageurs* helped each
other strap kegs and bales onto their backs in a sort
of rope harness. Genevieve watched in horror as Tiny
heaved three *pactons* on his back and adjusted the
thick leather strap around his forehead. She knew
that each of those packages weighed almost as much
as she did.

"If you keep watching him, he'll add a fourth for
pride's sake."

She started and glanced over her shoulder. André
wrestled into his shirt, which grew damp on his chest
and shoulders. Genevieve nodded toward Tiny.
"He'll hurt himself if he tries to carry all that."

"He'll do the entire portage with that load if it
kills him in the process." André stood close enough
for her to feel the damp heat emanating from his
body. "At least there's one advantage to having a
Frenchwoman around."

"What, exactly, does that mean?"

"It means my men are acting like roosters in a
henhouse, brawling and puffing out their chests for
your sake alone." He ran a hand over the spiky bristles
of his unshaven chin. "We'll either finish this portage
in half the time, or we'll end up with twice the
injuries."

"Your men are braggarts all, by the sound of the
stories they swapped over the camp fire last night. If I
weren't around, they'd just try to outdo one another."
She brushed a tendril of damp hair off her neck.
"Perhaps, if you strain yourself, you can think of
another advantage of having a wife."

His smoky gaze fell upon her, dipping to where her headrail clung to her swelling bosom. Her breath gathered in her lungs. No . . . she would not take it back. She had to say things so recklessly seductive if she was ever going to get this man in her bed. *For the future*, she told herself. *For survival, and for no other reason.*

"The only other women we've ever taken on these journeys were Indians. If you were a squaw, you'd be expected to paddle, to carry the canoe, to strike camp, to tend to the fires, and to carry nearly as much as Tiny."

"So heathens treat their women as badly as white men, then."

"Are you complaining?"

"I have reason enough. Since I've met you, you've tried to bury me, abandon me, divorce me, and now you're suggesting I work like a common laborer."

"Can you at least cook?"

"Cook!" She glanced toward the shore, where the cook heaved a huge copper cauldron on his shoulders. "It wouldn't take much imagination. We've been eating *sagamité* since we left Montréal, and the venison your cook flavors it with is getting as tough as leather."

"Sorry, wife, but we left the royal chef in Paris."

"It seems you left your wits in Paris, too, my husband, if you can't think of anything else to do with a wife but put her to work over a cauldron."

He thrust her case at her. "Here are the fripperies you insisted on taking with you. I warned you you'd have to carry them. They should feel like a hundred pounds in a few hours."

"You'll thank me for these fripperies when we reach that chewywagon place." She gripped the handle of her case, battered and wet, and nodded to the men upon the shore. "Maybe you should ask them what they would do if they had a French wife—Oh!"

"They would drag you into the bushes and roll you in the mud whenever the urge struck them." He swung her about to face him. "They would paw you like an animal in public. Is that what you want?"

Genevieve tilted her chin. She'd gone too far. She was supposed to act like an innocent, fainting young lady, when the truth was that since last night, part of her could think of little else but laying with this man when a woman like Marie Duplessis should dread it as a despicable duty.

"*Jésus!* Didn't the nuns at that charity house teach you anything?" His fingers tightened on her arm. "When a man makes a proposition like that, you're supposed to strike him or, at the very least, look at him in horror."

"I was under the impression that we were married, and such behavior was acceptable."

"Acceptable!?"

"If I can't believe my husband when it comes to such matters, whom can I believe?"

"You can't possibly be that innocent."

Genevieve tried to blush but knew she failed miserably. She looked away in a manner that she hoped was demure and shy.

André groaned and released her abruptly. "Christ! The ultimate innocence. Absolute trust in a husband."

She blinked, feigning surprise, sensing a crack in his armor. "Are you suggesting that what you said was improper?"

"No." He combed his fingers through his hair. "Not exactly."

"Then it's my duty to 'roll with you in the mud,'

no matter how messy it sounds." The devil whispered in her ear and she gave him voice. She leaned toward him. "There must be a dozen bushes along this portage. If it's your wish—"

"There'll be no bushes for us, Genevieve." André stepped back. A muscle flexed in his cheek. "You're making it very difficult for me to consider your welfare."

"I'm trying to honor my vows. Except for some scratches and bruises from twigs and roots, I can't imagine it could be unhealthy—"

"It's going to be a long voyage. Save your strength for survival, not seduction."

She let her gaze drop to the stretch of glistening golden chest revealed by the V of his shirt. "Seduction doesn't seem to take much effort."

"Survival will," he growled. He gestured to the edge of the clearing, where some of the men, already bent forward under the weight of packets and kegs, headed up a small path into the forest. "You'll need to follow those men. If some of my men catch up to you, let them pass. Wait wherever they pile the merchandise. We'll have to do several runs before we get it all to the end of the portage. And don't veer off the path. We won't have time to search for you later."

She couldn't resist. "I promise I won't be hiding in any bushes."

He dragged her close and spoke in her ear. "Don't tempt me, woman. It would be dangerous for you to become pregnant before we reach Chequamegon Bay."

Her smile dimmed. Genevieve knew there were ways for a man to prevent a woman from having a child, ways any man would know, certainly one as virile as André. She nearly opened her mouth and told him her thoughts, but stopped herself in time, for Marie Duplessis would never know such things.

Instead, she shrugged and hefted the case more firmly in her hand. "My mother always told me babies were found beneath bushes. Now I know what she meant."

Chapter Six

A rivulet of sweat ran down André's temple, soaking the leather strap attached to his harness and pulled tight across his forehead. His thighs flexed as he climbed a steep grade, straining from the weight of the load against his hips. It felt good to stretch those muscles after spending the morning pulling the canoe through the frigid rapids. A cool breeze filtered down through the scarlet leaves of a maple tree, chilling the perspiration on his face and chest and soaking the back of his shirt.

André strode through the woods, brushing away saplings, crackling roots, and leaves beneath his moccasins. He filled his lungs with clean mountain air, savoring the weight of the load on his back, the wavering heat of the sun on his head, and the pounding of his heart in his chest. He listened to the forest, full of the music of birds, the crunch of dead wood, the lazy buzz of what remained of the late summer insects. If he listened hard enough, he could hear the labored breathing and the shuffling gait of the canoeman some distance behind him, and it pleased him that his years in the deafening French cities hadn't dulled his senses.

He glanced at the furrowed rinds of the pines, judging the direction in which he walked by the growth of the moss on the tree trunks. He scanned the deep, green forest floor, judging the time of day by the length of the shadows. André felt the bite of mist on his skin and knew that if he hacked his way through the dense growth on the right, he would soon reach the cliff that overlooked the waterfall. He scanned the ground and saw the footsteps of each of his men imprinted in the dirt and scraped upon the rocks. Then, as he reached muddy ground, he found what he had been trailing for hours—the footsteps of the woman who had propositioned him twice in twenty-four hours, the woman whose kiss he couldn't get out of his mind.

He smiled grimly as he examined the imprints. Normally, the impression of her right foot sunk deeper than that of her left, because she carried her case in her right hand. Periodically, the pattern would switch, as if she was holding the case in her left hand. The pattern had switched three times in the last fifty paces. His stubborn, seductive wife was getting tired.

Good. He shifted the weight on his sweat-soaked back and heaved himself upon a ledge. His men had stared at him in horror after he sent her off into the woods carrying her own baggage; several of them had even offered to take her load upon their backs, but he had refused. He knew what he was doing.

A few days on the journey, and the temptation itched at him. *Sacré!* What man could resist a woman who propositioned him like a courtesan, then, when he kissed her, melted into a passionate innocent in his arms? It wasn't in his nature to say no. Damned auburn-haired, sharp-tongued beauty. To sleep with her was to consummate a marriage he didn't want and he wouldn't have. The sooner she became exhausted, the sooner she would cry to return to the settlements, and the sooner he would be rid of her and the temptation.

A dead tree trunk lay across the path; he paused as he reached it. A carpet of lichen undulated over the log, devouring the decaying wood. André eased down, the weight on his back straining his knees, and touched the splintered end of a branch that stuck upright from the trunk. On the ground beyond the fallen log was a deep gulch and, farther, two sets of evenly paced footprints.

He frowned and climbed over the log. André heard the voices long before he reached the height of the hill. He knew who they belonged to before he saw Genevieve and Julien standing in the sunshine, huddled far too close together.

"The landing is at the bottom of the hill, porkeater."

The two of them jumped apart as he strode into the clearing. Julien's face reddened beneath the edge of the copper pot he wore on his head. André's gaze paused on Genevieve, on the dirt streaking her pink skirts and caked in a lock of her hair. "Having some trouble, *ma mie?*"

She wiped the grit off her cheek. "Nothing a good scrubbing in the river won't fix."

"So you've finally discovered that the path isn't made for a lady's boot."

She plopped her hands on her hips—damned saucy hips, they were. "Don't fear, husband. I'll survive one little tumble in the mud."

"I trust," he growled, remembering their earlier conversation, "that you didn't have company in the mire."

"Julien," she grinned, flashing the boy a smile, "was kind enough to help me."

"Her skirts got caught on a branch," Julien explained. "She took a spill and I helped her to her feet."

"He's been helping me brush the muck off." Her eyes gleamed with mischief. "I never realized rolling in the mud is such a messy affair."

"Try harder to stay off your back, woman. There are no doctors in these woods."

"Your concern touches me, *husband*, but nothing's hurt but my vanity." She brushed at her puffed sleeves, adjusting the snagged ribbons while her lips twitched in humor. "Julien is doing everything he can to restore that."

"His job isn't to be a maidservant to my wife." André glared at the boy. "You should know better than to stop during a portage, especially along this stretch of the Ottawa."

The boy's fingers tightened on the dirty linen in his hand. "But Madame fell—"

"Madame is going to find herself in the slime often," he warned, meeting his wife's steady, twinkling eyes, "if she isn't very, very careful."

"Then I'll have to make sure I'm close to you, my husband, the next time I'm feeling reckless and unsteady."

Genevieve bent over to hide her smirk. Her head-rail gaped, showing the generous curve of one breast, and it took all his will to tear his gaze away from her and settle it on the red-faced young man at her side.

"It takes no more than a second for an Iroquois to scalp a man—or a woman. Why the hell did you stop here, in the open, in the middle of Iroquois country?''

"Oh, come, André." She straightened and brushed her hair off her forehead. "Wapishka told me there's been a peace treaty between those wigmakers and the French for three years now—"

"Savages like these will break a treaty whenever it pleases them." He shifted his weight and jerked his chin toward Julien. "You, pork-eater, are lagging behind. There are penalties for delays."

Julien glanced at Genevieve apologetically and handed her the dirty linen. "At least the silt will keep away the mosquitoes."

She smiled like the sunrise. "Thank you for your help, Julien."

The boy flushed and nodded, then bent his knees and reached for her case.

"Didn't I load you up enough?" André barked. Julien stared blankly at his boss, the case tight in his hand. André nodded to it. "You're taking on an extra burden."

"Madame is tired, and the case is heavy for her—"

"The lady will carry her own fripperies."

She curled her fingers around the handle. "You already have enough to carry, Julien—"

"But . . ."

"Go." She glanced at her husband. "Go before your master sprouts horns and cloven hooves."

Julien reluctantly released the case and headed into the woods. André glared at his wife, wondering how many of his men had carried her case along the way, wondering *exactly* what was the meaning of the secret little glance that had passed between her and Julien before the boy turned and strode into the forest.

"Don't be so harsh with him. He was only being

kind.'' She gazed at Julien's overloaded back, frowning. ''It's bad enough that he's been baptized in every cove since we left Lachine and now he's forced to wear a pot on his head for the men's amusement.''

André strode to her side. Sweat gleamed in the hollow of her throat and darkened a V into the headrail. ''Have you gotten bored so quickly of working your wiles on me, wife?''

Genevieve blinked, wide-eyed. ''I don't know what you're talking about.''

''That pork-eater is so smitten that he'll suffer more weight than he can possibly carry for your sake.''

A slow smile lifted the edges of her lips. ''I do believe you're jealous.''

''I'm wary.'' He brushed a bit of caked mud off her chin, then regretted the touch the moment his finger came in contact with her skin. *Christ.* A dirty, disheveled woman with knotted hair trailing down her back was *not* supposed to be attractive. ''Wary of a beautiful woman alone among two dozen men. Wary of the havoc she can wreak just with her presence.''

''Your men treat me like a fine piece of porcelain.'' She shifted the case to her other hand and kicked aside a little pile of acorns. ''Everything is 'Yes, madame,' and 'No, madame,' and 'May I lay the spruce boughs for your bed, madame.' I am the boss's wife, André, and all that havoc is in your head.'' Her nose wrinkled mischievously. ''Of course, I shouldn't tell you this. I should keep you guessing—''

''I don't take well to wearing horns.''

''Trust me, Julien won't give them to you.'' She swiveled and headed for the woods. ''So don't punish the boy for picking me out of the mud.''

''I'll have his hide hanging from the nearest tree,'' he growled, ''for idling away in the forest instead of doing his job.''

"No you won't."

"What?"

With her free hand, she hiked her skirts above her ankles, revealing a pair of splattered boots and delicate ankles, and ducked under a low bough, following the thread of a path through which Julien had just disappeared. "I said, you won't hang Julien's hide by the nearest tree."

"The hell I won't . . ."

"The secret is out, André. I know you're all bluster."

"What in blazes does that mean?"

She glanced at him over her shoulder, the fallen tresses of her hair swinging against her neck. "Julien told me the whole story. How long did you think you could hide it from me? The day you introduced me to that motley crew of yours, I knew there had to be a reason why Julien, who looks like he's never seen the inside of a tavern, was canoeing with acknowledged heathens and philanderers and God knows what other criminals on the other canoes."

"Julien is a convicted thief."

"Pah! He was an indentured servant who escaped from his master. He told me you saved him from the whipping post."

Damned wench. She probably batted those eyelashes and smiled that clean-toothed aristocratic smile and wheedled the entire story from the boy. "Julien is young and strong, and he's not the first man I've hired from prison."

"But you bought him from his master, set him free, and gave him a position in your canoe as a *voyageur*."

"He's cheap. He's working for me for the food I put in his mouth."

"Is that why you brought him on, a boy who, before Lachine, had never held a paddle?" She brushed past a sapling in her path and it whipped back, striking him in the belly. "Julien told me he had three more years of servitude with his master. You could have kept him working like a slave for you for three years and no one would have questioned it."

André frowned and watched her skirts sway back and forth with each step as she negotiated the rocky path down the side of the hill. The last thing he needed was Genevieve thinking he had a heart of gold, when his intentions for her were as black as they could be. "One year in the wilderness is worth three toiling in the soil. That pork-eater has no idea what he's gotten himself into yet."

And neither, my wife, have you.

"From what he told me, anything is better than his master's whip." The path twisted precipitously down and she released her skirts to grasp the sticky rinds of the trees as she negotiated the slope. "Though sometimes I wonder if being humiliated by two dozen merciless canoemen is much better."

"You're showing great sympathy for a boy who ran away from his obligations."

"Anyone looking into that boy's eyes can see that he's honest." Genevieve clambered over a jutting stone, lifting her skirts high enough for him to see the frayed stockings covering her shapely calves above the edge of her boots. "And you should talk, the man who took pity on a convicted thief." She glanced at him out of the corner of her eye. "Julien isn't the only man on this journey that you've set free. Wapishka told me—"

"*Jésus!* I see now why my men are slow on this portage." He shifted his shoulders to loosen the burden on his back. "They've been telling tall tales and waiting on you hand and foot."

"Wapishka used to be a slave, he told me. It was

that tribe—those wigmakers—who took him captive from the settlements. They took him to their village because they had never seen a Negro, but then they began to torture him." She switched her case to her other hand and flexed her reddened fingers. "Wapishka told me you saved his life."

"My men are braggarts."

"He was bragging about *you*."

"I was nearby, with the soldiers from the Carignan-Salière regiment. We were going to attack, anyway—"

"But you didn't wait."

"I don't relish the sound of a man screaming in agony as his burned fingertips are being chewed on by sharp-toothed children."

"A strong slave like him would have brought you a fine purse of gold." She whirled around a twist in the path and stopped for a moment, eyeing him. "His original owner would have paid you well for his return. You set him free and gave him work."

André nodded to a fallen trunk across the path. "Watch where you're going."

"I see where I'm going." She released the branch and toed her way down the rubbled hill. "I only fell once, and it was because a branch got tangled in my skirts."

"Take care, Genevieve. I doubt you'll take well to The Duke's medicines."

"Such concern for my welfare." She tossed a knowing glance over her shoulder and smiled widely. "The wolf I thought I married is turning out to be a gentle puppy. He saves young boys from the whipping posts and sets slaves free—"

"You're my wife. What tales do you think my men are going to tell? They know where their next meal is coming from."

"Mmm, and I think they know, too, that you wouldn't deny it to them, no more than you would deny milk to a child."

The path widened and André brushed past her. His gaze slipped over the disorder of her tumbling auburn hair, over the freckled tilt of her nose.

"I won't tell anyone," she murmured, wrinkling her nose at him, all mischief. "It will be our little secret. There's something charming about a strong man with a soft heart."

"You've listened to too many fairy tales, woman."

He ground to a halt in the mulch, swiveling around her. Genevieve gasped in surprise, then grabbed on to a sapling to steady herself on the uncertain path. Nose to nose they stood, so close he heard her breathing, the sweet, ragged breath of excitement. He focused on the dirt smeared over the pert tilt of her tiny nose; a child's nose, ridiculously small, but the full lips beneath spoke of a woman's sensuality. . . . Those lips parted, showing a glimmer of moist tongue, and André leaned closer, drawn to that mouth, to the quiver of those lips.

Wretched witch, staring at him, tempting him. He was no damned saint. She'd see soon enough, *oui*, soon enough, when those white hands of hers cracked with pain from cold and exertion, when those slim ankles of hers wobbled under the strain of climbing, when her white skin chapped with cold and wind; then she'd see the pith of him. How long would it take? How long did he have to watch her breasts rising and falling, soft warm mounds straining against her snagged bodice, before the journey finally took its toll and stole the roses from her cheeks? It was already taking too damned long. Someone had woven steel into this bit of lace.

Her lips quivered in the faintest of smiles; mocking

him, she was, the fool. He clutched her by the waist and thrust her against him. Her breasts surged against his chest, the nubbed hardness of her nipples raking his shirt.

"Careful, Genevieve." He whispered the words against her cheek, fluttering a tendril of hair curving soft to her shoulder. "These woods make savages out of the most civilized men."

The case clattered to the ground; her hands swept up his chest. He seized one hand and squeezed it, cruel and tight. "Remember this: There's one rule on this journey, woman. Don't slow me down."

He released her. She reeled back and snatched a sapling to steady herself. He turned away and strode down the hill, faster than safety allowed with the heavy weight unevenly distributed on his back. "From here," he called over his shoulder, "there's no turning back, Genevieve. No matter *what.*"

André increased his pace, increasing the distance between him and his muttering wife. Twice he slipped on the sleek rug of pine needles that matted the forest floor, maintaining his footing only by force of will. He needed to get away from her eyes, he needed to get away from the guilt that was nipping at his innards. She was beginning to trust him, the foolish wench. Damn fool men, conspiring to paint him like some sort of kind-hearted hero—and well they might, since they didn't know his plans for this woman. He hadn't even told Tiny, not yet.

He had no intention of bringing this spitfire all the way to Chequamegon Bay. He had no intention of spending the long, cold winter nights anywhere near her voluptuous little form. She would not be his *wife.* Ten days. Ten days, if all went well. Then they'd reach Allumette Island. She was still spritely now, but ten days traveling the rapid-strewn Ottawa River should be enough to exhaust his wife to the point of collapse; he would see to it. By then she would be screaming to return to Montréal, too bone-weary to continue any farther on the journey.

Then he would leave her with the Algonquin Indians and Jesuit missionaries who wintered every year on Allumette Island.

André trudged toward the shore, where the rest of his men were unloading their harnesses and loading the canoes floating in the water. Come next spring, as he returned to Montréal from Chequamegon Bay, he would pass by the island, pick her up, and bring her back to civilization. He could already imagine those green eyes snapping at him with all the power of nine months of pent-up fury. But it would be too late for her to wreak vengeance, for he would annul their marriage and then they'd both be free to do what they willed—he to return to the woods unencumbered, and she to marry some docile settler she could control.

Life *was* a circle, he mused darkly, just as the Indians believed. He'd seen his own life come around again, though he'd fought it tooth and nail.

Another French wife, abandoned in the wilderness for the winter. A grimace stretched across his face, tight and humorless, as dark as the shadows in his eyes. The fates mocked him. They mocked him, indeed.

"Hell and damnation!"

An icy wave slapped her awake. Genevieve straightened up off her wobbly bed of cartons and kegs and gasped, opening her eyes, as the frigid water soaked through her clothing. She coughed, sputtering, and glared blindly around her, searching for the culprit who'd woken her so rudely from her sleep.

"Ah, the sweet music of a lady's voice." André stood outside the canoe, gripping one side as he pulled it in toward the shore. His eyes danced. "Tiny, you'll have to watch your language. My wife is learning the native tongue."

As she looked around, she realized the *voyageurs* surrounded the canoe, having just leapt off in their usual synchronized fashion, sending up the spray of water that had awoken her. They were red-faced, trying to hold back their laughter. Genevieve flushed. She would have to learn to curb her tongue. She had spent too much time taking lessons in cursing from fishmongers' wives on the banks of the Seine.

She glanced at the rocky shore and groaned. "Is this another portage?"

"No." When the water was hip-deep, he signaled for his men to begin unloading the vessel. "We're done for the day."

Genevieve tried not to show her relief. For the past three days, they had done nothing but pole and pull upriver, only to stop what seemed like every half mile to unload and portage over terrain that was becoming steeper, rockier, and more and more overgrown. The Ottawa became so narrow and the water so swift that she wondered if the men were going to carry all the merchandise—six thousand pounds of it, according to Siméon—through the next five weeks of travel. The first few days, her muscles had merely been sore at night, but now they quivered with exhaustion at the end of each day. And when she awoke in the morning, it took all her strength to drag herself out of her bed. This morning, she barely remembered André carrying her out onto the canoe, until he woke her for the first portage. After each successive one, she would sink back down on her bumpy seat and drift back off into a jostled sleep.

She dragged her fingers through her nest of hair. Twigs and leaves fluttered to her lap. They scattered all over the canoe when André reached in without warning, swept her up, and carried her to the shore. Her stomach growled as she smelled the fires, set up ahead of time by the cook, who waited upon the bank.

Genevieve winced when he released her and her feet hit the shore. Blister upon blister had developed on her heels and toes after all the walking, for Marie's shoes were too small for her feet. She had tried wearing two pairs of stockings, but instead of cushioning her sores, they only made the fit of the boots tighter. She was tempted to walk barefoot from now on. Sharp, jutting stones couldn't do her feet any more damage than these wretched boots. Genevieve envied the men their soft deerskin slippers and even their shameless leggings, and found herself wishing she weren't pretending to be a lady, so she could freely find something to wear other than rigid boots and a boned bodice.

She leaned over to stretch the aches in her back, surreptitiously loosening the ties of her shoes at the same time. When she straightened, she watched as the *voyageurs* moored the canoes offshore, laying one end of a long pole on the gunwale and the other end on the beach, then swiftly unloading them and piling the merchandise on the banks. The sun gleamed golden on the water and shimmered off the sheer rock cliff that rose up from the other side of the river.

Julien brought her her woven case, smiling at her shyly. She nearly dropped it as she took it in her hand. Not for the first time, she wondered how a basketful of clothing and pins could weigh as much as gold bars after a few hours of carrying. She vowed that she'd get Julien or one of the other *voyageurs* to fashion a rope harness for her, so she could sling it across her back. Then, at least, she'd have two hands free so she could lift her bedraggled skirts and push aside the thick foliage that obscured the paths.

Genevieve dropped her case on the ground and sank down wearily upon it. She knew she should go wash herself and comb the debris from her hair while the men toiled, for she wouldn't get her dinner until André was free, but right now the only thing she could think of was eating. It seemed like days since her last hearty meal, though she had eaten her fill of cornmeal this morning. She worked, instead, on brushing the cakes of dirt from the ragged hem of her skirts.

André tossed his pack by her side, sending up a fresh spray of mud in the process. She frowned at him and wiped the splattered dirt off her cheek. His grin widened as he hunkered down next to her, looking at ease in his buckskin and fringe, as if the campsite were his own kitchen. He shoved a steaming pewter bowl into her hands. "Dinner."

She peered into the grainy, yellowish mixture. "*Sagamité* again?" She watched him spoon the gruel into his mouth. "Can't your cook fix anything else?"

"Get used to it. We'll be eating it clear through to Lake Superior, if the supplies last."

"Well I hope it all falls into the river and gets carried all the way to the sea."

"You shouldn't." He cocked a brow at her, his mouth full. "Then we'll be living on *tripe de roche.*"

"Anything is better than this."

"*Tripe de roche* is moss scraped off of rocks, flavored with whatever juicy caterpillars happen to be upon it."

Her stomach twisted. She whirled her wooden spoon in the cornmeal mixture. "Has your cook at least added some fresh meat instead of that leather he claims is leftover venison?"

André laughed and shook his head, his sun-washed hair shining in the sunset. "This isn't Paris, my wife."

"I noticed." She gestured to the boughs above her with a twirl of her spoon. "Who has hunting privileges in this land?"

He squinted into the stripes of sunset pouring through the trees, bathing him in a golden glow. He shrugged and turned his attention to his meal. "No one. Everyone. The land is free to all of us."

"Then let's hunt!"

He chewed around his words. "Sorry, princess, but we left the royal huntsmen in Montréal."

"It wouldn't take huntsmen to find fresh meat." She leaned toward him. "I've tripped over a dozen hares in the past few days. And the geese! They make enough noise to wake the dead. Yesterday I came so close to a doe that I nearly petted her."

"Hunting takes time."

"Why the haste, anyway?" She ate a spoonful of her *sagamité*, grimacing at the far-too-familiar gritty taste. "It's only September, and Julien told me it's a four- or five-week trip."

"That pork-eater you've grown so fond of has never taken a trip into the wilderness. He has no idea how long it will take."

"Somebody told him four or five weeks."

"It'll be four or five weeks if we paddle hard. If the weather doesn't turn. If the Iroquois stick to their treaty. If you don't slow us down. If we have no accidents . . ."

"Still, how much time could we waste hunting? An hour or two a day?"

"An hour or two tracking and killing a beast large enough to feed all these men, hours more to skin it and quarter it and roast it over an open fire. We don't have that kind of time. The men know it, too. We'll have plenty of time to fatten up when we get to Chequamegon Bay, but winter comes early in Canada. Early and hard."

Genevieve ate another warm spoonful and glanced around the clearing. A few hardwoods stood among the pines, gold in their autumnal glory. Birds still chirped high in the boughs. The sky was clear and the air warm, and winter seemed far, far away. "Mmm," she mused, swallowing, "I can just smell the snow on the wind."

"You'll see soon enough. If we make it to All Saint's Day without a snowfall, we will consider ourselves blessed."

"We'll starve first." She glanced over to where Tiny leaned back on a rock, puffing his pipe into full smoke. His leather shirt collapsed in folds where, only a few days ago, it had been stretched tight over his belly. "Even Tiny's bulk is wasting away."

"He was as big as a horse when we left Montréal, bloated from too much brandy and too many aniseed cakes." His pale almond gaze slipped intimately over her torn and stained dress. "You don't seem to be suffering from the steady diet."

She shifted her weight and felt the looseness of her bodice around her waist. "Ah, what a wonderful thing a boned bodice is."

"The *sagamité* must have sharpened your tongue."

"You can dull it with a piece of fresh meat."

"We'll have more fresh meat than we can eat when we reach Chequamegon Bay."

"We'll all be nothing but skin and bones by then."

André leaned over and snatched the empty bowl

from her. He smiled, only inches from her face, his eyes gleaming like a pale, tannic pool. "Don't worry, *ma mie.* I won't let you starve."

She frowned as he stood up and walked back to the pot of *sagamité.* The men squatted around the steaming cauldron, eating from their bowls with concentration, their wooden spoons flashing briefly before disappearing into their mouths. Genevieve knew André and all the other men were hungry for meat, too, and she suspected that he was acting like this just out of pique.

She never should have told him what Julien and Wapishka had divulged to her three days ago. Since that day, he had intentionally done everything to prove to her that her instincts were wrong. He warned her not to slow them down every time he crossed her path. He teased her unmercifully when she lounged around in the predawn light while his men raced each other to see which team would be the first to fill the canoes. He grinned like Lucifer whenever she reached the end of a portage, her face and arms itchy and red from insect bites, her clothes covered with soil, snagged and torn in spots where the skirts had caught upon branches, her hair tugged out of its chignon. He acted as if he had no mercy, and she was beginning to wonder if perhaps he didn't.

Genevieve rose from her seat, wincing as she put all her weight on her battered feet. She swept up her case and turned toward the woods, judging by the emergence of several men from the towering pines which was the best direction to head for her toilette. She wandered into the dim quiet of the clustered trees, humming one of the *voyageurs'* songs, until she heard the splash of a stream. Finding it winding over a tumble of stones, she placed her case upon a waist-high boulder near the edge of the creek and dipped her hands into the clear, cold water. She arched her neck and ran her wet hands over her skin, pushing the loose tendrils of her hair out of her face.

"Don't move."

She started as she heard André's whisper, only a few steps behind her. Genevieve whirled around and glared at him as he approached, as silent as a spirit. "Why . . ."

He clamped his hand over her mouth. His pistol was drawn and cocked, and he was staring at something to her right. He motioned for her to be silent, then released her mouth and pushed her behind him with one arm.

She followed the direction of his gaze, seeing nothing but a few branches by the creek swaying in the wind, six or seven paces away. She frowned and glared at him, willing him to turn around, but his attention was on the crackling underbrush.

Genevieve planted her hands on her hips and whispered, "Why did you follow me here?"

He reached back and pulled her tight against his body, until her cheek was crushed flat between his shoulder blades. He turned his head but not his eyes. "You have a bad habit of bumbling blindly into the forest."

Her voice was muffled against his shirt. "I know exactly where I am."

"You surprised two men from a very comfortable squat in the bushes during your walk to this creek. Did you know that?"

She frowned against the warmth of his deerskin shirt.

"I didn't think so. With all your humming and stumbling and breaking branches and making tracks, I'm surprised you didn't alert everything within miles of our presence here."

"At least I don't sneak around behind other people's backs." She tried to push her hair off her forehead. "I'm your wife. You don't have to hide in the bushes and watch while I bathe."

"I wouldn't. Someone else might." He nodded toward the swaying bushes. "We've got company."

Brushing the deerskin fringe out of her eyes, she peered around one taut bicep toward the underbrush. After watching for a few minutes, Genevieve realized that the movement was too erratic to be caused by the wind, but it was subtle enough for her to wonder how he had noticed it. By the way he was gripping the handle of his pistol, by the tenseness of his muscles against her cheek, he obviously thought the unexpected visitor was dangerous.

She stood on her toes to be closer to his ear, holding on to his sleeves for balance. "Is it an Iroquois?"

"If it were an Iroquois," he whispered, "we'd both have arrows through our hearts."

"Then what is it?"

"If you keep still and be quiet, it might be that fresh meat you've been craving."

She bit her lip and stood as still as she could, waiting for the creature to emerge from the bushes. She had seen lots of strange-looking wildlife over the past few days. Enormous stags with antlers like giant hands, fingers spread and palms cupped, facing heavenward. Prickly rodents the men called porcupine. Though she hadn't yet seen any, the *voyageurs* told stories of big, black bears with toothy jaws, of sleek, swift wildcats with sharp claws, of packs of wolves running wild in the forests.

She tightened her grip on his arms, pressing closer to his warmth, to the well-muscled curve of his back. The blue twilight gleamed off the resinous, knotty trunks of the pines, silvering the bark. The branches waved wildly. Whatever the creature was, it didn't seem disturbed by their presence.

André raised his pistol slowly as the beast waddled out of the underbrush.

Chapter Seven

Genevieve suppressed a smile and pressed her cheek against André's arm. The beast they had waited for with such anticipation was black and furry and as big as a lapdog. A pair of long white stripes ran along its back. It waddled to the edge of the stream, oblivious of their presence, nuzzling the ground with its black snout and then lifting it to the wind.

She released André and grinned into his eyes. "Is this one of the wild animals of the forest I should fear?"

He flashed her a look, then shoved his pistol into his sash. "You're lucky it isn't a wolf or a bear."

"The most savage thing I've encountered in these woods is you, and we both know just how savage you are."

"Do you?" His gaze, as deep and potent as rum, slipped over her body, over her loosened headrail, over her bedraggled appearance. He tilted his head toward the creature, who had noticed their presence and now stood still, sniffing the air and staring in their direction. "Do you know what that is?"

"I have no idea, but it looks as harmless as a cat."

"It's not running away from us." He rested his hand on the hilt of his knife. "How do you know it doesn't eat human flesh to survive?"

She rolled her eyes. "I suppose next you're going to be telling me it has piercing fangs and claws like knives."

"It might have venom in its teeth or poison on its fur."

"If you're afraid of it, my husband, I'll scare it away for you."

"Go right ahead." He grinned and crossed his arms. "I dare you."

She blinked in mild surprise. He was taunting her, as if she really feared this furry little animal, as if the creature could really do her harm. Genevieve glanced at it. She had never seen anything like it in France, but she could tell it was stiff and frightened. She was sure it would race away as soon as she approached. Unless he was telling the truth . . .

What rot. She frowned, angry at herself for letting him plant a grain of doubt in her mind. This beast was nothing but an oversized rodent. Her husband was taunting her, testing her courage, and she'd been in enough gambling halls to know a bluff when she saw one. Tossing her head, she strode toward the creature and waved her arms at it.

"Get away, little furball, before my husband faints of fear." Startled, the creature turned its back and raised its tail. She raced toward it, stamping her feet loudly on the ground, then laughed and pointed at it. "Look, André! Look at your maneater now. . . . Oh!"

An odor, more rank than anything she had ever smelled, exploded into the air. She covered her face with her hand and coughed, smothering in the vile, putrid stench, stumbling back, away from the animal who scurried, tail raised, into the bushes. "Jesus, Mary, and Joseph!"

His laughter echoed in the clearing. She turned and glared at him through stinging eyes, and saw him bent double in mirth, his hand pressed against his belly.

"You've just met your first *putois d'Amérique.*" His teeth gleamed. "The skunk has a unique way of warding off predators, wouldn't you say?"

"You *wretch!*" She looked down and saw wet spots upon her skirts. Her eyes teared from the odor and her nostrils burned. "That, *creature* shot poison at me."

"It's not poison, it's only scent." He covered his nose and mouth with his hand as she shook her stench-ridden skirts, trying to disperse the odor. "Now you know that something small and furry can still be dangerous."

"And something that's *not* so small can be as wicked as Lucifer!"

"You offered to scare it away."

"You dared me when you should have warned me!"

"If you were the kind of woman to listen to warnings, you wouldn't be on this journey with me now."

Genevieve stalked to the edge of the creek and dropped to her knees, lifting palmfuls of water to her skirts in a vain attempt to wash herself free of the stench. She should have known he would play a trick on her; she should have expected his treachery. A thousand vile curses rolled in her head and surged in her throat, most of them concerning his birth, his health, and the size and capabilities of certain parts of his anatomy. It took all her will to silently pour the frigid water over her lap and pretend to be a lady, when she wanted to curse him to the bowels of hell.

"Don't bother," he said. "It'll take days before the scent wears off, no matter how well you wash."

"You miserable wretch." She glared at him over her shoulder as water dripped from her chin. "You're nothing but a mangy cur —"

"You can do better than that."

"There are names for men like you." *Whoreson. Pox-ridden, thieving spawn of a babbling idiot.* Her chest heaved with the effort not to wish upon him the French disease or sundry other painful, embarrassing conditions that would affect the most sensitive organ of a man's body. Marie Duplessis would know nothing of them. Damn it, had *she* ever really been as innocent as Marie Duplessis? Had there ever been a time of innocence?

"I should go chase after that thing," she argued, "and throw it on you."

"I doubt it has any scent left after that shot." André coughed as she stood up from the edge of the creek and the wind blew in his direction. "*Dieu!* I've never known anyone to get hit so badly. You smell like burning flesh."

Her teary eyes narrowed. His face was red from trying not to breathe in too much of the stink. She stopped thinking. She reacted like Genevieve and threw all vestiges of ladylike behavior to the winds.

His laughter stopped abruptly as he saw her racing toward him, her auburn hair fiery, her eyes blazing green. He straightened and fled into the woods.

"Afraid of a little stench, André?"

"A *little* stench?" His laughter returned as he eluded her, running deeper into the woods. "You smell like the gaping mouth of hell!"

"A scent you will soon be very familiar with."

André laughed, crashing through the underbrush, and she followed in hot pursuit. He swung around pines to divert her, raising clods of mud in his wake, recklessly snapping branches and holding saplings so they would whip back and impede her progress. He headed into the thickest growth of bushes where, in her blind, headlong rush after him, her skirts tore and caught upon the thorns, slowing her down. She stumbled and cursed, not caring that the hanging branches pulled at the pins in her hair, sending them flying all over the forest, making her tresses tumble in knotted locks down her back. She didn't care that she was hiking her skirts well above her knees, that branches and twigs and saplings were pulling on the delicate wool of her stockings. His taunting laughter floated back to her, and she swore before the night was over, she'd rub her stench-ridden skirts all over his body so he, too, would pay the price of her foolishness.

The men, attracted by the sound of them crashing through the forest, wandered in through the trees to see what was about. André knocked Julien over as he rushed by, and Genevieve pushed him away as she followed. The sun had nearly set, making it more difficult to see in the shadows of the woods. She stopped for a moment to catch her breath and figure out which of the silhouettes she saw through the trees was André.

"You wretched coward." Genevieve hiked her hands to her hips, coughing as she took a deep breath and the stench burned all the way to the bottom of her lungs. "Your men are here now; do you want them to see you running away from a woman?"

A voice came from behind her. "They'll get one whiff of you, my wife, and they'll run, too."

She whirled in the litter, racing after him, keeping her gaze fixed on the fluttering fringe of his shirt, the bare skin of his thighs. The *voyageurs* laughed and clapped, urging her on as they watched from the periphery, their silhouettes stark against the orange-red fires of the campsite. Her feet swelled unbearably in her tight boots, but she ignored the pain. He was too swift for her, too sly and clever, and she knew he was taunting her, coming close but never close enough for her to do more than scrape the deerskin of his shirt with her nails. Once he teased her by trapping himself in a copse of pines, then slipping between the close trunks when she raced in for the kill. Just when she thought her lungs would burst from the exertion, fate intervened in the form of a tall, blond-bearded giant.

Tiny thrust his foot out from behind a tree and André flew to the ground. The giant's laughter echoed in the forest, like the roar of a great beast. "Since when has a little stench kept you away from a woman, André?"

"Mutiny!"

"It really isn't fair," Tiny continued, "with the poor girl having to carry her own case and all."

Panting, Genevieve reached them, feeling a joyous quiver of victory when she saw André on the ground, struggling to rise. She launched herself upon his body, slamming fully into his chest and bracing her hands on either side of his head.

"I've got you now, husband."

He placed his hands on her waist and tried to lift

her off him, but she pressed brazenly against his body, using all her weight to fight him. The men gathered around them.

"Christ, she stinks!"

"Worse than a savage in the height of summer."

"Eh, you all right, André?"

Silence.

"I think we'd better leave, boys."

Their footsteps faded into the forests. She hardly heard them, for her attention was focused on the man beneath her. He was wet with sweat from racing around the forest. She wiggled her body against his, rubbing him with the stench, fighting against him as he tightened his grip around her waist.

"I'm not the only one who'll pay the price for your little prank," she said, clutching a handful of his shirt as he tried to pull her off. "You'll smell as bad as me when I'm finished—"

"Careful, Genevieve."

"Careful? I'm going to mark you with this stench if it takes all night." She wriggled again and he made a noise deep in his throat. "That was a wicked thing you did, sending me off to get sprayed by that creature."

"No more wicked than what you're doing to me right now."

"This is what you deserve. I'm not going to be the only one stinking like the open sewers of Paris—"

"Stop wriggling."

"—and if you think you're going to change clothes, I'm telling you right now that I'll wriggle all over the next set, too."

"Genevieve."

A muscle moved in his cheek and his eyes glowed with a light she had seen before. Her breath caught in her throat and she suddenly realized that his laughter had long died; she suddenly realized how provocative her motion was, how intensely he held her in his embrace. He was no longer fighting to get her off, he was fighting to keep her still.

"Someone should have warned me about you back in Madame Bourdon's house." His gaze traveled over her tousled hair, the long column of her exposed throat, and his voice was as husky as rustling leaves. "They should have warned me that you laugh like a child but move like a woman." He slid his hands up her back to tangle in her hair. "They should have warned me that you were only half lady, and the other half . . . I'm not sure what the other half is. It's half wild, impulsive. Wanton. Have you always been like this, Genevieve? Or is it these woods that bring it out in you?"

She listened to his words—magic words, dangerous words—too close to the truth, validating all she had feared, all she could not control. His fingers snarled in her hair, combing through the tresses. His shirt was untied and hung open, showing the hollow in the center of his chest and the faintest gleam of sweat. She felt an unbearable desire to lower her head and lick a drop that pooled in the darkness of that hollow.

He pressed his hips against her abdomen. "Feel what you are doing to me, woman."

Her lips parted in a silent gasp as she felt the hardness of a man's passion pressing against her navel. She knew then what she had suspected when she first laid eyes on him in Montréal, what she had feared. She wanted him. The way a woman wants a man.

Even as she admitted the passion to her secret self, another revelation came to her. She wanted him, not just because he was her husband, not just because he could give her the security and the home that she always wanted, not just because fate had thrown them together in this strange situation, and not, most importantly, just because he was a man. She wanted *him,* André, the man who could carry two hundred pounds of weight on his back for two or three miles; the man who walked and lived and breathed as comfortably in this untamed wilderness as if it were his own parlor; the hard man with a soft heart.

He could make her a woman, here, now, on the littered carpet of dried nettles and grass and crushed, crinkling leaves, and she knew with absolute certainty that she wanted to give herself to him.

Oh, God . . . what is happening to me?

She'd never thought she'd feel like this, having wondered if it were even possible or if that feeling were just another fairy tale told to little girls so they would not lay in terror of the future. Now, something inside her began to ache, to yearn . . . some deep part of her that was still innocent, the part she'd hidden all those years ago, the part that still sheltered hope, which she'd thought she'd buried forever. . . .

Impulsively, she leaned down and pressed her lips on the salty skin of his neck. A pulse throbbed against her mouth. His throat vibrated with unuttered sound, his arms tightening around her. Her body trembled with a sudden infusion of heat and passion, a tingling so intense that she felt it right down to the tips of her toes. She had never been so conscious of another person's body. It was as if these strong, hard limbs, the blood flowing through the veins beneath her lips, the tense muscles of his abdomen, were all her own, for she felt the trembling in him like an echo of her own. She wanted nothing more than to be naked against him, to open herself to this man she barely knew yet somehow seemed to have known forever.

His hands slid down to her shoulders and lifted her up. From between their bodies rose a fresh wave of the stench, fetid and strong, warmed by the joining of their bodies.

She couldn't help it. The coughing erupted. She turned her head away and pinched her nostrils together to clear her head of the acrid stink, all to no avail, for the stench had intensified in the close warmth of their limbs. He coughed, too, and she rolled off him, clutching her face as the full effect of the stench rose in the air.

He rose to his elbows. "It smells worse on my deer-skin than it does on your broadcloth."

"Good!" she said petulantly, the mood long broken between them. "It's no less than you deserve."

"Mmm. Maybe it's divine justice." He stood up and brushed the dirt off his thighs and leggings. "In spite of the stench, that skunk did us both a favor." His gaze slipped over her. "You have a way of making me forget myself, Genevieve."

She wiped her teary eyes and silently cursed the striped creature. She wanted André to take her in his arms again, to make her feel that strange way again, but her eyes watered and her nose stung and she felt about as attractive as a woman with the ague. And with the air thick with the stench, the clearing was about as romantic as a pile of rotting meat.

He held out his open hand. "Come, let's get back to the campsite."

Reluctantly, she took his hand. He pulled her to her feet, then shook his head and stepped abruptly away.

"Do us all a favor tonight, *ma mie.*" His lips twitched. "Sleep downwind."

André hooked his carved pipe between his lips and drew the stinging smoke into his lungs. The rich scent

of tobacco rose in the air as the end of the pipe
glowed like a ruby. He had taken to smoking his pipe
more frequently since the incident with the skunk
four days ago, in a vain attempt to mask the stench,
and had discovered in the process how much he
enjoyed the pungent taste of tobacco. Now, among
a handful of his men, he leaned back on a stone just
above the muddy edge of the shore, resting his sore
shoulders and the cramped muscles of his legs after
a rugged portage past Chat's Falls, a crescent-shaped
dam of primitive rock that surged from the bed of
the Ottawa River.

Through half-closed eyes, he watched the end of
the path. For the first time in the ten days of the
journey, Genevieve was late in finishing a portage.
But he wasn't worried. Not really. He told himself
he was just enjoying the familiar sight of his men
emerging from the forest, laden with goods, not waiting for a certain spirited, auburn-haired wench in a
ragged pink dress to finally make an appearance.

André half-listened to the conversation going on
around him.

"Geese just don't twist their own necks and waddle
into the cook's canoe." Anselme Roissier glared at
the men as they crinkled open their *sacs au feu* and
stuffed their pipes with tobacco. "Someone is not
confessing. Someone here had to have trapped and
killed that goose."

Gaspard, Anselme's brother, shrugged. "Whoever
the hunter is, I'd like to raise a glass of brandy to
him for giving us meat for dinner."

"But no one has admitted it. Doesn't that mean
anything to you, to any of you?" Anselme raised his
arms in a dramatic gesture of frustration. "It didn't
just drop from the sky and land neatly in the cook's

canoe. This bird was trapped and its neck was broken and it was planted there."

André frowned. He had his own theory about who had planted a freshly killed goose in the cook's canoe that morning, a theory he wasn't willing to share. His gaze shifted to where Julien stood, thigh-deep in the river, wearing nothing but a garland of orange winterberries around his neck, while Siméon droned in Latin nearby. From the start of the voyage, Julien had gazed upon Genevieve like a lovestruck puppy. Though the boy always staggered in exhaustion at the end of each day, he had long assumed the responsibility of gathering fir boughs for Genevieve's bed at night, and now that the nights were growing colder, he'd assumed the duty of setting up a makeshift tent for her from the tarpaulins that covered the merchandise on the canoe. Genevieve's complaints about the food and the availability of game had become insistent these past few days, and it would be just like Julien to hunt to please that saucy-eyed wench.

Hunting and killing fresh meat. Bloodying his hands and feeding his woman. Bringing a woman freshly killed meat was the most primitive courtship, and it angered André more than he liked to admit. This woman was spoken for, even if their relationship remained unconsummated. The men thought otherwise, for when she had been sprayed with the skunk, he had returned to the campsite to face the mirth of two dozen *voyageurs*, all wondering aloud, in bawdy language, exactly how his lively, vengeful wife had marked him so thoroughly with scent. At the time, he had shrugged it off. Let them think he had torn off her clothes and tumbled her in the forest. Nothing would be more in character. The truth was, had the rank stench of skunk not interrupted what had begun between them, he might have forgotten himself and taken what she so freely offered.

The thought burned in him more harshly than the smoke burned his lungs. He kept thinking that there were other ways they could please one another without consummating their marriage. Blood rushed to his loins. There were ways. There were ways for an inventive man and a willing woman. . . . Christ, what was he thinking? He was going to leave the witch on Allumette Island. To caress her, to taste her in the most intimate places, to feel all that quivering energy against his naked body and then abandon her. . . . No, no, it was too wicked for even him to do.

Almost.

"Who do you think killed the goose, *frère?*" Gaspard raised his voice and waved his smoking pipe in the air. "If you know who did it, tell us, otherwise, shut up and talk of other things."

"All I know is we're still in Iroquois country." Anselme glanced nervously toward the edge of the forest. "There could be hundreds of them out there, sneaking around our camp, and we wouldn't even know it."

André knocked his pipe against a rock. Glowing red embers scattered all over the surface. "If they're sneaking around our camp, they wouldn't be hunting for geese. If they were here, you'd know it by now."

The young man shrugged. "Maybe they rubbed the bird with nightshade or filled them with poisonous fungus to weaken us."

"That is not the Iroquois way." Wapishka blew a blue stream of smoke into the air and stared down at his fingertips, still scarred from his experience with the warlike tribe. "The Iroquois are warriors. They would attack, not weaken us with poisoned game."

"You white men . . ." The Duke shook his head.

"You always look for reasons. There are not always reasons. It may be that a *manitou* is looking over us."

Wapishka leaned toward the Indian. "Why do you think such things?"

"I had a dream. I did not know the meaning until this morning, when we found the goose in the cook's canoe."

André frowned at the dark visage of The Duke. Dreams were considered divine revelations to the Indians of these parts. André had begun to wonder if some Indian fertility god had snaked into his own head and purged all Christian teaching, for the revelations *he'd* been receiving lately were not in the least holy. They all involved Genevieve in various states of undress and in various stages of sexual ecstasy.

"I dreamed of a bird."

He tore his attention away from his dangerous thoughts. They were part of his torment, as if the gods, angry that he spurned their revelations, tortured him by making him want her all the more. It didn't help that she grew more beautiful with each day. After a portage, her auburn locks sprung from their chignon, straggling down her back and flying wildly about her face. The sun had darkened the spray of freckles across her nose. With her skirts ripped and sullied, her headrail loose over her shoulders, exposing the white flesh of her glistening chest, she looked common, attainable, and so very, very approachable.

He wondered where she was now and why she was taking so damn long to finish this portage.

"This bird had plumage the color of blood." The Duke closed his eyes, summoning the memory. "It was hungry and weak, but an experienced hunter. It knew that it would do better to hunt in the night than in the broad light of day, where its enemies could see it and take advantage of its weakness. It saw a snow-white goose, and when the goose saw this blood-red bird, it raised its neck to sacrifice itself. And so the red bird survived by the sacrifice of the goose.''

"Don't let Siméon hear you," Gaspard whispered to the Indian. "He'll call that devil's talk."

"Your black robes tell me that the fish sacrificed themselves in Peter's net to feed the people. Is that not the same as what is happening now?''

Gaspard's smile dimmed. "That was a sacred miracle from God."

"You white men flaunt your faith and then have none." The Duke drew on his pipe. "The animals are sacrificing themselves for our sake. *Manabus* made it so."

André straightened when he saw Tiny emerge from the portage path, his face flushed and shining with sweat behind his bushy blond beard. Tiny was always one of the last men to finish the portages. André swiftly counted the *voyageurs* on shore and realized only two men had not yet arrived—two men and Genevieve.

"By the beavers of Saint Francis!" The giant caught sight of a naked Julien in the bay. He trudged to where the boy's buckskins lay, discarded in a heap in the mud, and kicked them toward the water. "Enough of this baptism! Blossom's going to be here any minute. . . . Have you no respect for a lady?''

André shoved his pipe in the beaded sack hanging from his waist and broke from the circle of men to approach Tiny. *Blossom* was the name the men had given Genevieve when she'd flounced back into camp after the incident with the skunk. There was another name he preferred for her, a name Wapishka had suggested, but few men could get their tongues

around such a twisting Indian word. *Taouistaouisse.*
Little-Bird-Always-In-Motion.

He caught up with Tiny as the giant shrugged the
load off his shoulders. "Where is she?"

"By Saint Peter's stones!" Tiny rolled his massive
arms. "You'd have her on a leash if you could."

"If it would keep her out of trouble—"

"She didn't look in any trouble when I passed her
some ways back." He massaged his arms with meaty
hands. "She should be slogging through the trees
soon."

The hair prickled on the back of his neck. Despite
the ruggedness of the terrain, despite the brutal pace
he always set, she always managed to make it to the
end of the portage, usually before the last few *voyageurs.* He had become accustomed to finding her
curled up in a ball on a rock, dirty and dozing, her
hair gleaming like raw copper in the sun.

André paced, willing her to appear between the
tree trunks. When the last two *voyageurs* arrived and
told him they hadn't passed her along the trail, he
pulled his pistol out of his sash.

"She's probably preening somewhere." Tiny
appeared at his side, his pipe smoking in his hand.
"You know women."

He remembered her as she had been this morning,
utterly unconscious of her own glorious dishevelment, barraging him with questions with all the
vigor of a lawyer in the royal courts as to why they
must rise before dawn.

"She's not preening."

"Then maybe she's resting." Tiny's bushy blond
brows lowered. "She's barely been able to keep pace
with us this past week."

André checked the priming of his pistol. He hoped
she had stopped in exhaustion and it was nothing

more than that. Despite her spirit, despite her continuing stubbornness, she was weakening fast. She had slept through some of the jerkiest stretches of rapids, so deeply that André had allowed the *voyageurs* to relieve themselves over the sides of the canoe while she reposed. Perhaps she had collapsed and even now lay unconscious somewhere on the forest floor.

The thought brought a grim sense of deflated triumph. This is what he had waited for, this is what he had planned since she had whirled into his room at the inn at Montréal. He'd intended to leave her at Allumette Lake, a few days upstream. If she had collapsed, it was for the best, for if she lasted much longer, he would be forced to take more drastic measures to wear her out. Yet even as he imagined her asleep somewhere in the bushes, he remembered her flashing eyes, the stubborn way she clutched that wretched case of worldly goods, and sensed that mere physical weariness would not defeat her—at least, not yet. The witch was made of stronger stuff than he'd thought.

Then he thought of other possibilities, more disturbing possibilities. He had spent the last week waiting for the all-too-familiar cry of *casse-cou* and the flash of a hatchet or the whir of an arrow. He knew it wasn't the Iroquois way to capture a single woman and not ambush the rest of his men, but a defenseless, copper-haired woman might prove too much to resist, even in a time of peace.

"By all the blazes!" Tiny stared at him as if he could read his thoughts. "There's a treaty, you know."

"The Iroquois abide by treaties as well as French priests abide by their vows of chastity."

"They haven't broken it in three years."

He strode toward the opening to the trail, heaving his pistol aloft. "Let's hope they haven't broken it now."

André edged silently along the path, his ears straining for sound. He heard Tiny's footsteps behind him as the giant followed. His gut had twisted into a knot as uglier and uglier possibilities roared through his mind. He shouldn't feel like this. She had brought this upon herself, but he had given up trying to explain why he suddenly felt so protective of this *Taouistaouisse*. It was all the more reason to leave her at a Jesuit mission long before Chequamegon Bay.

He wandered slowly down the path, scanning the muddy surroundings, searching for her distinctive imprint. She always hummed the *voyageurs'* songs when she walked, but he heard none of her music in the silent forests, nothing but the wind in the dry leaves and the muted rush of the Ottawa River. The leaves on the forest floor were crushed from so many footsteps, and he couldn't distinguish any single imprint. He couldn't even distinguish the scent of skunk, which had almost entirely worn off in the clean, crisp air.

Then he saw something. He lifted a hand to capture Tiny's attention, then pointed to a broken fern off to one side of the trail and a few spots of flattened grass beyond. He could tell by the pattern of the footsteps—a small, round toe and a deeper heel— that they were his wife's. There was no sign of struggle. There was no sign of animal markings. By all signs, she had willingly wandered off the path—something he had expressly forbidden her to do. As he followed the trail, André heard the quiet trickle of a brook and knew, instinctively, that this was the reason his wife had deviated from the path. He broke through the verdure and saw the silver thread of a stream.

He saw something else, too. His fingers tightened around the carved wooden handle of his pistol.

Genevieve stood motionless in the clearing, inches away from an Indian.

The savage's hand was wrapped deep in her fiery hair.

Chapter Eight

Genevieve's heart leapt as she heard a shout come sharply from the forest behind her. *Mother of God*, she thought, *two savages in one day*. By the look of utter terror on the face of the Indian woman who gripped a lock of her hair, she knew this new savage was unfriendly to both of them.

The Indian released her. Genevieve whirled around, but she saw no other savage behind her. Instead, she saw a familiar buckskin-clad man crouched in the litter, one glittering, tawny eye narrowed into a slit over the gaping barrel of his pistol.

"By the love of Saint Joseph!" Tiny emerged from the darkness and knocked André's pistol up. "Don't shoot! It's a squaw."

Genevieve whirled just in time to see the long sweep of the Indian woman's glossy black hair as she shot toward the woods. Genevieve cried out after her, but she knew it was useless, for the squaw didn't under-

stand French any more than Genevieve understood
the Indian woman's tongue.

"Go after her, Tiny," André barked, "before she
brings back her husband, her brothers, and every
other Iroquois warrior in the area."

Tiny splashed through the stream, chasing the
flashes of fringed deerskin through the shadowed
woods. Genevieve stamped her foot on the ground,
wincing as pain shot up her ankle.

Damn, damn, *damn!*

"What the hell are you doing off the trail?"

She whirled and glared at André. His lips were set
in a grim line behind his short beard, but she hardly
noticed his anger over her own frustration. "Look
what you've done!" She waved toward the woods
where Tiny and the squaw had disappeared. "She's
running away!"

"I would have dropped her like a deer if Tiny
hadn't interfered."

"Why? She meant no harm to you."

"She had a dagger in her hand and her fist in your
hair." He towered over her, the anger so fierce it was
palpable. "A few minutes later and you'd have lost
your scalp."

"I would have *given* my hair to her! It was the price
she wanted for her moccasins."

"What the hell are you talking about?"

"You have no idea how hard I've worked trying to
get her to understand. I've been pointing and jumping around and acting like an utter ass, and now it's
all for naught." Genevieve whirled and marched to
where her case lay on the ground, the contents scattered about on the grass. She swept up a pile of pins
and tossed them into the air so they rained around
her like a silver shower. "I've offered her everything
I have—scissors, pins, pewter spoons and knives, the

finest gloves I own—and she wanted *none* of it. They are as worthless to her as her beads and shells are to me."

"You were bargaining with this squaw?"

"It took me all this time to realize that this wretched mop of knots"—she tugged at her loose brandy-colored hair—"was worth more to her than anything I've been breaking my arms carrying. I was just about to make her an offer when *you* came rushing in here, waving your pistol like a damn Musketeer to the rescue, when the truth is you've ruined everything."

"You sell your life cheaply."

"I needed moccasins." She flounced to where her boots and stockings lay by the side of the creek, keeled over in the dark muck. "For a pair of slippers, I would pay a lot more than a lock of hair."

"Since when do you speak the Iroquois language?"

"I don't, but I damned well know a bargain when I see one."

"Do you, my foul-mouthed little aristocrat?" André shoved his pistol in his sash. "You'd have been wearing those moccasins for an eternity."

She swiveled away and plopped down on the grass by the edge of the creek, fisting a handful of crackling leaves. She didn't care how angry he was, she didn't care how she sounded. It was *she* who had lost what was probably her only chance to get a soft pair of slippers, and these past days she'd become obsessed with the desire. "The deal was for a *lock* of hair, nothing more, and that Indian was more frightened of me than I was of her."

"Her brothers won't be," he retorted, pacing with one ear cocked toward the woods. "And if Tiny doesn't catch the wench before she makes it back to her village, yours won't be the only scalp in danger."

"If they come in anger, it will be because you raised

a pistol to her, not because of anything that happened between us." Genevieve heedlessly yanked her skirts above her knees and dipped her feet into the stream to wash them free of dirt and grass, wincing as the frigid water scoured the sores on her toes. "I suppose you came looking for me because I was late. If you had a little patience, I would have made it to the end of the path in a few minutes and you wouldn't have been any wiser."

His shadow fell over her as he splashed into the stream. He seized one ankle and jerked it out of the water. She tumbled back into the mulchy earth as he lifted her leg higher.

"What the hell?"

She struggled to her elbows and tossed back her hair. His face contorted in horror as he traced a blister bubbling on her heel. He examined the rings of calluses and the angry blood-red splotches on either side of her foot, then his hand curled tightly around her bare ankle.

Genevieve bit the side of her lip. She hadn't wanted him to see her feet. She hadn't wanted him to know the extent of her pain, for she knew if he did, he might send her back to Montréal. She would *not* be sent away, not while she still had breath in her body.

"Not a pretty lady's foot, is it, André?"

"How long?"

"Long enough for me to know I need new shoes— shoes I would have bargained for had you not threatened to shoot the merchant."

"Why didn't you tell me?"

She yanked her foot from his grip, only to plant it firmly in the cold mud. "You haven't been a fount of compassion these last days."

"You'd rather risk your life than—"

"By Sainte Thérèse! Stop fighting! You're only wast-

ing your strength.'' Tiny emerged from the edge of
the forest, the Indian woman slung over his shoulder
like a sack of flour, her feet scissoring wildly as she
bucked against his hold.

"Put her *down*.'' Ignoring the sucking mud beneath
her feet, Genevieve scrambled over. "Did you hurt
her?''

"Hurt her?!'' Tiny tugged a dagger out of his sash
and flicked it to the ground, one meaty arm still tight
around the squaw's waist. "She nearly made a woman
out of me with that.''

"It's no less than both of you deserve for scaring
the life out of her.''

"Put her down.'' André slogged through the creek
to face him. "And pull the handkerchief out of her
mouth.''

Tiny heaved the woman over his shoulder and
turned her around, holding her by the arms. The
savage's face gleamed with grease, and her hair, as
black as a raven's wing, fell like a mourning veil
around her shoulders. The squaw snapped at Tiny's
fingers as he removed the handkerchief.

André asked the woman something in a guttural
language Genevieve had never before heard, not even
between The Duke and Wapishka. The woman tilted
her chin but didn't answer. André scanned her clothing—the short skirt; the red, black, and white quill
design on the hem and moccasins—and said something else.

Something flared in the savage's coal-black eyes.
She spat on the ground. Then, in a long rattle of
words, she spoke to André, pointing toward the forest
whence she had run.

When she finished all was silent, and Genevieve
glared at André. "Well? What did she say?''

"She claims she's from an Algonquin tribe that

camps close by, a proud and strong tribe of many warriors.'' He glanced at Genevieve, his gaze falling on her hair. ''She was searching for blackberries when she found the 'woman with fox hair.' ''

''Then she's not Iroquois.''

''She says the Iroquois are dogs.''

''Well, isn't this a fine kettle of fish?'' Genevieve tossed her hair over her shoulder. ''You're glib with the savage tongue, but you've got a few problems with French, eh? If you had listened to me, we could have settled this without all the flurry.'' She gathered her skirts and pointed to the squaw's feet. ''Now tell her that if she still wants a lock of my hair, I'll give it to her for her moccasins.''

''Moccasins?'' Tiny stared incredulously at André. ''By the passion of Sainte Thérèse! We thought she was being torn apart by wolves, and here she is, bartering for wares.''

''Are you going to ask her in her language,'' Genevieve said, ''or am I going to have to wave my hands around until she understands me?''

André barked something to the Indian. The squaw nodded swiftly, kicked off her moccasins, and held them out to Genevieve. The slippers were beautiful, *gorgeous*, finer than any delicately embroidered satin slippers she'd ever worn in Normandy all those years ago. She took them into her palms. The leather gave beneath her hand, soft, well-worn, and sewn with an odd red, black, and white quill design on the top, with flaps that could be tied over her ankles during the winter, all lined in the silkiest gray fur. . . . Genevieve tugged the savage's discarded knife from the ground and clutched a lock of her hair. She sliced it off and held the auburn curl out to the Indian. Genevieve had a feeling that the Indian took the lock of her hair into her hands with as much reverence as she took the smoke-ripened deerskin into hers.

It was, Genevieve thought, a fine bargain, though she was sure she had gotten the better of it.

Ignoring the men and the savage, she limped back to where her stockings lay by the stream. She kicked her skirts out of the way and washed her toes clean. Then she shook out a worn stocking, pointed one toe, and rolled it up her calf. She slid the stocking over her knee, twisted her leg to straighten the seam, then gartered it on her lower thigh. She did the same with the other stocking, and then, reverently, she took the moccasins and slipped them over her burning, aching feet. For a few moments, she did nothing but stare down at them beneath the froth of her dirty skirts.

They felt utterly divine—cushiony, unrestricted, and soft—and they were worth everything she owned. Even, she thought as she glanced up and saw André glaring at her in fury, her husband's anger.

Tiny stood near the savage, eyes politely averted from Genevieve, waiting for instructions from André. "Are we just going to leave her here, or are we going to bring her with us for a while?"

"Leave her," Andre snapped, still not removing his glare from Genevieve. "We've been delayed long enough."

"Oh, enough, enough! I'm coming."

She stood up, flounced to her case, and tossed everything haphazardly back in. It was just like him to remind her of the warning he'd issued that day in the woods. Oh, but she wouldn't slow him down. She wouldn't give him an excuse to send her back; she'd come too far now for that.

Genevieve reached for her mud-caked boots,

pounding them together so clots of dried mud fell to the ground.

"Throw those things out."

She started at André's angry bark, then pointedly tossed her old shoes in her case. "If a lock of my hair is worth these slippers, then someday even these stiff old shoes might be valuable barter." She bent over and tugged the ragged ties of her case closed. When she rose again, she stared at him defiantly. "If you're ready, my husband?"

"I'm ready." He strode to her and gripped her shoulders. "But you aren't, Genevieve."

She winced, for his fingers clawed deep into her shoulders. Genevieve struggled beneath the grip, but words died in her throat as she glanced up into his golden eyes. Fury vibrated in every line of his body, in every thick, hard muscle, in every sinew, and he squeezed her shoulders as if he were unaware of his own strength. And she stilled so he would squeeze no more.

"You've got a lesson to learn about the Iroquois, a lesson that only by the grace of God you've avoided." He jerked his chin toward the portage path. "They like to attack at difficult portages, like this one, when the men are loaded down and weak and tired, when the paths are so congested and narrow that the men can only walk in single file and the Iroquois braves can cut them down one by one with a hatchet to the chest. They won't balk at killing women and babies any more than they'd balk at killing a weak calf, and they would revel if any man or woman dared to stray off the path. When they're finished with their senseless mutilation, they dissolve back into the forest, leaving no trace of their presence but the lingering stench of death."

Abruptly, he released her shoulders and clutched

two handfuls of her hair, yanking back her head until she was forced to look into his burning eyes, the color of rum, of dark brandy, of spirits potent and dangerous.

"Do you know," he whispered on a rasp, "what the Iroquois do to prisoners, Genevieve?"

Tiny cast a shadow over them. "*Jésus*, André, don't—"

"The lucky ones die on the trail," he interrupted, ignoring the giant. "The ones that survive are lashed to a stake in the middle of the village. The Iroquois pull out their fingernails, one by one, and then tell their children to chew on the raw ends. They burn welts across their torsos. They flay the top of their heads and pour hot tar over them. The more the prisoner screams, the more they torture, and when they grow bored, they roast the prisoner, long and slow over an open fire, and eat the flesh in strips."

She clutched the fringe of his deerskin shirt and the words quivered on her tongue—*wretched children's tales*—but there was no doubt in his voice, no mockery in his eyes; they were full of a torment she'd never seen before. He shook her hard, and her head snapped back.

"Do this again, wife, and I'll leave you to your fate in this place—and leave my judgment to God."

He released her and she stumbled back. Her scalp tingled where he had yanked her hair, but the fury and pain of his words needled far deeper, far, far deeper. Without another word, he strode in the direction of the portage path.

Tiny loomed over her. His bushy brows, half blond, half white, drew together. "He shouldn't have done that." His gaze darted furtively toward André. "He's thinking of Rose-Marie."

André snapped, "Do I have to truss you up, wife?"

He was waiting for them, his hands on his hips. Wordlessly, she swept up her case and stumbled after as well as she could, for his steps were long and swift, and she had to run to keep up. Branches whipped across her face; sharp stones dug deep into the soft underbelly of her new moccasins, slicing the blisters and scratching new welts. But she hardly felt any of this, for a single question echoed in her head, louder and louder.

Who is Rose-Marie?

André crouched in the moss, his back to a lichen-covered boulder, hidden from a small clearing by the thin trunks of a few maple saplings and a dense mesh of dried, fallen branches. In the indigo light of pre-dawn, the spiny web of denuded boughs above his head gleamed with moisture. Periodically, huge teardrops beaded along the length, dripped from the bark, and splattered in the litter around him. The whole forest pattered with the wet aftermath of the recent rain.

Above the splattering of the drops, he heard another distant sound, the sound he had waited for all morning—the light, rhythmic crackling of twigs that heralded the careful approach of a watchful man. He peered through the netting of branches toward the cook's canoe, no more than twenty paces from where he hid. Yesterday evening, while the rain threatened and growled overhead, he had ordered the cook's canoe to be newly caulked with pine resin—not because it needed the waterproofing, but so the stench of heated resin would be so strong that the canoe would be placed far from the others, and the cook himself would seek shelter from the coming rain under less offensive-smelling canoes in the main campsite. Now the vessel lay, belly-up, in the mud, waiting for the advancing hunter to deposit his latest kill.

The dampness of the soaked earth oozed through the soles of his moccasins. His muscles cramped from the uncomfortable position. Anger stirred in him as the footsteps grew swifter and louder. In moments, he would put an abrupt end to the hunter's secret courtship of Genevieve. It didn't matter that André had chosen to spend the rainy night beneath a crowded canoe with his men, rather than in the warmth and protection of a makeshift tent with his wife. However odd his relationship with Genevieve might seem to the other *voyageurs*, no man would get away with courting his wife beneath his very nose.

He straightened his back against the stone as he heard another sound, a familiar melody on the still morning air. He strained his ears and frowned in incredulity, for what he heard was humming—Genevieve's humming. Then he realized that the swift, light footsteps that he had thought were those of a wary hunter belonged instead to his fleet-footed wife.

Her humming stopped abruptly as she strode into the clearing. Her headrail sagged over one arm, showing the curve of a rounded breast. Her long hair lay in a tangled braid down her back. Despite himself, his loins tightened at the sight of her, bathed in bluish light, disheveled and unkempt from sleep. A linen sack swung over her shoulder and she held a palmful of something in her hand. As he watched, she popped whatever it was into her mouth.

He crashed out of his hiding place, filling the forest with the snapping of the branches and frightening a flock of sleeping birds into the sky. Genevieve whirled at the noise, and a shower of round little berries scattered all over the forest floor.

She dropped her linen sack with a thunk. *"Saccajé chien!"*

"What the hell"—he swept up one of the berries, now mushed and unrecognizable—"is this?"

"André!" She slapped her hand to her breast. "Had you antlers or claws, you couldn't have scared me more! *Mon Dieu*! Why did you crash out of the bushes like that?"

He grabbed her hand and turned it over to see smears of purplish juice, the same juice that stained her generous lower lip and now her bodice where she had gripped it. "Where did you find these berries?"

She glanced at the mangled fruit he held in his hand. "There was a bush heavy with them back some ways—"

"A bush of what?! Winterberries? Baneberries? How the hell do you know they're not poisonous?"

"They're blackberries." She yanked her hand from his grasp. "I know what blackberries look like. Wapishka showed me days ago."

André smelled the juice of the berry, tasted it on the tip of his tongue, then tossed it away. He never knew what to expect of this reckless wife. His anger still hadn't faded from finding her bargaining with some strange Algonquin woman. He was sure her impulsiveness and unpredictability would be the death of her if he kept her on this voyage much longer. Picking wild berries in the dark and eating them without thought! He should wring her neck with a leather leash and tie her to the campsite—or better, turn her over his knee, pull up her skirts, and give her a good, long spanking. He pushed the thought out of his mind. The idea of touching her firm, white buttocks with his bare hand didn't in the least sound like punishment.

Instead, he glowered at her and planted his hands

on his hips. "What are you doing awake? Tiny hasn't even called *Lève* yet."

"I couldn't sleep. The rain kept me up all night."

"You've never had trouble sleeping before, wife. I usually have to do everything short of kicking you to get you up in the morning."

"What are you doing here, waiting in the bushes like a wildcat, ready to pounce?"

"I wouldn't have pounced if you hadn't bumbled in here so unexpectedly. Now take your fripperies"— he reached for her linen bag—"and find another place to do whatever women do in the morning."

"Leave that alone!" She seized a handful of the linen as he lifted it off the ground and yanked it toward her. "Don't you have any respect for a woman's privacy?"

"Since when is helping my wife with her load an invasion of privacy?"

"Just get your hands off it!"

He released it abruptly. She grabbed the other end but not soon enough, for the linen tumbled open in a sweep of white. The contents fell with a thump to the mud.

"Now look what you've done!" She fell to her knees and swiftly blanketed the contents, but not before he caught sight of a mottled coat of gray fur.

"What the hell? . . ."

He tore the linen away, exposing the creature beneath. It was a hare—a *hare*—and its gray coat had already begun to give way to thick winter-white fur. Incredulous, he fell on one knee and combed his fingers over the damp pelt. The hare was still warm. He could tell by the disjointed way the rabbit lay that its neck had been wrung—just like all the geese that had mysteriously appeared in the cook's canoe.

She clutched the linen to her chest and leaned

away from him. In the darkness, her eyes were full of defiance and fear.

They are in it together. Anger flushed his cheeks free of the morning chill. He hadn't expected this. André knew some sort of *tendre* had sprung up between his wife and that boy, but he had foolishly thought Julien was too exhausted to graft him horns. Now he found his wife prancing around the woods in the predawn with a freshly killed rabbit in her hand, humming and looking by all accounts as if she had just had a good tumble in the mud. Rage shot through his veins. He curled his fingers into his hands to stop them from itching, to stop himself from shaking her in fury, for he could kill her now for making a fool of him, for giving herself to another man when she was *his.*

André shot up and peered into the dimness beyond the boulder. His words emerged through clenched teeth. "Where is he?"

"Who?"

"Don't bother protecting him. Nothing . . . *nothing* can protect him from me now. You'll see what a saint I am, woman. . . ."

"I don't know what you're talking about." Genevieve stumbled to her feet and swiped the mud and twigs off her skirts with the linen. "Who am I supposed to be protecting from you?"

"Julien." One ragged nail pierced the callused flesh of his palm. "I'll shake you until your teeth rattle if you don't—"

"That's a fine way to speak to your wife," she snapped. "And how would I know where Julien is? Last time I saw him, he was being baptized near Calumet Falls."

"Is that when he snared this hare for you?" André

let his gaze rove insolently over her exposed bosom. "Or is that when you paid him for his services?"

Shock filled her eyes and her mouth gaped open. She slapped her hands over her face and turned away, but not before he saw something else blossom in those green eyes. Fear. Fear and guilt.

Guilt. He clenched his teeth on a roar and swung around, shattering the bark of an elm with his fist. Cheating little wench, she'd not gotten what she wanted from him and so she'd turned her wiles on an easier catch—damn sly creature. André kneaded his bruised and throbbing knuckles, rage hazing his sight, thinking even through the anger, with the slightest twist of admiration, that she was a resourceful one, this little aristocrat, determined and clever and strong.

"The gander might play, husband," she argued, her voice quavering, "but that doesn't mean the goose does, too."

"Are you denying that Julien caught you this hare?"

"Julien can barely walk after a full day's work." Genevieve tossed her plait over her shoulder, tugged her bodice down, and met his gaze evenly. "What makes you think that between the endless baptisms and the constant work, he'd have time to snare me a rabbit? Or I'd have time to *pay* him, as you so crudely put it?"

André stared at her, trembling from the intensity of his anger, realizing from the steadiness of her gaze and the conviction in her voice that she and Julien were not making a cuckold of him—not yet, at least. Furious relief rushed through him like water on a blazing fire, and he thought only of one thing: She was still untouched, she was still innocent, and she was still his for the taking.

And he was a damned fool.

"You're jealous."

Damn right, but I'd sooner trust an Iroquois before I'd admit it to you, woman.

"If you joined me in my tent," she continued softly, "you'd stay a lot drier and a lot less ornery, and you would never have reason to suspect I was wandering off with another man."

He kicked the hare with his foot. "Someone is hunting for you, and you know who it is."

"Is that why you're here, lurking in the bushes?"

"Tell me," he demanded, stepping closer and lowering his voice, "who you've charmed into doing your bidding, Genevieve."

"Unfortunately, not you. I've been complaining about the food—or lack of it—since we left Lachine. You haven't done anything but laugh at me and tease me and tell me to wait until we get to that chewywagon place—if I don't starve first."

"I'll ask one last time."

Her bold gaze faltered and then fell. She wrapped the linen around her hand, up her wrist, then unwrapped it and toyed with it as if she were considering folding it. Finally, she shrugged and draped the cloth over her forearm.

"It's very simple." She tilted her chin. "I found him."

"You found him?"

"Yes. It was . . . in a snare of some sort. I assume it was laid by Indians. I came upon him as I was looking for a place to brush my hair. He was just lying there. Since we haven't had fresh meat in a while, I wrapped him in one of my old shifts and decided to bring him here, to the cook's canoe."

Indians caught hares in nets or killed them with arrows or darts, he knew that well enough. But there

was no sign of any blood on the hare's sleek coat.
And if it had been caught in a net, it would still be
alive, not lying on the ground with a broken neck.
Not unless his aristocratic wife had wrung it herself,
and that possibility was too preposterous to consider.
Nor would an Indian leave fresh game dead in the
forest, where it would be ripe for attack by foxes,
wolves, and whatever other creatures came upon it.

He met her vivid green eyes. "Did you find the
goose in Indian snares as well?"

"Yes."

"You're lying."

She frowned and swiveled away. "If you're going
to insult me—"

"Indians kill geese with bows and arrows, and there
wasn't a drop of blood on those birds." He snagged
her arm. "Who are you protecting, Genevieve?"

"I'm protecting no one."

"Think of a better explanation than that, *wife*.
You're not leaving this clearing until you do."

She jerked in his embrace. "You wouldn't believe
me if I told you the truth."

"I won't believe your lies."

"Very well." She jerked herself free, then rubbed
her arm where he'd held it. Faint morning light silvered her skin. "*I* caught the hare."

"Stop it . . ."

"It's the *truth*."

Damned fool woman, he'd wring her neck if she
didn't stop spitting lies at him. But she stared at him
again, evenly, with a determined, haughty expression:
How dare you mock me. How dare you doubt my word.

"Laugh if you will, but it's true," she retorted.
"My mother used to hire a hunter in season." She
mangled the linen between her hands. "I had a very
unconventional upbringing. My father died when I

was quite young, and my mother had to raise me alone. I was alone a lot. I used to follow the huntsman as he stalked through the woods of my mother's estate. I used to watch him catch small game in the forests. He always told me I was a quick student.''

Genevieve untied the linen and shook it out in front of her. She pointed out the stones sewn in the corners of the old shift, explaining how she had climbed a branch overhanging a gaggle of migrating geese that were resting in a shallow pool, then dropped the makeshift net upon them to capture one of the birds in the flock. Faltering, she told how the previous night she had dug a pit and covered it with grasses and moss to trap the rabbit after she had seen fresh pellets in the area.

She tossed the linen to the ground and paced about the clearing, wringing her hands together. André remembered The Duke's strange dream, the dream of a red bird and a goose, and the revelation took on new meaning. He shook his head. It was one thing for an aristocrat to bargain like a peddler out of desperation, but it was another thing altogether to. . . . It couldn't be possible. It *couldn't* be possible.

She was a French noblewoman, damn it. The vast wilderness should be as alien to her as a drawing room in the Louvre was to him. Yet here she stood, telling him she'd calmly wrung the necks of rabbits and geese so she'd have a bit of meat for dinner. Here she stood, her long white neck tight with tendons, her slender wrists flexing as she tugged her delicate fingers that no chapped, reddened skin could hide, pacing back and forth, her back as straight as a ramrod. She was an aristocrat, petty and poor, but part of that useless breed nonetheless. Not only could this glorious creature withstand a trip that tested the mettle of men, but she could provide meat for the pot as well.

Damn it, she wasn't supposed to act like this. What did he know of her, this little sylph he'd married? He didn't *want* to know anything. He'd spent all this time pushing her away, trying to tamp down a normal man's lusty urge to mate with a healthy, attractive woman so that he wouldn't consummate this unlikely marriage and bind himself to another burden in civilization. He didn't want to know her, because to know her was to take responsibility for her, to care for her, and thus to hate himself for what he must do. And here she was, defying all his expectations, shattering his preconceptions like so much delicate church glass . . . making him think things he had no right thinking.

"You wrung the necks of those geese, didn't you, Genevieve?" He flexed his bruised hand. "And the hare, too?"

"I know it's not ladylike, but it seemed so foolish to live on that mush when the forests teemed with game." She whirled in her endless pacing and stopped in front of him. "If I had a pistol, I would have shot some grouse. The huntsman taught me how to shoot straight enough."

My God. My God, I've married a lady and discovered a woman inside.

Something cracked inside him, like the movement of a great stone door to a tomb smothered in too many year's growth of woody vines, a tomb in which he'd buried feelings he'd not wanted to bring forth ever again. Who was this tenacious, single-minded, utterly unpredictable creature who looked, spoke, and walked like a Frenchwoman but had the skills and the spirit of a squaw?

André found himself sweeping a tendril of hair off

her face and tracing the point of her chin. "What kind of creature are you, Genevieve?"

She blinked up at him. Fear blossomed in her eyes—no, it wasn't fear. Fear was too timid a word for the emotion. It was terror. Stark, unadulterated. She was as frightened to reveal herself to him as he was to crack open the tomb in his heart.

"Tell me," he urged, his voice barely a whisper, wondering why now, *why now*, after all these years? His gaze fell to her lips, still gleaming from the juice of the blackberries, and he willed answers from them. *"Tell me."*

"I am no more . . . and no less than what you see," she stammered, bracing her hands against his shoulders. "I don't know what you mean. . . . I don't know what you want to know."

"Who are you, Genevieve?"

Chapter Nine

Genevieve's mother had been a courtesan—the most notorious whore in Carrouges, Normandy.

For twelve years, Jeanette Lalande had serviced a nobleman she hated above all men on earth. As a young girl, betrayed, disowned, and bitter, Jeanette had learned to use her power over her patron to live the life she was accustomed to . . . and raise Genevieve, her only child, in the same luxury.

Then the unexpected happened. Jeanette Lalande fell in love. Suddenly, Jeanette was willing to risk everything to be free.

Genevieve often wondered if her mother would have paid the price for freedom had she known her daughter would still be paying it so many years later.

* * *

"When Armand returns from Paris, we'll leave this place for good, Genny. Would you like that? To see the whole world beyond these mountains?"

Genevieve clutched *Maman*'s hands tightly. The pale Norman sun streamed through the windows, lighting her mother's golden curls. Mother had promised a special surprise for her thirteenth birthday, but Genevieve had not expected this. She didn't want to leave Carrouges. The mountains of Normandy, which thrust up behind the ivy-covered manor house, the well-tended garden, and the wild forests, were her own little kingdom. Genevieve knew the location of every rabbit hole, every birds' nest, every deer path in the forested hills. Here were her writing slates and her books and their beloved harp. Outside of the forested perimeter was a hostile country. A place where people peered at her and whispered *bâtarde*.

Her mother released her hands and sighed deeply. "You don't want to leave, do you, *ma petite*?"

Genevieve couldn't lie, no matter how much she hated to see her mother's pretty face so blotched and red. *Maman* cried so much lately, ever since Armand, Genevieve's music teacher, had been called away to Paris. Genevieve hoped the handsome tutor would quickly return to the country, but as soon as she wished it, she took it back, for when Armand came, he would take both of them away from here.

"I was afraid of this." Her mother rose from the seat beside her on the sapphire-blue velvet couch. "I've spent the last thirteen years protecting you, giving you the type of home that I once wished for, but the truth is, Genny, this place that you love so much is nothing but a gilded cage." She turned tear-filled eyes upon her daughter. "I had hoped I could wait until you were a little older, but there's no longer any time. I must tell you everything, Genny, so you will understand."

Genevieve understood more than her mother knew, for the servants acted as if she were deaf, dumb, and blind. They gossiped endlessly about her mother's behavior. Since Armand's arrival, their opinions had grown harsher and their words for her mother coarser. Genevieve knew *Maman* was the mistress of the Baron de Carrouges, a man Genevieve had seen only once from a distance, for she was banned from the main part of the house whenever he visited. She knew, too, that her mother and Armand were lovers.

But when her mother spoke, she didn't speak of lovers. She spoke of other things, of wondrous things, of subjects long forbidden between them.

"My father was a *financier* in Paris." Her mother spoke the words as if Genevieve had never broached the subject before, as if it were perfectly natural to answer all the questions her daughter had once ached to know and had long given up asking. "He loaned monstrous amounts of money to the Queen Regent when Louis XIV was still in his minority. In return, he was given the right to levy taxes and collect the king's revenue." She lifted one fine, arched brow and turned toward the windows. "In my youth, it was rumored he was wealthier than some Princes of the Blood."

Genevieve's world tilted off its axis. A grandfather, richer than royalty? Who loaned money to the Crown? Until this moment, she had not known of any other relative but her mother; she had only dreamed of a distant family, rife with dozens of frolicking cousins, soft-bosomed aunts, and old misty-eyed grandparents. She sat, too afraid to blink, frightened that any motion she made or any word she uttered would bring *Maman* to her senses and stop her from telling the tale she had ached to know from the moment she was old enough to speak.

"On my fifteenth birthday, Father took me from the convent and brought me to the townhouse he had just built, in a fashionable section of Paris north of the Louvre." Her lips twitched. "Every day I had a new dress, satins unlike anything I had ever imagined, with jeweled clasps and rope upon rope of pearls. Father lined whole rooms with emerald-colored silk, and he told me he did it just to show off the brilliance of my eyes. Heirs to great estates, sons of barons, of viscounts, of other noblemen, came and dined with us. Father hired Italian acting troops for weeks on end for our entertainment. And he would make me play the harp, looking upon me with such pride that I thought no daughter had ever had such a perfect father. Genny, I thought I had entered Paradise." *Maman* stepped back, away from the window, out of the light. "When I met Hamlin, I was sure."

Her mother's eyes suddenly turned inward, as if they were focused on a time long past but remembered as vividly as if it were only yesterday. Genevieve leaned forward, for there was something in the timbre of her mother's voice when she said the name Hamlin that made her tremble.

"I remember the first time I saw him," her mother continued. "He stood in the doorway of the salon, watching me as I played the harp, as if I were the only woman in the room. He was the most handsome man I had ever seen, all tall and straight in his military uniform, with gold braid hanging from his shoulders and a brilliant scarlet sash across his chest. I was told his name was Hamlin de Lautersbourg, and that he was a nobleman from Alsace, which the regent had just won in war. I fell in love with him at first sight.

I nearly burst with joy when Papa allowed him to court me.'' A strange light illuminated her mother's features. ''Hamlin had a wonderful gilded Italian carriage, and to me it seemed like freedom itself, for except for my journey to Paris, I had never been outside of the convent walls. He took me outside the city, with Nanette—who was my maidservant then as she is now—as my guardian. We ate long lunches *alfresco* in the country; we rode on the *Cours de Reine* in the evening with the aristocracy and danced on the turning circle to the music of violins. Hamlin took me to watch cattle drives through the narrow streets of Paris; he brought me to view the strange flat-bottomed boats filled with melons or wine or coal that crowded the Seine.'' She released a gentle laugh. ''Once, he even stepped out of the carriage and bartered with a fishmonger for the day's catch of carp, just for my amusement.''

Genevieve had never heard *Maman* speak of anyone like this, not even Armand, who was the only person Genevieve knew who could bring color into her mother's face.

''I was so involved with him,'' she continued, ''that I hardly noticed the trouble brewing in Paris. When I found a dozen dead cats in our courtyard one day, I thought it was nothing more than some unruly peasants complaining, as they always did, of their lot. I didn't understand how much Father was hated by the peasantry for the taxes he levied, how much he was envied and despised by the noblemen because of his fantastic wealth. Father grew more and more anxious to leave Paris, to seek refuge in our summer house near Rouen, but he hesitated, and I vainly thought he hesitated for my sake, for to me, to go to Rouen and leave Hamlin was a fate worse than death.'' She clutched the patterned velvet drapes of the high window. "I didn't realize then that to my father, no expense was too high, no risk too great for an aristocratic son-in-law."

Her mother stared, sightlessly, toward the hills of Normandy. "You see, one thing eluded my father, Genny, one thing all his gold and all his power could not buy: true aristocracy. I was prettier than my younger sister in his eyes, most likely to catch the attention of an aristocrat willing to lower himself to marry a rich woman of bourgeois blood. The noblemen of Paris would always look down upon him, a mere tax collector, but my father had vowed that their sons would address his grandchildren as 'my lord.'

"I didn't notice the changes until much later, when I was alone and had an eternity to reflect upon it all. Nanette accompanied me and Hamlin on fewer and fewer of our journeys outside the city. Instead, my father entrusted another nobleman to be our guardian—a man. The very man who had introduced Hamlin to our salon, an aristocrat of rank and title whom my father respected and trusted. I was foolishly grateful to this nobleman, for he was lenient and generous in allowing Hamlin and I to be alone and . . . celebrate our love.

"Within six weeks, I knew I was carrying Hamlin's child." *Maman* looked at Genevieve, her green eyes full of shadows. "You have his hair, *petite*. Sometimes, I hear his laughter in yours."

Genevieve's heart stopped. For years, she had dreamed that her real father—whoever he was— would come back to *Maman* and drive the baron away, for despite the fact that the baron paid for her food, clothing, shelter, and education, Genevieve always knew, instinctively, that she couldn't be the Baron de Carrouge's illegitimate daughter. *Maman* hated him so much but still loved her, and the baron had never once asked to see her in nearly thirteen years. Now, she realized all her suspicions were true. Her father was an Alsatian nobleman that *Maman* had once loved. It was almost too much for her to absorb. Genevieve resisted the urge to barrage her mother with questions, for this sudden honesty was too new, too fragile, and she feared *Maman* would stop if she dared to ask the questions boiling in her mind.

"I was frightened," her mother continued. "I had to tell Father, for although Hamlin promised to marry me, he told me that we must wait for approval from his family, and it was long in coming. But instead of Father's fury, I was faced with his joy. Father was so sure he had trapped this wealthy aristocrat into marriage." She absently traced a pattern on the drapes. "My father sent a message to Hamlin, demanding that he come and do what he must, but the message was promptly returned. Unopened. It seemed that Hamlin had recently left Paris. My father, frantic, sent inquiries all over France and even to Alsace, but Hamlin was nowhere to be found. Soon enough, my father discovered that there was no such man as Monsieur de Lautersbourg. Hamlin simply didn't exist."

Genevieve gasped and felt tears surge to her eyes. Hamlin *must* exist. He was her father.

"My father sought out the man who had introduced Hamlin to him, the same man he had entrusted as our guardian." She met Genevieve's wide-eyed gaze, her voice as cold as snow. "I suppose you know by now that that man was the Baron de Carrouges."

The Baron de Carrouges. The man to whom her mother was courtesan.

Mother straightened her shoulders beneath the thickly boned emerald silk bodice and took a deep breath. "It seems the nobleman had paid Hamlin, some ne'er-do-well without a drop of noble blood in his veins, to ruin me and thus my family. He said it was my father's punishment, for daring to think his common blood was as good as that of an aristocrat." She tilted her chin. "Well, it was good enough for something, for when Father disowned me and threw me out of his house, the baron was waiting in his carriage outside, like a vulture hungry for the spoils. It seems he had wanted *me* from the start, but he knew my father would never approve of his interest— for the baron was, and still is, married—so he ruined me so my father would no longer want me. I became his mistress because he made me an offer and I had no other choice." She met Genevieve's gaze squarely. "But I bargained with him, like a true bourgeois, I suppose. I told him he would have to give me a home, far from Paris, and that he would have to pay for your upbringing. After all his trouble to get me into his bed, I suppose he had no choice but to agree.

"So here I am, Genny, all these years later, still courtesan to the man who destroyed my life. I would have remained here until you were safe and settled somewhere, but I met Armand, and he has shown me that I have been dead all these years. He has proven to me that I'm not too old to be happy."

Her face softened as the memories faded away, as she locked them away in their secret places and thought upon the future and the face of the man who had changed everything for her. She walked to her daughter and sat on the couch by her side. "He has promised to marry me, Genny, despite my past, despite all the risks. Now do you understand why we must leave? Do you understand why we must flee this place and never, ever return?"

* * *

Maman's fork clattered loudly on her dish as the unmistakable sound of carriage wheels rumbled up the pebbled path. She rose from her seat abruptly, upsetting her full glass of red wine. It stained the white damask tablecloth like blood.

"Go, Genevieve." She paled. "Wait in the gardens."

Genevieve took one last bite of her favorite dish, a meat pie with truffles and mushrooms. The crust melted in her mouth like flakes of snow. Washing it down with a glass of watered-down wine, she pushed away from the table and raced out of the room, passed through a white and gold parlor, and pushed open the high glass doors to the garden. As she lifted her face to the wavering July sun, she wondered who had finally arrived at the manor house—the baron or Armand?

For two weeks, her mother had been as agitated as a wild bird caught in a net, fluttering to the window with every rattle of the wind, with every muted scraping of pebbles across the drive. Armand was late, and the summer was nigh. Genevieve knew that any day now, the baron would forsake the pleasures of the Parisian court and arrive at his Norman estate to while away the hot summer months in the country. Soon after, he would visit his mistress and demand his due. After a season with Armand, *Maman* couldn't bear the thought of seeing the man she hated. Mother and Armand's well-laid plans had become a race against time.

For her mother's sake, Genevieve hoped the visitor was Armand. But as she headed toward the forest, which crept right up to the edge of the well-tended lawn, she couldn't help but feel a spurt of selfishness. If it were Armand, he would take her away from this place, from her *home*.

Recklessly, she raced to the edge of the garden, running her hands over the bristling, razor-straight edge of the bushes and feeling the short, prickly grass beneath her feet. If she hid before *Maman* found her, she could spend one last afternoon in these woods before she was forced to leave them forever.

The humid July air shimmered with light. A recent rain had soaked the earth, filling the air with the scent of rotting leaves and damp wood. Birds chattered in the trees overhead. The churchbells of the village rang, their clanging echoing on the hills. Genevieve strode up the highest slope, and when she reached the top, she climbed nimbly up the twined limbs of an oak. Hidden in the leafy canopy was her own secret castle, built of old broken branches and bits of rope. She spent the afternoon there, peering through the leaves onto the thatched-roof houses of the village huddled in the valley below. She played queen of her own country, and her subjects were as numerous as the birds and squirrels and hares and deer.

Once, long ago, she had surprised two young boys fishing in the baron's stream. They were younger than her and frightened by her sudden appearance. She knew that they could be punished for poaching, but she was hungry for companionship of her own age and allowed them to stay. They showed her where berries grew wild in the woods. They taught her how to fish in the stream with twine and a little leaden hook. They taught her how to snare rabbits and grouse and how to find bird's eggs among the litter or high in the trees. She had watched in fearful fascination as they skinned and gutted a rabbit, then roasted it over an open fire.

They were her friends, her first and only friends. The servants in the manor kept their children far away from her. She was the daughter of the lady of the house, they told her; she must play with her own kind. But there didn't seem to be any of her own kind . . . until these two boys. But one day, coming upon them quietly, she had heard them talking about her. She heard the words *whore* and *bastard*. Enraged, she ordered them out and told them never to step foot in her kingdom again.

As the shadows stretched far toward the east, Genevieve knew that soon it would be her kingdom no more.

Reluctantly, she wandered down the hillside at sunset, using a knotted branch as a walking stick, her heart breaking with every step. As she passed the gardens and approached the leaded glass doors at the rear of the manor, she heard the sound of many muted voices coming from within the house.

Something was wrong. Genevieve entered the white and gold parlor and noticed that all the servants were clustered in the hall that led to the dining room, their dark gray skirts quivering as they attempted to peer over the people in front of them. She charged into the pack, pushing the servants aside. They turned, cursing, but when they saw who it was, their faces paled and their words died on their lips.

They let her pass. She noticed that the dishes from dinner still lay neatly on the table, and the wine *Maman* had spilled stained the tablecloth in long, burgundy streaks. Nanette, her mother's maidservant, spoke quietly with the gardener and shook her gray head.

"Nanette, what has happened?"

Nanette turned around. Her face was as pale as fine wheat flour. Nervously, the maidservant glanced at the floor, and it was then that Genevieve saw the lump of green silk.

"Maman?" The silence deafened her. She approached. Nanette clutched her arm and held her back, but not before Genevieve realized that her mother's skirts were dark with blood.

Blood.

"Someone came to the manor." Nanette nodded to Genevieve's motionless mother. "He came, did this, and left before any of us saw him."

The air was as thick as honey; it clogged her nose, her throat, and pressed painfully on her ears until they rang. Her limbs tingled as if she had rolled on a bed of pins. She choked on the scent that permeated the room. The distinctive odor of lilacs and oranges hung in the air like a fog.

Her own voice sounded strangled and foreign. "He did this."

Nanette looked at her sharply.

"The baron . . . he killed her."

A dozen gasps filled the air. Nanette took Genevieve's shoulders in her hands and shook her firmly. "Hush! You don't know what happened here."

"The room stinks of him. Can't you smell it?"

"I smell nothing, child, and neither do you." Nanette's scraggly brows knotted. "For all we know, it could have been that music man . . ."

"Never Armand!" Her eyes flared. "It was the baron. I know it!"

"You stupid child." Nanette's pale eyes flared in anger. "If you have any sense . . . if you want to live, you'll hold your tongue when the baron arrives."

"I'll tell the constable," she retorted. "He'll arrest him."

"Arrest the Baron de Carrouges! For killing his own whore?"

Genevieve slapped the old crone, and the surprise and vehemence of her attack took the woman off guard. She stumbled back and clutched the dinner table to regain her balance.

"To think I pitied you, you little cur." Nanette rubbed her work-hardened hand on her reddening cheek. "You're nothing but an orphaned bastard now. No better than any one of us."

The room began to swim. Nanette's contorted face was the only stationary object in it. The old woman leaned over and clutched Genevieve. "I had a good position in Paris before your mother spread her legs for that imposter. Then I was sent here with her, to suffer for her mistakes. If you're smart, you little chit, you'll keep quiet. If you don't, you'll find yourself begging in the village." Her gaze skimmed over Genevieve's pale pink silk dress, covered with twigs and nettles from playing in the forest, and her fingers dug into the girl's shoulders like talons. "If you're lucky, he'll provide for you and all the rest of us as well . . . if he thinks you're ripe enough to do what your mother trained you to do." Her wrinkled face filled with scorn. "You were born to be a whore, Genevieve. Just like your mother."

The baron arrived the next morning.

Maman's body lay wrapped in a sheet upon the dining room table. The stink of lilacs and oranges permeated the air as Genevieve entered the room. Her stomach swam with nausea as she saw the baron, standing with his back toward her, with one of his gnarled hands laying upon *Maman*'s forehead.

He turned as Nanette cleared her throat. His cold gray eyes fell upon her like a frigid gust of wind. She had never seen the aristocrat. Until yesterday, he was nothing more than a blur of colorful satin she had glimpsed, once, through the windows of her bedroom. He had the most soulless eyes she had ever seen.

With the pressure of her hand on Genevieve's shoulder, the servant forced her down into a curtsy. Nanette had made her wear her best dress, a brilliant yellow satin decorated with pale peach ribbons, and the old servant had trussed her up so tightly that her small breasts surged above the edge of the bodice. She felt his gaze upon them, examining, assessing, evaluating.

She straightened and waited. The muscles in her throat knotted. For a long time, he said nothing. When he finally spoke, his voice sounded as if it emerged from within the echoing halls of an empty tomb.

"Do you play the harp?"

She blinked at him. Such an unusual request from the murderer of her mother. Such a strange request from the man who had paid for her music teacher. She tilted her chin. "I play." Then she added boldly, "Armand taught me."

The gray eyes glazed and hardened to steel, then a strange, twisted smile contorted his features. He reached out and wound a lock of her mother's golden hair around his finger. "I'm saddened to inform you that your music teacher is dead."

Her heart stopped. She felt as if someone had just pressed a solid block of ice against the back of her neck. Frigid trickles slid down her spine.

"One must be careful where one walks these days, with so many ruffians about, especially in Paris. They'd slit a man's throat for the clothes he wears." Without looking at her, the baron gestured to the harp with his free hand. "Now play for me, daughter

of Jeanette. I paid a pretty sou for that tutor. I want
to see if he was worth his price.''

Nanette pushed her toward the instrument, but
her feet were rooted to the floor. The baron leaned
upon the dining room table and waited. She smelled
Nanette's sour-milk breath as the servant leaned over
her shoulder, pinching the tender flesh of Genevieve's upper arm. ''If you value your life, you will
play.''

Somehow, she found the ability to move. Woodenly, Genevieve walked across the room to the gilded
instrument standing in the corner. She sat upon
Maman's red velvet stool and leaned the instrument
between her legs. She ran her fingers over the strings.
Genevieve remembered *Maman*'s favorite melody—
Armand's favorite, too. She glanced at the white-
sheeted form on the table.

For you, Maman.

Then she filled the room with the music of angels.

When she finished, her hands fell to her lap. She
had never played so well. It was as if Armand himself
plucked at the strings, as if her mother sang the melody in her head. Genevieve looked up to see tears
streaming down the baron's face, but the sight had
all the emotional impact of watching raindrops slip
down the face of a statue.

''You have your mother's touch.'' The baron rose.
His wide satin skirts whirled around him. His sword
clattered against a chair. He approached her and
snaked a finger down her cheek. ''After your mother
is buried, Genevieve, you will take her place in this
house.''

Genevieve escaped as soon as darkness fell. She
raced through the woods in the darkness with a sack

of bread and meat she had stolen from the kitchens. She hid in the tree house, praying at the sound of every churchbell that she would not be found. On the second day of her absence, the baron sent the servants to find her. When they failed, he unleashed the hounds.

But the hounds could not find her. A single night's rain had washed away her scent. They were confused by the trails of deer that crisscrossed the hills. Once, through the uneven floor of her perch, she watched the baron ride past her, cursing, his face distorted in fury.

For three months she lived in the hills. She fished in the stream by the tree house with a stick, a pin from her hair, and her corset strings. She baited traps for grouse and rabbits. She gathered strawberries when they ripened, and ate wild greens and roasted chestnuts. When the air grew cool, she snuck into the orchards to pluck apples and raid the villager's gardens. She was always hungry. She ached for the taste of bread. When the air grew chill, she thought about winter and knew she could not survive much longer in the forest.

Genevieve snuck down into the village one evening and stole a common broadcloth skirt and a bodice from the laundress's establishment. She tossed away the silken rags of her clothing and set off, barefoot, for Paris. Surely, she told herself, there would be work for a woman who could read and write and do sums and sew as well as she, and it was better than dying in the woods alone.

The trip was long and dangerous. She slept in trenches beside the roads. She stole her dinners from the village markets and the orchards that lined the pitted passage. Merchants driving their carts between villages took pity on her and gave her rides through the countryside. She traveled ever westward until, a month later, she finally walked through the towering gates of Paris.

Genevieve had never seen so many people, so much activity. The narrow, twisting streets reeked of the stench of yesterday's fish or the odor of human sewage. Water raced down the center gutters, and with it ran the guts of slaughtered animals and the refuse of tanneries, blacksmiths, starchmakers, candlemakers, and whatever other trade resided along the route. She searched in vain for her mother's family, hoping that time would bring forgiveness and compassion, but no one knew of any Lalandes living in the area north of the Louvre.

She knew then that she would be alone forever.

When she could, she stole her supper from Les Halles, a crowded, bustling marketplace. She slept beneath the bridges of the Seine with beggars and waifs and thieves of all kinds, and every day she sought work, to no avail. One morning she awoke to a magnificent clatter and discovered a glittering procession of gilded carriages driving over the bridge above her head. It was the court, she was told, returning to the Louvre for the season. That day, she found work among the dressmakers of Saint-Denis.

She shared a dingy, rat-infested room with three other girls. It wasn't much, but it was the only home she had had since Carrouges. Whenever the court left the Louvre for Vincennes or Saint-Germain or the hunting lodge in Versailles, she would find herself without income and thus threatened with losing the safety of her room. It was not long before one of the other girls taught her how to pick pockets. One of them would attract a victim's attention by lifting her skirts or tugging on her bodice. While he was distracted, the other, would slice off the heavy pouch that hung beneath his doublet. Then they would both disappear into the labyrinth of the Parisian streets. They lived by stealth and nimble fingers, and as the court spent more and more time in Versailles and less in Paris, they moved to the only place they could afford—an even tinier room near the notorious *Cour des Miracles*. Here was the center of the Parisian crime underworld. Here, all the cripples and invalids who begged during the day suddenly found their sight, their health, and their lost limbs in the evening.

Soon, King Louis XIV stopped coming to Paris altogether. The men who infested the narrow, stinking streets around the *Cour des Miracles* closed in around Genevieve and the girls like wolves. One by one, the girls resorted to prostitution. Genevieve resisted. She cut purses on her own. She took greater and greater risks and had to search markets farther and farther away in order to feed herself. Soon, the other girls tossed her out of their lodging, for she could no longer pay her share and refused to earn it on her back. Her mother had lived that way, and she swore she wouldn't. Once again, she slept under the bridges of the Seine.

But she was no longer thirteen years old. Despite the constant hunger, the three years since she'd left Normandy had given her body a woman's curves. Genevieve never went unnoticed as she wandered through the streets of Paris. The men of the *Cour des Miracles* kept telling her she could earn a fortune on her back. Her virginity alone, she was told, could be sold for fifty livres. Why not earn some money before it was stolen from her?

Genevieve began to wonder if she should listen to these toothless men. She began to wonder if she should have stayed in Carrouges and agreed to the baron's offer. A bed was a bed, after all, and clean linens and a single partner were preferable to bare lice-infested, straw-filled mattresses and the whole disease-infested population of Paris.

You were born to be a whore, Genevieve. Just like your mother.

She took the money.

But as she was being led to the room where the deed would be performed, the lieutenant of police attempted something he had never before dared. He marched into the *Cour des Miracles* with two hundred armed men and took it back for the people of Paris.

Genevieve was saved from herself. She was sent to the Salpêtrière.

Chapter Ten

Who are you, Genevieve?

The question rang in her ears. André gripped her shoulders, willing her to answer him. She wanted to tell him. She wanted to scream, *I am Genevieve Lalande.* She wanted to pour out all of the grief, all of the suffering, all of the desperation that had brought her to this man and to this place in the Canadian wilderness. She wanted to be held and kissed and told that it would never be like that again—that he would give her a home, that he would protect her from the world.

She scanned his face, the fine, straight nose, the dark brows, the dark, scruffy growth that covered his cheeks and chin and could now be called a beard. The dusky predawn light cast pale blue shadows on his skin and gilded the streaks in his shaggy, sun-washed hair. He was strong. *Stubborn.* Determined, capable. *Secretive, evasive, half-wild. Handsome.* . . . He was more than she had ever expected to have in a husband; he was more than she had ever dared hope. How well she had played her part! His eyes were full of confusion, of wonder, of desire. He thought he had married the finest daughter of the *petite noblesse*, impoverished but well-bred, orphaned but protected by the Crown. Now he had caught her with a rabbit, a rabbit whose neck she had twisted with her bare hands, yet he still didn't suspect the truth. From his expression, she knew he was bemused and amazed that a woman of her kind "adapted" so well to the wilderness.

Genevieve should be relieved that he had not guessed the truth; she should be praying thanks to God. Instead, she ached to cast aside this disguise and tell him everything. She wanted him to want *her*, not Marie Duplessis.

But Genevieve was the daughter of a murdered courtesan. She was a thief, a pickpocket, a poacher. A liar. A bastard.

A whore.

Yes, a whore in all but deed—for she'd taken the money, she'd sold her soul for a bite of bread. The remnants of the honor-price still jingled in her case. That day, she'd realized that she'd been destined for this fate all her life: What's in the marrow will always come out in the bone.

She turned her face away. She was a fool—a senti-mental fool. Those years in Paris should have sucked her dry of sentiment, not left her with this tiny pocket of hope. If André knew the truth, all that wonder would disappear from his face. She couldn't bear the disgust, and more, she *wouldn't* suffer the conse-quences: an annulment in the spring, the frantic search for another husband, the threat of being sent back to Paris. She was acting like a besotted young girl to consider risking everything she'd worked for just to be comforted in this man's strong arms.

"Look at me, Genevieve."

His voice was ragged. She met his tawny eyes and a frisson of something glorious quivered up her spine. She thought, *This is how Maman must have felt when she looked at Hamlin. This is why she was so willing to throw away all modesty, all care, for the love of Armand.* Perhaps a woman would do anything—risk anything—for the chance to be loved.

No. She gasped as he raked his hands through her hair and dragged her against his body, solid, full, demanding. She couldn't tell him the truth. Fifty years from now, she wanted to wake up next to this man and still find him staring at her . . . just like this, just like this, just like this. . . .

There was only one way to keep him. There was no place for sentimentality in her world—there hadn't been, not since the day her mother was murdered. She had come to Québec to start a new life. She had left Genevieve Lalande behind—forever. Whatever the cost, he must never know the truth.

She gripped a handful of deerskin fringe and softened against him. "Everyone has secrets, André."

"Tell me yours." He squeezed her body, as if he could force the truth from it. "Tell me which is the real Genevieve: the one who swears like a drunken seaman, or the one who stitches the men's shirts like a girl out of the convent?"

"Neither—or both." *Too close. Too close to the truth.* "They never could make a lady out of me at the Salpêtrière."

"A lady doesn't belong here in Québec." He buried his fingers in her loose plait. "*You* should have stayed safe from swine like me in Paris."

Genevieve fluttered her eyes closed against the truth. "Make me your wife, André."

"Damn you." His fingers tightened in her hair. "Damn you."

"André . . ."

"Be quiet and let me kiss you."

He kissed her. Ah, the kissing. She'd never get enough of this, never in a hundred years. The sweet, hard merging of lips and bodies and souls into one— so pure, so powerful, overwhelming her senses so she could not think. *This* was lovemaking. *This* was the meaning of the feelings that had surged within her from the moment they'd met. When the kiss ended, Genevieve clung to him as if the earth had fallen away beneath her feet.

She pressed her cheek against the warm curve of his neck. Her heart pounding hard in her chest, she wrapped her arms around his wide shoulders and waited for her body to stop trembling. Her toes skimmed the forest floor.

His breath, fast and hot, warmed her hair just behind her ear. "It's useless, isn't it?"

"What is?"

"Fighting you." Hungrily, he kissed the line of her jaw. "I'm damned tired of trying to swim upstream against the rapids."

She arched her neck, giving him access to the tender skin of her throat, but he wanted something else. He kissed her again, nudging her lips apart, tracing the line of her teeth, seeking the warm, honeyed recesses of her mouth. Genevieve surrendered herself to him, tilting her head at his urging, opening her lips wider, welcoming his tongue and his hands in places where she had never wanted any man to touch her. His caresses were magic, pure and heady, swirling a fog in her head until all she could think about was lying with this man under the open sky and giving him anything—anything—he demanded.

André lifted her off her feet. She felt the gentle prick of nettles against her back as he lay her down on the damp forest floor, on top of her makeshift net. His body fell atop hers, heavy and large. She softened beneath him, for the feel of his muscled limbs, of his long, strong form covering her like the warmest blanket, was the sweetest sensation she had ever known. He released her lips to kiss her temple, to breathe warm, moist air into her inner ear, and then to bury his face in her hair.

He tugged anxiously on the ties of her bodice. Genevieve tried to assist him, but her arms were like leaden weights and her fingers were clumsy and uncertain. She had always wanted him like this, since the first day she had seen him in Montréal. There was no sense to it. She had only known him for a few weeks, yet he filled her every thought, he haunted her every dream. He had become as necessary to her as food and water and air. Then realization struck her, as clear as a bright winter morning.

Genevieve blinked open her eyes and stared sightlessly at the latticework of boughs above her head, at the few soggy amber leaves still clinging to the black branches. *Of course.* She should have guessed sooner; there was no other reason for these feelings. Her heart trembled in sudden fear.

She was afraid to love. To love was to hurt and to die a little.

The thought scattered away as quickly as it came, as he pushed her bodice apart, lowered his head, and engulfed one sensitive, aching nipple in his hot mouth. She squeezed her eyes shut. Oh, to think that for fifty livres she'd been willing to give this away. . . .

The past was gone . . . gone. He continued, relentlessly lathing the peak of her breast, drawing it deep into his mouth, holding her still beneath him, coaxing another and yet another moan from her until she was arching against him, weaving her hands in his silky hair, kissing his head, smelling the scent of damp river water in the long tresses. It no longer mattered that the earth was cold and damp against her back, that heavy drops of rain pattered around them, falling from the trees. All that mattered was the touch and taste and smell and sight and sound of him, poised over her body, hungry and wild.

Genevieve squeezed her eyes shut as he released one breast to taste the other, and the cool air chilled her nipple to hardness. She was no longer the master of her own body, for it writhed and arched beneath him, communicating in a language she had only begun to understand. She didn't care. She helped him rearrange the cloth of her skirts, which were twisted and tangled beneath her legs. She welcomed the feel of his callused fingers on her calf, encouraging his touch as his hand rose past where the threadbare stocking was gartered above her knee, to scrape the bare flesh of her inner thigh. She felt so vulnerable, so dependent, so tiny against his bulk, all her senses following the trail of his fingers with trembling anticipation. A wonderful, alien sensation throbbed through her limbs, growing stronger as his hand slid between her legs. He nudged her thighs apart, then he touched her, masterfully, and her entire body jerked in response to the waves of pleasure reverberating through her form.

Unconsciously, she closed her legs tightly.

"Let me touch you, *Taouistaouisse.*" His voice was soft but urgent. "Let me feel you against my hand."

André gazed down upon her, his tawny eyes bright,

his breath coming fast between his lips. She opened
herself to him again. He pressed a knee against her
thigh and stroked her. She arched as the sensation
shot through her anew.

"Genevieve . . ."

She couldn't seem to catch her breath. His kisses
stole it from her mouth, his tongue tracing her lips
as his fingers conjured powerful magic in her body.
She wrapped her arms around his neck to hold on
to him, for he was the only thing that wasn't whirling
madly about her. His stroking continued, endlessly,
creating a bubble in her abdomen that grew tighter
and thinner and tauter, threatening to burst.

"Please . . ."

She didn't know what she was asking for. She didn't
know what she wanted—except that she wanted for
him to continue touching her and kissing her, murmuring nonsense in her ear, moving his great, large
body over hers, protecting her with his warmth. The
stroking of his fingers grew rougher and Genevieve
broke away from his kisses, gasping for breath. She
found the fringed hem of his shirt and plunged her
hands beneath it to feel the warm skin of his back.
His tumescence strained against the deerskin of his
breechcloth as he pressed urgently against her thigh.

Then his finger slipped inside her, almost but not
quite, breaking the bubble of anticipation that had
stretched to unbearable tautness in her body. Genevieve arched up against him and felt his finger slip
still deeper. She released a ragged moan.

"Oh, God, Genevieve . . ." He spoke against her
cheek, his breath coming fast between his lips.
"You're ready for me."

Yes.

Suddenly, the bubble burst. She cried out against
his chest, digging her fingers into his lower back,

arching up against his hand until the throbbing passed and she was left breathing as heavily as if she had run the length of a rocky portage, pressing her forehead against his soft deerskin shirt.

Swine. André squeezed his eyes shut. No, he thought, he was lower than swine. He was a snake, slithering around on his belly like the devil in the garden of Eden.

She trembled in his embrace. Her ragged fingernails still dug into his back, anchored firmly in his flesh, though her body's intimate throbbing had long faded. He focused on the meager pain and the guilt roaring in his head, for both prevented him from taking what every muscle and every sinew in his body screamed for: final release in the soft, willing moistness of her womanhood now quivering in the palm of his hand.

His lungs screamed for air. He couldn't move, because he knew that if he attempted to roll away from her, he would instead roll upon her, push aside her lithe thighs, and thrust into her eager, supple body. He tormented himself with the feel of the silken tresses on his cheek. He wanted this woman as he had wanted no other in a long, long time. *Sacré*, she was as warm and responsive as a well-trained courtesan, yet as innocent as a lamb, for as he touched her, he had felt the tight restriction of her maidenhead, that thin, fragile piece of flesh that proved to the world she was not yet his wife.

And she must never be.

André forced himself to think of the consequences. A wife would expect him to buy three by forty *arpents* of Canadian land for a few coppers and a couple of chickens a year, to give up fur trading and spend his time tilling the rocky soil. A king's girl would expect him to fill their house with furniture and earthenware and linens imported from the motherland, to drape her in lace from Brussels and silk from Lyon, to clutter his life with more things than any one man could carry. But he had grown up on the edge of the settlements, within easy reach of the bountiful forests, and saw no need to buy a plot of land when the whole uninhabited world stretched westward; he saw no need to fill a house with clutter when all a man needed was a sharp knife, a keen eye, and quick wits to thrive. He'd tried that once.

Never again. *Never.*

Yet he had taunted her, teased her, tempted her with all these things even though he knew he would never have another wife, not even the impetuous, passionate one purring in his arms.

Damn it, why couldn't she have been like every other Frenchwoman he had ever known? Why couldn't she have collapsed in exhaustion before they ever reached Long Sault? Any other Frenchwoman in her situation would be sobbing at the sight of her own ragged dress. Any other Frenchwoman would have demanded to be sent back to Montréal at the first sight of a savage. This one bargained with one for her shoes. This one hunted geese and rabbits. This one grew lean and strong and rosy-cheeked and beautiful from the fresh air and the exertion.

"Don't stop, André."

Her voice, breathless, rose between them. Genevieve looked up at him with eyes as soft as dew. He realized he was still touching her, stroking her gently, and she was waiting for him. Abruptly, he removed his hand from her warmth and jerked her skirts down over her thighs. "We're finished."

Her gaze wandered down to where his passion pressed forcefully against her body, as if she knew, instinctively, what the bulge in his breechcloth indicated. "You said . . . I was ready for you."

He suppressed a groan. She was still ready for him, and he couldn't seem to get the feel of her, hot and inviting and moist, out of his mind.

"André? What is it?" She brushed his beard. "Why have you stopped?"

"I told you . . . we're *finished.*"

"We can't be," she argued gently, then flushed. "I . . . know there's more to ravishing than this."

He glared down at her, wondering why he was cursed with an innocent wife who seemed to know most things solely from instinct, and what she didn't know, she found out by wile. "Are you complaining?"

"No." She lifted herself upon her elbows. "I just thought—"

"Don't think."

"Then show me," she whispered, brushing her lips against his. "Let me make you feel as you have made me feel."

André struggled with a fresh surge of desire as her soft, generous lips pressed against his mouth. He throbbed forcefully, and he could tell by her gentle gasp that she felt the motion against her belly. He pulled her head away by her long plait, which had unraveled during their lovemaking, and stared deep into her green eyes.

"For your own good, Genevieve, don't tempt me."

"Oh, but I shall tempt you, my husband, for I have been waiting for you to kiss me and touch me like this forever."

That damned little smile. He tightened his grip on her hair, forcing himself to ignore those inviting lips, those green eyes that had grown as soft and gleaming as rain-drenched moss. The sight, the smell, the touch of her, was headier than brandy, and he was dangerously close to growing drunk on her. "Listen to me. Do you want to birth your first child here, in the forests?"

Genevieve blinked, surprised at the change in subject. "I haven't thought about it."

"I have." *Too much, too often, have I thought about filling you with child.* "I've seen Indian squaws fall back from their tribes and hide in the bushes to give birth, alone, only to follow their tribes when they're strong enough to do so." His gaze swept over her frame, the slender wrists, the delicate ankles peeping out beneath her skirts, the aristocratic bones. "If you grow big with child out here, you'll have no help, no midwife, no doctor. Do you think you're hardy enough to birth a child like the natives?"

The seductive light faded from her eyes, replaced by something else, something hard, something contemplative. "There must be some way to prevent me from growing big with child," she argued, "else you and every other man on this voyage would have a thousand half-breed children running around in these woods."

His lips tightened. André knew so many ways they could enjoy each other's bodies without conceiving a child, but thoughts of tasting her, of feeling her hands on his body, of teaching her all the nuances of lovemaking, were all too powerful for him to bear while his body still strained for her. He pushed them from his mind. He might be a bastard in many ways, but he knew he had no right to accept a gift that he had no intention of keeping.

"Don't play with the bull, Genevieve, and you won't get caught."

André removed her hands from beneath his shirt and yanked the fringe over his back. He untangled his limbs from hers and stood up, cursing the misty cold that rushed between their bodies, cursing the day he first lay eyes on her, cursing the unexpected passion that had put him in this situation. He brushed at the mud that clotted on his legs and hips.

Her voice rose, as soft as the mist that hovered over the river and drifted along the forest floor. "You have secrets, too, my husband."

The wind rustled the leaves drying on the boughs overhead, fluttering down a confusion of golden leaves. She brushed one off her bare shoulder, where her hair draped and covered one breast. Her bodice gaped open, and her shift drooped over the curve of her bosom.

Yes, he had secrets, so many secrets: One of them he couldn't keep from her much longer, for Allumette Island was a day's ride away. After their intimacy, he'd be a swine of the lowest kind if he held back any more secrets.

It would make her hate him, he thought. It would stop her from tempting him as she tempted him right now. It would give her a chance to protect herself from him, because he was damned close to letting what little honor he possessed fly to the wind.

"It's time to tell you the truth, Genevieve."

"Here it is, then." As if realizing that there would be no more embraces, she shrugged herself more securely into her bodice and rose to her feet, brushing litter off her skirts as they cascaded over her legs. "I knew there had to be a reason why seducing you has become such a Herculean task."

"I will never have a wife. Never."

Again.

She planted her hands on her hips. "If you haven't noticed, you already have one."

"You're not my wife until this marriage is consummated."

"After this"—she gestured to the muddied piece of linen on the ground, twisted in the imprints of their entwined bodies—"I thought it was."

"As pleasurable as that was, I didn't finish what I started." The ache in his loins testified to *that.* "I won't take you to my bed, Genevieve."

"What's this foolishness?" Her brows knit together. "How can you touch me like *that* and then tell me you'll never make me your wife?"

"I was forced into this marriage; I wanted none of it." The words seethed like acid on his tongue. What had begun as a joke to be played upon a willful aristocrat had turned into an ugly betrayal of trust upon a woman whose stubborn resourcefulness he had grown to admire. "There was no other way to get a trading license."

"I know that well enough. So you have your trading license and you have a wife," she retorted. "What difference does it make if you sleep with the unwanted baggage?"

"Christ." He glared at her, standing erect in the clearing, her bosom heaving beneath an open bodice. "I'm doing this for your own good."

"Well, thank you very much, but I shall decide myself what's for my own good."

"Do you have any idea," he growled, daring to move closer to her flashing eyes . . . eyes that grew more fiery by the minute, "what kind of husband I'd make?"

"One who doesn't know his own mind, obviously."

"An absent one," he retorted. "The kind of husband who disappears for seasons, for years." *The kind of husband who won't see to his responsibilities at home because his heart, body, and soul are always somewhere else.* "There's more to this journey than a trading license. I spent three years in France, for God's sake, in a crowded city, fighting with fools to get my inheritance so I could return here and do exactly what I'm doing now. Do you really think I'm out here to collect beaver pelts?''

"I don't care if you're out here hiding from the king's judgment." She jerked the ties of her bodice closed with shaking hands. "I'm out here because I'm your *wife* and I intend to remain so, and by the way you behaved today, it looks like it won't be too difficult a task. . . ."

"There's a whole world out there." He pointed to some distant wilderness. "A world no white man has explored—yet. My home is right here. Here, where there are no walls, no roof, no land to till, no taxes to pay. No responsibilities—to man or woman. I'll never return to civilization. This is where I will always live."

"Even out here, you need a place to sleep and shelter for the winter," she retorted, her white hands fluttering in agitation. "That home is mine as well. . . ."

"That home will be nothing but a temporary little hut that I abandon every spring." He resisted the urge to grip her shoulders, to shake the truth into her. "You need a husband who will stay with you in the safety of the settlements, who will provide for you, and who will give you the home you want—not a bare, empty bark hut in the midst of the woods."

A lock of her hair fell over her furrowed brow. "A bare, empty bark hut is better than nothing at all."

"Don't be a fool." Was it his imagination, or had he heard a plaintive tremor in her voice, a soft yearning? "You can't come with me into the unknown, year after year after year hauling loads on your back like some Indian squaw," he argued, dismissing the thought as soon as it came. "And if I were to keep you as my wife and leave you in Québec, you'd give me horns. Obviously," he growled, glancing at their imprints in the mud, "you need a man who'll love you, often and good."

"But not you."

Green eyes, steady and hard, pinned him to the spot. He shook his head once. "Come spring, you and I are returning to the settlements to annul this marriage."

"Liar." She curled her hands into her hair, tearing the matted length into sections. "In Montréal, you said we'd see about—"

"I know what I said in Montréal. I know every lie I told you—from the day you walked into my room to only moments ago, when I made you think that I would make love to you and make you my wife. In Montréal, you were fool enough to threaten to go to the governor and have our marriage annulled in my absence. If you'd done that, my trading license would have been revoked and all I had worked for destroyed. Did you think I was going to let a single woman ruin everything on the eve of my departure?" He jabbed a finger in her direction. "You were supposed to be screaming to be sent back to Montréal by now."

"But I haven't, and I *won't*." She slapped one section of hair over another, then jerked the plait tight. "You're trapped in a situation of your own making, *husband.* For the winter, at least, we will live in your house in that chewywagon place. 'Nine months is a long time for a man and woman to be alone in the woods. . . . '"

"If you survive." He thought of the voyage ahead: the Joachim Rapids; the Mattawa River with its eleven rocky portages; the dark waters of Lake Nipissing; the boiling rapids of the French River; the dangerous, rocky channels of the Lake of the Hurons; and finally,

Lake Superior, the inland sea. Though she had made
it this far, the worst was yet to come, and he didn't
want to find her lying bleeding on a portage path,
mauled by a bear or broken and drowned on the
shores of a river.

"I'll survive, André." Genevieve tossed back her
long, loose plait and something hard glinted in her
eyes. "I *will* survive . . . I always have."

He looked at her face, at the tip-tilted nose with
the spray of freckles across the bridge, the generous
lower lip, the glittering green eyes, the tendrils of
claret-colored hair that flew like wisps about her face,
and the rain of autumn leaves between them. Then
he walked away, so his back was to her, so he wouldn't
have to face her.

"No, *Taouistaouisse*. My mistake, thinking you'd
never make it this far, thinking you'd weaken and
beg to be left behind. Now, you've forced my hand."
He gazed through the trees, toward the river he could
barely hear gurgling beyond. *You'll be safe. Safe from
the rigors of the journey, safe from the Iroquois, safe from
danger. Safe from me.* "There's an island a day's ride
from here, Allumette Island. An Algonquin tribe winters upon it, as well as a handful of Jesuits. Wapishka's
wife and children are there." He waited for something, for anything, for the feel of her nails in his
back, for the pounding of her fists, for the shrieking
sound of her defiance. "You will be well cared for.
Come spring, I'll return by this route and pick you up.
When we get to Montréal, we'll annul this marriage."

"I don't understand."

André turned and looked at her, bright-eyed,
incredulous, still disheveled from their aborted lovemaking. His stomach twisted into a knot. He had
looked upon another woman in such a way before;
he'd seen those same eyes bruised with confusion

and misplaced trust, and he'd said much the same thing.

Cursed, he was, cursed to relive the past. He'd done everything in his power to avoid this, yet now it looked as if God himself had reached his hand down from the heavens and brought him back to that place, to that moment, to that very same situation, then leaned back to see if André would act in the same way.

André swallowed the acid that rose to his throat. This time he knew the consequences, but it made no difference. A man could not change his own nature.

"I'm going on to Chequamegon Bay." His throat parched with self-loathing. "But you, my wife, are staying behind, at Allumette Island."

Chapter Eleven

Genevieve sucked in air but her lungs would not fill, for the air had thickened and solidified, and the river mist that swirled around her calves anchored her to the ground more firmly than irons.

Tomorrow, I'm leaving you on Allumette Island.

She waited for him to explain. He couldn't possibly mean it. Not after all the wonderful things he had said. Not after the way he had kissed her. Not after touching her so intimately. . . . Her body, still warm from his embrace, trembled with the memory, but the trembling grew frigid. She had surrendered herself to him, wantonly, opening her heart and her soul and inviting him in, and they had shared a strange, glorious experience. Yet, now he stood before her, insanely insisting on leaving her on some wild island with strange savages.

Genevieve willed him to retract his words, to explain this madness. He cursed beneath his breath, slapped his hands onto his hips, and swiveled away from her gaze. There was more to this than he was telling her; she sensed it. He was not this cold-blooded despite all his bluster. Moments ago, he had wanted to merge fiercely with her body; she had wanted the same. Men never denied their own lust, weak-willed creatures that they were, and never with a woman as willing and eager as she. There was something more, some undercurrent, some secret. . . . She could think of no other reason why he would insist so suddenly on thrusting her out of his life.

The knowledge had prickled her since the day she'd bargained with the savage for moccasins, since the day Tiny had slipped and revealed a bit of André's past, and now she blurted out the question without pretense.

"This is because of Rose-Marie, isn't it?"

André flinched, then he gouged a footprint in the mud as he jerked around. "What did you say?"

"Rose-Marie." She rubbed her raw palms against her sleeves. "You're leaving me because of her, aren't you?"

"Who told? . . . No . . ." He held up the flat of his hand. "Tiny, wasn't it? He's the only one who knows, and he's too loose-lipped for his own damned good."

Tiny hadn't said a word other than Rose-Marie's name, but it was more than enough. "A woman always knows when there is another woman on a man's mind."

André swept his knife up from the ground and smeared his leggings with the mud on the blade. "If you know about Rose-Marie, then you understand how dangerous this world is, how unfit a place it is for a Frenchwoman."

"What rot."

She'd spoken without thinking; but she'd spent too

much time on the streets of Paris with shifty-eyed
cutpurses, worn-out whores, toothless gamblers, and
drunks, people to whom life was cheap. She'd take
this world over that, for at least here the water was
clean and the food was plentiful, and the only men
to worry about belonged to a single tribe of warlike
savages she'd yet to lay eyes upon.

"This place is no more dangerous for me," she
argued, "than it is for anyone else on this journey."

"Every man here looks after himself, but *I* must
look after you." He shoved the knife under his belt,
tightening his grip on the handle. "You're a woman,
a Frenchwoman, in a world you know nothing about.
I can't protect you from it just as I couldn't protect
Rose-Marie."

Jealousy bit her hard, for there was a kink in his
voice when he said her name. Whoever this Rose-
Marie was, she still held a part of André tight in her
grasp; she still could control him from afar. *A sister*,
she thought, clinging to hope. *A beloved friend.* May
the woman be nothing more.

"What could you possibly have done to her that
was so evil?" Genevieve hated the bitterness in her
voice, she hated the creature of envy chewing at her
heart. "Did you lie to her about your intentions? Did
you drag her hundreds of miles into the wilderness
under false pretenses? Did you?" She dragged her
gaze away from the muddy linen, where they had
kissed and embraced only moments ago. "Did you
abandon her among savages in the middle of the
wilderness?"

"Tiny didn't tell you."

She tilted her chin. This is what loving a man would
do to you, she thought, muddle your senses, soften
your heart, fill you with worthless sentiment.

"I killed her, Genevieve."

Angry words died in her throat. Her skin chilled to ice, as if the heavens had opened and drenched her in frigid rainwater. She shivered, suddenly conscious of the cold ground beneath her moccasined feet, the faint howl of the morning wind, the bite of the air on her bare chest, the *plunk-plunk* of raindrops on the marshy earth. She hugged herself against the cold, against what was to come.

"I killed her, Genevieve," he repeated, flexing his hands, holding them up to her. "As surely as if I had taken her pretty neck between these hands and squeezed. It would have been more merciful if I had." His fingers curled into his palms. "It would have been more merciful than leaving her for the Iroquois."

"You're talking madness."

"Yes, it was all madness." His eyes shone dull, like pale gold coins, turned inward to some other time and place, as he looked away to scan the half-naked maples and the deep green spruces around them. "It was madness for me to roam these woods in those days. The Iroquois were on the warpath. They'd hunted the beaver on their own lands into extinction and were fighting for control of this river so they could become middlemen in the fur trade. There were bloody clashes between them and the settlers all the time . . . *all* the time." His tousled, sun-washed hair flew into his eyes; he didn't push it away. "But I defied them. I was eighteen years old. I was immortal."

Eighteen. Genevieve bit her lower lip. *So young, so young.* She tried to imagine André at Julien's age— wide-eyed, eager, brimming with excitement, half-savage—much the man he was now without the innocence, without the shadows in his eyes, without the caution that seemed so much a part of his nature. *Surely too young to be married.*

"The danger was part of the attraction." He yanked his knife out and fingered the silvered edge, nothing showing in his face but a quiver around one eye. "I snuck past the Iroquois war parties and traded with the western tribes, and brought furs into Montréal nonetheless. My forays made me a rich man." He stretched his lips in a mockery of a smile and laid the blade on the flat of his palm. "That pleased Rose-Marie. She'd come from a family just like mine: Both of us had escaped France after the wars of the Fronde. Both of our families had been rich and powerful, and now we had nothing. It was assumed I would marry her. Being an honorable fool, I did."

Oh, God. Part of her heart crumbled. *Oh, God, another wife. Another woman in his heart.*

"Yes, Genevieve," he snarled, "I had a French wife once before."

She willed her face still. She would not let him see, she *could* not let him see how the knowledge tore at her. Fool, fool she was to have opened herself to him. Fool, fool to hope for the impossible, a woman who'd been willing to sell her soul for a few months' ration of bread.

"Rose-Marie filled our log house on the outskirts of Montréal with the stink of France past." He stabbed a furrow into the rind of a spruce on the edge of the clearing. The pale green inner flesh flaked to the ground. "She wanted a home, just like you, just like any Frenchwoman, a home like she'd been used to. But I had a home, a life . . . here in these woods. Then, as now.

"I smelled the stink of charred wood as I crossed the Montréal island that summer after we'd married.

The Iroquois had raided.'' He ground his teeth as he buried the knife into the flesh of the tree. ''I remember hoping that they had taken her prisoner and not killed her—for then she'd still be alive, then she might survive.'' He barked a humorless laugh as he cracked out a chunk of pale living wood. ''I remember thinking I might *save* her.''

Genevieve hid her trembling hands in the folds of her skirts while André examined the chunk of tree-flesh. He flaked off a few ragged slivers, ran his fingers over the grain, then turned the hunk of wood over and over in his hands to figure the shape of it, to figure what he could carve of it that would best do justice to the wood. She stood as silent as a statue, aching for him because for all his quiet, for all his easy telling of the tale, for all his feigned distraction, his voice had grown husky, and she knew that now he waited for the moisture to return to his throat.

''Damned fool woman.''

He turned his back on the spruce and its gaping green wound, oozing clear sap around the edges. Genevieve dug her fingernails into her arms. She didn't need to know the rest; she'd heard enough from him about Iroquois torture. Her heart reached out to André for what he'd lost, but at the same time she wondered how she was ever going to battle against the loving memory of a woman who was no more than a ghost.

''I got my wish. She'd been taken prisoner, with some others.'' Heaving his arm back, he launched the block of wood deep into the woods, where it clattered with a crack to the ground. ''I even caught up with them.''

''André . . .''

''No, Genevieve, you'll hear it all, then maybe you'll come to your senses. I caught up with the Iroquois war party just in time to see my wife throw herself off the canoe into the river, with her hands and feet bound." His smile turned ugly. "Killing herself. To save her honor. Presumably, for me."

Honor. Suddenly, Genevieve could picture Rose-Marie in her mind's eye: sweet, lovely, full of grace and purity . . . and honor. Like Marie Duplessis. The kind of woman who would kill herself before bargaining away her honor in the alleyways of Paris.

"Unlike my wife, I choose survival over honor, woman." Suddenly, he stood before her, his eyes glittering strangely, his hands on his hips. "*You're* staying at Allumette Island—where it's relatively safe, where the risks are known. You're not coming into the unknown with me. I will have no more women's blood on my hands."

He looked powerful, standing with his feet planted firmly in the earth, the butt of his pistol and the well-worn handle of his long knife sticking out from his Indian sash, the muscles of his chest and arms straining against his buckskin, his bare thighs visible and hard, his lips tilted in mockery, hiding a pain that she now knew furrowed deep inside him. Part of her yearned to reach out and touch him, to give him the comfort he needed, but his eyes defied her.

He clutched her chin hard. "I won't have a wife. I already have a mistress, and this wilderness has proven herself a jealous, vengeful creature."

André released her chin. He strode to where the rabbit lay, discarded on the ground. He picked it up and tossed it in the cook's canoe. Then he returned and lifted the muddy makeshift net from the ground, stamping on the imprint of their bodies until nothing remained but a muddy morass.

She didn't understand this; she didn't know how to fight it. All she wanted to do was love him—yes, *love him,* she thought, with sudden fervent conviction. The truth had come to her in the midst of passion, but she knew it was true even now, for never had she felt such yearning for a man; never had she felt such warmth in anyone's presence as she had with André.

Genevieve thought of her mother and Armand, both risking their lives for the chance to be together, fighting against all the powerful forces trying to tear them apart. There were no such forces between her and André—they were married, they were together— yet he spurned a chance at the kind of happiness that only comes once in a lifetime, all because of the guilt from a past he couldn't let go. She watched as he strode about the clearing, her heart growing colder by the minute. The only conclusion she could reach was the one she feared most.

He doesn't love me. Genevieve squeezed her eyes shut to prevent her tears from spilling. He loved his damned life in these forests, he loved his freedom, perhaps he still loved his former wife enough to enshrine her memory by never taking another; but he didn't love *her,* for if he did, he would never consider abandoning her to her fate.

Listen to me! Talking about love as if I could ever have it, talking about it as if I deserved it. What had made her think a man like André would ever fall in love with a woman like her? What had happened to her these past weeks? She had lived in the dirty underbelly of Paris; she understood the cruelty of humans and the heartlessness of the world, she knew the power of a man's lusts. All along he had planned to abandon her like a leaky canoe. She was a stone-headed dullard to believe there was anything more to his lusty embraces these past weeks than the need to deceive her until they reached Allumette Island.

All for the damn trading voyage, all for a dream that had already destroyed his late wife.

She blinked her eyes open, trying to clear them even as she tried to clear her mind. What had made her so weak that she dreamed of things that only existed in young girl's minds?

Angrily, Genevieve tried to swallow, though her throat was as dry and parched as a desert. She had come to these godforsaken shores to find a husband and to have a home of her own. Somehow, silly dreams of romance had cluttered her mind, obscuring reality like a mist, and now that they had been blown away by the harsh winds of truth, she could see that her dreams were nothing but shadows of her own making, as ephemeral and flimsy as clouds.

Genevieve tilted her chin. He still had a home. *She* still had a home, at least until the day this farce of a marriage was annulled. Just because her heart had been crushed to a bloody pulp in this man's hands didn't mean she was going to give up *all* her dreams, not after what she had been through to hold on to them. She wanted a home now more than ever, for in it she could hide and lick her wounds.

André wadded the muddy linen in his hands, his jaw set. The coldness of reality settled over Genevieve's shoulders. She wasn't completely powerless. He still wanted her body, her damned treacherous body; in the end, it always seemed the only thing she had to barter. From the beginning of this wretched journey, her plan had been to seduce him and consummate the marriage. There was no reason her goals should change now. If she succeeded, then she would have what she came to Québec to get—a husband, a home, a new life, and security.

Somehow, she would learn to live without his heart.

"*No.*"

She hadn't realized she'd said the single word until she heard the echo among the trees. He stopped his fussing and stared at her. She calmly jerked the laces of her bodice tight, crushing the curve of her bosom beneath the boned garment, crushing what remained of her sorry little dreams.

"Genevieve . . ."

"What makes you think that I'd let you abandon me in these godforsaken woods?" she snapped, cutting him off at the quick. "I wouldn't let you abandon me in Montréal, and I sure as hell won't let you abandon me here."

"I thought you'd see reason, woman."

She yanked the last ties into a knot. "I see no reason in leaving me with savages so close to Iroquois country—"

"We're at peace with the Iroquois. The voyage is much more dangerous—"

"The voyage has always been dangerous, but I've done well enough." Her eyes narrowed on him. "You deceived me, André. You made me think that we could be husband and wife. Well, you're my husband for now, whether you like it or not. You're going to take care of me."

"I'm trying, you damned fool—"

"I intend to spend the winter in my own home, not in a skin tent with savage strangers." She lifted her hands to her hips. "If next spring we must annul this marriage, then so be it, but until then I'm going to live in my own house!"

His chin tightened, and flames lit his eyes. "I could tie you up—"

"Yes, you could," she retorted. "But I'm telling you now that as soon as I'm untied, I'll steal a canoe

HEAVEN IN HIS ARMS 241

and follow you, and nothing—*nothing*—will hold me back.''

"You're not that stupid."

"I believed *you*, didn't I? That makes me the biggest fool on earth."

"Damn it, Genevieve." He curled his fingers into fists. "I'm trying to keep you alive."

"Then you'll have to keep me with you." She hurled the words with all the pain in her heart. "I won't be abandoned like Rose-Marie."

Their gazes met and locked, and she knew her arrow had drawn blood. *I don't care,* she told herself. There was too much at stake. There was no more room for softness in her heart, not any more. Somewhere on the river, a loon cawed a mournful wail. The dry pine needles above their head rustled in a gust. In the distance, Tiny cried, *Lève! Lève!* raising the men from their slumber, heralding the start of a new day.

André walked toward her, that rolling, graceful, silent stride, until he stood in front of her, his eyes as hard as amber. "You leave me no choice."

"I thought you'd see reason."

"What did you think, *Taouistaouisse?* That you could force a man into marriage?"

She blinked up at him in the growing light, seeing the violence latent in him, seeing the anger and the ruthlessness in the tightness of his jaw. A man such as this had done many things to survive, perhaps many as ugly as the things she had done. How similar they were, deep down inside; brother and sister in spirit, survivors both. And the thought frightened her, for Genevieve knew to what lengths *she* would go to have her way.

"Listen to me. You've been warned. You know my

intentions." His gaze roved lazily over her body. "There are some weapons you'd best not use against me."

He wound a tendril of her fiery hair around his finger. The heat of his breath brushed her face. A pulse throbbed in his throat, and she wondered what madness had come over him. "What do you mean . . . weapons I should not use?"

"I am only a man. I have only so much strength to resist a beautiful woman." He brushed his finger against her cheek and lowered his head, until his lips were only a breath away from hers. "The next time you try to seduce me, *Taouistaouisse*, I will take it as an invitation that you will be my mistress—and nothing more."

He made no other move to touch her, though if she swayed even slightly toward him, or him toward her, their lips would touch and passion would ignite, and she knew all her fears would scatter away like deer before wolves.

Genevieve's gaze flickered from the potent attraction of his lips to his heavy-lidded eyes. He expected her to staunch this passion that raged between them still, despite all that had happened, but she feared she had no more control over it than she had over the winds. She had been depending on this desire to drive him to consummate this marriage in spite of himself, to make her his wedded wife, to give her the security she craved. . . .

She leaned away from him, suddenly breathless.

"Now I think you begin to understand." André released her hair and let it brush, whisper soft, against her skin. "If I were so willing to entice an innocent on this long journey, with no intention of marrying her, then I'm capable of much worse. I will take no more responsibility for what happens between us."

He brushed a knuckle under her chin. "There's no place for honor among savages."

André backed away, his eyes bright and gold, full of danger and promise. He turned abruptly and strode into the woods toward the campsite.

She gripped her shoulders, her blood chilling to ice. By the love of Mary, what a fool she'd been. *What did you think, Taouistaouisse? That you could force a man into marriage?* Sentiment . . . it had made her soft.

Genevieve buried her face in her hands. She'd forgotten. She'd forgotten the lesson taught to her long, long ago, in a very different world. The Baron de Carrouges had taught it to her. Rich men lived by different rules. If the baron could kill her mother and still walk free, then another man of similar wealth could certainly rid himself of an unwanted wife— even if she were pregnant with his child.

Terror, cold and unadulterated, flooded through her veins. She hadn't felt so helpless, so frozen with fear, since the day the Baron de Carrouges had touched her and said she would take her place in her mother's house.

Oh, God . . .

If she seduced André, perhaps she *wouldn't* have a home, a husband; he might get rid of her nonetheless. Then she would be abandoned and pregnant in a hostile world, forced to do whatever she could to survive.

Just like *Maman.*

"By the blessed milk of the Virgin Mary!" Tiny jerked up from his seat in the canoe and glared at Julien. "What are you doing, lying back like a whore on Sunday? We've entered the French River, porkeater!"

Julien put aside his unlit pipe—a small carved vessel made of red pipestone that he had recently bought from the Nipissing Indians—wordlessly reached over his shoulders, grabbed two handfuls of fringe, and stripped his shirt off his back. Then he stood up and dove smoothly into the oily black waters at the mouth of the French River.

Genevieve's bright head emerged from the deer-skin blanket she clutched around her shoulders, against the wind. When she saw Julien splashing around in the water, she glared at Tiny, who struggled to light his pipe from a flaring piece of tinder.

"I trust you aren't just going to leave him bobbing out there like a piece of dead wood."

"Of course not!" Tiny dragged deep on his pipe, then exhaled the blue smoke. "Come, pork-eater! Sing *Parmi les voyageurs*."

Julien, desperately trying to keep his head above the frigid water, began the song with a gurgle:

> *Among voyageurs, there are some good men,*
> *who scarcely eat but often drink,*
> *with pipes in their mouths and mugs in their hands,*
> *they say, Friends! Pour me some wine!*

Agitated, Genevieve straightened. "Tiny, the water must be close to freezing!"

"Hear that, pork-eater?" His blue eyes glittered as he stared at the red-faced boy. "Blossom thinks you're cold."

The boy stopped his singing abruptly. "The water's as warm as ale, O Mighty One."

Tiny's lips split into a smile, showing his tobacco-yellowed teeth. "More like piss-pot warm!"

"Tiny."

The giant's grin faded as Genevieve glared at him.

He waved his pipe expansively. "Arise, boy! You've been baptized in the waters of the French River."

André frowned as he stood in the rear of the canoe. He twisted his paddle so the vessel wouldn't drift as the men settled back for a pipe break. His little spitfire of a wife had a way with them all. One look from those flashing green eyes and they collapsed like marionettes whose strings had been cut. And damn it, he was no better—because he *allowed* it, as he'd allowed so many other concessions. Like the rope harness he'd allowed Julien to fashion for her. The skin of her hands had already cracked and bled as she carried her case over the portages, and André didn't want to bother with bandaging them every night—so he told himself. He was a lying bastard.

The stubborn wench should have stayed on Allumette Island.

André twisted his paddle to heel the boat toward Julien. Blue curls of pipe smoke twisted up into a sheet of cold gray sky. Ten days, and already the warmth and color of the hardwood autumn leaves had settled into a brown mush of carpet on the earth. Gone were the warbles and chirps of the late migrating birds. The gentle forests that once rimmed the banks of the river gave way to ice-polished sheets of rock rising like ancient castle walls, and feathered crags bearing scraggy, stunted pines. Genevieve was as cold to him as the Arctic wind.

At the end of one of the innumerable portages on the Mattawa River, André had found her curled on a rock, shivering like a wet dog, her hands wrapped in bloody, ripped rags of her dirty petticoat. *Did the wench fear nothing?* He wanted to strangle her for her stubbornness. Instead, he gave her an extra pair of his leggings to keep her legs warm, and when they reached the windswept waters of Lake Nipissing, the first thing he did was buy her a blanket from the Indian tribe that lived along the shores. Never once had she turned to him in thanks.

He was a damn fool for expecting it. She was the ice princess now, haughty and distant, as cold to the touch as marble, and just as stiff whenever he carried her to or from the canoe. But *he* knew the fire that burned inside; it tormented him every night when he slept under the canoes with his men, heard her mumbling in her sleep beneath the tarpaulin, and imagined her, rosy-cheeked, beneath him, her lashes casting shadows on her cheeks, her lips parted and her head thrown back . . .

"Steady," Tiny warned, the canoe rocking as Julien clutched the lashed gunwale. *"Steady!"*

André dragged his attention back to the situation at hand, twisting his wide paddle deep as Siméon and Gaspard grabbed the boy beneath the armpits and heaved him over. *The wench will be the death of all of us*, he thought, cursing his distraction. He set himself to straightening the boat as the boy lay shivering, naked but for breechcloth and leggings, as the men laughed and taunted Julien for looking like a plucked chicken in the morning sunshine.

The boat swayed. *She* was staring at Julien, at the lean muscles of his back, muscles that had finally emerged beneath his young flesh, muscles that now bulged hard and knotted, after hundreds of miles of paddling and portaging. André didn't like that look; he didn't like the way she assessed each of his men as a potential husband in the past ten days.

"Take your place, pork-eater." André dug his paddle deep into the water and felt the first pull of the upcoming rapids. "We've got five miles of rapids to run."

The men knocked their pipes on the sides of the canoe. The embers sizzled as they hit the water. Shaking, Julien took his place and retrieved his paddle. Genevieve shrugged off her deerskin blanket—the one *he* had given her—and tossed it across the boy's wet back.

André barked for the men to get to work and concentrated on the slice of the canoe through the water. He navigated the vessel down the deep, elongated bay, around shoals and fingers of smooth granite rock. He dug his paddle deeper, too deep, and The Duke glanced back in surprise as the canoe bucked. André scowled and he shifted his paddle, then set his mind on the task to come. The French River was the first west-flowing river they had encountered during the journey, and soon they'd be riding down a brutal sweep of raging white water. He'd have to keep his mind on the watery road ahead and not on the quagmire of a relationship he had with his wife if he intended to keep his men, his wife, and all his merchandise dry and whole.

The men knelt and lifted their paddles out of the water as they passed through a narrow channel and rounded an island bristling with pines. The water rippled and eddied as the current clutched the belly of the canoe. Ahead, a narrow staircase of rocks fanned across the river. André bobbed from the knees as the canoe bucked beneath him, scanning the river for haystack waves that concealed no harm and ragged crests of foam that hid boulders and, beyond, dangerous eddies and holes.

They shot down in the rapids—Little Pine Rapids—and it was like sliding down a sheet of ice. Gritting his teeth, André watched for standing waves and souse holes, barking out orders to the men to keep in the narrow thread of water that wound through the danger, that would bring them most swiftly down the river, twisting and turning his paddle like a rudder. A black strip of soaked stone marked the low water level on either side of the shore, and rocks André had never before seen on this route now crested above the froth. Faintly, he heard the excited cries of the men in the canoes following as they, too, entered the white water and felt the rush of power beneath their feet. But soon even that noise was drowned out by the thunder and roar of the water as it tumbled over its bed of stones. His men, all well trained but for Julien, knew how to drag their paddles against the current, or paddle with it, or veer the bow or stern to one side or another, or raise their paddles as they faced an oncoming wave; they knew how to react instantaneously to his commands, and André felt the rush of exhilaration as they tumbled down the water as smoothly and easily as if they had raced like the wind across a choppy lake.

The rapids followed in succession: Big Pine Rapids, Double Rapids, the treacherous Ladder, Little and Big Parisian Rapids, the Devil's Chute, and Crooked Rapids, five miles of unceasing white water, five miles of the cold wind biting his skin above his beard, filtering like ice through his hair, feeling the canoe below him as if he were an extension of the vessel, as if he were riding a horse bareback across the hills of Provence as he had done with his brothers as a child. The men whooped and laughed as the vessel careened through narrow chutes, as it slid down slick tongues of current, as spray as clear and sparkling as diamonds rose and splattered over them. André's heart pounded in his chest, hard and loud, and when the rapids finally spit them out on a long stretch of calm water, he, Wapishka, and The Duke, smiling and triumphant, rent the silent, scraggy woods with piercing Indian shrieks.

Heaving and exhilarated, he glanced down at Genevieve, expecting to find her clutching the canoe as if her life depended upon it, expecting to find her shocked and quivering from fear. *There, woman, is a man's risky pleasure.*

But she swiped water from her face and laughed with all the rest.

"By the head of Saint John!" Water gleamed in Tiny's beard as he twisted at the sound of her laughter. "We ought to give you a paddle, Blossom, and see how you ride the waves!"

"It's like . . ." Water dripped from the bright length of her braid as she twisted it. "It's like tumbling down the side of a hill!"

André suddenly thought of her as a little girl, rolling down the side of a slope, giggling, her skirts rising above her knees.

"Julien had my knees clattering with all his talk." She nudged him playfully. "He told me it was like dropping off the edge of a cliff."

The boy shrugged, shamefaced. "I've never run the rapids before, either."

"Reason enough for another baptism," Siméon suggested, his teeth visible beneath his black beard.

"Why bother?" Wapishka gestured to the boy's soaking shirt. "He's already been baptized by the river herself."

"There are more rapids, aren't there?" Genevieve asked. "Somewhere downstream?"

"There are more," André snapped, "but we won't run them."

"Why not? It's so much faster than portaging."

She tilted her head and looked up at him, and for a moment she was his *Taouistaouisse* again; bright-cheeked, excited, all the haughtiness melted away. The rapids had done this, the rush and tumble of the water, the buck and roll of the canoe in the fresh open air; the danger and excitement of it stripped away all pretense and revealed the pith of a man— or a woman. André's hands tightened on his paddle. *What kind of creature are you, woman? What does it take to make you scream?*

"It's dangerous, that's why," he argued. "The water level is too low. We could tear a hole in the bottom of the canoe and lose everything."

Her gaze skittered away, as if she suddenly remembered to whom she was talking. She shrugged beneath her deerskin blanket, which Julien had long returned to her in favor of his shirt. "If it can't be run, then it can't be run, but it's just so much more fun to rush down with the current than plod along the shore."

He thought of the falls ahead that gushed into the river, leaving a sliver of turbulent water for the canoes to pass by; he thought of the jerky drop just beyond, and the breath-stealing rush of froth and mist before the ribs of the canoe connected again to the water. A wicked grin twitched his lips.

"I didn't say it *couldn't* be run, *Taouistaouisse.*"

Tiny, Wapishka, and The Duke glanced over their shoulders in astonishment. Genevieve tilted her head, a sparkle of excitement lighting her green eyes.

"We'll walk the shore and take a look at the run." He twisted his paddle and steered the canoe toward the shore. "Then we'll do it."

André's footsteps crunched on the bare stones as he and The Duke picked their way along the edge of the steep cliff that formed one bank of the river. Nothing obstructed the view down the edge of the precipice into the deep ravine that held the swirling white water of the rapids, for here, as along the shore of most of this river, scarcely any dirt covered the bones of the earth. Only stunted jack pines and scrubby, dry vegetation flourished atop the hill, their gnarled roots digging deep into fissures of rock.

The water flowed low in the ravine. In places, only the tips of rocks thrust from the river, easy to see from above but nearly impossible to see from the rim of a canoe. Still, as André scanned the length of the rapids, he knew they could be run if the canoe was empty of merchandise and only two skilled men manned the vessel.

With Genevieve as a passenger, of course.

Break, woman. It was a damned cruel thing to do, but he'd reached the limits of his control. Soon, they'd pass the farthest western point he'd ever traveled. Ahead lay territory charted by only a few Frenchmen, and beyond that, by none but the Indians. Now he was fully in *his* world, his savage world, where life was short and hard and a man didn't fight against his pleasure.

Break, woman. For there can be no such thing as a Frenchwoman with the courage and grit of an Indian squaw.

Now she'd get a taste of what it was like to live in *his* world, always riding the edge of control, swept along by the forces of nature, in a place where only those quick of wit and courage could survive.

"We must watch those ridges." The Duke squatted and pointed down the ravine toward a ragged line of stone that thrust out into the center of the river, the shells knotted in his hair clanking as his slick black ponytail slipped off his shoulder. "We must remember to bear away from them when we reach this curve."

They discussed the run all along the route to the camp. All his canoes had landed and the merchandise lay scattered about the rocky shore like so much flotsam. The men had already eaten their gritty breakfast of *sagamité* flavored with blackberries, and a haze of blue smoke hung in the air from the pipes and the cooking fire. The cook clanged his copper pot clean near the shore.

André saw Genevieve perched upon a boulder while Wapishka regaled her with a story that, by the amount of hand waving, was exaggerated utterly out of proportion. André's loins tightened at the sight of her, her breasts straining against her bodice, her legs crossed at the ankle and swinging back and forth, her lips parting in a laugh.

She looked at him suddenly.

"Come." He bowed and swept out an imaginary hat, then gestured to The Duke, who waded out to the empty canoe. "Our carriage will be departing soon."

"I thought we weren't running the rapids." She leapt gracefully off the boulder and jutted her chin toward the water, where The Duke ran his hands over the sides of the birch bark vessel. "The canoe is empty."

"It's just you and me, woman." He grinned as her eyes widened. "And The Duke. We'll be doing the run with an empty canoe. It's the only way to be sure we don't damage the boat."

"What use is that?" She shrugged herself into her blanket. "The men will still have to portage all the kegs over that rock."

"I'm not running the rapids to save time, Genevieve. I'm running them for you."

She blinked at him, then her chest inflated and that steely, defiant look lit her eyes. "If that's the case, I'd rather not."

"You were all-fire eager to run the rapids an hour ago."

"I thought it was the quickest way down."

"It *is* the quickest way down."

"But that's useless if it's only me, you, and The Duke who are going to benefit from it. I'm perfectly capable of climbing the portage by myself."

"I thought," he growled, frustration curling his hands into fists, "you would enjoy the ride."

"I would." Her dark lashes rose as she met his gaze evenly. "But I'm not willing to pay the price for your kindness."

He clutched her arm as she tried to turn away. "Frightened, Genevieve?"

"Suspicious." She tugged her skirts clear to her knees, so he could see the leggings strapped around her leg. "These leggings, the blanket, and now a ride down the rapids. What are you trying to do, André?"

"I don't need a woman freezing to death or collapsing on the trail."

"It would save you a lot of bother. No woman to slow you down on the voyage." She leaned toward him, arms akimbo. "No annulment proceedings in the spring . . ."

"Quiet." He lowered his voice when he realized some of the men had turned to stare. "If I'd wanted you dead, I'd have done it by now."

Genevieve set her jaw and glared at him, and he saw all of his treachery in her eyes. "I might have spent too much of my life in charity houses like the Salpêtrière," she retorted, "but I know one thing: No man gives a woman gifts unless he wants something back from her."

It was on the tip of his tongue to say *I don't want anything from you,* but he stopped himself, for it was a blatant lie. He *did* want something—he wanted *her.* He had had enough of this cold, angry Genevieve. He wanted back the woman who laughed, he wanted back the woman who tried to seduce him at every turn, and he wanted her without commitment, without entanglements, without complications.

But most of all, he wanted to kiss her pouting lips, then caress her until she was senseless with desire, until she begged him to take her, until she melted like a block of snow in the sunshine. His breechcloth tightened at the thought. He wanted to pull her in his arms, press his loins against her, smother her parted lips with kisses, feel her sex with his fingers, and make her throb for him, as she had that day on Calumet Island. He knew he couldn't. He had no right—and that was what was tormenting him, this last shred of honor he'd not yet shed. *She* had to initiate any lovemaking between them—and she'd damned well better do it soon, before he forgot himself.

Then he remembered how she'd looked, only moments ago, when they had run the five miles of rapids. The exhilaration and the power of the white water had affected her as it had always affected him: It made her forget, for a brief moment, that he was the enemy. She had been eager and open. Passionate. They had shared a moment.

André admitted, in some deep part of himself, that he didn't know whether he was running the rapids to frighten her . . . or to seduce her.

"Ride the rapids with me."

Her pupils widened, darkening her eyes, and he knew with a rush of heat that she wanted him, too.

"It won't be a gentle ride," he barked. "It'll be rough and dangerous—"

"With you, I suspect it always is."

"Say yes."

The tension stretched between them, sweet and hot. A pulse throbbed in her throat; her lower lip swelled. A flush crept over the creamy skin of her breasts. He no longer knew whether he was talking about the rapids or talking about making love to her. He just wanted her to say yes, to come to him willingly, to submit, to surrender.

"*Yes.*"

André didn't give her time to change her mind. He swept her up in his arms. Her rounded hip brushed against his abdomen. The softness of her breasts crushed against his chest. She was so small, so fragile, this tough little bird, and she had said *yes*. He splashed out into the water, splaying his hands over her thighs and back, staring at her lips as if they were food and he were a starving man. If there weren't two dozen men watching them from the shore, he'd wrestle her to the bottom of the canoe and have his way with her, right now, right here, kiss her until she lay naked and eager and willing in his arms.

The canoe rocked wildly as he released her in the center, among the cedar ribs. Nodding to The Duke, who stood at the bow, the two of them tumbled over the gunwale. Without the weight of the merchandise to equilibrate the vessel, it wobbled wildly with every move, and with Genevieve struggling to a sitting position, it took all of André's skill to keep the vessel upright as he and The Duke steered it into the current.

There was no more time for thought. Just beyond the landing point the river funneled into a steep-walled canyon and the drop for the rapids began. André dug his paddle into the water and felt the ferocity of the current tugging at the red-painted end. The run would be short and tight, and it required his full attention to avoid the danger of the rebounding waves and the tips of rocks that just barely jutted from the surface of the water. At the end of it, he would send The Duke away and he would be alone with her.

He would melt the ice princess; he would make her ask for it, and then there'd be no guilt.

The Duke called out a terse warning as the canoe slipped down the first drop, gliding on a rush of current, splitting the lacy white spray and flinging it aside. Flung against one side of the canoe, Genevieve quickly righted herself. Above the roar of the water, André heard the yells of encouragement filter down from the edge of the gorge as some of the *voyageurs* who had already begun the portage watched the progress of the canoe from above. The painted prow dipped beneath a wave and then shot up again, splashing frigid spray over The Duke's naked chest and soaking Genevieve in her seat in the middle of the vessel. The rumble grew louder as the ravine narrowed and all sound reverberated off the pinkish granite walls.

For a few yards, they rode a high ridge of water, formed by the velocity of the current between two large rocks. Beyond, the river swirled and scoured the granite walls with the force of its passage. André rose from his crouch in order to read the river, which had turned into a long swath of turbulent white foam. The vessel slid with gathering speed down slick tongues of current. He dug his paddle into the current, stroking one side of the canoe or the other to veer the bow away from ragged crests of lacy spray that hid boulders and ridges. They reached the ridge that thrust out from the right wall of the ravine, and he and The Duke struggled against the force of the current to veer the canoe far to the left. His thighs burned with the strain and his arms ached from fighting the elements, but he barely noticed the pain as the canoe glided past the dangers, the prow dipped into a standing wave, and a wall of frigid water battered over the bow. André shook his head, flinging droplets of water around him.

The run wasn't over. The roar of the upcoming

cascade filled the ravine. The canoe careened around a bend and then he saw Récollet Falls, a long sheet of white foam plunging from the height of the gorge into a vortex at its foot, in the middle of the river. The canoe soared down, closer to the fury of the cascade, and André and The Duke put all the musculature of their backs into veering the vessel into the slim path between the mist rising from the crash of the falls and the perpendicular wall that formed the other bank. The fog rose as thick as cream around them, soaking them instantly. The vortex of the falls yanked on his paddle and he battled it, as the canoe edged its way around the thunderous sheet of spray and found its way down the next, and milder, chute.

He looked down at her. She had her back to him and was kneeling in the canoe. The whole run had taken less than a dozen heartbeats, but they must have fallen ten meters in less than fifty of length. Genevieve turned around to look up at him, her cheeks scoured red from the cold air, her breath misting through her lips. Her bosom heaved above the constriction of her boned bodice. Drops of water sparkled in her hair, but nothing could match the brilliance of her eyes or the blinding light of her smile as she laughed, the music of the sound blending with the roar of the waterfall.

And for a moment, nothing existed but him and Genevieve. Not the pounding of the cascade, not the aches and strain of his muscles as he fought the rushing water, not the wind in his hair or the icy water dripping off his chin, not the thick mist clogging his breath. She looked as if she had just been made love to, fiercely and thoroughly, as if *he* had just made love to her, and he wanted her with a sort of blind violence. Every sinew, every bone, every muscle, ached with urgency for her. He *needed* her. He needed to plunge his sex into her soft, tight body . . . to hold her hips flat against him . . . to feel her energy throbbing around him like the power and fury of the rapids . . . to spill his seed into her . . . to conquer her as he had just conquered the white water.

Amid the muddle of his lust a thought came to him, hazy but sure—*Genny, Genny, Genny.* She was as unpredictable and as stubborn as this great stretch of untamed land—full of mystery, full of secrets, constant only in that she was ever-changing. A man could wrestle to master her and conquer her, but it would never be more than a veneer, for the wildness inside her could never be fully tamed. A man could spend a lifetime exploring her, understanding her, living with her, making love to her, and it would be like riding these rapids—wild, exhilarating, bordering on the brink of control.

He saw the passion in her eyes, too, as her smile faded and she continued to stare, the water flowing from her face over her long white neck, to slip between her breasts and spread a wet stain in her cleavage. Mouthing his name, Genevieve rose to her knees and moved toward him, stumbling as the canoe wobbled with the unexpected motion. It wasn't until he heard The Duke cry out something that André knew he had taken his attention away from the river too long.

The canoe keeled as it slid down an unexpected high ridge of water. Off balance, André thrust his paddle deep into the river to try to regain control. Knocked to one side, Genevieve fell against the gunwale. The canoe tipped from the uneven distribution of weight. She cried out and clutched the gunwale, but the force was too strong. Suddenly, her skirts were in the air, like the opening petals of a flower, and then she was sucked beneath the surface of the water.

"No!"

The vessel rolled in the other direction and his feet lifted from the ribs of the canoe. André felt weightless for a moment, suspended in the air, and then the cold river clutched him.

The water gurgled around his ears, gorged his nostrils, and flushed past his ears, creating a painful vacuum. The warring currents yanked him downstream, deeper into the river. André extended his legs and flattened his feet to rake the rocky riverbed, searching for footing as needles of rock sliced his moccasins and tore the callused skin of his feet. Gasping, he swam up from the icy chill, filling his lungs with air, coughing out the river. He jammed his toe into one hold and lost it, then found another as the current thrust him toward a smooth rock jutting above the surface. He winced as he slammed into the stone, but before the current could whoosh him around it, he grasped the slimy skin and dug his fingers into the grain. Lodging his feet in the cracks beneath the surface of the water, his thighs bulging, André fought against the pounding of the river.

He climbed onto the stone. His ribs ached where he had been pushed against the boulder. The canoe suddenly rushed past him and knocked against a rock downstream. The craggy boulder sliced through the bark hull like a knife through soft butter. He saw The Duke's dark head as the Indian clung to the stern of the vessel and, somehow, found a foothold in the riverbed.

André peered through the dripping curtain of his hair, desperately looking for Genevieve. A log whooshed by, bobbing high on the current, crashing in a spectacle of wet splinters a dozen meters downstream. He searched the rocky shore for a glimpse of her faded pink skirts, for the sight of her auburn hair. The deep gorge had widened and there were places along the shore where she could hold on. *If* she could hold on. If she could keep her head above water in the rush of the rapids. If the river hadn't thrust her against one of its embedded rocks and knocked her unconscious.

He yelled her name, but his voice was lost in the tumult. There was no sight of her. No sound. His heart pounded in his chest. He slid down the opposite edge of the boulder, submerging himself in the eddy behind the stone. The current swept on either side of him, encasing him in a triangle of whirling water. He balled himself up and thrust his body into the current. It assaulted him and shoved him downstream. The water was chest-deep and swift, and André struggled to keep his head above the river, struggled to slow his forward motion by planting his feet firmly against the gritty riverbed. He searched the shore, the treacherous scattering of jagged rocks, desperately seeking a scrap of pink petticoat, a length of copper-colored hair. A sudden drop in the riverbed forced him below the surface and he struggled against the undertow, only to be spit up like a bobbing piece of wood a few meters downstream. He lost control. Ahead, he saw a treacherous scattering of boulders funneling the river into a dozen different arteries. He could not avoid them. André braced himself for a knocking, but instead a crosscurrent whirled past a verdant outcropping of the bank and thrust him into the sudden shelter of a swirling cove.

His knees scraped against the pebbly bottom, and the deerskin and the flesh tore. He shook his head to dislodge the water clogging his ears, dragging himself unsteadily to his feet. The eddying current pulled weakly at his knees as he scanned the cove, searching for her. His breath came fast and deep. A

pile of flotsam lay on the pebbly shore, thrust there
by the same current that pulled him into this small
bay.

Oh, God, Genevieve.

André stumbled through the water toward the
other tip of the crescent-shaped cove. His heart thud-
ded against the walls of his ribs. He reached for the
rough, thin trunk of a jack pine, pulling himself out
of the cove and onto the sheer edge of the bank.
Digging his fingernails into the lichen, he clambered
up over the bare rocks. His breath burned in his
lungs. A hundred disjointed thoughts flooded his
mind. He remembered Genevieve vividly, laughing
with him on the floor of the forest, her hair the color
of aged claret in the last light of day, her eyes sparkling
with life, her clothes stinking of skunk. Genevieve, a
daughter of the *petite noblesse,* slogging through the
woods with the intrepidness and courage of any
coureur de bois, looking regal and seductive nonetheless in her torn, mud-stained skirts, her cheek livid
with scratches. Genevieve, lying huddled beneath her
blanket in the twilight, bantering with the *voyageurs*
as they sucked on their pipes and bragged about their
adventures by the campfires.

Oh, God, Genevieve. Genny.

He had been a fool, distracting himself with
thoughts of her when he should only have been thinking of the danger. He knew the rapids were treacherous and unpredictable, that the water level could
cause dangerous funnels that disappeared when the
river rose. He'd dragged her with him because they
would frighten her, hoping to scare the living wits
out of the wench so she would cry *Enough! Enough!*
and he could be rid of her. He could say *Yes, yes, she's
like all the others,* then send her away from him before
he let himself do something he'd sworn he'd never

do. Christ, he should have stifled his own lusts for a time when he could get Genevieve alone, someplace safe, and instead he might have killed her . . . *killed her* . . . more blood on his hands . . . more blood on his hands.

Genny's blood on his hands.

Then he heard the cry. A weak wail, like the meow of a kitten, and it was swallowed up almost immediately by the rumble of the rapids. André yanked himself to the top of the boulder and stumbled to his feet. He raced to the edge of the outcropping and searched below, where a motley collection of timber and leaves and debris had gathered, forming a dam between the bank and a rounded boulder a few meters away from the shore. He heard the cry again, and then he saw a bit of faded pink among the foam.

André scrambled recklessly down the outcropping, slipping on the slimy moss, shifting a spray of pebbles into the water, clawing the stone with his free hand as he bumped his way toward the water. A fallen log had lodged with one end against a boulder on the bank and the other against a boulder in the water, and among the shattered branches bobbed Genevieve, her skirts tangled in the tree. The current pounded her against the log, battering her back incessantly.

"Genevieve!"

She opened her mouth to speak but coughed instead as the water pounded her. Her hair lay in dark tendrils all over her face. She slipped below the surface for a moment, her skirts tugging on the branches, but she struggled up again and clutched the trunk with both arms.

André splashed into the water, heedless of the stinging of the icy liquid on his raw knees and thighs. The log was unstable, likely to be dislodged at any moment. The current here was fierce. He clutched the trunk for support as he worked his way toward her. She watched him, her eyes wide with fear. Bits of wood—twigs and splinters—dug into his bare side, propelled there like needles by the force of the rapids. The riverbed dropped suddenly and he struggled to regain his balance. The water rose to his chest, but Genevieve was only an arm's length away.

He held out his hand and she reached for it. Clasped it. Tiny frozen fingers in his hand. He yanked her toward him, but her skirts were tangled in the log's branches. Heedlessly, he ripped the worn material from the netting of branches with his bare hands, leaving bits of cloth and thread hanging from the ends. Her skirts fell into the water and were swiftly sucked beneath, pulling her with them. Genevieve gasped and her grip slipped on the trunk, but he pulled her toward him until their bodies slapped together.

Her cheek was as cold as ice against his neck. Her body bucked with the force of a cough. He closed his eyes and smelled the scent of her, rising from the warmth still trapped in her hair. The current pulled heavily on her skirts and yanked on his legs.

"Hold tight."

He headed back toward the shore, each step careful, the bundle held tight in his arms. Something banged against the log, dislodging it from the shore. It shot past them as they climbed out of the water, disappearing beyond the outcropping. He fell to his knees on the rock, dragging Genevieve up with him.

André held her while she coughed the last of the river from her lungs, hacking until he knew her throat was sore and raw. He ran his hands over her body, warming her, searching for injury. She was as skinny as a wet kitten. The remnants of her skirts clung to her legs, and her leggings sagged over one foot. She'd lost her moccasins in the rapids and her right foot protruded, bare and unprotected, but nothing seemed broken. He boldly felt the swell of her breasts, felt her heart beating rapidly beneath her bosom, then he dragged her hips closer and lay atop her, his body sheltering her from the cold air, his loins pressed into hers, where they belonged.

Where they belonged.

He framed her face in his hands. She trembled like a wild thing, her lips tinged purple from the cold. Her skin was so pale and translucent that he could see the bluish veins beneath the surface of her cheeks, and her freckles stood out like flecks of cinnamon. A gritty streak of mud stained her forehead and a dozen welts seared her skin where she had been struck by debris. He knew he should just hold her, for she was weak and exhausted, hurt and dangerously cold, but those damned eyes, those damned bruised, frightened, grateful eyes . . .

Her lips were as cold as ice, but the inside of her mouth was not—it was warm and fragrant and soft and welcoming, and he tasted the sweet, crystal purity of the mountain water on her tongue. This was Genevieve, his wife, spit back at him from the hell into which he'd sent her. The fierce wanting gripped him. He kissed the one woman on earth he had forbidden himself to touch.

Her heart pounded loudly against him. He pressed a hand against her chest, against the sound, feeling the proof of her survival vibrate against his fingers. Beneath her shivering skin he felt the coursing of her blood, the trembling of muscle, the rush of air in and out of her lungs. Genevieve broke free to catch her breath. He tasted the sweet river water running in rivulets over her temples, dripping from the soft lobe of her right ear, dampening the heat of her long neck, pooling in the fragrant hollow of her throat.

Her chest filled and collapsed with every deep, ragged breath. André rolled her nipple, as hard as a pearl, against his palm. He looked up into her eyes . . . eyes that had brightened to the color of sunlight falling on a shaded forest pool. Relief poured through him, mingling with passion, with that blind, reckless yearning. *She's alive, alive, alive* . . .

"I knew . . . you would find me." Her voice was husky and raw. "I knew . . . you wouldn't . . . let me die."

And suddenly he realized that his breechcloth was full with passion, that he was seducing her here, on the banks of the river, when he had just pulled her from the maelstrom of the white water. What the hell was he doing? What the hell was she turning him into, this red-haired chit of a girl? She was hurt, she was frozen, and he could think of nothing else but laying with her.

André gathered her limp form in his arms and rose to his feet, guilt stabbing through him. How had she crawled so deep under his skin? Why did he push her and push her, test her over and over, though he knew—damn it, he *knew* she could survive anything she faced? Now he'd pushed her over the edge of a canoe into some of the most vicious white water he'd ever run. In some black part of his heart, did he want her dead? Was he destined to murder every wife he had?

No. He gripped her tightly, feeling the contours of her wet body press against him. He was her enemy, yes, her enemy, for she wanted something from him that he would never give. She would never be safe in his presence. He'd wanted her *frightened*, not dead. He'd wanted her so frightened that *she'd* run away from *him*. For he knew, from somewhere deep inside, that he couldn't let her go.

He was fighting to protect her from himself. And then he knew the truth.

The raw emotion roared inside him, primitive and undeniable, an emotion he dared not name.

Chapter Twelve

Genevieve drifted on a warm cloud. She felt as tranquil and comfortable as a well-fed babe swaddled in soft cloth and held against her mother's breast. Sounds drifted in and out of her consciousness: the voices of the *voyageurs* as they argued, the wind soughing in the trees, and something flapping, like the billowing sails of a ship. The scents of spicy pine fires and sweet tobacco smoke floated around her. She heard rustling nearby and felt gentle hands massaging the arches of her feet.

It was this languorous sensation that tempted her from the edges of her slumber. Genevieve blinked her eyes open and examined her surroundings. She was inside a tent, a tent whose sides collapsed and extended with the battering of the wind. In the corner, a strange collection of round stones radiated feeble waves of heat. A heavy deerskin blanket smothered her from the chin down. She pushed the soft,

smoke-ripened leather away from her face and peered
around the rest of the tent.

"Awake, *Taouistaouisse?*"

She saw his eyes first, gold and intense. He sat just
inside the entrance to the tent, cross-legged, wrapped
in a woolen blanket. Beneath the blanket his chest
was bare. His beaded bag swung against the hollow
of his chest as he kneaded her left foot.

"You've been out since yesterday afternoon." He
ran his thumb over the pads of her toes. "I was beginning to think you'd sleep till All Saint's."

The foggy remnants of her languor skittered away
as she remembered the terrible sucking of the rapids,
the white blindness, the icy rolling, and the feel of
the frigid water gorging her lungs. Genevieve sucked
in a ragged breath and felt the soreness in her chest.
She didn't dare move, for even lying still, she could
feel the aches in her joints, the bruises on her skin,
the sting of a hundred scratches.

His warm hand tightened around her ankle. "Are
you all right?"

"I don't know." She swallowed dryly. "Am I?"

His hand gently traced the bone that ran over the
top of her foot to her big toe. "You're safe now.
Nothing's broken. Your legs and arms are scratched
up, and you'll be blue with bruises for a few days."

She carefully wiggled her fingers and tested her
limbs, wincing as pain shot through her body.

"Lie still, little bird."

She groaned as she tried to twist, and every muscle
and joint screamed in complaint. "I feel like someone
has spent the night scraping me against a washing
board."

"Lie still."

His hair fell over his brow as he concentrated on
her foot, rubbing the hollow behind her anklebone

with his thumb, then digging his fingers gently into her arches. It felt good, the slow, soothing caresses, and she was reluctant to speak anymore, reluctant to distract him from his work, for the warmth of his touch seeped up her leg and eased some of the soreness in her muscles. She watched the way his hair fell over his face, the way his large-boned hands spread over her sole, the way his fingers found all the tense points between her toes and gently pressed them until she closed her eyes, easing into forgetful slumber.

"It was my fault."

Genevieve blinked open her eyes. She looked down at him, confused. His concentration remained on her feet.

"The rapids below the falls are dangerous." He put her left foot down and picked up the right, warming her toes in his palm. "But they're more unpredictable when the water is low. I wasn't paying attention." The blanket slipped off his shoulder, showing a long, strong clavicle and a deep hollow behind it. "My mind was on other things."

She remembered something, a flash of a memory, powerful and vivid. He stood at the stern of the canoe, soaked from head to toe, the white swath of the falls roaring behind him, his teeth bared in a reckless smile. His deerskin clung to the muscles of his chest and arms like a second skin. His hair was swept back from his face and his eyes were like molten gold upon her.

"I managed to climb on a rock in the white water after the canoe tipped. I saw The Duke save himself and the canoe, but I couldn't see you." His hands curled over her toes. "I swam the rapids myself, and I still couldn't find you."

Genevieve eased herself up on her elbows, watching the intensity of his features as he kneaded her foot.

She remembered when he had found her, but only vaguely, for it wasn't long after that that she had fallen into the darkness. She remembered the strength in his arms as he bore her up, the warmth of his chest as he held her tight against him. She remembered feeling safe. She remembered thinking that no man who caressed her like this could hate her, no man who held her with such desperation could wish her harm.

Strange thoughts. Born out of sentiment, she supposed, or out of the terror of the moment. She dismissed them. "I'm here. What difference—"

"If I had been a minute later, you'd be at the bottom of the Lake of the Hurons."

She shivered, with a cold that came from her heart, not from the chill air around them. For all her struggles in Paris, she'd never come so close to death before, had never felt its breath on her skin.

She shook off the feeling. "It was an accident."

"Do you believe that?" His eyes flickered up at her. "Or do you think I'm trying to send you to the Great Hunting Grounds before your time?"

She drew in a soft breath. The Great Hunting Grounds was The Duke's version of Heaven—the place beyond the sea where all departed spirits thrived, living on the souls of the animals they had killed during their lifetimes. She wondered why he'd think she'd suspect him of such a thing . . . and knew the answer even as the thought formed. *Rose-Marie.*

Something inside her reached out to him. How long would he torment himself with a past over which he had no control? How long would he look into her face and see the ghost of his dead wife? He must have loved that woman deeply, to hold on to such guilt for so long. The thought brought a new stab of jealousy.

"What's this?" She hated herself for the petulance in her voice. "Is the wolf feeling remorse?"

"You thought I had a scheme. You said as much before we left Montréal. I put you in danger. *Intentionally.*"

"You warned me over and over about the dangers of this journey." Genevieve straightened to a sitting position, ignoring the pain shooting up to her shoulders. "It's a little late for a case of conscience—"

She cut herself off, for his hand had tightened over her foot like a vise. She looked down and realized the blankets had fallen to her waist, and she was naked. The pink tips of her breasts tightened into buds beneath his perusal.

Genevieve clutched the sagging deerskin, then crossed her arms over her chest.

"I tried to ease my conscience." His gaze slipped over the deerskin as if nothing covered her body. "When we made camp, I stripped off your clothes and hung them up to dry. I told myself I needed to tend to your cuts and bruises."

Her hair fell over her shoulders as she lowered her head. *He* had stripped her naked. "Indian women joined us at Allumette Island," she murmured, remembering the small canoes of the squaws, which had grown in number every day behind the flotilla. "You could have sent one of them to care for me."

"I wanted to do it. It was my fault you were so battered." His hand felt hot on her foot. "You have freckles on your thighs."

She drew in a sharp breath. "How gentlemanly of you to notice."

"I kissed them, Genevieve." His voice flowed over her like trickles of sand. "I was supposed to be tending your wounds. Instead, I followed the trail up your inner thigh. You moaned in your sleep."

Her heart pounded in her chest. Her thighs quivered like bowstrings. She probably had moaned. She probably had opened her legs wider, inviting him to explore more. For two weeks she had battled to suppress her desire for this man, since the day on Calumet Island, but her body stubbornly refused to listen to the dictates of her mind. Whatever else had happened between them, she could not deny this primitive, uncontrollable passion.

He leaned closer to her. His hand slipped up, under the covers, to caress the taut muscle of her calf. "You were in danger then, too, *Taouistaouisse*."

"Did . . . did you . . ."

"I wanted to." His fingernails dug into her calf. "I wanted to take you right there, while you lay beneath me. But I didn't. I want you awake when I make love to you. I want to see your eyes."

She could no longer feel the bruises and stinging welts that riddled her body. All she could feel was the hollow ache in her abdomen and his callused hands on the bare skin of her calves. He made no move to caress any higher than the tender hollow behind her knee, though she silently screamed for him to clutch her thighs, to lean forward just a little more and kiss her. . . . But Genevieve knew though he might be a ruthless, lustful, determined wolf, he had some scruples. He wouldn't take her unless she allowed him.

So here she was, in the very position she'd wanted to be in since she set out on this wretched voyage. But everything had changed that day on Calumet Island. She couldn't give herself to a man who promised her nothing in return but poverty and hardship. By sheer luck, she'd saved that one precious part of her, as the only treasure she truly had, to be given to the man who'd be her husband and protector. . . . She couldn't give it to a man who would, without second thought, abandon her in the middle of a forest full of savages. Not to a man who wouldn't live up to his vows.

Even if he did give her blankets and leggings to keep her warm. Even if he did ride the rapids for her comfort, and then hold her in desperation when he pulled her out of the white water.

She couldn't give this part of herself to a man who didn't love her as, God help her, she loved him.

Her head throbbed. She squeezed her eyes shut. She was too confused to sort this all out, not now, when she had just awoken from her slumber, and his touch was making her weak and trembly. He shouldn't take advantage of her weakness, but she should expect no less from him.

"Damn it, Genevieve, you shouldn't look at a man like that."

He slid his hands down to her ankles, settling back with a growl of a sigh. When she opened her eyes, he'd reached between his legs and lifted up two pieces of buff-colored deerskin decorated with dyed porcupine quills.

"Here," he said gruffly. "You lost your moccasins in the river. I bought these from one of the squaws."

He yanked the whisper-soft material over her foot. She forced her voice not to quiver, not to show how close she'd come to succumbing. "Are we breaking camp?"

"Not yet." He slipped the second moccasin on her other foot. "The men spent yesterday afternoon patching the hole in the canoe with birch bark and caulking it watertight. It needs to dry well before it'll be ready for use. Tomorrow is soon enough to travel."

Her brows knitted. She'd been on this voyage long enough to know the rhythm of the campsite. If the canoe wasn't already watertight, she'd smell the pungent scent of heated spruce gum in the air, or she'd hear the *voyageurs* working upon it. But all she could hear was good-natured laughter, an occasional outraged shout, and the clatter of dice on stone.

He was lying to her.

"I'll bring you some *sagamité*. One of the men shot a deer yesterday, so there's fresh venison." He yanked the blanket down over her legs. "Your clothes should be dry by tomorrow. I'll get you some brandy."

Genevieve pulled her brows together more. He had jealously guarded their precious, illicit stores of brandy since the first day out of Lachine, when all the men were given a single ceremonial tote of the fiery liquid. He had driven the men onward in the worst of rains, even forcing them out on Lake Nipissing during a storm, and now he was allowing them to take a day off to rest, when their journey was far from over and the air seeping through the ragged edges of the tent was nippy with the threat of winter.

He's doing it for me.

She watched him as he rearranged the heating stones with a stick, wondering if she'd ever understand the man who sliced deep wounds with one hand, then healed them with the gentle caress of the other.

"André . . ."

His name slipped through her lips without conscious thought, and a quiver warmed her body as he turned and fixed her with those molten golden eyes.

What am I doing? Her breath rushed through her lips. She couldn't close her eyes. She couldn't block out the sight of him, tall and strong, his shaggy hair falling over his shoulders, his chest bare and hard . . . *my husband.*

No . . . not her husband yet, but a man torn between honor and his own passions; a man torn by guilt and the fear of making the same mistake twice; a man who kept pushing her away . . . to protect her, perhaps? She didn't know. She couldn't think now, not with so much emotion muddling her senses.

She shouldn't feel like this—a woman like her— but she'd never felt like this before, and some secret part of her wondered if she ever would again. Some secret part of her whispered, *Love him. . . . Know what it is to love a man. Have a memory to hold against the others that still lurk in the shadows. . . . Purify me, André, baptize me.*

"There must be . . . a way." She bit her lower lip on the words, hating herself for not having the sense to keep quiet, for not listening to that instinct of self-preservation screaming in her head, for allowing herself to hope again. "For us to . . . to prevent . . . complications. Like before. Isn't there?"

André didn't think. He'd long moved beyond the point where he could think clearly when it came to the woman looking up at him with hope and desire in her eyes. He reacted to those innocent, hesitant words by clutching a handful of the deerskin blanket and yanking it clear off her body.

There she lay, all rosy flesh on a pelt of fur, naked as the day she was born, her thighs pressed together and her knees raised, her arms crossing instinctively over her full breasts. His mind conjured up a thousand images of how he could love that body, how he could caress and kiss and suck her flesh into ecstasy, imagining how she would feel and taste, the texture of her deepest flesh.

He dropped to one knee, prying open her thighs, viewing her moist inner core, touching her with one bare hand. She bucked and gasped in surprise, then relaxed and looked down at him with eyes soft with wanting. She grew hot and moist, welcoming his hand.

Something inside him cracked. *I'll give you what you want, wife.*

He fell atop her, between her legs, then clutched them at the backs of her knees and lifted them up, up, so her sex lay open beneath the tumescence straining against his breechcloth. He ground himself against her, seeking the heat pulsing beyond the thin barrier of deerskin.

Color rushed to her cheeks as she squeezed her eyes shut and thrashed her head back, arching against him. He released her legs and clutched her wrists, dragging them high above her head, holding her tight beneath him with one hand.

Her neck tasted of salt and musky woman. With his tongue he felt the vibrations of a groan flutter in her throat. Sweet, foolish, reckless, dangerous woman . . . *look what you've done to me.* The mindless heat burned away all pretense of tenderness. She was all yielding flesh beneath him, soft and small and trembling. And he took, and took. He turned her chin and kissed her hard, sinking his tongue deep into her mouth as it gave way to him, then clutched one breast pressing against his shoulder, beading the nipple between his fingers, scraping it against his palm, then sucking on it—hard, deep—drawing it against the back of his throat.

What does it take to make you scream, woman? Even now, when she should be fighting against this assault, she ground her hips up to him instead, bucking beneath the restraint—a wild virgin, deaf to all but the cries of her own body. He should give up trying to frighten her away; but the woman would not run, the fool of a woman would stay, damn her.

He reached down and tugged free the ties of his

breechcloth, shoving the leather between them out of the way.

Hot, slick, *wet*. He ground his shaft against the crease of her womanhood, back and forth, back and forth, the damp essence of her licking his most sensitive flesh from tip to root. This was the closest they could get without him taking what he wanted, the closest he could come to temptation. She quivered beneath him and he felt every throb; she struggled to loose her hands from his grip.

No. He would not loosen her. If he did, he'd lose every last bit of restraint, that tiny leash that kept him from plunging *in* at an angle each time he drew back, each time he felt the heat of her center blast against the tip of him; that's where he wanted to be, that's where he belonged.

Her body tensed and she growled a tight cry. He dragged his hand under the hollow of her back, then wedged his fingers beneath her buttocks, lifting her hips against him even as she arched, even as she cried out and swelled against his loins, reaching her climax already, already.

He squeezed his eyes shut and buried his face in her neck, his fingers digging deep into the soft flesh of her bottom as the same swelling tightened his tumescence to the thin edge of bursting. *I belong inside you, woman. I want to touch that center of you forbidden to me. . . .*

Then he pulled back and the tip of him lodged in that throbbing, hot place . . . and for one crazed second he bucked, slipping slightly between those lips. He felt his soul cushioned there, welcomed, soft, home, he wanted to be here, to explode here, and then the bursting rushed up on him . . .

And in one shout of frustration he pulled away and ground his shaft on her belly, releasing the flood of passion, easing the tightness on the soft hollow of her abdomen until the strain ebbed away . . . to an aching throb of frustration.

André rolled off her. His heart hammered against his rib cage as he stared up at the bellowing tarpaulin of the tent. The air was full of the sound of their harsh breathing, while outside the men went about their day, laughing, joking, and a bird in some nearby branch lilted a mournful song.

Genevieve nudged her cheek against his arm. He lifted it and guided her into the nook of his throat, rolling her warm body tight against his side.

She sighed, long and contentedly, then tilted her head to look up at him, a smile quivering on the corners of her lips. "Maybe . . . maybe we can have a wonderful winter after all."

"Maybe, Genny. Maybe."

He kissed her to hide the truth. At the touch of her warm, soft lips, passion stirred anew in his aching body. It wasn't enough, this half-loving. By God, he was greedy. He had to have all of her—or nothing at all.

As the kiss deepened, as their bodies rolled together, André knew he would not be able to suffer this mockery of lovemaking for an entire season. For now, yes, for now . . .

But for her sake, he must give her one last chance to escape, before he took what no man, no woman, and no conscience could deny him any longer.

"It's right over this ridge."

Genevieve glared at André. He leaned toward her and held out his hand. The golden rays of the setting sun poured over the hill and silhouetted his muscular form. It seemed as if they had been climbing this steep slope for hours, though she knew the campsite lay just below them, nestled in a tiny cove against the hill. Her body still ached from the incident in the rapids, and from the choppy ride from the mouth of the French River to this island in the Lake of the Hurons, and from their frequent, acrobatic lovemaking these past days. For the hundredth time, she wondered what was so important for her to see that he insisted she climb this wretched mountain.

Genevieve clutched his hand, curling her fingers in his. "This better be worth it, or I vow you're carrying me down."

André smiled and pulled her over the slick, moss-covered boulder, holding tight until she found firm footing. Then he released her and wound his way to the height of the hill.

Genevieve followed at a slower pace, picking her way among the loose stones and the grasses poking stubbornly from the fissures in the rock. She loosened the deerskin blanket around her shoulders, for the exertion of the climb made her much-mended dress stick uncomfortably to her skin. She watched him beneath lowered lashes as he sauntered to the height of the hill.

They'd reached a wary peace since they'd started loving in the tent every night. The tight fury that had always shone in his eyes whenever he looked her way had now been replaced by something else. Something hard, something bittersweet and fatalistic. For all their intimacy, for all their teasing love-words, she was no closer to André's heart than before she'd succumbed to her own weakness.

Genevieve kicked aside a loose rock and followed its path with her gaze. There she went again, expecting more than she could ever have, expecting some sort of *caring*, of all things, just because she'd revealed her body to a man. She knew better. Men and women were different creatures. For a woman, even a woman like her, it *meant* something to open her body to a man. For a man, it was just another function like coughing or sneezing—except it gave much more pleasure and required at best a willing partner. She'd told herself to be pleased with this uneasy, tentative friendship, with the hot, healing passion they shared beneath the furs—and to expect no more.

She *was* pleased . . . sort of. Genevieve ran her hands up her arms, memory coursing warm ripples of passion through her blood. For all the swift fierceness of that first time, André had become a most careful lover. The kissing, the touching, the heat of their bodies pressed so tightly together under the deerskin blankets in the chill of the night. . . . Yet she was honest enough with herself to recognize that always . . . always at that most crucial moment when she wanted most to be close, he wasn't there. For all the pleasure, she'd learned to live with a vague disappointment, a yearning for something greater.

Genevieve shook the troubling thoughts from her mind as she met him atop the ridge. The wind blew up over the side and struck her, cold and forceful, lifting her braid from her shoulders and chilling the spots of sweat on her chest and under her arms. She looked at the scene and sucked in her breath.

They stood on the highest point on Manitoulin Island, the apex of a long ridge that stretched westward, rising out of the meadow like the exposed bare spine of the earth. An amber glow bathed the bald, wrinkled granite as the cold northern sun sank in the west. From this elevation, she could see the entire length of the isle, the random scattering of other rocky outcroppings in the bay, and the whole sparkling extent of the Lake of the Hurons, which spread like an inland sea to the southern horizon.

André didn't give her an opportunity to enjoy the view. He took her arm and drew her to the very edge of the ridge. "The Duke told me they would be here." He peered down into the valley below. "He said for centuries they've been coming. Look."

Her brows knitted as she noticed a large shadow hovering in the valley. She gasped when she realized the shadow was moving.

"They're called *wapiti*—elk."

There were hundreds of them, chewing on what remained of the straggly grass that carpeted the valley. They were large and buff-coated, some with many-branched antlers. Smaller ones frolicked along the edge, scampering across the meadow and raising their snouts to the chill wind. Others stood partially submerged in a shining ribbon of a stream that wound its way into the waters of the Lake of the Hurons.

"How did they get here?" She looked behind her. Even from the height of the ridge, she could see the whitecaps on the choppy bay waters. "They couldn't have swum that bay from the mainland. We nearly tipped a dozen times between the mouth of the French River and here."

"The Duke says every winter a herd of *wapiti* walk to this island upon the ice of the frozen bay and become trapped here when the ice breaks. They fatten on the grasses over the summer, and in the fall his people come and hunt them." André shrugged and straightened. "At least they used to, before the Iroquois scattered the Hurons westward."

She had never seen so many animals—*wapiti*—in one place. In France, even in the densest forests, the deer did not run so thick. Here, the beasts ate unmolested, enough to feed a dozen Indian villages for the winter, fighting and bumping each other for space across the grassy meadow.

Genevieve hugged her blanket around her shoulders, listening as the mewling of the elk rose up the side of the hill with the wind. It was as if this place had not changed since the beginning of time. It was as if the world was new and fresh, as if it were the eighth day of creation, and she and André stood high atop the earth, watching it all.

"It's beautiful here." She whispered the words, as if afraid to break the silence. "It's like Eden must have been."

He looked at her, his eyes shadowed. "Most people think of it as barren and merciless."

"There are aristocrats in France who would kill to hunt here."

"But this isn't a gentle place. There are bears and wolves. Wildcats. Don't you find it savage?"

"No." Paris was savage. Civilization was savage. This was as natural as God meant it to be. "A person could live here, grow fat on the land, and never want for anything."

"Not even a soft feather mattress? Or lace or jewels?"

She frowned. Those were things an aristocrat would want, that Marie Duplessis might want, but those were things that Genevieve Lalande had long learned to live without. She shrugged as nonchalantly as she could. "Well, of course, those things could be imported."

André laughed, showing a flash of white teeth, and she watched him until the sound faded. He'd been so unpredictable since the incident in the rapids. One moment he was warning her of the danger she was in, and the next he was burning his hands bringing heated stones into the tent, or tenderly brushing her hair out of her face when he thought she was sleeping, or dragging her up a hillside to show her an enormous herd of elk. She wished she could reconcile the two men. The first one she didn't fully understand, but this one, the one who laughed beside her, she loved with the full of her heart.

They watched the sun sink beyond the horizon and the sky fade slowly from sapphire to indigo. They did not speak. Somehow, it felt right, to be standing here, alone with André, with the whole world spread at their feet.

And as the moments stretched and he didn't touch her, she realized that there was another reason he had brought her to this place, for he was not a man to wait for the loving. She waited, sensing the tension growing in his body as the night closed in around them.

"We must talk, *Taouistaouisse.*"

She pulled the blanket tight around her shoulders and looked up toward the sky. The first evening stars winked down at her from the heavens. "So there is more to this than a lesson on the fauna of the Huron country?"

"I wanted you to see this." He paced unsurely, weaving his hair into disarray. "But since the accident, my men have been like mother hens around a wounded chick, and I need to be alone with you, away from them."

Genevieve shivered, but not from the coolness of the evening. There was a seriousness in his voice. She wasn't sure she wanted to hear what he had to say; she didn't want anything resolved between them, not yet. She wanted to enjoy this half-life for now. Half a life was better than none.

"The Indians at Lake Nipissing told me that the Black Robes—the Jesuits—have settled in a place a day's ride from here." He crouched down, picked up an egg-shaped rock, and ran his fingers over the smooth surface. "They've built a mission near the river that flows out of Lake Superior into this lake. They've called it Sault Sainte Marie. We'll be there tomorrow."

Her spine stiffened. A Jesuit outpost, a day's ride away. Suddenly, she knew what he intended to tell her. "We've had this conversation before."

He palmed the rock from one hand to the other, digging his nails into the grain. "You'll be safe at the mission. The Jesuits will treat you well."

"My answer is still no."

He flinched, as if he had been struck in the back. "You don't understand—"

"No, *you* don't understand." She had hoped he had brought her up here for another reason, and she couldn't hide her anger that the skunk hadn't changed his stripes. "Did you think that ride in the rapids made me daft?"

"I thought it might have knocked some sense into you." His fist closed over the stone. "You'd be better off wed to a man who can give you a home. A man who will stay with you—in Québec."

"Yes, I would." She stepped toward him, and he stood up abruptly. She had never seen him so edgy, so uneasy. "But until this marriage is annulled, I'm your responsibility. You've got a house out there. We're not far away from it now. I'm staying in that house this winter. I thought I made that clear; I thought we had an arrangement."

"As long as you're with me, you're in danger. I told you yesterday—"

André cut himself off, then vaulted the rock into the darkness. He turned his back to her, shook his head, and planted his hands on his hips.

Her anger dissipated as a suspicion lodged in her mind. It was a wondrous thought, something she almost didn't dare believe.

Genevieve approached him. She placed her hand on his back, just below his shoulder blade. His muscles were taut and firm beneath the deerskin. "André . . . why are you trying to get rid of me again? After all that's happened?"

"We—you and I—we can't live in the same house." He didn't turn around. "Not over the winter. It wouldn't work."

A hot flush bathed her cheeks, but she didn't move. He wanted to send her away to someplace safe, to someplace where he wouldn't have to face, daily, his own desire for her; someplace where he wouldn't have to fight it anymore. *It is as powerful for him as it is for me.*

When she spoke, her voice was breathless. "Why wouldn't it work?"

"I haven't changed my mind about annulling this marriage next spring. But if you stay with me, things will happen between us that I can no longer . . . control."

"But—"

"No buts." He turned around and clutched her shoulders. "This is your last chance. If you don't go with the Jesuits, then I'll do things to you. I'll take you the way *I* want, whether you want me to or not."

Her breath caught in her throat. It was as if a storm had suddenly blown into the valley, and they were two turbulent clouds, facing one another, the tension stretching so taut between them that she could do nothing but wait for the lightning to ignite.

And she knew the truth, in that second of hesitation, in that eternity when they gazed at each other and saw the matching naked need reflected in each other's eyes. This is what he'd hidden from her these past nights; this is what his body had screamed to her but his mind had denied. She knew, with a certainty as ageless and strong as the mountain beneath her feet, that he was in love with her.

He was trying to protect her from himself.

Raggedly, he said, "Stay with the Jesuits."

She shook her head blindly. Her heart pounded in her chest. He was trying to send her away so she would be safe from him. He was denying his own desires for her protection. But if he loved her, he would never hurt her, despite all the meaningless vows he repeated by rote.

Genevieve thought about all the risks she had taken to come to Québec, to marry this man, and to join him on this voyage. Now, the acrid taste of death had sharpened her hunger for life, dulling her fear of the risks. There was one last gamble she could make, one final cast of the dice, and the prize was Paradise itself. *He loves me.* She felt as reckless as a drunkard wagering the last of his begging money on sevens, a drunkard who knew the dice were weighted in his favor.

She boldly cast the bones.

Genevieve let her deerskin blanket slip off her shoulders, to fall in a pool by her feet. She leaned toward him, brushing his shirt with her breasts, flattening her hands on his shoulders. "I don't care anymore, André. I want you to . . . to do those things to me. *All* those things."

His eyes flared. His fingers dug into her shoulders until they hurt. "I warned you. God help me, I warned you."

They were nothing but words. His body and his kisses and his hands spoke more eloquently and more truthfully, and it was these she listened to, not the incoherent murmurings of his voice, for it was these that told her of his love, that spoke of his desire so strongly that she felt it in the marrow of her bones. He buried his hand in her hair and eased her head back, pressing his mouth against hers. His other arm wound around her like steel, crushing her body against his until she could feel every muscle in his frame.

He pulled away, watching her face as her lips parted, begging for more. "Sweet Jesus, Genny."

Her hand slid up the front of his shirt, grasping the open ends of the edge. She wished she had the strength to rend the skin in two so there would be nothing more between them. His lips captured hers, hard, slanting across her mouth possessively. His kiss screamed of aching hunger, of angry desire too long denied. His beard brushed her cheek, her chin, as soft as a bird's feathers. She opened her mouth at his urging and felt the glorious roughness of his tongue against hers, tasting her, drinking her passion like a man dying of thirst. She succumbed to him, saying wordlessly, *Take my body. Take my soul. Make love to me, André.*

They tumbled to the ground, landing partly on her deerskin blanket, partly on the cold granite. The butt of his pistol and the handle of his knife dug into her abdomen as his weight fell upon her. He kissed a trail of fire down to her collarbone and she wove her fingers in his soft hair. He untied the laces of her bodice, then brushed aside the edges and closed his hand over her full breast. Then he raised his head, met her eyes, and captured her lips once again.

She ran her fingers over his beard, cupping his face, drawing him closer and drinking the love from his lips. His anxious fingers centered on the nub hardening at the tip of her breast, poking through the threadbare chemise. She groaned, deep in the back of her throat. He released her lips, and her head fell gently back against the pillow of granite. He took the ridge of her chin in his mouth, the curve of her throat, the edge of her jutting collarbone. Then, after a chill moment as he shifted his weight, his hot lips closed over her distended nipple, chemise and all.

Her hands, lost in his hair, curled into fists, capturing long tresses between her tight fingers. The worn fabric of her shift cooled in the evening air whenever he moved his lips, chilling the nub to tautness. Impatiently, he yanked the edge of her chemise down, exposing her naked breast to his gaze, taking the throbbing peak into his hungry mouth.

André . . . She didn't know if she had spoken his name or if it just lingered in her mind, a silent murmuring of her passion. He was taking possession of her, with his warm lips and callused fingers and strong will, taking possession of her like he never had before. Vaguely, she felt him tugging up her skirts. She loosened her grip on his hair and spread her fingers over the taut muscles of his back. She felt his fingers skimming her deerskin-bound calves, hesitating on the flesh just above the ribboned garter of her hose. Genevieve arched instinctively in his arms, wanting him to touch her as he had before, to give her that sweet, sweet joy, wanting more than anything to finally give that full joy to him. His fingers continued their unerring journey up the inside of her thigh, until they brushed against her secret curls.

The thickness of his deerskin shirt scraped against the rosy peak of her breast as he slid up to meet her gaze. Their breaths misted between them, for the sun had long set and the earth had given up the lingering threads of the day's warmth. She felt none of the cold, not even the icy hard granite against the back of her head. Her blood pumped hot beneath her skin and he warmed her like a blazing fire with his gaze alone. The stars twinkled in a sky as soft as dark purple velvet, and they seemed to swell and come closer as he touched her.

She was lost. Utterly. It was as if she were caught in the rapids again, drawn irrevocably along with the rush and gurgle, helpless against a force much more powerful than herself. But there was a difference. Now there was no terror, no choking blindness, nothing but a pleasure so exquisite, Genevieve thought she might happily die from it. He brushed his lips against hers, murmuring her name with a tremor, urging her deeper into the vortex. He kissed the hollow beneath her earlobe, the pounding vein in her throat, the tender white skin between her neck and her shoulder. He returned, relentlessly, to her lips, taking her bottom lip between his, then her top one, teasing her with his tongue and his gentle fingers at the same time.

She flattened her hands on his shoulders, then dragged them down between their bodies, feeling his heart pounding like a blacksmith's hammer in his chest. His fingers paused for the briefest moment, then plunged into her, moving in swift, hungry strokes in and out of her quivering body. His tumescence throbbed against her hip, and she wanted him to touch her with his sex, to fill her with a husband's need, finally, finally.

"Make love to me."

She barely recognized her voice, it was so husky, so strangled, her throat so tight with desire. He shifted his weight off her and she felt the frigid air bathing her bare thighs. Genevieve made no attempt to hide herself, though one breast was exposed to the yawning sky and her skirts were piled high on her hips. She wanted him. She wanted him to see how much she wanted him.

His pistol and knife clattered to the ground. He ripped off his sash and fumbled beneath the hem of his shirt. Rolling his weight atop her, he braced himself with his elbows on either side of her face. He nudged her knees apart with his but she needed no prodding. She arched against his hips and his throbbing member pressed intimately against her inner thigh.

André brushed the hair away from her face, his fingers lingering on the curve of her jaw. He looked down at her with such intensity that she lifted her hand and brushed his soft beard. He kissed her hand, one finger at a time. André shifted his hips and pressed against the warm entrance to the core of her body, stopping as she felt him lodge against something—something she knew instinctively was the thin membrane of her maidenhead.

"Only a moment's pain," she whispered. Every sinew in her body strained toward the promise of release. "I would suffer worse for you."

It was a single, sharp pain, a startling twinge, forgotten a moment later.

Then he filled her.

It was a sensation more exquisite than a cool bath in the still, humid heat of summer, more shocking than the tingle of the wine of Champagne on her tongue, more explosive than the fireworks she had seen the day Louis XIV had married the Spanish Infanta. André throbbed deep, deep inside her, as if he had become a part of her body. She lifted her hips higher, taking him in, possessing him even as he possessed her. They were one, man and woman, lover and mate.

Genevieve moaned and squeezed her eyes shut.

This is what she'd missed all those times before; this was the fulfillment. His weight fell against her and he murmured something unintelligible in the hair above her temple. Her hands found their way beneath the hem of his fringed shirt, tracing the tense muscles of his back, feeling the heat of his skin. He moved in her and her soul moved with him.

He stroked. Again. Deeper.

And suddenly, she was the summer sun, aflame in passion. Suddenly, she was the wine of Champagne—all sweetness and bubbles and gathering pressure. Then, as he stroked again, touching a part of her that had never before been touched, she became the fireworks, exploding in the air in a frenzy of color, showering like a thousand glowing sparks over the great open sky.

Chapter Thirteen

André lay atop Genevieve, his face lost in her hair, his loins still buried intimately in hers. His breath eluded him. He struggled to inhale and then exhale, to slow the racing of his pulse, to find his bearings, but his senses seemed to have scattered to the four corners of the earth.

He had wanted her this way for so long, had fantasized about caressing her, had spent entire nights straining *not* to do this. Nothing in his imagination could match the feel of her warm body throbbing around him, the salt-and-woman taste of her skin, the delicious sound of her cries of pleasure, and the heat and pressure of her womanhood sheathing him, even now. There was more than a little madness in this joining. He had lost part of himself—the part that reasoned, the part that knew better than to spill his seed into a woman's body.

André pushed the thought aside. There had been

too much between them, and she had been so wet, so hot, so eager, so tight. He couldn't stop, he couldn't pull away—not anymore. He knew he would feel guilty later, when he found his senses and realized the possible consequences of his lack of control, but he didn't want to think about it right now. His body and his mind were still reeling. Nothing mattered but the feel of her naked flesh against his, the final echoes of her pleasure pulsating through her frame, and the brush of her hot breath against his neck.

Genevieve shifted languidly beneath him. He kissed her temple, then lifted himself on his elbows to look down upon her face. Her lips were soft and parted, her cheeks dark with a flush. Her eyes mirrored his own lingering surprise, his own sense of dazed rapture.

Her mouth trembled in a hesitant smile. "We've done it."

"Yes, *ma mie.*"

She closed her eyes and sighed, then tightened her arms around him. "This is a thousand times better than wintering with the Jesuits."

He couldn't quite smile. Her comment reminded him that he had tried to send her away; he had tried to save her, and he had failed. The guilt pierced his lethargy, and this time he could not push it aside.

"Come." He shifted his weight. "You must be cold."

She clutched his arms as he tried to rise. "Let's stay here for a while."

"We'll stay." He traced her lips with one finger. "But I'm crushing you, and the ground must be hard against your back."

She released his arms, wincing as he gently pulled away, separating their loins. His guilt increased. He had had little experience with virgins—except for

Rose-Marie, and that seemed like a hundred thousand years ago. His tastes had always veered toward women of lesser virtue, and in the mad fog of their lovemaking, he had no idea how badly he had hurt her. André looked down and saw bloodstains on her inner thighs.

"It's cold." Genevieve sat up and tossed her skirts over her legs, then wrapped her arms around herself. She pulled her rumpled deerskin blanket from beneath her hips. "Come keep me warm under this."

"You're bleeding."

"That's what happens the first time, isn't it?" She pulled the blanket across her shoulders. "Proof of my virtue and all that."

"We should clean you up—"

"Not now." She spread her arms, holding the blanket behind her like a cape. "It's not likely I'll bleed to death, but I will freeze if you don't hold me and keep me warm."

He lay back down on the ground, reaching for her and pulling her small body fully on top of him. A dozen pebbles dug into his back, and André realized how hard a bed he had given her for her deflowering. She spread the blanket over her back, kicking it down so it covered his legs and protected them both from the cold air. She sighed deeply and pressed her cheek against his chest.

For a long time they lay in silence. André listened to the murmur of the late autumn night and smelled the tart but distant scent of rain on the wind. He stared blindly up into the star-filled sky as he ran his hands through her tangled hair and down the length of her back. His mind raced with so many conflicting emotions, with so much guilt, yet lying with her body warm and still atop him, he felt an unusual, rare sort of peace.

"André?"

"Mmm?"

She plucked at the ties of his deerskin shirt. "Is it always . . . like that?"

Genevieve lifted her head and looked at him. He gazed into her wide, innocent, hopeful eyes. Laying with a woman had never been like this. At this moment, he, too, felt like a virgin—right down to the sharp pain he felt, deep in his gut, because in the end he would bring her nothing but sorrow.

He told her none of these things. Instead, he brushed her hair off her flushed face and let his hand linger on her cheek.

"For us, *Taouistaouisse*, it will always be like that." *That much, at least, I can promise.*

André stood in the stern of the canoe, squinting against the afternoon light. The waters of Lake Superior swelled heavily beneath the belly of the laden vessel. He peered at the steely clouds in the distance, then scanned the rocky southern shore for coves. After a week upon this lake, he was brutally familiar with the scents and sights and signs of these waters. Twice in seven days, he had peered in the distance and seen what looked like white water breaking on a reef, only to discover that it was a storm, descending unexpectedly and with fury. Fortunately, both times he and his men had survived unscathed by paddling desperately through the black, choppy water to the protection of the scalloped shore. But he didn't relish another brush with fate. And right now, the air smelled suspiciously like an oncoming squall.

A rough swell bobbled the canoe as they veered off into deep water. A groan rose from the deerskin-covered form at his feet.

"*Oui*, I smell him too, Blossom." Wapishka pulled back in another powerful stroke. "But this Indian guide wouldn't leave the shore if it weren't safe. He knows Missipeshu better than us."

André frowned. Missipeshu was a spiny-backed, horned creature of Ojibwa legend who, with one swipe of his tail, could swirl up the wind and the waves on Lake Superior. He didn't welcome another battle with him, not now in the middle of a bay. André glared at the forward canoe and wondered if the Ojibwa guide he had hired at Sault Sainte Marie really knew what he was doing. Normally, he would never hire a guide when he could explore the land himself, but since they had left Manitoulin Island, the morning frosts had grown more persistent, the nights colder. He knew that if he did not arrive at Chequamegon Bay soon, the lake would grow grim with ice, and he and his men would be forced to walk the last long leagues across frozen land to the bay. So he had hired an Indian who knew the way, an Indian who now blithely forged across open water toward a distant peninsula in the midst of a gathering storm.

"That Indian is in league with the Iroquois!" Tiny lifted his paddle and waved at the forward canoe. "Blossom can scent that Indian's own demon, blinded beneath a blanket. I can smell him with my white man's nose. That Indian is sending us right out into the dragon's mouth!"

"Missipeshu can't be out here." Genevieve's pale face peeped out from the edge of the blanket. "With the way my stomach is churning, I'm sure I swallowed him."

Without missing a stroke, Tiny said, "Didn't my squaw's brew do you any good?"

"Missipeshu didn't like it at all." She sat up and pulled the deerskin tight around her shoulders. Her hair sprung unruly from its plait. "He's been chasing his tail all morning."

André gazed upon the figure of his wife. Despite her words, she looked better than she had in days, and for the first time since they entered Lake Superior, she hadn't lost her breakfast over the side of the canoe. Her skin was pale, but it was no longer as green as boiled peas. The noxious, watery brew that Tiny's new "wife" had prepared and André had fed to her last night, seemed to have made her feel better.

It was ironic that after all the portages, all the white water, and nine hundred miles of rivers and lakes, it was this final leg of the journey that was physically breaking her. The first day out on Lake Superior, she told him that the rocking of the canoe on the enormous lake reminded her of the sea voyage from France to Québec. He remembered what she'd looked like after that voyage. He didn't want her sick. He wanted her strong and healthy and determined and bold. More than anything, he wanted her to turn to him in the cold, dark night and press her body against him, so they could share once more the passion they had discovered on Manitoulin Island.

André tightened his hands on the cedar handle of his paddle. It had been a week since they had made love. He had restrained himself in the days that followed, determined to hold his passion in check until she was fully healed, but it was a difficult task. He had taken his place beside her in the tent. Every night he felt her soft breasts crush against him. Every night he lay beside her with an erection as hard as the granite upon which they slept. What had happened to that control he was so proud of? Under the influence of her touch, he had about as much restraint as a gangly fourteen-year-old fumbling with his first girl. He'd be more worried about his lack of control now, if she hadn't stiffened and blushed three nights after their lovemaking, when he reached for her and she told him that it was "her time." Though the news left him aching with frustration, at least he knew she wasn't pregnant. In the future he would be more careful. It was the least he could do for a woman who had decided of her own free will to give him her greatest gift.

He stifled the powerful surge of guilt. She gave herself to me fully warned, he thought. She knows what not to expect.

"Why are we so far from the shore?" Genevieve asked.

"We have to portage over that peninsula." André nodded toward the low strip of land in the distance. "It will take less time than following it around."

"If we make it across this bay," Tiny mumbled.

The Duke knelt in the bow of the boat. He took his paddle out of the water and balanced it across his knees. The Indian pulled a twisted stick of tobacco from the pouch hanging from his belt, cut off a hunk, lifted it ceremonially in the air, then tossed it into the water.

"By the Martyrdom of Saint Joseph!" Tiny stopped paddling. "There's barely a carrot left of that tobacco."

The Duke shrugged. "This Ojibwa's Missipeshu asks only for a sacrifice."

Siméon shook his black-bearded head. "Pagan rubbish!"

The Duke calmly dipped his paddle back into the water. "The tobacco will do us little good if we drown."

Wapishka and Tiny looked at one another, then at Julien and the Roissier brothers behind them. Their paddles clattered against their knees as they dug into their near-empty pouches for the last vestiges of precious tobacco. Curled brown leaves fluttered to the lake and bobbed on the swells in their wake.

"It's all your sacrifices to false gods," Siméon warned, "that will bring God's fury upon us."

Tiny closed his pouch and settled his paddle back in the water. "For all you know, Missipeshu and God may be one creature with a different name."

"Blasphemy!"

Genevieve reached for her battered case and unknotted the ragged ties. Gripping it tightly on her lap, she riffled through the contents. "I have nothing to offer," she murmured. "I don't think Missipeshu would appreciate pins or linens."

André's loins tightened as she held up bits of feminine frippery. Limp lace, a knot of corset strings, a frilly edge of a shift. Deeper in the case, he saw an enticing swatch of green velvet. He found himself wondering what it would be like to see her dressed like a civilized Frenchwoman in the midst of this wilderness—stiff-backed from a boned corset, her breasts thrust up against a scooped neckline, her legs rustling beneath yards and yards of underskirts. But as soon as the image materialized in his head, he started thinking about stripping the layers from her body until she was naked as the day she was born.

Groaning, he reached inside his pouch and pulled out the end of a stick of tobacco. "Here. Offer this."

"Don't you want some?"

"Missipeshu would probably prefer it from your hands."

She solemnly held the tobacco in her palm, closed her eyes, then tossed it into the water.

"Look what you've all done," Siméon raged, "corrupting a good Christian—"

"Oh, put a pipe in it, Siméon," she exclaimed.

"And paddle, will you? Before Missipeshu stirs and we become the next sacrifice into these waters."

André didn't know whether to bless the tobacco sacrifices or just plain luck when all his canoes and all the squaws who followed pulled into the mouth of a river on the peninsula, just as the squall burst overhead. It rained furiously, then the storm passed as quickly as it had come. They paddled upstream to a lake as far as they could go, then spent the last light of day portaging across the rest of the peninsula. They camped on the shores of the west side just as the sun sank below the horizon.

Restored to shaky health and pleased to be on land, Genevieve ate more than her share of the dwindling reserves of *sagamité*, even daring to complain about the lack of meat. She looked at him so longingly as she entered the tent that it took all his will not to chase in after her and to hell with his responsibilities.

But his canoe had been damaged during the trip across the peninsula. He and The Duke had stumbled over some rocky ground and dropped the vessel, ripping a hole in its belly. If he intended to be in the water tomorrow, it had to be fixed immediately.

André stayed up late into the night with Tiny, Wapishka, and The Duke, mending the tear and caulking the belly with heated spruce gum, swearing and cursing all the time. By the time he crossed the campsite to their tent, set a short distance away from the men, the fires had burned to embers and the men snored loudly beneath the overturned canoes.

He opened the flap and crawled in. Beneath the tarpaulin the air was warm from the heat of her body, smelling faintly of tanned leather and dampness. He kicked off his wet moccasins and slid up beside her, pulling a deerskin and a red woolen blanket over him.

Instinctively, she rolled up against him. She was all softness and curves, all warmth and fragrance. Her breathing was deep and even against his chest. He squeezed his eyes shut and cursed to himself, vowing that he'd make one of the Roissier brothers or Julien caulk the canoe next time—even if they knew nothing about it.

Her voice startled him.

"What took you so long?"

André ran a hand over her head, pushing the hair out of her face. He couldn't see her expression in the darkness, but he sensed her alertness. His blood coursed in anticipation. "I had to repair the canoe."

"I've been waiting for you."

Her small hands found their way up his chest to wind around his neck. Her breasts, those warm, heavy globes, pressed against him. Hungrily, he searched for her lips in the darkness, finding instead her smooth forehead, then her nose, before finally landing on her generous mouth.

He drew slowly away from her lower lip, tasting the spicy remnants of Tiny's squaw's medicine. Control, he thought. He wasn't going to climb on her in lust if she was still as weak as a newborn calf.

"You've been ill, *Taouistaouisse*."

"The Indian medicine helped."

He rubbed his hardened loins against her thigh, asking huskily, "Are you well enough for this?"

"Mmm." She kissed him. "I've been waiting for that medicine all night long."

Her lips parted. André drank in the sweet, hot breath of passion. All rational thought fled. He plunged his tongue deep into the silken cavern of her mouth, toyed with her tongue, traced her teeth, tasting the cherry-sweet essence of her. He filled his hand with a breast and felt the peak tighten against his palm, ruthlessly tweaking it beneath the layers of her bodice and shift until it stood out sharply against the fabric. Each gasp of pleasure she released spurred him on, for he wanted to hear her cry out beneath him; he wanted to feel her body throb around him in ecstasy; he wanted to taste and touch and hear and see her pleasure.

Genevieve removed her hands from about his neck, pulling at the laces of her bodice until it gaped open, giving him free access to her breasts. André buried his hand in the warmth beneath her shift, feeling the tautness of her nipple bead against his hand. He released her lips to feast on the fullness of her bosom, to suck greedily on the dark areola until it throbbed, every flick of his tongue against its rigid bed making her entire body arch against him.

He felt that urging again, the same urging that had driven him over the edge of sanity on Manitoulin Island. It was as strong and powerful as the winds across Lake Superior. He released her breast and slid against her, letting her feel the proof of his desire. André silently cursed her clothes. He wanted to hold her bare body against his bare skin. He wanted to fold her nakedness in his arms, to merge their bodies into one, to hold her tight against him, not just now, in the midst of their passion, but tomorrow and the day after.

He tried to push it out of his mind. Possessions had a way of cluttering up a man's life. He must be mad to be thinking about having a woman, now and always—but right now, in the midst of desire, he could think of nothing better than merging their bodies and making her his. He wished he could see her in the darkness. He wished he could watch her face as he drove into her.

André nudged her knees apart and slid his hand

up her leg, under her skirts. She was ready for him, oh, so ready, and he felt a thrill of victory as he realized she wanted him as much as he wanted her. And he would have her. He would give her a woman's pleasure, and for this night and the winter to come, he would utterly possess her.

He squeezed his eyes shut as he rolled atop her. When he spread her legs and entered her tightness, he felt the heated passion of her sex sheathe and throb around him. André braced himself above her, buried his lips in her hair, and felt their hearts pound wildly as one.

La Vieille, the old woman of the wind, blew soft and light and whirled around the sandy spit of land called Chequamegon Point, to swirl in the bay of the same name. André and his men had improvised a sail from the tarpaulins that covered the merchandise and some straight branches of birch wedged among the kegs and bails. It puffed full, now that the wind was blowing from the right quarter, and propelled the vessel deeper into the bay. The men took their ease, sharing the last of their tobacco, tossing the ashes into the water as a ceremonial sacrifice in order to remain in the good graces of *La Vieille* during this last stretch of their long journey.

André's gaze was fixed on a spot in the distance, where the endless forest of sugar maple, aspen, and birch trees gave way to a cleared section of the shore. He thought he saw movement upon the bank—movement of the human kind. He knew for sure that the pale blue smoke that curled up beyond the spiky tips of the red and white pines indicated a settlement of some sort. It could be an Indian village. He could only hope that the smoke came from the fort his men were supposed to build around the structures Nicholas Perrot had abandoned last spring. If it didn't, André knew he would have to search every one of the low, flat islands that lay in the north part of the bay until he found it.

All his worries disappeared as he neared and distinguished the flash of a dozen bright red *capotes*—the distinctive caps worn by the men of Québec.

"That's it." His blood surged with excitement. "They're straight ahead, where the smoke rises."

Genevieve clutched his leg and rose to her knees, leaning to one side in an attempt to see past the gaping sail. "I can't see anything but trees. Show me where it is!"

He reached down and took her hand in his, pulling her unsteadily to her feet. The canoe wobbled wildly and twisted in the water, for already the Roissier brothers were tearing down the makeshift sail. After six weeks of paddling, the men intended to enter their home under their own power. Tiny broke the excited babbling with a rendition of *Salut à Mon Pays*.

She struggled for balance on the craft, peering off to the distant shore. Her deerskin blanket fell to a puddle at her feet. Her fine dress, once rose-colored, was now nothing but a faded rag, webbed with mending and hanging in tatters around her legging-covered knees. But the sparkle in her eyes made her look as beautiful as if she were dressed to be presented to the Court.

André felt a twinge of apprehension. He had been dreading this moment since the day he realized she was going to stay with him all the way to Chequamegon Bay. Over the past few nights, after their long bouts of frenzied lovemaking, she had asked him so many questions about the area and the life they would lead during the winter months. There was so much excitement in her voice. He had been tempted to tell her the truth . . . but he didn't have the heart to crush her illusions, not yet. Soon, there would be no more hiding yet another secret he had kept from her.

He reached for her, spread his legs for better balance, and pulled her back against him. Then he dipped his paddle in the water to steer the canoe landward. Soon enough, she would discover the truth. In the meantime, he planned to share her excitement at their arrival. "Can you see the bits of red? Those are the hats of the men of Québec."

Genevieve stood tense, rising up on her toes and peering anxiously off to the shore. Her hair tickled his beard and felt like silk against his throat. He thought of this morning, when he had woken up with her poised over him, bright-eyed, wet-lipped, laughing as she lowered her small body upon him.

"I see them!" A shiver of excitement shook her small frame. "There are so many people!"

"Most of them are Hurons and Ottawas. There are a few savage villages nearby, and maybe even a Jesuit trying to save their souls."

She looked up at him, smiling slyly. "And I thought we'd be alone in the wilderness."

"We'll be alone often enough, *Taouistaouisse*, and we'll have more damned privacy than we ever had at the campsites."

She giggled at his throaty growl and leaned against him. The canoe approached the shore with growing speed as the men increased the tempo of their paddling with the tempo of another song. An icy wind raised goose bumps on her fair skin. "I can hardly believe it," she murmured, snuggling back against him. "We're finally home."

Home. Apprehension twisted like a knot in the center of his gut. She could have stayed in Québec with

Marietta Martineau, safe in a warm cedar-shingled building with a stone fireplace, a straw mattress, and thick woolen blankets. For the sake of living in her own home, she had taken this dangerous journey with a strange man through the untamed forests to Chequamegon Bay. He had convinced her to come, with lies. Now she was about to see her home, for the first time, and he dreaded her response.

Everything had been going so well. There was no talk of the coming spring, no discussion of what he would do next summer, after they returned to Montréal. It was as if she had resigned herself to enjoying what she could now, here, and left the future to take care of itself. He liked the situation as it stood—he didn't want it to change—and he didn't want to think of the future, either. Right now, the future was a hazy thing, undefined and far, far away.

They approached the shore. André recognized the leader of his advance contingent and raised his hand in greeting. A crowd of Indian maidens sang their own song of welcome to the newcomers. The Duke pounded the blunt end of his cedar paddle on the thin glaze of ice that rimmed the edge of the broad cove, cracking a wide path so the men could work the canoes through to the shore. André urged Genevieve back down and helped push the ice away.

When he could see the sand beneath the water, he leapt off the side and plunged his legs into the frigid bay. The water froze the skin of his thighs so badly, it burned. He turned to wade to the shore.

"Wait!" She rose to her knees and held open her arms. "Take me with you."

"No . . . stay here," he ordered, more harshly than he intended. "I'll come and get you later."

"André!"

His stomach twisted, more painfully than the slosh

of the icy water against his bare thighs, but he didn't turn back.

A thick-thighed *voyageur* with a mane of dark hair stopped dead in his tracks as André approached. He pulled his red cap off his head and stared at the canoe. André turned to find his wife standing, arms akimbo, in the vessel. Her deerskin blanket gaped open, showing the tightness of her boned bodice and the magnificent fullness of her breasts above. The song the men on shore had been singing died off in a strange, distorted note. André suddenly realized that everyone—the *voyageurs*, the Indian maidens, the few Indian men who stood aside—were all staring at his wife.

He frowned and turned to face David, the leader of his advance contingent. "It's good to see you made it."

The dark-haired *voyageur* didn't acknowledge André's words. His gaze was fixed beyond, on Genevieve.

André tried again. "Is everything built as I ordered?"

The man's glazed eyes focused on André for a moment, then returned to the woman on the canoe. He gestured to her dumbly. "That's . . . that's a Frenchwoman."

"I'm glad you're familiar with the species," he said dryly. "By the way you're all staring, you'd think she was some new breed of moose."

"How did she . . . why is she . . ."

"She's my wife." André frowned as a surprised murmuring arose among the other *voyageurs*, while the Indian maidens huddled to one side, wide-eyed and gesturing wildly among themselves. "If you're through gaping at her like an ass, you can show me the fort."

Recovering, David nodded and replaced his cap. He walked away from the shore toward the shelter of birch and aspen trees. Not more than fifty paces from the shoreline, a high stockade stood in a clearing. Scattered around, near the walls, stood a dozen small bark huts—Huron huts—probably belonging to the Indian wives of the Frenchmen.

"There's a Jesuit here by the name of Marquette," David said, his voice returning to normal. "He's got a little bark chapel called Saint Esprit about a half league down the coast, and he visits once a week, on Sundays. When we arrived here a few weeks ago, all that was left of Perrot's post was his house, a storehouse, and a building large enough for the men to share. We had to cut the trees and sharpen the ends to set up the stockade, and that took most of our time. This past week we've been replacing some of the boughs that thatched the roofs because all of them leaked, and we whitewashed the inside of all the buildings with a white clay . . ."

André barely heard David's report as he strode through the tiny Huron village. It was empty now, for everyone congregated on the shore where his men were unloading the merchandise for the last time. Blue smoke curled out of the open holes in the center of the bark roofs. A tiny grouse carcass cooked over an open fire, unattended. A webbed snowshoe leaned against one of the huts, discarded as the mender ran to the shore to greet the newcomers. A deerskin, with half the meat scraped off, hung on a pole dug into the ground. A wide bowl lay tilted, half filled with ground cornmeal and half filled with corn.

He eyed the stockade critically, noting the tight fit between the wooden palisades. He gripped one and shook it for stability as he passed through the gate.

It was as solid as stone. The scent of pine smoke hovered in the air, for to one side of the open fort, two broad flanks of moose meat hung from a stand, slashed, drying in the air with the help of the wood-fire smoke bathing its flesh. Leaning against the side of what he assumed was the warehouse were a half-dozen willow frames with dark, silky beaver fur stretched over them. The trading had already begun.

". . . plenty of food. The deer sometimes wander right into the village. There's a couple of Ottawa and more Huron villages about an hour's walk south, and they've got enough maize and squash and pumpkin to feed all of us at least until Christmas. We've started setting seines into the river for the whitefish . . ."

André walked to the corner of the stockade, where a tiny dwelling stood apart from the storehouse and the large house set aside for the men who didn't have Indian wives. There was a window cut into the logs, and an oiled skin flapped lightly against the wall. A mud and stone chimney sagged on one side.

"We were planning to wall up the window in this and use it as a smokehouse," David said, "but I suppose with you having a wife and all . . ."

André stared with growing dread at the tiny cabin. It was so small, he could cross the width or length of it in four strides. The chimney would have to be cleaned and partially rebuilt, or the house would fill with smoke every time a fire was lit. But even if he cleaned the chimney and walled up the window, the wind would still whistle coldly through the cabin. The logs that formed the walls were ill-fitting, and the mud that had been used to clog the chinks chipped and flaked. The dried boughs that thatched the roof were held down by poles that hung askew upon the peaked top.

He stared ruefully at his new home, thinking that no self-respecting settler in Montréal would house their pigs in this place.

"There you are! Why didn't you take me with you?" Genevieve strode through the gate. "I had to ride on Tiny's back to get off that canoe, and those Indian women were poking and prying at me as if I were a fat goose to be slaughtered."

He turned to face her. Her hair, tangled and falling out of its plait, glowed in the light. Her cheeks flushed with excitement and indignation. Wapishka, Tiny, and Julien followed close behind her, glowering at the crowd of Frenchmen who wandered in, staring dumbstruck at the ragged Frenchwoman in their midst.

"And how long have your men been in the woods?" Genevieve asked David, pulling her deerskin around her. "They're staring at me as if I were a pet bear at the Saint-Germain fair."

"The Indian women have never seen a French-woman," David explained, as André stared mutely at his wife. "And my men ... you'll have to excuse them, ma'am. They've never seen a Frenchwoman out here."

"They'd best get used to it, because I'm here to stay." She peered around, examining the inside of the stockade for the first time. "Where's our house, André? Is it here or is it somewhere else?"

His tongue felt like a molten ball of lead in his mouth. In his lifetime, he had walked twenty-mile portages in the driving rain, he had willingly run the wildest of rapids, he had faced and fought a group of brandy-crazed Indian warriors—and he had lived through all of it. Yet right now, in the face of Gene-vieve, he felt as weak and unarmed as a naked child.

"That's it." His voice was a croak. He jerked his head toward the cabin. "That's our . . . home."

His neck muscles stiffened to stone as she walked around him and stood before the house, her hands on her hips. She approached it, brushed away the length of deerskin, and peered into the single window. A clod of mud fell from the top of the sill. He waited, motionless, bracing himself for the outburst he knew was to come.

"It looks . . . as if it needs some work."

The lump in his throat choked off all words. She approached and took his hand. Then, incredulously, her lips stretched in a soft smile.

"When it's done, André, it's going to be absolutely beautiful."

Chapter Fourteen

Flakes of freezing snow bit into André's face above the edge of his beard. The frigid air stung his lungs as he drew in an icy breath. He lifted his leg, wincing as his sore thigh muscle tightened and quivered from the exertion, and took a giant step forward, planting his webbed snowshoe on the sinking snow. Leather straps dug deep into his shoulders as he leaned forward and dragged his laden toboggan one step deeper into the blizzard.

"God's wounds!" Tiny's bellowing voice was battered and dispersed by the howling wind. "This snow is as thick as bear grease! We should stop and camp until it blows over."

André glanced at the giant, who pulled a toboggan next to him. A white crust covered Tiny's deerskin coat and the leggings that stuck out beneath. Ice clung to his mustache and beard, where his breath had frozen around his mouth. His blue eyes gleamed between slitted lids in his red face.

"We're not stopping." He took another aching step. "The fort is ahead."

"By the balls of Saint—" The giant waved his arms in the air, gesturing to the world. "It's a blizzard. . . . We may as well be walking in the clouds!"

"A ration of brandy says we'll find it within the hour."

"Much good brandy'll do me if I'm frozen until spring." Tiny placed his meaty hands on his hips. "Make it two!"

"Two it is."

André peered into the blinding snow. He and his men had been walking since dawn, when the blizzard had been nothing but a gentle sprinkling of calm flakes. Now it raged and howled, and the snow fell from the sky as thickly as the wind lifted it from the ground, swirling around them and completely obscuring the horizon. As they pulled their heavily laden bark sleds, the dark shapes of trees loomed in their path. To André, they were familiar trees in a familiar layout, and he knew that they were only paces from the stockade.

For two weeks, he and five *voyageurs* had wandered through the lands west of Chequamegon Bay. En route, they met up with Indians from the Cree tribe and traded their European goods for the wealth of beaver furs that now sagged heavily upon the tobaggans. But he gathered much more than fur. In the hot Indian lodgings, while he and the natives smoked tobacco in long red stone pipes, André listened eagerly to their stories of a brackish body of water west of Lake Superior, and a great river they called the "Messipi," which led south and west to another

potential sea. On some future trading trip, he vowed
to follow the threads of those stories. But he had
promised Genevieve he would be home for Christmas
Day, and Christmas Day was tomorrow.

His back and shoulders ached from pulling the
heavy toboggan. His legs wobbled beneath him. The
snow lay soft and deep and powdery, and even with the
webbed snowshoes laced tightly onto his moccasins,
André nearly sank to his knees with each step. He
leaned forward, fighting the icy wind, thinking of the
warmth and comfort that awaited him at home.

Home. He smiled inwardly, despite the pain. That
was Genevieve's word. Before her, he had never
thought of his temporary abodes in the wilderness as
homes; they were simply stopping places, interrup-
tions in a constant journey westward. Wherever he
laid his head was his home, whether it be on spruce
bows on the hardness of a granite bank, in an Indian's
wigwam, or nestled in a hole dug deep in the snow.
But over the weeks that they had lived together in
the small cabin in the stockade, André discovered
that there was a pleasant difference between a home
and a resting place. He also discovered that there
were some distinct advantages to living with her within
the privacy of four solid walls.

The thought charged him with new energy. He
bent his head and surged forward. One step. Two.
The toboggan pushed the new snow forward as it
rode on the ice crust beneath. He stopped to kick
away the drift that had gathered to impede its progress. In the white haze beyond his toboggan, he saw
the indeterminate shapes of the other three men
forging their way through the blizzard.

Tiny stopped in his tracks. "By the blessed womb
of the Virgin Mother!"

André looked ahead. Through the swirl of snow

he saw glimpses of Huron bark houses, the flicker of wavering fires gleaming through the uneven bark walls. His dry lips cracked into a smile. The stockade could not be more than twenty paces ahead. As if to prove his point, a wavering voice called from the heavens.

"Qui vive?"

André cried out his name, mounds of snow tumbling off his shoulders as he straightened. He heard the vague squealing of the gate. He headed toward the sound. Out of the whiteness, the stockade door emerged, yawning open in welcome. He glanced at Tiny in silent triumph.

"Aye, you'll get your brandy," Tiny grumbled. A gleam entered his eye as he glanced from André to the fort. "But only if you can beat me to the gate."

His laugh pierced the howling of the wind. In a minute, both of them were running—as quickly as they could through the depth of the snow with rackets on their feet and two hundred pounds of fur dragging behind them. They wove past the Huron houses and surged toward the open gate of the stockade. André reached the doorpost a moment before Tiny and victoriously shrugged the straps of the toboggan off his aching shoulders.

"'Twas not an even race!" The icicles were quickly melting off Tiny's beard from the heat of his breath. "I had my strength sapped by that Cree woman and you've been a monk for two weeks!"

"Tell that to the Huron squaw waiting in your hut," he warned, "and she'll cut your 'strength' right off."

A crowd of men burst out of the long building that served as their quarters and hurried across the snow. The sound of banging copper emerged from the gaping door, a sign that the cook was already preparing for tomorrow's Christmas feast. The men barraged

André and the others with questions as they unloaded the furs strapped in heaping piles on the toboggans. Wapishka handed André a pewter cup with brandy, which he drank in one gulp, the liquid burning the back of his throat and lighting a pleasant glow in his belly.

He peered toward the tiny cabin in the corner. Golden light sifted through the oiled deerskin that stretched across the small window. He wiped his beard and mustache against the frozen sleeve of his deerskin coat, then picked up his pack, pulled off his red cap, and strode home.

The succulent aroma of roasting meat greeted him as he swung open the door. The dry heat of a hearth fire blasted out of the tiny room, thawing his frozen limbs. Genevieve leaned over the hearth, basting a hunk of glistening meat. The firelight made her long plait glow a rich amber. She whirled around as he plunked his pack down inside the door. The spoon clattered to the floor as she launched herself across the room.

"You're home!"

He bent his knees and lifted her up into his arms. She pressed against him, small and warm. André closed his eyes and breathed in the sweet fragrance that emanated from her hair. "I promised you I'd be back for Christmas."

"But the snow is heaped as high as my shoulder against the walls of this fort, and there's a blizzard—"

"All the more reason to race back here."

"*Bête!*" Her arms tightened around his neck. "You could have frozen to death in the storm."

"I couldn't," he murmured. "Thoughts of you kept me warm every night."

He held her tight, flush against his body, trying to

feel her warmth through the layers of his deerskin. "You missed me, *Taouistaouisse?*"

"Not a bit." Genevieve tilted her chin defiantly. "Wapishka and The Duke and the Roissier brothers kept me entertained in your absence."

"Did they?" He squeezed her until she squealed. "I trust I won't have to emasculate them in the morning?"

"For losing four beaver pelts to me in dice?" Her eyes twinkled wickedly. "I believe you're jealous, my husband. I'll teach you how to play, if you'd like."

"There's only one game I'm interested in right now."

"Is there?" She slid down the length of his body. "And I thought you'd be too exhausted from your trip."

He kissed her parted lips, showing her exactly how much energy he had left. Her breath was hot, eager. Her hair felt like heated silk against his frozen hands.

She struggled away from him. "I feel like I'm kissing a snowman."

André glanced at the wet spots that stained her chest, where the encrusted snow on his shirt had melted between them. He traced a throbbing vein in her throat. "There's another part of me I'd rather you melt."

"And your fingers are cold."

"I know a very warm place I'd like to put them."

She released a surprised gasp and André kissed her again, more demandingly. He tugged anxiously on the laces of her deerskin dress. She clutched his hands and pulled gently away. His loins tightened at the light of promise in her eyes.

Her voice was as husky as fire. "You'll have to undress, my husband." She glanced at the puddle growing at his feet. "You'll catch your death in all those wet clothes."

He shrugged off the deerskin robe that covered his body and hung it blindly on a peg beside the door, then let the other fur wrappings follow. When he wore only his deerskin shirt and leggings, she took his hand and led him one step deeper into the hut. The flickering, red-orange light of the fire cast fantastic shadows above the guns, pistols, knives, snowshoes, and sundry scraping tools that hung on pegs on the walls. He sank in the luxurious pile of furs that served as their bed and took up nearly half of the room. She fell to her knees in front of him.

Genevieve started at his feet, painstakingly picking apart the frozen knots that held the teardrop-shaped webbings to his moccasins. When she finished, she tossed the icy rackets aside, pulled off his sodden moccasins, and placed them near the fire. He watched her every move. The dress covered her from the neck to the knees, but he loved the way her hips swayed beneath the deerskin. Cinched with a belt decorated with dyed porcupine quills, the simple garb showed off the fullness of her unbound breasts and the narrowness of her waist. Leggings covered her legs to the knees, and he knew that above them she was naked.

The thought sent blood rushing to his loins. He was painfully aware that the only thing separating them was his own breechcloth—a single layer of soft, smoke-ripened deerskin. André clutched her by the waist and drew her closer, burying his head in the bare, scented nook of her throat. Her hands worked busily over his body, stripping him, while his hands hungrily roamed over hers.

His pistol and knife clattered hollowly to the boards that formed the floor. She fiddled with the snow-encrusted edge of his sash, then tossed it close to the hearth. He lifted his arms as her fingers curled around the hem of his shirt and she pulled it up, over his head, spreading cakes of snow on the floor and the pelts. He ran his hands over her body, from shoulder to hip, lifting her skirt so he could wrap his fingers around her strong thighs.

Her laugh was deep and husky as she pulled away to undo the lacings that held up his leggings, the last piece of clothing but for his breechcloth. As she tossed them away, Genevieve placed her hands on his chest, feeling the aching muscles of his shoulders, and it was if she burned him with fire.

"Two weeks," she murmured raggedly. "Two weeks."

He lifted her, spreading her legs until she sat upon his lap, proving that no amount of trudging through blizzards would exhaust his hunger for her. Her dress rode up her legs. He felt her bare limbs against his, the skin of her inner thighs as soft as butter. André dragged her up his lap until she was placed squarely on his aching groin. He kissed her, slanting his lips against hers, drawing her tongue deep into his mouth and then filling her mouth with his. Her nipples hardened beneath the deerskin and lightly grazed his chest.

He drew away. "Take it off."

Without a murmur, she untied the lacings at her throat, loosened them, then lifted the deerskin dress and the shift she wore beneath it over her head. Now all she wore were her leggings, tied tight against her calves. Bathed in the glow of the fire, her breasts stood proud and heavy. He laved one taut nipple with his tongue and felt it tighten into a knot against his lips. He pressed her pelvis against his, feeling the crisp curls of her secret place scrape his bare thighs.

André slipped a hand between them and felt the moist heat of her womanhood.

His sex threatened to burst from his breechcloth. What shaman's spell had this creature cast upon him, to make him want her and only her, to make him turn away from the promise of distant saltwater seas, to return to the warm glow of this tiny hut? It wasn't as if there were no other women available, for the Cree chief had pressed several wives upon him, all of them comely and lithe. He had felt nothing for them, though their dark eyes had danced in promise. He wanted only Genevieve.

I love her.

The thought came without preamble, without doubt, without angst. It wasn't the first time it had come. It had slipped into his mind a hundred times since the day she fell into the rapids on the French River. And each time it entered his consciousness, he fought against it less.

There was no time to dwell on it now. She was all fire and passion in his embrace, and his own desire overcame the thought as quickly as it had come. André stroked her while he kissed her breasts, her neck, her lips, feeling her grow warm and slick in his hand, feeling a power, a victory in making her want him so badly—as badly as he wanted her.

She pressed against him, murmuring his name, cradling his head in her trembling hands. He could stand it no longer. He tore the breechcloth from between them and lay back in the pelts, lifting her by the waist and positioning her over his aching member. He squeezed his eyes shut as he felt her muscular tightness sheathe him in heat and passion. And then she moved, rhythmically, naturally. André felt himself buried deeper and deeper inside her heat, and he grasped her hips, pressing her still closer, aching to reach still deeper, deeper, into Genevieve.

She cried out. He held her firm against him as she shuddered and her body pulsated in his embrace, and before he could think, before the last of her contractions gripped his member, he tilted his hips and surged into her, exploding into the warm, soft body of the woman he loved.

Genevieve stayed atop him, his member snug inside her, long after they finished their lovemaking. Damp spots stained the pelts where ice had melted and soaked the furs. Through the cracks in the hut, he could hear the howling of the blizzard, but inside all was silent and warm. The dry heat of the fire filled the room, the wood crackling and rearranging itself on the floor of the hearth. As he lay, his heart pounding, André was aware of nothing but the form of the woman lying damp and exhausted against his chest.

Yes, he loved her.

The thought returned, unbidden, taunting him. He had wanted no other woman since the day he'd met her; he could think of no other woman.

André stared up at the tangle of spruce boughs and poles and bark that formed the roof of the hut. He flattened his hand against her back. This wasn't supposed to happen; he had never wanted it to happen. Lurking in the back of his mind was the knowledge that this would cause complications, this would muck up the simplicity of his life. There were repercussions beyond the warm cocoon of this room. Loving was never a simple thing. It meant responsibilities and ties; it meant a curtailing of freedom, the one thing he treasured above all else.

"Mmm." She snuggled against him, her breasts warm and heavy on his abdomen. "That feels good."

André realized he had been tracing tiny circles on her back. He kissed the top of her head and traced larger ones. She was curled so defenselessly, so comfortably atop him, that his heart ached just looking at her. He pushed all his burgeoning doubts away. It was Christmas Eve. He was in the middle of the wilderness, exactly where he had struggled to be for three years. He was lying in a hut in the midst of a pile of furs, in front of a blazing fire, with a lusty, naked woman in his arms . . . a woman he loved. There was no room in this idyllic existence for doubts.

Genevieve turned her face so the opposite cheek lay against his chest and the firelight cast shadows on her features. She gazed toward the hearth. "I made beaver tail for you, hoping you'd be back by tomorrow."

He breathed in the mouth-watering aroma of the delicacy and his stomach growled in response.

She shifted in his embrace. "You're hungry. . . ."

"No, don't move." He held her more tightly. "Stay here a while. Tell me what happened while I was gone."

She settled on his chest. Her voice was lazy. He listened to her unconscious lilt, the distinct Norman accent. He wondered from what part of Normandy her family hailed, but he didn't want to interrupt her to ask, not now. There'd be time enough to know the all of Genevieve. Tonight, he wanted only to listen.

She sounded so contented, almost joyful, living in this hut. He wondered if she would tire of the life, if she would yearn for the comforts of civilization, for the feel of silk against her skin. She was a daughter of the *petite noblesse,* a feisty one but an aristocrat nonetheless, and André feared this winter in the wilderness might be no more than a novelty to her. The doubts nudged the edge of his consciousness and again he pushed them away. All that mattered was that she was here and she seemed happy, and she filled what once were long, cold winter nights with warmth and lovemaking and conversation and laughter.

"Father Marquette visited last week," she continued. "His eyes nearly fell out of his head when he saw me. He had just arrived and I was perched outside one of the Huron huts, weaving a snowshoe and trying to get my tongue around the Algonquin words Tiny's new wife was trying to teach me. When I welcomed him, he looked at me as if I were some kind of demon."

André's lips twitched. He could imagine the Jesuit's expression when he saw a Frenchwoman with auburn hair dressed in Huron clothes in the middle of the wilderness, greeting him as well as any member of the French court.

"Julien had a devil of a time convincing him that I was married to you. When the Jesuit left, he called the fort a 'veritable brothel of iniquity.'" She swallowed a laugh. "Of course, that was right after the drunken Huron warriors left."

He tensed beneath her.

"Don't worry," she murmured. "Everything is fine now. For a while everyone was worried, the way those Hurons were screaming and running around naked in the snow, pulling on their scalp locks and brandishing their hatchets . . ."

"Hatchets?"

He stopped scratching her back. His stomach twisted into a knot. André knew what madness the savages descended into whenever they drank more than their fill of spirits. He'd seen them kill their own brothers, their own wives, while gripped in the fever of drunkenness. When it was all over, they'd blame it on the brandy or the rum, saying the demons had taken over; certainly, they weren't responsible for their actions.

He had ordered David not to give any brandy to the natives. The brandy was only for the Frenchmen. He nudged her head up and glared into her eyes. "Genevieve . . ."

"Oh, bother, I didn't mean to say anything. It's all over now, so there's no need to worry. Right after you left, a dozen Hurons arrived with all kinds of pelts slung over their backs. They came to trade, but they didn't want pots or beads; they wanted brandy." Genevieve wiggled beneath him, urging him to continue scratching her back. "David refused. They camped outside for a few days. They challenged the men to an Indian game—the *voyageurs* called it *La Crosse*—and Julien and Anselme and some of the younger men took them up. The *voyageurs* won, which seemed to anger the Hurons, and it angered them more when they returned to camp and found Gaspard in the tent of one of their squaws."

André groaned.

"Wapishka nearly killed him. So did the Indians. But after a lot of talk, David assuaged them by giving them brandy and gifts and shutting them out of the fort. That's when they spent the night yelling and running around." She yawned. "The next morning they packed up and left, and that was it."

The thought of a crowd of Huron warriors dancing in a brandy-crazed haze around this wooden fort made his blood pump hard through his body. Genevieve was here, defenseless, and he was out roaming the wilderness, ignorant of her danger. What the hell was Gaspard thinking? Weren't there enough savage women around from whom to choose a wife? Why did he have to sleep with another Indian's squaw?

They were too far into the wilderness to start making enemies out of tribes with whom they were allies, and any slight would be enough incentive to send the Indians on the warpath.

He suddenly remembered Rose-Marie, white-faced and determined, launching herself over the edge of the Iroquois canoe, her belly swollen with his child, *his babe. . . .*

"André . . . I can't breathe."

He loosened his grip, then rolled over until she lay beneath him, cushioned in the pelts. Her brows drew together in curiosity as he traced the soft curve of her cheek.

God, he had been a fool to drag her all the way out here. He could not protect her always, not in this place where the dangers were unknown. He would do what he had to do, what he'd vowed to do a long time ago. Come spring, he would bring her back to the settlements, deep in the protection of the settlements, safe from the savage unpredictability of the wilderness.

I won't let you die, Genny.

His heart chilled with fear. *Fear.* He knew the feeling: wet palms, cold sweat, trembling. He might fail again. He might lose another wife. Another babe. More blood on his hands, more crimes on his conscience.

"What is it, André?"

The words surged on his tongue—*I love you, Genevieve*—but he knew better than to say them. To say them was to give her false hope. He wouldn't keep her . . . he couldn't.

So he kissed her swiftly, greedily. They had this day, this night, and the nights to come, no more than that. She responded, arching her lean, curvy body against him. André buried his hands in her hair, his loins stirring anew. He was hungry for her. Again. This time he delayed sating himself, instead sharpening his appetite by tasting her in places she had never been tasted before, by pleasuring her twice before sinking himself deep into her warmth and wetness.

Then he lost his fear, his doubts, his heart, and himself in the open arms of his loving wife.

Genevieve's joy was like a great bubble in her chest, expanding and growing tighter and tauter and fuller each day until she thought she would burst.

It was Christmas Day. She woke up in the shelter of her home—her *own* home. The fire wheezed in the primitive hearth, providing little warmth from the frigid morning air seeping in through the ill-fitting logs of the cabin, but she didn't mind. Nor did she mind the small puddle that lay on the floor beneath the skin-covered window. She had slept in draftier rooms, certainly in dirtier houses, and definitely in more dangerous places. Here, in this cabin, she was as warm and safe as she could ever want to be. She lay snug beneath a half-dozen thick bear, fox, marten, and lynx furs, her nose pressed against her husband's broad chest.

Genevieve had everything she had ever wanted in the world. A home. Safety. A place where she belonged. But more than that, she had a man she loved, and he was home from his wanderings. André was like a gift from the heavens—wonderful and strong and totally unexpected—and she had never been happier.

He shifted, and she felt his lips on her temple. *"Joyeux Noël, ma mie."*

A slow smile slipped across her face. It was a merry Christmas—the merriest one ever. Her last Christmas had been in the Salpêtrière, her only gift a day off from laundering and an extra piece of two-day-old bread. How far she had come in a single year. Genevieve rubbed her face between the plates of his chest, wrinkling her nose as the crisp hairs tickled it. Outside the warm cocoon of their home, she heard male voices—lusty cries of *Joyeux Noël* and calls for food and brandy—but Genevieve felt no urgency to rise and join the imminent festivities. She lingered, her thigh draped between his, savoring this precious, private moment.

"Listen," she said, her voice muffled against him.

"Barely dawn and they're already calling for brandy," he mused. "Father Marquette will harangue them for hours if they're bug-eyed drunk during Mass."

"No, not the men. Listen." As the *voyageurs'* voices faded, silence wrapped around the little house, broken only by the crack of an icicle snapping away from the eaves and sluicing into the snow just beyond the walls. "Can you hear it?"

"Yes, *Taouistaouisse.*"

"It's like there is no one around for hundreds and hundreds of miles."

"No screaming peddlers. No clomping of horses and clattering of carriages. No stink of civilization." He poked his head above the furs and glanced at the embers of the fire. "Of course, it would be nice if we had someone around to add a log to the fire. . . ."

"I'm warm enough."

"This hut has more drafts than a wigwam." André glanced down at her, nestled firmly against him. "What will you give me if I stoke the fire?"

"Breakfast."

He nodded to the pot hanging in the hearth. "It's already made."

"Breakfast doesn't always come in a pot, my husband."

André chuckled and pulled away, emerging naked from their tent of furs. Through heavy lids, she watched the sleek, well-muscled body of the man she loved as he threw more kindling and a new log onto the fire. He squatted and poked at the flames. Genevieve reached out and traced the hard, sinewy muscles of his upper arm. When the fire blazed high enough for her to feel the heat on her face, he tossed away the poker, smiled wickedly, and dove beneath the furs. His skin felt like ice and she scrambled to the other side of the bed, trying to get away from his chilled limbs just as he reached for her, trying to steal warmth from her body. They rolled in the tangle of pelts, laughing. The touch of their limbs soon created a different sort of heat. The laughter died away, drowned in quiet gasps and deep-throated moans. They kissed and caressed and he feasted on her, in a way that made her squirm in passion, and then he filled her and stroked and they both reached that sweet explosion of pleasure while wrapped in each other's arms.

The fire quickly filled the room with dry heat and the spicy scent of burning resin. The furs, kicked off during their lovemaking, lay twisted around their limbs. Sated, Genevieve kissed André on the throat and rose reluctantly from their bed. She searched for her deerskin dress and leggings amid the tangle of discarded clothing on the floor. Once dressed, she stirred the *sagamité* in the pot she had hung over the fire the evening before, spooning out two bowls for their breakfast—it was the least she could do for him, she teased, for making the room so warm for her.

Genevieve chattered while he ate, encouraged by the bright look in his tawny eyes. It had been lonely in the fort while he was gone. In anticipation of his return, she had stored up anecdotes like a squirrel stored nuts, and now, their passion sated for the moment, she yearned to share everything with him. She told him about the mistakes she had made trying to ice-fish, about the lessons in how to scrape and oil and treat the sundry furs the men brought back from hunting trips, about her first shocked taste of smoked moose meat. She told him she had bartered nearly everything in her woven case—a handful of silver pins for another deerskin dress, two linens for a log mortar and wooden pestle to crush corn into cornmeal, her old corset strings for a deer jaw scraper— and André commented, with a twinkle in his eye, that it was about time she sent that woven case to the bottom of Lake Superior. When she was finished eating, he walked to the door and fiddled with the ties to his pack, the one he had taken with him into the wilderness. He pulled out a deep-piled gray pelt, wrapping it around her shoulders.

"My Christmas present to you," André murmured, yanking her closer and kissing her on the lips. "It's a caribou pelt. I bought it from the Cree."

Genevieve buried her fingers into the lush fur. She felt like a queen in coronation robes—certainly ermine could not be as soft and warm as the fur now draped on her shoulders. All she had for him for Christmas was a pair of snowshoes she had painstakingly woven until the webbing was as tight as a harp's strings, but suddenly she felt that nothing short of her heart would be adequate.

Then she had an idea.

"I can't give you your present until later," she murmured, wrapping herself in the pelt. "I'll give it to you tonight. After the feast."

His lips twitched beneath his beard. He glanced at

the bed of tangled furs. "And I thought I already received my presents."

"So did I." She shrugged deeper into the robe, and looking into his eyes, she felt like she was wrapped in pure love. She wanted to race with him. She wanted to run through the snow. She wanted to scream her joy to the entire world. "Let's go outside," Genevieve said. "The games must have started long ago."

He put on his long deerskin coat, strapped on his belt and weapons, then they pushed open the door to their home. Feeling the crack of the crisp, cold air, Genevieve blinked, for the blanket of pristine new snow blinded her with its brightness.

When her eyes adjusted to the light, she noticed that the stockade gate gaped open and all within the perimeter was silent.

"The men aren't here." He tilted his head. His breath misted in front of him. André glanced over the pointed ends of the palisades toward the north. "I hear them. They're near the lake."

They half walked, half ran through the gate of the stockade, and she led him like an excited puppy. Outside, every proud pine sagged under the weight of a new cloak of fresh white snow, and the world was muffled and wonderfully silent. Their leather-bound feet crunched through the virgin glitter as they headed through the woods toward the lake. The air was so crisp it bit her lungs as she drew in each breath, but it was as invigorating as a shocking cold bath in the summertime.

Genevieve and André met up with the men and the Indian women on a small slope. They had dragged all the empty toboggans out of the stockade, and now they took turns riding the bark sleds down the slope and over the solid surface of the lake. André took her hand and helped her climb up the ridge, then

commandeered one of the sleighs. He sat on it and
planted her, caribou robe and all, firmly between
his thighs. With a push, they slid down the slope at
breathtaking speed, the frigid air whizzing through
her hair as she laughed aloud at the thrill of it.

They spent the morning frolicking like children.
Genevieve raced down the slope on the toboggan
with him, then raced up again, jumping up and down
in excitement and complaining when he dallied.
When she became too breathless to speak, André
picked her up and tossed her in a snowbank, and she
retaliated by pelting him with hard-packed snowballs,
a skill she was familiar with from her winters in Paris.
But Genevieve soon found out he had much more
experience. She gave up—willingly—when he had
pinned her down flat on her back. Then they played
with Indian snowsnakes—long, thin wooden sticks—
which were thrown on a cleared patch of ice on the
lake to see how far they could slide, with an extra
portion of brandy going to the winner.

By the time Father Marquette arrived, Genevieve
was so exhausted she could barely stand, and her
body steamed in the cold air. André picked her up,
tossed her on a toboggan and, looping the straps over
his shoulders, started tugging her home. Tiny, not to
be outdone, directed his squaw to sit on his toboggan
and began pulling it behind him. Soon others joined
the race, and the laughter of the women mingled
with the arrogant cries of the men as they ran forward
like sled dogs, racing for the gate of the stockade.

They all piled into the men's quarters, toasty warm
after the cold of the outside. They stripped off their
frozen outer garments and left them hanging on the
pegs that lined the wall. The men stood solemnly
while the Jesuit said Mass. The mouth-watering
aromas of the feast wafted around them, teasing them

all into madness, and as soon as Father Marquette finished, they rushed to set up the tables and benches in the middle of the room. The squaws brought in wooden and bark trenchers of meat: juicy hunks of elk from an animal that had been caught and killed only days before and stewed with the last of the dried blueberries; flat silver-gray slivers of precious beaver tail; heaping plates of wild rice that André and the men had purchased from Ojibwa Indians during their travels; a tender, sweet meat that tasted like pork and turned out to be beaver stewed decadently in its own skin; roasted porcupine; platters of aromatic sturgeon from the lake; the ever-present *sagamité;* and brandy—plenty of it—five day's worth of rations for each man.

They spent the afternoon eating. Tiny began to sing and the men joined in, banging their wooden and box-turtle shell cups on the tables in rhythm to the music. Some of the Indian women swayed to the melody and the men tried to teach them to imitate the stately dances of the nobility. Genevieve laughed to see them mincing around the log cabin like aristocrats in cork-heeled shoes rather than woodsmen in deerskin and breechcloths. Their voices grew so loud and their antics so wild that the hanging snowshoes rattled against the log walls. As the celebration continued and the songs became more and more bawdy, she slipped away from André's side. She whispered in Wapishka's ear to keep her husband in the men's quarters for an hour or so—she had to complete his Christmas present before the night was ended. Then she slipped out the front door and scampered across the fort in the crisp blue twilight to their home.

An hour later, André concluded that all the arm wrestling matches and drunken toasts to the beauty and fertility of the Indian women had been done solely for the purpose of keeping him away from his missing wife. Brushing his men off, he left the room and headed across the packed snow toward his cabin. He swung open the door.

Startled, she whirled around and faced him.

His breath caught in his throat. Her hair shimmered like polished copper, drawn up smoothly in the back of her head, with a froth of curls brushing her cheeks on either side of her face. Not since Montréal had he seen her wear her hair like this. It showed off the grace of her throat and the fine bones of her face. His gaze drifted down and he felt as if someone had ripped the air from his lungs.

Her body was encased in a length of emerald green velvet, her breasts molded like round, ripe fruits above the edge of the low, wide neckline, her shoulders emerging like snowy caps on a green sea. The stiff bodice cut down to her small waist, and her skirts flared out in deep folds.

Shyly, she pulled out a pair of snowshoes from beneath the furs on the bed and walked toward him, her skirts whispering against her legs. "Wapishka's wife taught me how to weave rackets." She shrugged, and the tops of her breasts bobbled seductively. "I worked on them while you were away."

He drank in the sight of her, all shimmering white skin, all curves. The spray of freckles across her nose showed starkly against her skin. Her eyes glowed dark green, full of hesitation and hope. He lifted a finger and touched her cheek, noticing for the first time how fair she was compared with the callused skin of his hands, how tiny were her face and her features.

His little aristocrat. Weaving rawhide thongs through a bentwood framework and presenting them to him like the finest silk embroidery.

He took the rackets from her and ran his fingers

over the taut webbing. "They're beautiful, Gene-vieve."

Her lips parted. He bent down and drew her lush lower lip into his mouth, releasing it before the passion became too strong for him to control.

"Take off your clothes."

She began tearing at the ties to her bodice. He put the rackets aside, leaning them against the wall, then stopped her by engulfing her hands in his.

"No, little bird, not like that." He felt the pounding of her heart beneath his hands. "I want to watch you take them off . . . slowly. Lace by lace. Petticoat by petticoat."

Her lips curved in a smile—a courtesan's smile; she'd been born to be loved like this, he was sure. Genevieve backed away from him, and he leaned against the door and watched. She bent over, giving him an unobstructed view of her full breasts and the tempting dark shadow between them. She lifted her skirts from the floor to show one slim, delicate leg encased in a sleek white stocking. An emerald ribbon held it up at the thigh and she picked at the knot, drawing the satin between her fingers, showing a glimpse of naked flesh just above the edge of the stocking. She let the ribbon flutter to the floor and slowly rolled the stocking down, over her knee, over the swell of her calf, and then off the tip of her pointed toe.

She tossed the stocking aside. André struggled for control as she leaned over and repeated the process with the other leg. He wanted those bare limbs wrapped around his hips. He wanted to cross the two strides that separated them and throw her on the bed and make love to her—now—but he was fixed to the spot as he watched his aristocratic wife slowly strip herself bare of the trappings of civilization . . . all with a seductive half-smile on her face and a wild light in her heavy-lidded eyes.

Tonight, she was his pampered mistress, his highborn courtesan, and she played the part solely for him.

Her bodice was next. It seemed to take forever for her to remove the lacing from the holes hidden beneath a flap of green velvet on the front of the garment. Slowly, the bodice eased and the weight of her full breasts pushed the edges apart. She shrugged it off. Through the thin veiling of her shift, he saw her rosy areolae and watched them peak as she loosened her skirts. She wiggled her hips seductively and stepped out of the pool of velvet.

The fire blazed at her back, showing the blurred outline of her body through the knee-length shift. He leaned away from the door but stood, waiting breathlessly, his loins afire, as she crossed her arms, gathered the linen in her hands, and lifted it. His gaze followed the rising hem, lingering on the auburn pelt of her loins, the gentle curve of her stomach, the ripple of her ribs, finally, resting on her flushed face as she tossed the shift aside.

He took one step toward her.

"No." She held out her hand. "Not yet."

The air burned his lungs. He curled his hands into fists and waited. With both arms, she reached up, bent her head forward, and pulled the pins from her hair. They tinkled as they hit the wooden floor and long, copper curls fell from the neat roll to tumble over her shoulders and rest against her breasts. He couldn't swallow; his throat was too dry. She tipped her head back and shook out her long hair, then smiled slowly and opened her arms.

"*Joyeux Noel*, my husband."

He crossed the space that separated them, folding

his hard arms around her naked body. He knew his lips bruised hers with their insistency, that his beard razed her cheek and chin. He couldn't help it. She was naked, defenseless against him, and he wanted this soft aristocrat with the same urgency that he wanted the rough little savage she had become. He clutched her firm buttocks, spread her legs, and drew her up against him, scraping her naked inner thighs against his cold, damp deerskin, rubbing the icy, crackling leather against her loins until she was crying out in need.

André carried her to the bed and dropped her upon the pelts. He tore the shirt off his back, then unlaced his leggings. The fur ruffled against his shins as he knelt on the bed. Instinctively, she opened her legs to him and he saw her rosy womanhood, gleaming amid the auburn curls in the firelight. Lowering his head, he tasted the noble flesh, breathing in the scent of her, suckling on the nub of her pleasure until she buried her hands in his hair and cried, *"Please."*

He fumbled with his breechcloth, tossing it aside. Clutching her hips, he filled her. She contracted around him on the first, long stroke. André thrust deeper. Genevieve arched up and cried out. He told himself to wait ... *wait* ... to stretch this joyous moment, but when he felt the third pulse of her womanhood, he filled her with love.

The next morning dawned clear and cold. Genevieve slipped out of bed before André stirred and dressed quickly in her deerskins. She tossed another log on the fire and stirred the pot of *sagamité*. She smiled secretly to herself as she gathered the scattered clothing she had stripped off her body the evening before, then flushed hotly as she remembered the long night of lovemaking just passed.

"Come back to bed."

She glanced over her shoulder, recognizing that subtle rumble in his voice. His eyes had not fully opened, but behind their sleepy lids they glittered like stars.

"I thought you'd sleep through the morning."

"Come here."

"Are you going to ravish me again?"

"Yes." He sat up, crawled to the end of the bed, and riffled through his pack at the foot. "First I have another Christmas present for you."

"But you already gave me the caribou robe—"

"It hardly matches what you gave me last night, *Taouistaouisse*."

She sat on the edge of the bed and peered over his shoulder. He pulled a book from the bottom and placed it in her lap. She ran her fingers over the tooled leather, admiring the designs in what appeared to be gold leaf. "*Gargantua and Pantagruel*, by François Rabelais." She stared at him in surprise. "I know you didn't buy this from the Indians."

"I brought it with me from Montréal."

Genevieve lifted the heavy tome and weighed it in one hand. Her eyes narrowed. "After all that complaining about the fripperies in my case, you actually carried a book all the way from Montréal?"

"At the time," he said dryly, "I didn't expect to spend the winter in the company of a lusty woman who not only could warm my bed, but could speak French as well." He nodded to the tome. "That was going to keep my sanity between trips into the interior. I've not gone completely savage, you know."

She opened the book. Though the leaves had not yet been cut, the pages smelled musty and old from dampness. Genevieve fingered the fine grain of the paper. She had expected a pistol or a knife or some kind of weapon necessary in the wilderness. The last thing she expected from him was something as precious and expensive and civilized as a book.

"This place can get lonely," he explained. "I thought you might want to read it when I'm away."

"I'd rather we read it together, a few pages a night."

"We could do that." He pulled her back against his bare chest. "It might keep my hands off you for a few hours a day."

"Talk like that and I'll toss it into the fire."

He pulled her down on the pelts. The book fell out of her hands, tumbling to the floor, while his hand spread greedily over her deerskin-bound breast.

They were interrupted by a pounding on the door. André lifted himself off her and frowned. Over his shoulder, he yelled, "What is it?"

"Ah . . . sir, I need to speak to you about something—"

"Listen, pork-eater, is the fort on fire?"

"No, sir, but—"

"Are the Sioux attacking?"

"No."

"Then leave a married man alone in the morning."

"Sir, we have guests." Julien hesitated. "I think you'd better come out here."

André cursed and rolled off the bed. He searched for his clothes and hastily put them on. Genevieve sighed, pushed her skirt below her knees, and turned her attention to the *sagamité*, thinking that there were definite disadvantages to being married to the leader of a wilderness stockade.

He opened the door and faced a red-faced Julien, then closed the door behind him to keep the heat in the hut. She heard them talking just outside, then noticed a sudden silence.

Curiosity got the best of her. She grabbed her caribou robe and draped it over her shoulders, then stepped out into the frigid cold of the early morning.

André stood with his back to her, ramrod-straight. He and Julien stared across the width of the fort toward the gaping gates of the fortress. Framed in the wooden opening stood a small band of Indians. In the front, a proud-featured Indian squaw stood, her long, sleek black hair falling over one shoulder. She gazed calmly in their direction.

Genevieve placed her hand on his arm. "Who is she, André?"

He didn't look at her. His bicep was as hard as a rock beneath her hand.

"She's my wife."

Chapter Fifteen

Genevieve stared at André through a red haze, as if a fortress full of cannons had turned their dark muzzles toward her, then fired in unison, leaving her body shattered and bleeding on the pristine white snow.

She gripped his bicep and spoke, her voice hoarse and croaky. "André . . . *I'm* your wife."

He looked down at her suddenly, as if only now he became conscious of her presence. Something flashed in his gold-brown eyes. "Genevieve, it's not as it seems."

The ground dipped beneath her feet like a canoe on the swells of Lake Superior. Questions clogged her dry throat and choked her. Her entire body trembled—but with what emotion, she could not say, for a hundred emotions struggled for dominance within her. Disbelief, denial, fury, and betrayal all flooded her senses, but beneath them all flowed a stormy, whirling sea of pain.

André gripped her shoulders. "Genevieve, this is a dangerous situation." He shook her gently. "It's best if you go back inside the house."

She shook her head, at first hesitantly, but as the haze of her shock began to disperse, she shook it more and more vehemently. This couldn't be—*she* was his wife. Only moments ago they had been snug in their home, on the verge of lovemaking. Now this woman appeared. . . . She glared at the squaw, noticing the beads and shells woven in her hair, the fine designs on her moccasins, the eagle feathers—signs of success in battle—hanging from the hair of her escorts.

"You're going to have to trust me, *Taouistaouisse*." A muscle moved in André's cheek as he leaned down, forcing her to face him. "If this situation isn't handled with care, you and me and all the men could find ourselves in the middle of a war. An ugly, bloody war. Do you understand?"

Genevieve looked up into the intense, tawny eyes of the man she loved, the man whose child she longed to bear, the one man she'd trusted with her most precious gift . . . the man to whom she had dedicated her life. She wondered if he were like the other *voyageurs*, like all other men, unable to stay faithful to one woman, marrying and discarding them as he pleased.

"I will tell you everything, I promise." He squeezed her arms reassuringly. "But right now you must go back into the house. For me . . . and for every other Frenchman in this stockade."

He released her. She felt the cold wind slap her cheeks. Julien placed his hand on her arm and tried to draw her away. Suddenly, she realized that all the men of the fort stood in the yard, watching them with curiosity. Her cheeks flooded with color. They all knew . . . they all knew. She had lived in blissful ignorance while all of them had known.

Genevieve set her jaw and yanked her arm free of Julien's grip. She would not be pitied—and she would not show her weakness here, in front of the world. She had her mother's proud blood in her. Wrapping her robe tightly around her, she turned and walked alone into her home.

Inside, her shoulders drooped. Trembling, she leaned back against the wooden door. The heat of the fire blazed against her icy skin and she smelled the ashy odor of burnt *sagamité*. She heard André's footsteps crunching in the snow as he walked away from the house and toward that woman. Genevieve listened to his muffled voice as he spoke in the guttural Indian tongue but she could not distinguish the words of the language she had only just begun to learn.

For him. She had tried to learn the Algonquin dialect for him. She had spent the winter learning the skills of setting up a household in the wilderness for one reason only: to prove to this man she loved that she was worthy to be his bride, that there was no reason to set her aside come spring. Now, all her work was for naught. He had a profusion of wives. The thin veneer of control that pure shock had provided crumbled away like a wall of sand.

She dropped to the floor. Strands of hair caught on the rough boards of the door and pulled painfully on her scalp. Cold winter air flooded in from beneath the frame, chilling her back, but she barely felt these twinges of physical pain. The heart-wrenching sword of betrayal cut deep inside her, releasing a wellspring of anguish, blocking out all other sensations. She curled up into a ball, hugging her caribou robe around her, hugging her shivering body. Hot tears gathered in her eyes.

She had given him everything. She had given him the one gift she truly owned, the one gift that was truly hers to give, the gift she had managed to save despite all odds. But not only had she given him her virginity, she had also given him her heart, and now it lay in bleeding tatters in her chest.

One tear burned a trail down her cheek. She remembered a thousand things he had told her in the weeks of their journey from Montréal. How many times had he resisted her, only to have her press against him, taunt him, seduce him in the only way she knew how? He had told her he would never have a wife. She had believed his resistance was nothing more than the reluctance of a man who did not want the responsibility of a wife—a man who feared the joys of loving and family because of what had happened to Rose-Marie—but now she wondered if he had kept another horrible secret from her.

A wife in the wilderness. An Indian bride.

What a fool I am. Genevieve leaned her head back against the door and gulped in air. She should have known this would happen. He was a man. More than that, he was a passionate man, not the type to live like a celibate monk in the forests when the woods swarmed with young, healthy, lusty Indian maidens offering up their bodies to him without conditions. What need did he have of a French wife and all her demands when an Indian woman would serve his needs better?

The thought wandered into her mind that he might have just taken this woman as his wife while away on his latest trading voyage. The thought pierced her like a poisoned arrow, the pain too excruciating to bear. This was why he loved his life in the wilderness. Here, he was free to take whatever woman pleased him, whenever he wished, free of all encumbrances . . . encumbrances like a possessive French wife.

Genevieve felt the tiniest frisson of anger and she grasped it desperately, holding on to it as a shield against the pain. He had lied to her. The thought intruded that she had lied to him just as severely, but she pushed it away. Her lie would never hurt him, for he would never discover the truth; he would never know who she really was. He must have known that sometime during the winter, she would discover that he found his pleasure outside, as well as inside, the walls of this home.

She sucked in long, deep breaths. The anger grew, dulling the agony. She wiped away the hot trails of tears. Men were faithless creatures. She was a fool to think otherwise. How else did thousands of whores all over France make their living? How had her own mother survived through the years? How else had *she herself* planned to survive those last horrible days before being sent to the Salpêtrière? Genevieve knew at least four *voyageurs* in the fort who had French wives in the settlements as well as Indian wives and half-breed children living in little bark cabins outside this fort. Why would André, the leader of these men, be any different?

She shucked the caribou robe off her shoulders and struggled to her feet. Her legs felt as weak and trembly as if she had walked a seven-mile portage uphill, but somehow she crossed the room and stood before the blazing fire. He was a man like other men, but there was one glaring difference: She was head, heart, and soul in love with him, and no matter what happened today, she knew with certainty that that would never change.

Genevieve didn't know how long she stood motionless in front of the fire, breathing in the coarse odor of burnt *sagamité* rising out of the pot. All time seemed suspended until the moment she heard his footsteps hesitating outside the door to their home. She squared her shoulders and turned to face him, dry-eyed, as he opened the door and stepped inside.

The concern in his eyes unnerved her. Her neck muscles tightened into cords. She struck, nonetheless, for the bow had been drawn too taut for too long.

"Well, my husband, have you picked a wife, or is the array of choices too bewildering for you?"

André had the grace to look shamefaced. He tugged on the beaded Indian sash, tossing it aside along with his robe, then uneasily rubbing the back of his neck. "She's the daughter of a powerful Ojibwa chief."

"Wonderful. A savage of rank." Her eyes narrowed. "Tell me, what's her name? 'Deer Who Runneth Wrongly After Randy Buck' or 'She-Wolf Who Trails After Mate'?"

His eyes flickered. "She's known as Running Squirrel."

"How charming." She gestured toward the pot of ruined *sagamité*. "Should I throw a serving of acorns on the fire for the fleeing rodent?"

"She won't be staying."

"Good. There's barely enough room in that bed for the two of us, and I don't want her gnawing on all the furs." She crossed her arms in front of her. "So. Tell me. Will she be burrowing herself in some tree stump outside the fort, or are you going to build her a nest within the walls?"

"You can put down the knife, Genevieve." His voice was low. "She and her people are leaving tomorrow morning—for good."

She tried not to show her relief, though it bathed her in a sudden tingling warmth. She stared at him, her lips pressed tightly together, waiting for him to continue. He stood by the door, his arms limp at his sides, his tawny gaze steady and even.

"I married her four years ago while I was wintering in Ojibwa country. . . ."

"Four years?!" The words burst from her lips. "You've been married to her for four years?"

"I would have told you . . . but, frankly, I forgot about her. In the spring after the marriage, I returned to Montréal to fight against the Iroquois. When that was over, I discovered I had an inheritance waiting for me, so I left for France."

"You, my husband, have a bad habit of abandoning your wives."

He flinched as if struck. She choked off her own flash of guilt. *He deserves it*, she mused.

"Tell me," she continued, "did a priest preside over this blessed union, or did some Indian shaman do the honors?"

"We married in the way of the country."

Genevieve made an exaggerated gesture of relief. For whatever it mattered, she was still legally married to him. All the rattle-shaking of the Indian ceremonies held no sway in the courts of the settlements. "It's good to know you're not a bigamist as well as a liar."

He stiffened. "I didn't lie to you, Genevieve."

"No? Over and over you told me you would *never* have a wife, and now I discover I'm the third!"

"The only reason I married her was for the benefit of the trading alliance. . . ."

"And the only reason you married me was for a

trading license." She blurted out the question whose answer she feared the most. "Did you enjoy your savage marital rights with her while on this last trip?"

"No. I never saw her. She heard of my presence from one of the tribes we visited while out in the interior, and then she traced me here."

"The Rodent Queen went to a lot of trouble to sniff you out."

"It seems I'm plagued with persistent wives." His face was soft, full of gentle compassion. He was teasing her. "You're jealous, aren't you?"

"I'm furious," she retorted. "You should be sly enough to keep your wife and your courtesan apart."

"She didn't come invited. She had a half a dozen warriors by her side and they were prepared for battle."

"There was war the moment you told me she was your wife."

"I didn't meant to tell you so bluntly." He spread his hands and shrugged. "She surprised me. Some of the Ojibwa's main villages aren't far from here. If the men thought the daughter of one of the boldest chiefs in the tribe was shamed in any way, there could be war." His teeth flashed briefly behind his beard. "I saw bloodlust in your eyes, little bird. I wanted you in this house before the fur started flying—or the arrows."

"It must have been a tender reunion—I didn't hear a battle. I'd have gnawed your face off for abandoning me for that long."

"Not all wives are as possessive as you."

"You told me she's leaving." Her eyes narrowed. "Where is she going? I suppose it's not so far that you can't drop in every once in a while and firm up those trading alliances. . . ."

"Her new husband wouldn't appreciate that."

"What new husband?"

"The one she took while I was away."

"Lies, bigamy, adultery." She threw her hands in the air. "You're all going straight to hell!"

"The Indians are more practical about marriage than the French." He closed the meager distance between them. She flinched when his hands fell upon her shoulders. "When I didn't return to her village for a few years, she assumed I was dead. So she found herself another husband. She's already borne him a child. When she discovered I was alive, she came to ask to be released from our tie and be given to her second husband." He gave a self-conscious laugh. "She came here to get rid of me, little bird, not to be my wife."

"She has more sense than I thought."

"More sense than you." He rubbed the back of his knuckles against her cheek. The logs in the fire crackled and rearranged themselves on the stone floor of the hearth. "All those weeks on the journey, I tried to convince you I wasn't the right man for you, that there was a better man waiting somewhere in Montréal who would give you all you wanted. You never listened."

"You can't get rid of me as easily as you got rid of that squirrel."

"I noticed." His fingers moved to her chin. "I've always had my hands full with you, in more ways than one. When would I have time for a concubine?"

"You'd find time. After all, you're a man." She twisted out of his grip. There was too much to absorb and her emotions were tangled like a fishing net. His tenderness only made it worse. There was nowhere to run in the tiny cabin so she stood, rubbing her arms, her back to him, far too conscious of his tall, strong warmth only a footstep behind her. "Men do things like keep one woman in the wilderness and another back at home in the settlements."

"One wife is more than I can handle."

"One wife at a time, perhaps—"

"Genevieve—"

"—one wife a night, or one wife in every port—"

"Stop it."

"Now at least I know why you don't want me."

"I do want you. That's the whole problem."

"There are a thousand Indian women roaming these woods who would do for you what I do," she retorted, "and they would never ask anything in return."

"What other woman could hunt for grouse one day, and the next dress in green velvet and strip like a courtesan for my pleasure?" He stood close enough so she could feel his body heat from the back of her calves to the back of her head. "I couldn't stop wanting you, though I knew it was best for you that I didn't take you to my bed."

"And now you're sorry that you did."

"No."

Her lips parted. Genevieve waited for him to say something. She turned around and faced him. Their gazes met and locked, and she felt the floor drop beneath her feet.

"I don't want any other woman but you, *Taouistaou-isse*."

It was too much for her to hope, it was too much for her to believe, but the words hung in the air between them.

"I'll be damned to hell for telling you this," he said, "but I love you."

His arms wound around her. Her doubts and fears

and confusion vanished like morning fog beneath a hot summer sun. The bubble of joy reinflated and swelled tautly in her chest.

"Oh, God, André . . . I love you, too."

And all the world was right again.

André glared at the fat, furry creature who stood in his path. The yearling beaver sat up on his hind legs, his broad, scaly tail stretched out behind him. Bits of chaff from the poplar branch he had been chewing littered the fur around his mouth. He squinted up at André, bared his orange-red incisors, and released a querulous churr.

Genevieve's musical laugh filled the woods. She separated from the cluster of Indian squaws who worked around a maple tree, tapping it in order to collect its sweet sap in a little bark pail. She crossed the damp ground, carpeted with blooming bright red trillium and blue lupine, and covered with a dense, wet blanket of dark green moss. Warblers sang loudly in the budding trees above their heads and drops of the morning's rain pattered to the soft earth. Water darkened the deerskin of her dress at the shoulders, where she had been showered with the rain.

"It's all right, my little protector." She scooped up the indignant beaver and nuzzled her face in his dark brown fur. "Isn't he wonderful? He does that to any man who approaches."

André wondered what madness had possessed him to buy the tame yearling for his wife as a pet. She had seen the creature waddling behind one of the bands of Indian traders who arrived weekly at the fort during the late winter. Apparently, those Indians had crushed its lodge and killed its parents a year ago, leaving the kit helpless and its pelt too small to be of any worth. As a result, the squaws had raised the kit and now, a year later, it was as tame as any domesticated dog—at least around women. It hissed and churred at him whenever he approached, and the beaver and his wife were inseparable. Only by locking the creature outside for the night was he ever free of it.

He glared at the beaver with undisguised dislike. "One wrong move and I'm turning him into a hat."

"Hush!" She squeezed the dumpy ball of fur protectively to her chest. "No wonder he growls every time you're around. You look at him as just another pelt."

"He's not just another pelt," André explained. "He's the pelt that's been eating up the fur frames and chewing on my snowshoes."

"The snow is gone—you won't be needing them anymore."

"He's also in the process of gnawing a hole in the corner of the cabin."

"You'd better watch out," she murmured, a sparkle in her green eyes. "If he gets into the cabin at night, he might mistake a certain part of your anatomy for a fresh branch of poplar."

"If he does, he'll join his brothers in the storehouse."

"You just don't like him, do you?"

"He'd taste good boiled in his own skin."

"André!"

"*Jésus*, Genevieve, it's a beast, not a human." He felt a strange stab of jealousy. The beaver's eyes were closed and he made a purring sound against her breasts. Lately, that creature got more attention from his wife than he did. "If you can put that ball of fur down for a moment, I need to talk to you."

Her green eyes shuttered. In the passage of a single

moment, she withdrew completely behind some kind of invisible door. He frowned and wondered for the hundredth time what had happened between them these past few weeks. Her withdrawal dated from about the time he had purchased the damn yearling for her, or maybe a little before. It had grown worse as the ice cracked into huge floes on the lake and the spring rains began to melt the winter snow. It was as though the more the earth thawed, the colder she grew.

It wasn't as if their lovemaking had waned. It was as hungry and passionate as ever—perhaps even more so, because whenever he got close enough to touch her, he demanded the most intimate contact, the most thorough lovemaking. It was the only time he felt he was reaching her. Inevitably, they shared a moment of hungry intimacy and then she withdrew, far, far into herself, far away from him, and no amount of teasing or kissing could draw her out.

"Let's talk later." She gestured to where the Indian squaws worked, pounding a tube into the rind of a maple tree. "We've got six or seven pails full of sap that have to be boiled down before sunset."

"There are other things for you to do. We're leaving for Montréal the day after tomorrow."

"Oh, no!"

The exclamation was so heartfelt, so fearful, that he gazed at his wife with new intensity. She covered her lips with her hand and whirled so her back was to him.

"It's only April." She glanced through the trees at the gleaming surface of Lake Superior. "The ice only just broke up in the bay. There must still be ice somewhere on the lake. . . ."

"The party I sent out to reconnoiter returned today. The shores are free enough to leave."

"I thought we'd wait until it was warmer." She bent and released the furball to the ground. "There is still frost on the ground in the mornings, and there's snow on the hills, and the stream just west of here is roaring with the spring outflow. . . ."

"We'll be on the lake for at least a week before we hit any rivers. By then, they'll be free of ice."

She pulled an amber-colored rock from the pouch at her waist and began sucking nervously on the chunk of maple sugar. Genevieve had developed a voracious appetite for the hard, sweet chunks in the past weeks. His loins tightened as he remembered an evening when he had softened one of the rocks and rubbed it all over her body, then slowly licked off every drop of the sweet, buttery substance.

"Our leaving so early wouldn't have anything to do with the Sioux, would it?"

He started abruptly out of his wandering thoughts. "What do you know of the Sioux?"

"There are rumors that the Sioux are going to attack and massacre us all. The women told me." She raised a brow at him. "Is it true?"

André frowned. He had tried to keep her ignorant of the rumors, but her ability to understand and speak the Ottawa dialect had gotten too good over the winter. It was true. The Sioux were threatening to attack. The threat made him edgy. A wealth of furs lay within the fort, and their powder and shot was almost spent. He and his men had a choice: They had to abandon the fortress or face a war they couldn't win.

Another time, another place, he might have railed against the situation, for he stood to lose a great deal of money because of the threat of the Sioux attack. Right now all that concerned him was getting Genny far, far away from the danger. "The Sioux have been fighting for a long time over the right to harvest wild rice in the marshes south of here. They resent the Huron and Ottawa interlopers who've moved in." He shrugged. "It's just a rumor."

"A strong enough rumor that the Ottawa canoemen aren't going to Montréal with us."

"*Sacrebleu!* Have you been listening at the door of the storehouse?"

"The women know more about this than you think." She removed the gleaming rock of maple sugar from her lips. "I know if the Indians don't join us, then we'll have to leave half the furs here."

"Not half," he said angrily, frustrated that she knew so much about his arrangements when he had tried to keep them all secret. "Just a portion. I've trusted some Ottawas to come to Montréal later in the season with the remainder of the furs, when the Sioux threat has passed."

"By that time," she mused, "they'll be eaten by moths and mold."

"And we'll all be alive and well to bargain next year." And next year, he vowed, he wouldn't rely on the capricious nature of the natives. He would make arrangements for men from Montréal to come here in the spring with new merchandise and with enough canoes to transfer the furs back to the settlements. This way, he could set up a permanent post in the wilderness—a necessary advancement if he ever intended to stretch the tentacles of the fur trade farther west.

It also meant that if he wanted, he would never, ever have to personally return to the settlements again.

André staunched the pain ripping through his heart. He had wanted to speak to her for weeks about his plans, but she had been so distant, and he was loath to push her farther away . . . not before he had to. Now that the reconnoitering party had returned with news, there was no more excuse for delay.

He stepped toward her and ran a hand over her hair, warmed by the spring sunshine. Encouraged by her stillness, he said, "I've been wanting to talk to you, but you've been acting so strangely. What is it, *Taouistaouisse?*"

"It's nothing." She gathered her wits and returned the sticky rock to her pouch. "I just didn't think we'd leave so soon."

"We've been preparing to leave for weeks."

She tossed her plait over her shoulder. "I try not to stay inside the stockade. It's too crowded, with the canoes scattered all over the place. And the stench of heated pitch makes me sick."

"I thought you were avoiding me."

"Don't be silly."

"Am I, *Taouistaouisse?*" He nodded to the beaver who waddled his way over to a sapling. "Sometimes I think you'd rather spend time with that yearling than with me."

"You can't possibly be jealous of a beaver."

"You were once jealous of a squirrel."

"That squirrel wore a dress. This is just a pet."

"I'm jealous of anything," he added, leaning close enough to smell the maple sugar on her lips, "that gets to nuzzle your breasts."

She looked directly at him. "Does that include babies?"

"Babies?"

"According to the squaws," she said, placing her hand on her abdomen, "I'm going to have one before the first snows of winter."

The air rushed out of his lungs, and his gaze dropped to her splayed hand. He had taken four trips into the interior over the winter, each about ten days to two weeks in length, and although as soon as they were reunited they spent every day and every night making love, André had somehow thought the long weeks of frustrating celibacy would somehow prevent his seed from taking root in her womb. He always knew in the back of his mind what they were risking, but he'd convinced himself never to think more than a few hours ahead, never beyond the taste of her next kiss.

Her fingers splayed over the deerskin, and he noticed for the first time the slight, almost imperceptible fullness to her belly. A powerful sensation rippled through his veins, his chest inflating as he took a deep breath and felt himself charged with some sort of primal, elemental pride. He had marked his woman in the most basic, natural way. He had taken Genny and filled her with his child.

"I didn't realize it would come as such a shock," she said dryly. "This is what usually happens when a man and a woman marry—and you certainly haven't done anything to prevent it."

André reached out and removed her hand, covering the gentle swell of her abdomen with his own. He felt her muscles contract beneath the deerskin at his touch. This was the result of all those long nights and slow, lazy days of lovemaking. This was the product of the love he felt for this maddening, exciting, sensuous woman. He marveled that in her small body, nestled somewhere deep in the warmth of her womb, beneath his hand, lay the beginnings of his son or daughter.

Their child. His and Genevieve's. An entirely new life. *Life.*

"*Sacré chien!*" She covered his hand with hers and pressed it close to her belly. "Say something, André. Don't stand there like a mute."

He glanced at her face. Though her voice was hard,

her eyes searched his with an intensity that bordered on desperation.

Inanely, he said, "We're going to have a child."

"Well, it's not going to be a beaver. Are you happy or not?"

"Ah, Genny . . ." His fingers dug gently into her abdomen. He felt it again, the thrill of wonder, the rush of male pride, and it left him without words. "How long have you known?"

"I've been sure for about two, three weeks."

"Why didn't you tell me?"

"You were so involved with the preparations for returning to the settlements—"

"Not so involved," he argued, "that we couldn't make love every single night."

"I thought you'd be angry."

"For filling you with my child?"

She looked at him mutely, but her eyes betrayed her. They were so full of uncertainty that he let go of her abdomen, stepped closer, and framed her face with his hands. He kissed her gently, for suddenly she seemed like a fragile little bird in his arms, trembling and small.

"How could I be angry at you," he murmured, deep in the silken threads of her hair, "for something neither you nor I had the power to prevent?"

"Tiny told me . . ." Her breath trembled. "He told me . . . about Rose-Marie. About . . . the babe."

His hands stilled in her hair as his thoughts darkened. Yes, there'd been a baby once before. Unborn. His and Rose-Marie's. Strange, but he'd never really thought about it too much, never really allowed himself to acknowledge it. He'd not known about the babe until he saw Rose-Marie throw herself off the canoe, killing herself and the child in her womb. The babe was gone before it had ever been real.

Now, feeling the soft swell of Genny's belly, André felt a spurt of anger at his late wife, for selfishly taking that child with her, for not being strong enough to survive at any cost.

"You want this baby?" she asked.

"Of course I do."

"I thought you'd be angry. You seemed so anxious to go back to the settlements, and now we'll have to stay here."

"Stay here?"

She tilted her head back. "I'm pregnant. I can't travel all the way back to Montréal."

"You're not staying here with the Sioux thinking of war. . . ."

"But last fall you said the journey would be dangerous if I were pregnant."

"You can't travel if you're as big as a house." His hand slipped down between them, to the slight swell of her abdomen. "You've got a few months before you grow awkward. We've got to get you back now, before it becomes too dangerous for you to travel. The sooner you're back in the settlements, the safer you'll be."

"No!"

He frowned at her adamancy. "Do you want to give birth here, in the middle of the forests, with no one but Indian shaman and squaws to attend you?"

"I don't care about midwives and straw mattresses. The Indian women do well enough without them." Genevieve stepped back, out of the circle of his embrace. Her hands moved protectively over her abdomen. "I want to stay here with you."

"You know I'm going to Montréal with you."

"But what happens in Montréal, André?" She tilted her chin. "Will you find a way to annul this marriage . . . a marriage that is about to bear fruit?"

So that is it, little Taouistaouisse. Suddenly, he understood why she had kept so quiet about the child these
past weeks. The snow was melting and he was preparing to depart, and she was wondering if he would
cast her away.

His blood ran cold, for in a sense, he was planning
to do just that.

Genny, Genny, Genny . . . Stubborn little witch. He'd
come full circle again, with this woman, full with his
child, to be left alone in the settlements. He'd do the
same with her as he'd done with Rose-Marie all those
years ago. It was a decision he knew, instinctively, she
would not like, and so he had never said a word.
Better to spend a winter in harmony and wrestle with
the demon in the spring.

It was the only way. He could not give up the dreams
of a lifetime, the dreams of finding the China Sea
beyond the next range of mountains, up the next
river, into the next valley; he'd be a shell of a man
if he were forced to live in one place for the rest of
his life, his dreams burning a hole in his brain. Nor
could he take her with him. Though she had struggled
and survived this single voyage into the wilderness,
she had not been heavy with child. The settlements
were safer than these woods, and that is where she
belonged, she and his babe, to live healthy and safe.

If he were a stronger man, he'd let her go. He'd
give her to a better man. But this was his punishment:
to suffer the pain of separation and worry when he
was away from her, and to suffer the chains of civilization in order to be with her.

Perhaps it was all his pagan musings that made
God mock him so. Again, he'd have a wife in the
settlements. A wife and a child. He was tearing himself
in two, splitting his existence between two forces he
loved equally—the wilderness in which he had spent

his life, and the woman he had grown to love as much as life itself.

"My father left his land to me, outside of Montréal, when he died," André said, toeing a rock out of the mulch. "I'm going to restore the house on it when we return."

Her lips spread in a blinding, incredulous smile. "You won't set me aside?"

"*Jésus.*" He kicked the pebble across the ground. "Do you think I could just cast you away?"

"But last fall you said—"

"Forget what I said last fall. I was a fool."

"But I thought nothing had changed." She leaned into him and spread her hands on his chest. "I thought you'd still wander the woods."

"I will wander the woods." He clutched her hands and held them tight. "But when I return, I'll come home to you."

She blinked, finally understanding. The light that had begun to grow in her eyes dimmed like a candle snuffed out by the wind. She yanked her hands out of his grip. "Then you *are* abandoning me."

"Only for part of the year. I'll be back in the summers. You'll have a home, Genevieve, just like you always wanted—only it will be in Montréal."

"I like this home." A defiant light returned to her eyes. "I'll return with you in the fall. . . ."

"You'll be as round as you are tall, little bird." He reached out and brushed a strand of hair off her temple. "It'll be too dangerous. . . ."

"Dangerous, dangerous!" She crossed her arms. "That's all you talk about is danger."

"I'm not going to watch you die on the trail from a miscarriage," he argued, "nor am I going to watch you bleed to death in my arms after a difficult birth somewhere on the banks of the Ottawa River. I want

you safe—in the settlements—for the sake of you and
the sake of our child."

"After all we've been through," she murmured,
"do you think I'll really stay put come the fall?"

"You've never been pregnant," he warned. "Come
autumn, you'll won't be as swift and agile as you are
now. You'll be willing to stay. And there are ways,
little bird, to keep you at home . . . ways that I probably
should have used long ago."

André knew she wouldn't like this unhappy com-
promise. He also knew that she would have no choice
but to agree with it, at least for now.

Genevieve dropped her gaze, but her chin was as
high as the heavens. "So we're leaving the day after
tomorrow?"

"Yes." He stepped closer to her and ran his knuckles over her soft cheek. "You mustn't work too hard.
The trip will be exhausting enough, and I want you
healthy when you give birth to our child."

Her lips softened and her chin dropped. "I'll do
nothing to risk the baby. You don't have to worry
about that."

He heard a hiss coming from the ground and he
glanced down to see the beaver on his hind legs again,
his beady eyes fixed on him. She bent down and
picked up the yearling.

"Poor thing." She nuzzled his fur. "He doesn't
want to leave, either."

"He's not coming with us."

Genevieve arched a brow. "Isn't he?"

"Over my dead body."

Yet somehow, by the tilt of her chin, André knew
that the beaver would be the tenth passenger in the
canoe back to civilization.

Chapter Sixteen

The men sang.

Their music rang above the distant roaring of the rapids of Saint Louis, echoed in the unbroken shore of pines and carried over the foam-streaked waters of the Saint Lawrence River. The song broke in mid-verse as the men rounded the last wooded bluff and caught sight of the line of peaked-roofed houses, the rough log palisades set back from the shore, the frowning military fort and great stone mill of the settlement of Montréal.

Julien's paddle clattered against the kegs as he rose to his feet. His splotchy, whiskered face broke into a proud smile. He had completed his first journey into the interior and he would never again be called a pork-eater. Genevieve caught a glimpse of Tiny's yellowed grin as he glanced over his shoulder and winked at the Roissier brothers, pointing toward a cluster of brightly clad women gathered near the landing point. Siméon bowed his head and murmured a prayer, then gazed up at the sight of the cross perched atop the Hôtel-Dieu, appearing stark against the blinding clear blue of the sky.

The men looked at each other silently, then they filled the air with a series of piercing Indian shrieks.

The beaver barked a plaintive cry, waddling swiftly across the length of the canoe to huddle against the green velvet of Genevieve's skirts. Absently, she ran her hand over the yearling's sleek pelt and watched the town come into sight.

Two wide-hulled vessels bobbed in the middle of the Saint Lawrence, the unfurled sails of one still bleached and salt-stained from the distant sea. Set back from the muddy shore, a cluster of compact dwellings faced the river, huddled against the encroachment of the surrounding forest. Atop the square bastioned fort of stone that formed the western defense, a line of soldiers in their bright white and blue uniforms stood with their muskets aloft. A staccato series of sharp reports rent the air in welcome and wisps of blue smoke hung against the blinding sky. Before the smoke dispersed, the clangor of churchbells rang through the air.

The canoe rocked wildly as the *voyageurs* sat down and picked up their paddles anew. Despite the fact that they had canoed well over a thousand miles in the past five weeks, and had spent the morning portaging past the rapids of the Long Sault and Saint Louis, the men dug their paddles deep into the boiling waters of the river as if they had just begun the voyage. Tiny started another boastful *voyageur*'s song while the men, lean-armed, worked frantically, tipping, thrusting, battling the strong current of the mighty river, steering the painted nose of the battered birch bark canoe toward Montréal's muddy shore.

After five weeks of icy lakes and swollen rivers and long, muddy portages, after five weeks of living solely on dried, roasted pemmican, a tough, tasteless beaver meat packed in tallow, after nearly nine months away from the settlements . . . they had finally returned to civilization.

Yet despite all the gaiety and anticipation and laughter around her, Genevieve's spirits had dropped to the frigid, murky depths of the Saint Lawrence River. This was the end of the journey for André and herself. Soon enough, he would leave her on these shores to rejoin the love he had left behind—the great Canadian wilderness.

As if sensing the darkness of her mood, André crouched behind her. He brushed the heavy trail of hair off her damp neck. "The worst is over now, *Taouistaouisse.* We'll be at the inn in a little while."

She looked up at him. His hair, streaked blonder by the days on the open rivers, fell over his forehead and shaded his eyes. Eyes that had stared at her naked, slightly swelling abdomen in wonder during the dark nights when they'd camped on the banks of the river. Eyes that had witnessed her retching over the side of the canoe much too frequently since they'd left Chequamegon Bay.

Twice, André had forced the entire contingent to stop and camp until he decreed she had regained enough strength to continue. Had she not argued vociferously against it, he would have laid her on a deerskin stretcher and carried her over the long portages. There was something wonderful about his incessant concern, his willingness to climb trees to find birds' eggs for her dinner, to send the men out to hunt for fresh game to feed her strange and frequent cravings—but she was insistent about completing this journey under her own power.

It had proven only one thing. She would never survive an autumn voyage into the interior while heavy with his child. He knew the truth. Although they never spoke of it, he knew also that she had learned the same painful lesson.

Genevieve turned away from his concerned gaze and stared at the approaching shore. "You owe me, Lefebvre."

"Owe you?"

"For five weeks, you've been telling me all the wonderful things you're going to buy for me as soon as we reach the settlements." She jerked her chin at the wide-spaced row of merchant's booths lined up on the Commune, the muddy space between the houses and the river. "All I see here are beads and kettles and blankets."

"The Indians who come in from the interior trade on the shore," he explained, running a cool finger down her neck. "On Saint Paul Street, there are shops with every kind of frippery you could imagine, straight from France."

"You've dug your own pauper's grave, *Onontio*." Tiny laughed. "She'll spend all your furs before the week's through."

André ignored him and continued to toy with her hair. "Tell me the first thing you want."

"Brandy!" Tiny exclaimed, before Genevieve could answer. "Brandy and a good long stick of tobacco. Just wish Wapishka was here to enjoy it with me."

Disappointment glazed Tiny's face. Wapishka had left the contingent at Allumette Island to settle with his wife and children in their Indian village. It was too dangerous for the Negro to come to the settlements and enjoy the fruits of his labor, so he had said his goodbyes a week earlier.

"I'm going to eat a whole goose," Julien exclaimed.

"Stewed in its own juices, and with it a loaf of white bread."

"That's not what you told me last night," Gaspard interjected, his eyes dancing, ducking as Julien splashed him with water.

"You should all go directly to the chapel and seek absolution," Siméon grumbled. "After this past winter, your souls are in mortal peril."

"Why waste time seeking absolution now," Anselme argued, "when we'll just have to seek it again later?"

Genevieve mused while the men argued, becoming more and more conscious of André's warm breath against her throat.

"The first thing I want," André whispered, "is four solid walls and one soft bed."

She bit her lip to prevent herself from smiling, closing her eyes as his lips brushed the lobe of her ear.

"Do you realize this will be the first time in five weeks that I'll have you all alone?"

"Five weeks and two days."

His hands tightened on her shoulders. Though they had managed to sneak away, out of sight of the men, several times during the voyage, their lovemaking was always hungry and anxious, for they never knew when the next opportunity would present itself. The few times they had made love beneath the tent in the middle of the night were slow, quiet interludes, where they had to bite their lips to prevent themselves from crying out.

"Tell me that's what you want, *Taouistaouisse*, and we'll be at the inn before these men finish their next song."

She giggled as he kissed a sensitive spot just below her ear and her skin shivered with goose bumps. Her eyes flew open as an idea struck her. "Gooseberry jam."

André fell back on his heels. The men turned to her in surprise, then they struggled with laughter.

"There's nothing wrong with wanting jam," she argued. "The nuns served it to me while I was sick at the Hôtel-Dieu in Québec." Her mouth watered just thinking of it; certainly it wasn't such a strange request. Genevieve blinked up at André. "You *did* promise me anything."

"Mmm." His brows drew together in frustration. "Anything else?"

"Boiled eggs." She ran a hand over the beaver's back. "And aniseed cakes."

He winced. "No wonder you're sick all the time."

"You'd be sick, too," she retorted, "if you had a babe growing in your belly."

He pressed a warm kiss against her neck, his beard scraping her skin. "I promise you'll have your gooseberry jam, your eggs, and your aniseed cakes before the night is through."

They neared the shore at a landing point just west of town, where a slew of canoes already lay upside down on the bank, a bevy of merchants in their silver buckles and wide-brimmed beaver hats critically scanning the merchandise being unloaded on the banks. Shouting, quarreling for space, the *voyageurs* splashed into the water and pulled the canoe close to shore, then began unloading the tightly wrapped packets of beaver pelts.

André leapt off the canoe and sank to his hips in the water. He reached for her. The beaver dove neatly off the side of the vessel and swam his way through the line of men toward the shore, his long leash trailing behind him. The men upon the shore stared at him in stunned confusion.

"He won't get clubbed ... not here, anyway," André said as he noticed her anxious look. "None of these men know how to cure a pelt."

Genevieve gestured to the cluster of wigwams and camp fires just to the west of the landing point. "And I suppose you're going to tell me the Indians don't know how to cure pelts, either?"

"They'll take one look at the way that creature waddles after you, and they'll think it's a spirit and leave it alone."

"He's staying with me."

"At the inn?" André's lips clamped shut on a sharp shake of his head. "Not a chance, Genevieve."

"He'll be killed out here and you know it."

"My men will watch him."

"Your men will be either sotted to the gills," she retorted, tightening her arms around his neck as he walked toward the shore, "or hiding in some dramshop all night."

"Not until all these furs are safe in some merchant's warehouse."

"Then until then, we'll have to take him into the inn."

He released her as they reached the shore. Her feet, encased in her old, rigid boots, sank deep into the mud. She waited for him to answer. Several times during the trip from Lake Superior, they had awoken to find the beaver nosing his way between their bodies, seeking a warm place to sleep. André had threatened to strangle the creature, but instead he'd fashioned a leash for it and tied it up close to the water. After a few nights of angry, mournful hisses and cries, where André made hungry love to his wife in order to keep her from running out to it, the yearling finally quieted down and accepted its fate.

"I'm not going to have him interrupting my nights away from the wilderness, Genevieve. . . . "

"I'll tie him up. Away from the bed."

"One whine out of him," André warned, "and he takes his place among my other pelts."

Genevieve frowned and watched her husband stride away to speak with Tiny. The beaver perched at her feet and ran his front paws over his head, cleaning his soaking fur. She crouched down, ignoring the bite of her boned bodice on her swollen stomach, and ran her hand over the beaver's damp coat. Besides her well-worn moccasins and deerskin dress, both of which she had lovingly folded and put away in her ragtag woven case this morning as she'd changed into her French clothing, the yearling was the only real memento she had from the long winter spent in Chequamegon Bay. Someday soon, the beaver and her child would be all she had left for company.

She tilted her chin and breathed in the warm breeze, angrily blinking back the bite of tears. She had no right to be so desolate. This time last year, she would have given her life for the things she would soon own: a plot of land and a new home; a place in this exotic wilderness; a new name and a new identity. She would have died in ecstasy to know that she would also have a strong, handsome, rich husband who loved her—and whom she loved. Her hand drifted to the growing swell of her abdomen beneath the waistband of her velvet skirt. The babe was a special gift—icing upon the sweetcakes . . . the extra drop of brandy that made her cup runneth over.

So why did she feel as if her whole world were crumbling around her?

André was suddenly beside her. "Are you all right?"

"I'm fine." She straightened and smoothed her fingers over her belly, her head swimming at the sudden motion. His hands gripped her firmly.

"It's just the heat," she insisted.

"Your freckles are showing."

Genevieve frowned and glared at him. He always said that when she looked pale, and he knew it irritated her to no end. "If you fed me more often, I wouldn't feel so faint."

"Ah, now the color is back in those cheeks." He leaned closer to her. "If you're feeling faint, maybe we should go directly to the inn so you can lie down. . . . "

"Absolutely not." She shrugged away from him and headed toward the Commune. "I'm so hungry I could eat a moose."

The beaver waddled behind them as they passed the wide-spaced rows of temporary booths made of rough-hewn logs. A string of men, bent under the burdens from some newly arrived vessel, made their way from the shore to the marketplace. Throngs of Indians armed with bows and arrows, war clubs, or cheap guns meandered among the rows, some of them completely naked but for the eagle feathers on their heads, the paint on their faces, and the briefest of loincloths. She smiled as she watched a merchant in wide bright blue satin breeches block the view of a naked savage from the sight of his young daughter.

To Genevieve, it was like a savage version of the Saint-Germain fair. The singing that rose above the babble of a dozen languages came from drunken *voyageurs*, not drunken Musketeers, and the items being sold were beads, pots, iron tools, and red blankets, not jewels, lace, and exotic timepieces. The currency wasn't dirty sous but thick pelts of beaver fur. A priest, who stood out among the gaudily dressed merchants in his black robes, checked for the illegal sale of brandy to the Indians. Genevieve even caught sight of a pickpocket among the crowds.

Never again. She hugged the thought close to her heart. *Never will I have to do that again.*

André picked up the beaver as the crowds grew thicker. They strolled along the Rue Saint Paul, past a closely spaced row of mercantile establishments, stores, trading posts, and warehouses. The scent of bread wafted out of one of the stores and she stopped in her tracks.

"I smell aniseed cakes."

He shook his head, sniffing the air curiously as she headed straight for the bakery. She pointed directly to the aniseed cakes lying on one of the tables and the baker wrapped up a dozen as André paid. Returning to the street, Genevieve stopped in a tavern and convinced the wife of the owner to boil a half-dozen eggs while they waited. André stood by as the rotund woman jawed endlessly about her first, second, and third pregnancies. Genevieve's mouth watered and her stomach growled angrily as they searched, in vain, for gooseberry jam in the establishments along the street. Finally, after what seemed like hours, she boldly approached a Jesuit in black robes. Appealing to his merciful nature, Genevieve managed to charm him into giving her a precious jar of gooseberry jam from the seminary stores.

Loaded with bundles, André finally steered her toward an inn at the end of Saint Paul Street.

"The Sly Fox," she exclaimed as she saw the sign swaying in the wind.

"The last time I stayed here," he said, "a beautiful woman insisted on spending the night in my bed."

"You were foolish enough to refuse."

"I intend to rectify that mistake, little bird."

She tossed her head. "Not until I eat dinner."

They strode into the inn. The common room was filled with bearded, buckskin-clad *voyageurs* drinking something out of tin cups. It didn't take long for Genevieve to realize that this room had been transformed into a dramshop, and the bright-cheeked, bright-eyed, loud-mouthed men were drinking their fill of brandy. It seemed most of the houses along this street had turned into dramshops of one sort or another. André warded off the men's curious glances with one piercing glare, but as soon as his back was turned to get a key from the innkeeper, Genevieve felt a dozen gazes return to the bodice of her low-cut velvet. She hefted up the beaver, holding him protectively against her chest, and was relieved when André shifted his bundles under one arm and placed his free hand on her waist to lead her upstairs to a room.

"You're not to leave the room," he said gruffly, "unless I or one of my men is with you."

"But—"

"Unless you want me hanged on the Commune for murder, Genevieve, there'll be no buts." His chin tightened. "White women—beautiful white woman—are as rare here as gold coins and just about as coveted. Those men probably haven't seen one in almost a full year."

She didn't argue. Men hadn't looked at her like that since her days on the streets of Paris, a hundred lifetimes ago. André's hand pressed against her back as he led her toward a room in the back of the inn. He slipped the key into the door and pushed it open, slamming it closed behind him and sliding the bolt into its sleeve.

"Put that creature down."

His voice was husky and ragged, and she released the beaver to the floor. He waddled away, sniffing around. Genevieve walked over to the window, leaned on the bed, and opened the shutters. Golden light flooded the room. Just outside the window, a plum tree stood, its pale pink flowers filling the air with fragrance.

Suddenly, André was behind her, his hands winding around her body, resting possessively on her swollen belly. His beard scraped the tender flesh of her neck. She tilted her head to give him better access to her collarbone.

"I'm hungry for you, *Taouistaouisse.*"

His kisses grew insistent. Her knees weakened, and she leaned heavily against him. It had been so long since they had made love with utter abandon. His fingers worked at the ties of her bodice, freeing her breasts from the restraint. His hands slipped beneath the velvet and cupped each breast over the worn linen of her chemise, his thumbs working magic over her taut nipples, which had grown tender and sensitive during her pregnancy.

Then her stomach growled, loud and insistent, and he stopped abruptly. "That child is likely to eat us out of house and home." He reluctantly released her. "Let's feed him so we can get down to more serious business."

Light-headed and woozy with desire, she sank on the bed. He walked over to where he had dumped the packages and tossed them on the worn coverlet. She reached for the package of aniseed cakes and ripped it open. Her mouth watered as she bit into one, savoring the taste of licorice.

Genevieve had finished two more before he had completed peeling the shell off one of the hard boiled eggs. He handed it to her and she bit eagerly into the rubbery texture, sucking out the crumbly yolk, finishing the white, then licking her fingers clean.

When she looked up, André was staring at her. He handed her another egg, watching as she bit off the top and eased out the round yellow yoke with her tongue. She arched a brow at him as she finished the white. "What about my gooseberry jam?"

He searched among the debris for the tin. "I'll give it to you on one condition."

"Beast! You're going to withhold gooseberry jam from a pregnant woman?"

"I will," he said, "unless you take off your bodice."

She sucked in her breath. His eyes were dark in passion. A smile hovered on her lips as she slowly arched her back and peeled off her open, gaping bodice. Her nipples hardened and poked against the threadbare linen.

André leaned over the bed toward her, rising to kiss her lips. She met them, brushed her lips against his, then pulled away. "My jam, husband?"

Reluctantly, he sat back. A muscle moved in his cheek. He fumbled with the knife hanging from his belt, then opened the tin and spread some of the crimson jam over a torn end of bread.

Genevieve took the warm bread from his hands and raised it to her lips, moaning as the tart sweetness of the jam filled her mouth and made her teeth sing. She finished every bite of the bread, then licked her fingers clean, looking at him expectantly.

"No more," he said, his voice hoarse, "until you take off your skirt."

"That's extortion, husband." She held out her hand, but he made no move to give her any more. Abruptly, she stood up and removed her skirt. Her boots tumbled to the floor. She lifted her shift and untied the ribbons that held up her stockings, sending them flying to the middle of the room.

The tin of jam tipped dangerously in his hand as

she sat back down on the bed dressed in nothing but a shift.

"I think that means I get at least three or four more pieces," she demanded, her attention drifting nonetheless to the bulge beneath the hem of his shirt.

"Are you still hungry?"

"Starved."

André glopped the jam on the bread, handing her three pieces in rapid succession. She ate them, licked her fingers clean, then waited for more. He stared with intent at her shift. She didn't need any prompting. Her blood pounded hard in her body, fueled by the promise in his eyes. She sat up and pulled the offending garment over her head. The warm summer breeze flowed in through the plum blossoms and caressed her naked skin. She waited for him to move.

"Are you still hungry?" he asked.

"Not for gooseberry jam." Her body throbbed with a different sort of hunger, a different sort of need. "Not anymore."

"Then it's my turn to feast."

He clattered the jamb on the windowsill. With one rapid sweep, he cleared the bed. Debris flew across the floor. The beaver squealed and scattered into a corner. André leaned over and pressed her down so she lay flat on the mattress. He kissed her hungrily, his lips parting hers, his tongue exploring deep into her mouth. Genevieve wound her fingers in his long hair and pressed him close, wanting him to possess her, to keep her with him forever.

Even as his kisses grew more heated, more demanding, even as his hand closed over her breast and lifted her peaked nipple to his hot mouth, she knew she could never really have him, not the way she could have a home or land or even security. His life, his spirit, his dreams, all resided in the wilderness.

She couldn't hate him for it, she couldn't blame him
for it, for she had fallen in love with that half-savage
man, and he would not be the same if he didn't crave
the freedom he knew only deep in the woods. Trying
to capture him was like trying to capture the wind.

She had him now. Genevieve held him, like an
eddy of tropical air in a cove, whirling about for a
time before siphoning its way out. She would hold
him for this brief moment and treasure it forever.
There was so much she wanted to share with him.
His hand slipped between her legs. She gasped and
parted them for him, eagerly inviting this invasion of
her body and soul.

Gently, he pulled away from her. His breath came
fast between his lips. André rid himself of all his
clothing, tossing his garments in the growing pile on
the floor. Bare flesh met bare flesh, and she lay back
and closed her eyes.

Genevieve opened them abruptly as she felt him
rub something sticky and cold over her left breast.

His eyes sparkled with devilry, and his finger and
her breast gleamed with gooseberry jam.

"It's my turn to feast," he murmured, just before
his hot mouth descended.

She groaned and buried her fingers in his hair.
Yes, feast, my love. Soon there would be nothing but
famine.

"We're here."

André waved vaguely toward the northern shore
of the Saint Lawrence River. The canoe lurched as
Genevieve clutched the rim and teetered to one side,
peering beyond her husband's stiff shoulders to the
bank. A tattered wooden pier jutted out onto the
river from a snarl of brush and saplings.

The beaver churred upon her lap as Genevieve curled her fingers into its slick coat. All along the river route from Montréal, patch after patch of newly cleared land had stretched from a sliver of the river's northern shore deep into the forest beyond. Neat little log houses had perched just beyond the river's edge, belching blue kitchen-smoke from stone chimneys. But here, so far away from the main settlement, a nest of growth shielded from the river the merest glimpse of André's father's house.

The house that would soon be hers.

Her belly quivered, stronger than the vague flutterings of the babe. A cool breeze, tinged faintly with sea-salt, lifted a tendril of hair off her cheek. Somewhere in that tangle of wild woods stood the fulfillment of her dreams, the home in which she'd spend the rest of her living days, the place where she'd raise one child, perhaps more, God willing. Now, so close to it, Genevieve trembled with the old, familiar yearning, along with a strange, shimmering emotion that swelled to bursting in her chest.

The sweetness of success, she told herself. She'd fought for this and prevailed.

The canoe's rim slid alongside the pier. André wedged his paddle into one of the missing slats, grinding the vessel to a halt. Genevieve heaved the beaver off her lap and dumped it onto the platform, then gripping the damp edge of the canoe, she gingerly stepped out of the rocking vessel. André leapt out as gracefully as the mountain cat she'd seen on the trip back from Chequamegon Bay, all bunched muscles and economy of motion.

Tears swelled and blurred her vision. She ducked her head and brushed the chaff from her skirts as André pulled the canoe deep into the brush and tied it to a clutch of brush. What a foolish woman she was becoming, collapsing into tears at the merest memory. All the way from Montréal, her emotions had shifted like the winds. That's what pregnancy would do to you, the baker's wife had told her. Make a woman all weepy and strange. Well, *she* wouldn't give in to it. She wouldn't shame herself in front of André or ruin this moment of triumph, all because of a woman's weakness.

"Look, André." Genevieve tipped her chin at her beaver, who had dropped the wedge of wood he'd been chewing and set to chipping away at the trunk of a sapling upon the shore. "Do you still think him useless?"

André's jaw tightened. "It'll take more than a single beaver to clear this shore."

"Then I'll have to find him—or her—a mate."

She leaned close to him and smiled, but her smile faded as his expression remained stony, his gaze fixed on the woods. He'd been in a strange mood all morning, silent and grim, avoiding her eye throughout the trip from Montréal. In some deep place present in all women, Genevieve knew it was a memory that had cast this shadow upon his face. Memory of the charred remains of another house, on the far end of his father's holding; the shadow of a home in which he'd left another wife, many years ago. A memory all of her loving and all of her care could not dislodge.

She wound her fingers around his upper arm and battled a fresh surge of tears. "Are you going to stand here all day, or are you going to show me my house?"

He shook off his stillness and strode up the crumbled muddy steps of the pier. "The house could be in ruins. Seven years is a long time to leave a place untended in this country." André bent a sapling out of his way. "Impulsive wench. You should have let me send someone ahead."

As if she cared what it looked like now, as if she cared if it were a palace or a hut, after all this time. "Oh, bother. What difference does it make? Did you expect me to sit idly in Montréal all summer?"

"I could have had the house repaired. I could have brought you here like a man should bring his bride."

Genevieve patted her swelling middle. "We're well beyond the honeymoon, André."

"At least," he argued, gritting as he arched a branch out of her way, "I could have had this land cleared."

"Don't clear it."

"What?"

She followed him through an overgrown thread of a path. Around her, spruce saplings bristled next to maple and slender white birch. Tufts of ferns and wild grasses choked the ground. Hot sunlight splattered through the low, uneven canopy. The buzzing of cicadas filled the air and a rabbit, startled out of its hiding place, flashed white feet as it ran away.

"I said . . . don't clear the land."

Leave it like this, as wild and untouched as the forests beyond Montréal.

"It'll be cleared, Genny, straight to the shore." He shook his shaggy head sharply. "I won't have you living like a squaw, not my wife, not anymore."

Memories flashed through her mind—of making love under the stars, of a smoked-filled log hut and a bed of furs, of long winter nights of loving. Oh, there it goes again, what was she to do about it? She dipped her head to avoid a low branch. She was tired of rocking on the thin edge between laughter and tears. Would there ever be a time in this wretched pregnancy when she wouldn't be blind with emotion?

Genevieve tripped; a thin flagstone flipped, spraying chunks of loam before it cracked on another amid

the weeds. She reached for André to steady herself
. . . and clutched an arm as stiff and tense as stone.
She glanced to where his steady gaze was directed, up
the path of uneven paving stones, to a shape looming
beyond a fencing of trees.

"Welcome." A muscle flexed in his cheek. "Welcome to your home."

Home.

Angrily, she brushed the tears muddling her vision
out of the way, then buried her hand in her skirts and
brushed by André. The patchwork of paving stones
wound around a thick-trunked sugar maple, an older
tree left standing after the original clearing—for
shade in the summer, she supposed, or perhaps for
syrup in the spring.

The wilderness had stretched its tentacles over and
around the building, softening its rough edges with
a luxuriant blanket of waxy green ivy, spotting the
framework of timber with red columbine and nodding wild roses, still dewy in their new buds. Ruddy
cedar shingles hung askew upon the patchy roof and
peppered the ground below. Genevieve crackled
through a dried-up garden, frightening a flurry of
birds out of the eaves, then rattled the shutters, but
they were closed tight. Peeling a woody vine off the
sill revealed the silver-gray gleam of stone.

She ran her fingers over the rough rock. Every
house she'd seen on the way from Montréal had been
made of crude logs set upon one another; this house
had a framework of timber filled with layers of hewn
stone. A stone house. What an oddity in this land of
endless forests. She remembered a tale her mother
used to tell her, of three men and their houses of
straw, sticks, and stones. Only the house of stone
stood against the wolves.

"My father nearly went bankrupt building this

thing." André leaned against the sugar maple, scowling at the house. "Used every able-bodied man from Québec to Montréal to cut and transport the stone. He wanted a manor house in Québec, a true *seigneurie*, finer than the one he'd lost in France." He gestured to the bristle of wild land. "He was planning to terrace the gardens before he died, like he heard King Louis was doing in Versailles."

Her mother's house had been made of stone, strong Norman rock yearly scraped free of lichen. The front gardens had been pruned and shaped into geometrical patterns of bushes and straight-edged hedges, a sharp contrast to the wild Norman woods tumbling out behind the manor. Funny, she'd spent so much more time amid the wild forests than skipping along the straight, pebbled paths.

She rubbed her damp hands along her skirt. "Can we go inside now?"

André scraped a rusted iron key out of a fissure in the stone sill of the opposite window, then turned it in the lock to creak open the front door. Silt sifted onto his shoulders as he stepped in. He brushed it off, disappearing into the dim interior.

Genevieve stepped into a hallway and waited for her eyes to adjust to the darkness. In the next room, wood clattered as André yanked open a pair of shutters. Golden light sifted through a mesh of dust and spilled through the portal, illuminating a stairway in the hall, with a carved railing that curled up to the second floor. André strode past her to the next room, clattering open yet another set of shutters.

She wandered into the room André had just vacated. *It must be the air,* Genevieve thought, as her breath thickened in her lungs. She ran two fingers up the leafy vines carved into the wooden frame of the parlor portal. A crystal chandelier draped in dusty spiderwebs chimed in a soft breeze, its facets capturing the pale sunlight. The brass of an ancient timepiece gleamed on a mantelpiece of marble, its hands frozen at twenty of two. The chairs were turned gently toward the hearth, awaiting a lady and her basket of needlework.

She leaned against the portal, her hand to her breast. *My God . . . my God.* Not even in the most delirious of her fevered dreams on the ship from France had she imagined there'd be such opulence in this New World or that she'd be the mistress of it. André had never mentioned anything; he'd had her thinking it was a tumbled-down old place. She stumbled deeper into the room, in search of a place to sit . . . and saw the harp standing in the corner.

Her breath hitched in her throat. Somewhere deep in the house, André cursed as he struggled with yet another set of shutters. Genevieve clutched her chest and approached the instrument, daring to stretch out one reverent hand and touch the gilded frame, daring to lightly strum the dusty strings.

A shaky laugh of wonder fell from her lips. All this time, and the strings rang true . . . or perhaps her ear was not what it had been, in those days when Armand taught her and *Maman* sat by the window watching with the softest of smiles on her lips. Genevieve ran her fingers over the basket of roses embroidered on the stool. A faint perfume, sweet with remembrance, billowed from the cushion as she sat upon it.

She raked her nails across the strings, then probed her memory for a tune. The music swelled in her, that lovely melody. . . . She could not remember the name, but Genevieve found herself plucking the strings, rolling her hands in that familiar way, yearning to hear that song again, to remember

Maman and those golden days, when the world was gentle and simple and enclosed by an iron gate and a series of hedges, when she was still innocent, her mind pure and refined.

But all that emerged from her stroking was a screech of chords, a twanging mockery of the music of angels that she remembered. She released the strings abruptly and curled her hands into fists, to stop the cacophony. A sob heaved to her throat. What was she thinking, touching this instrument after so long? Did she think she could revive the skills of her childhood after all that had happened? Did she really think she could bring back the dead?

She blinked open her eyes and scanned the room, something sinking in her breast. This was a *lady's* house, the hearth of a fine family name. She did not belong here.

"You never told me you could play."

André stood in the portal, his hands loose at his sides.

"You have an ear of tin." Genevieve jerked up with a swish of skirts and turned her back to him, feigning interest in the marble top of a chest of drawers. "I can't play at all."

"My mother played."

She trailed a hand over a moth-eaten bit of embroidery framed on the wall, forcing the hitch from her throat. "She must have been . . . a fine lady."

"She could play like an angel. It was the only time she wasn't weeping, the only time she wasn't mourning all she'd left behind in France."

Bitterness seeped through his words. How hard it must have been for him, she thought, dragging her mind away from her own sorrow long enough to notice the shadows in his eyes, the stiffness of his shoulders. He'd told her he'd been barely twelve when his family was forced to move to New France, young enough to view the change as an adventure. Yet he'd lived in this house, watching his parents build this odd castle and spend their lives pining away over the past.

No wonder he escaped into the wilderness, she mused, where pretty objects meant nothing and a man was forced to live for the moment.

Genevieve approached him, her hands out-stretched. "I'm sorry, André . . . "

"It was a long time ago." He stepped back, turned away from her, then gestured toward the stairs. "Come upstairs. My mother had a carpet from the Savonnerie specially made for the master bedroom."

Her empty hands fell to her sides. She watched him climb to the second floor. Grief lay as thick as dust in this house. Now it was her duty to exorcise the ghosts, to fill the house with warmth, to make it a home.

She screamed a silent cry, then squeezed her eyes shut and grasped the carved portal to keep herself from falling into a heap on the floor. What a fool she was, a sentimental idiot. This place was more than she'd ever wanted, more than she'd ever dared dream. She'd be a rich woman, safe in a sturdy house; to the world around her, she'd be the perfect lady of the manor. With a child as well, *a child of her own*, to hold and to love. She should be singing praises to the skies, dancing in reckless abandon, for she'd triumphed, she'd survived and prevailed beyond all her imaginings.

But it was all a mockery. Marie Suzanne Duplessis belonged here, sewing embroidery and plumping pil-lows, not Genevieve Lalande. Genevieve was a fraud, her life was a fraud. She'd never wanted to hope for more than this, and now she couldn't help it. She'd been betrayed by her own convictions. Everything had changed.

Love had changed her.

She gripped the railing of the stairs and climbed to the second floor. With each step, she steeled herself to feign bright joy for the three months that remained before André returned to the wilderness. She wondered how she was going to live without him in this tomb of a building, for months and months untold, how she was going to live with the lie that was herself.

She wondered, for the first time in her life, if she could really survive.

Genevieve pushed open the inn's wooden shutters. She winced as the blinding morning light poured in over the tangled linens. But for the warblers chirping among the plum blossoms, silence reigned in the street.

Finally.

All night, she and André had been serenaded with the shrieks and whoops of drunken Indians, the sounds of brawling men, the pounding of feet as people raced along the thoroughfare. The street below looked as if an army had marched through the mud, for footsteps had pummeled the dirt into a morass. Embedded in the sod were discarded breechcloths, caps, and other clothing, along with empty and broken bottles of brandy. Two *voyageurs*, looking worse for wear, snored below her window against the wall of the inn.

Madness reigned in Montréal. It seemed as if no one cared what murder or mayhem was being committed in the streets. Not once had she heard the voice of soldiers. André had told her that Montréal was always like this during the spring, when the *coure-*

urs de bois returned from the interior and Indians from distant tribes came to trade their furs. It made him even more short-tempered than he'd been at his father's house yesterday. She'd tried to ease his anxiety the only way she could: by kissing him, by making love to him.

Genevieve smiled as she found the empty tin of gooseberry jam on the floor beside the bed, a remnant of their loving of two nights ago. She tossed it in the pile of debris to be removed from the room. Startled, the pet beaver reared back from the tin and waddled to the cut-off barrel that stood in front of the blazing hearth. Climbing in, the creature rolled and frolicked in what was left of the cool bathwater. She and André had bathed in that barrel earlier this morning. Looking at it now, Genevieve wondered how they'd managed to fit into such a small space.

She flushed. She knew exactly how they had managed to fit. They had shared a desperate lovemaking, merged their two bodies into one, and then sank into the tepid river water.

She straightened from picking up the remnants of a loaf of bread, tossed the ends in the growing pile, and ran her hands over the velvet bodice and skirts. Her stomach was growling again. He had left only a few moments ago to find her some goose liver pâté— if such a luxury could be found in this wilderness. She wanted him back already, tracing the fullness of her naked belly with eyes full of wonder and awe.

A knock on the door startled her. André would never knock, she thought, then realized that as he left, he had probably told the innkeeper to send someone up to remove the bath and clean up the room.

"Come on, beaver. You'll scare the devil out of whoever has to pour out this bath." Genevieve reached in and grasped the slippery creature in her hands, soaking her velvet in the process. He flattened his webbed feet against her as she walked toward the door and swung it open.

She stared, startled, at the group who greeted her. She had expected a couple of the innkeeper's boys, the same ones who had lugged the pails of steaming water up the stairs to her room this morning. Instead, she was faced with a soldier in full uniform, a woman swathed in a voluminous cloak, and a very officious-looking man in a blue satin doublet with scarlet ribbons around his knees and falling from his shoulders.

The beaver bared his orange-enameled teeth and hissed. The officious-looking man stepped back in surprise.

"He's a pet," Genevieve said quickly. She shifted the squirming bundle of beaver into the other arm. "May I help you, monsieur?"

His eyes never left the beaver. "Is your husband here?"

Genevicvc hesitated, peering at the three. They didn't seem to be a threat, at least not physically. "He's not here at present, but he should be back any moment now. He's gone to find some breakfast."

The officious-looking man turned and held out his hand for the woman who stood in the shadows. She walked forward until she was standing directly in front of Genevieve.

"Tell us, mademoiselle." The officious-looking man gestured rudely to Genevieve and spoke to the woman. "Is this the woman we are looking for?"

The woman drew the edges of her hood back until it fell against her shoulders. Chestnut-colored hair tumbled in neat, well-coiffed curls on either side of her face. She lifted her lashes and her tear-filled eyes met Genevieve's stunned green gaze.

The beaver squealed in protest as Genevieve's arms tightened around him.

"Forgive me, Genevieve." A single tear spilled out of Marie Suzanne Duplessis's eyes. "Forgive me."

Chapter Seventeen

André clutched a small clay pot of goose liver pâté and hastened toward the inn. It had taken him a full hour to convince the tavern owner's wife to part with the delicacy, and it had cost him two beaver pelts in the process. The truth was, he would have paid a king's ransom, anything to coax a smile to Genevieve's face.

She tried so valiantly to hide her feelings from him, but he knew the meaning of those long, unexpected silences, the hours she spent petting the beaver and staring off at the river. During the trip from Chequamegon Bay, her spirits had sunk deeper and deeper the closer they came to the settlements. Even her infrequent laughter held a quiver, and her eyes brimmed with sadness. Over the weeks, he had discovered that there were only three ways to make Genevieve happy: tease her, feed her unusual cravings, or make love to her.

The situation tore him to pieces. He had considered bringing her back into the interior with him. He reasoned that childbirth was a natural process, that the Indian women could help her during the birth. Certainly the natives knew more about the birthing process than any French midwife, for in all his time in the woods, he had only known a handful of squaws who had died in childbirth, while in the same period, he had known of a dozen Frenchwomen who had died of the same in the settlements. The more he thought about it, the more possible it seemed. Then he remembered how Genevieve had suffered through the voyage from Chequamegon Bay, when her pregnancy had been only a gentle swell in her abdomen. She would never survive the voyage come fall. Furthermore, he could never ask her to take that risk.

She belonged in his father's house, seated behind the harp, strumming sweet music with white hands.

He tightened his grip on the jar of pâté. Now was not the time to think of such things. They had the entire summer before them. Now was the time to store up memories, in preparation for the long, lonely winter.

André burst through the doors of the Sly Fox Inn. He kicked away broken chair legs and brandy bottles that littered the floor as he strode through the common room, then took the stairs two at a time. He heard someone call his name, but he ignored it; his wife and his child were hungry. André approached his room and pushed open the door.

"Genevieve?"

The cut-off barrel in which they had bathed still stood in the middle of the room. The beaver whined and waddled toward him, his chewed-off leash trailing behind him. The fire had died down to embers.

Genevieve was nowhere to be found.

"Monsieur, I tried to find you. . . ."

André whirled around and glared at the innkeeper, who stood in the doorway, rubbing his hands nervously on his stained apron.

"Where is she?"

"They took her away."

"Was she ill?"

"No, no, monsieur."

"What is it, then?" His heart pounded. "Who took her away?"

"Monsieur Lelièvre took her." The apron knotted more firmly in his hands. "He came just after you left and demanded to know which room she was in."

André clutched the innkeeper by the shoulders and heaved him up flat against the door. "Who the hell is Monsieur Lelièvre?"

"The . . . the sub-delegate to the Intendant." The innkeeper's voice emerged as a squeak. "Sweet Mother Mary, I couldn't stop him! He had a soldier with him."

"Where is she?"

"He said . . . he said he'd be waiting for you." The innkeeper coughed as the neck of his shirt dug deep into his throat. "In the western fort."

André stepped over the body of the soldier he had just knocked down with a blow to the face. A chair fell as the barricade he had erected against the outside door began to crumble beneath the efforts of the soldiers on the other side. He ignored it and scanned the room, striding over to the only other portal, the door that had to lead to Lelièvre's inner offices. He kicked the carved door open just as the barrier fell. A soldier cried for him to stop. André ignored him and entered the inner office. His glare riveted on the man in blue satin who calmly stood up behind a rosewood desk.

André stopped a few feet from the desk. His chest heaved and a rib twinged where one of the soldiers had struck him with the butt of his musket. He flexed his sore fists and felt a ribbon of blood drip down his temple and over his cheek. Glaring at the man in the shimmering satin, André saw the crimson ribbons falling from his shoulders, the pristine white lace at his throat, and debated whether to kill him outright or to make him suffer.

But first he needed to find Genevieve. It was that, and only that, that checked his bloodlust.

"Put your muskets down, men." Lelièvre waved one beringed hand toward the soldiers who rushed in behind André. "I've been waiting for this man."

André's nostrils flared as he watched Lelièvre walk to a side table with a marble top and calmly pour some brandy into two tankards.

"I was told you were once a soldier, Monsieur Lefebvre." The glass bottle clinked against the side of the pewter cups. "A good soldier would determine whether he could enter at will before he attempted a full-scale siege."

"Where's my wife?"

"Yes . . . your wife." Lelièvre held out a tankard but André ignored it. He shrugged and placed it on his desk. "I suppose with such a goal in mind, a man doesn't think much of strategy. I trust there aren't too many casualties?"

André took one step forward. Behind him, muskets clicked into readiness.

"Monsieur, this situation is utterly distasteful as it is." Lelièvre sat down in his chair and gestured to another on the other side of his desk. "It will be easier if you sit and let me tell you about the whole sordid affair.''

''If you don't bring me my wife,'' André began, his voice deceptively quiet, ''there's going to be one more casualty.''

Monsieur Lelièvre lifted a brow, and to André's rage, a ghost of a smile passed over his lips. ''I've always found you *coureurs de bois* to have tempers that explode more quickly than saltpeter.'' He toyed with a curl of his long periwig and gestured again to the chair. ''Dampen your powder. Violence won't help your wife, who is safe and in my custody. Now please. Sit.''

André ignored the offer. He took two steps and laid his fingertips on the top of the rosewood desk. He heard the soldiers move restlessly behind him.

''I don't give a damn that six loaded muskets are aimed at my back.'' The words filtered through André's clenched teeth. ''I don't give a damn that your chandelier is made of crystal or that you have the king's own brandy in that tankard. I don't give a damn who you are. If you don't tell me where my wife is and why you took her away, I shall rip your heart out through your throat even as your soldiers shoot me down.''

André heard a quiet feminine gasp. He turned his head sharply. In the corner of the room sat a young woman in black clothing, her blue eyes wide with fear, her hand clamped over her mouth.

''Get her out of here.'' André pointed at the woman. ''There's no need to shock her with the sight of your bloody innards.''

''You don't understand.'' Monsieur Lelièvre swallowed and pressed back in his chair. ''You don't know who she is. . . .''

''I don't give a damn if she's the Queen of France.''

"Tell him," Lelièvre stuttered. Beads of sweat broke out on his forehead. He looked at the girl. "Tell him your name."

André reached across the desk and crumbled a wisp of lace in his hand. He dragged the delegate up off his seat until he smelled the onions on the man's breath. The soldiers cried out sharply. André tensed, waiting for the slam of musket balls in the muscles of his back.

"Stop! No, please!" The girl leapt up and waved frantically at the soldiers. "Don't shoot, please!" She turned her frightened blue gaze on André. "Monsieur . . . you must listen. Please listen."

He glared at the woman. She hesitated, then shrank back and gripped the arm of her chair.

"Tell him," Lelièvre implored, his voice hoarse and uneven.

"My name," she said, "is Marie Duplessis."

André frowned at her. "That's my wife's name."

"No." The woman dropped her gaze and fretted with her hands. "Your wife's name is . . . Genevieve Lalande."

André stared at her, as expressionless as an Iroquois. A memory returned, swift and vivid.

Don't call me Marie. There were a thousand Maries in the Salpêtrière.

Then what shall I call you?

Call me . . . Genevieve.

He glared at the girl. She and Genevieve were the same height, but their coloring was completely different. This woman wore fine white gloves and a well-tailored dress of black wool. The toes of her expensive leather boots peeped out from beneath the hem of her skirts. Her hair was parted in the middle and hung in ringlets on either side of her face. Her skin looked as if it had never seen the kiss of the sun.

Disbelief roared in his ears. "What's the meaning of this?"

"If you would . . . kindly . . . release me," Lelièvre said, his voice choked and dry, "I could explain everything."

André shoved the delegate back into his seat. Monsieur Lelièvre coughed and readjusted the tightness of his cravat, then reached for the tankard he had offered to André and finished the contents in one gulp.

The woman sobbed quietly. Lelièvre gestured to one of his soldiers and waved wordlessly at her. She glanced up in surprise as the soldier took her arm and began leading her out of the room.

"No." André barked. "She stays."

"Please, monsieur, for decency's sake," the delegate murmured, "let the child leave."

"He must know the truth," the woman interrupted, between sobs. "Tell him everything. Everything."

"He will give me no choice."

Lelièvre waited until the girl had disappeared through the doorway and her sobs could no longer be heard in the halls of the building. Then he pulled down the edges of his doublet, took a deep breath, and gestured to the opposite chair. "It's a rather complicated story, Monsieur Lefebvre. Complicated and fantastic . . ."

"You have five minutes." André glanced at the gilded, imported timepiece clicking above the mantelpiece. "Starting now."

After a shocked pause, he began swiftly. "I assure you that it is not in my nature to arrest a woman, especially to arrest her while her husband is away. In light of"—he rubbed his reddened throat—"recent events, I believe I was wise to do so. I wanted to avoid a public scene, not for my sake, mind you, but for your own, and there's no longer a doubt in my mind that you would have fought to the death." The delegate gestured to the doorway. "That poor child is the real Marie Suzanne Duplessis, the woman you thought you married in Québec this past fall. The woman in my custody—the woman you know as your wife—is named Genevieve Lalande."

André waited in stony silence.

"You see, there seems to have been an incident in Paris, at the Salpêtrière, the charity house." He rushed on. "Both Marie Duplessis and Genevieve Lalande lived in that charity house, but in very different sections. Last year, when the king's girls were chosen, Marie Duplessis was one of them, Genevieve Lalande was not. When the time came for the girls to be transferred to the ships, Mademoiselle Lalande took Mademoiselle Duplessis's place among the women of good family—with brute force." He waved to the empty doorway. "As you see, Mademoiselle Duplessis still hasn't recovered from it. She was kidnapped, tied up, forced to switch clothing—and then Mademoiselle Lalande took her place in New France. She married a man of your stature by using Mademoiselle Duplessis's own good name."

Call me Genevieve.

André's ears rang with shock. He stood, motionless, staring at the delegate. She had never said a word, never hinted at a secret identity. He thought of all those months in the hut on Lake Superior, when she had told him stories of her mother's harp and the hills in which she had grown up. How much were lies? How much was true? How much did he really know about the woman with whom he had fallen in love?

"You must be shocked, Monsieur Lefebvre, to discover that your wife is not a woman of quality." Lelièvre raised his brows and looked down at his open hands. "It will shock you even more to know that Genevieve Lalande was one of the unfortunates of the institution. She was picked up on the streets of Paris, from a section of the city in which few innocent women dwell. She was put in the section of the Salpê-trière reserved for—" he faltered, glanced up at André, then forged ahead, "for women of easy virtue."

Something snapped. André leaned over the desk. "My wife is no whore."

"Please!" The delegate raised his hands in defense. "I am only telling you what has been told to me by the Mother Superior of the institution. After so many months with the woman, you would know better than I the nature of her character."

He suddenly remembered the look on her face when he caught her with a goose in her hands, a goose she had just captured and killed. *Everyone has secrets, André.* He remembered her bartering with the Indian for a pair of moccasins, stowing away her old, muddy boots for future trading like a merchant's wife. He remembered her swearing like an angry *voyageur* in his cups. He remembered her insistence on having a home, her determination to survive the voyage into the interior at all costs. But most of all, he remembered the first night they made love, under the velvet autumn sky in the land of the Hurons, when he had taken her maidenhead and made her a woman.

She was no woman of easy virtue. He had taken her virginity that night, a virginity she must have battled hard to save if she once spent time on the streets of Paris. He wondered about everything she had kept secret from him; he wondered about her life before he had married her. André knew the delegate's story was true. The entire scheme smacked of Genevieve, for it was fantastic and risky, and she was so determined that it had almost succeeded. Why had she done it? What would drive her to spend the rest of her life masquerading as a petty noblewoman, in constant danger of discovery and imprisonment? Was her life in the Salpêtrière so brutal? Was the chance to come to the New World her only hope?

Who are you, Genevieve?

The questions swarmed in his head. He searched for some sense in the madness. He wanted her here. He wanted to hold her and look into her eyes and ask her all the questions that raced in his head. There was more to this story than this petty official was telling him. There was a whole history he didn't know, and he wanted her to pour out her soul, to tell him everything she had been unable—or too afraid—to tell him before now.

Then he realized he didn't give a damn what her real name was. He didn't give a damn how she had found her way to him. He didn't give a damn how many years she had spent on the streets of Paris or what she had done to survive them.

She had survived. A woman such as Genevieve wouldn't throw herself overboard and take a child with her into death, for something as useless as honor. A woman such as this would fight to her last breath for one single moment more of *life*.

Genevieve was his wife. He loved her. He wanted her back.

Monsieur Lelièvre stumbled onward, his voice an annoying drone. ". . . I wondered why you took her into the interior until two weeks ago, when the ship arrived carrying Marie Duplessis and orders from the authorities in Paris. I suppose your wife insisted on it; she must have known that we would catch up to her sooner or later. Unfortunately, it's obvious that your wife is well in the family way. No one could blame you. She was your wife and you were alone with her in the wilderness for a very long time. Normally, that would make it very difficult to obtain an annulment, but considering the circumstances, I'm sure we can arrange something. . . ."

"There will be no annulment."

Monsieur Lelièvre started in his chair. He looked up and faced André's steady glare. "I understand you are concerned about the child."

"She is my wife and she will stay my wife."

The delegate's brows rose high on his forehead, almost disappearing beneath the curls of his dark periwig. He spread his hands in his lap and shrugged. "If that is what you wish . . ."

"I want her freed."

The delegate started. "I'm afraid that is not possible right now."

"Make it possible."

"Monsieur Lefebvre . . ." The delegate straightened in his chair. "I'm sure you understand now that the situation is complicated. . . ."

"It can be very simple, Lelièvre."

"She took the place of a king's girl, and in the process put in question the reputation of every king's girl ever brought to these shores." Monsieur Lelièvre shook his head. "The Crown doesn't take well to being fooled. They want her kept under guard until the case is heard by the courts."

André's eyes narrowed. He knew how this system worked. Nothing was impossible if a man were rich enough to pay for it. His gaze scanned the room, noticing the tric-trac board on a side table, the walnut commode, the Gobelin tapestries gracing the walls. This delegate didn't pay for these expensive trifles with his meager salary—he paid for them with furs.

"In a warehouse not far from here," André began, "I have stored a winter's worth of beaver pelts."

A gleam lit the delegate's eyes. He leaned forward and toyed with the empty pewter tankard. "I have heard that you were in partnership with Nicholas Perrot."

"I wintered on the western end of Lake Superior, the same place where Perrot wintered the year before. You do remember the haul of furs he brought to Montréal this time last year?"

"The finest, silkiest, blackest beaver these settlements have ever seen."

"Find a way to free her," he said softly, "and my share of this year's haul is yours."

The tankard clattered against the desk. Monsieur Lelièvre stared at him in incredulity. When he spoke again, his voice was hoarse. "You are aware, monsieur, that bribery is a punishable offense."

"Consider it a donation toward the building of Montréal's fortifications. Payable upon the safe return of my wife."

The delegate stood up abruptly. The light from the tallow candles burning in the chandelier above gleamed off his silver buttons. Beneath the edge of his long, curled periwig, his brow creased in deep furrows. "If I could, I would give her to you immediately. Unfortunately, it has already been arranged that this situation will be handled by the *Conseil Souverain* in Québec."

André's stomach tightened into a knot. The council was the highest authority in New France. Yet he knew any official in this settlement could be bribed. It was just a matter of determining the price. "If you are powerless, then take me to someone who isn't."

"I'm not powerless." Lelièvre's brow furrowed

more deeply. "This is a delicate situation. Let me think what must be done."

The delegate paced. André stood stiffly, curling his hands into fists. He wondered where she was now—if she was within the palisades of this fortress or if she had been transferred elsewhere. He wondered if she was being kept in a small, empty room without windows. He wondered if she was still hungry or still craving the goose liver pâté he had scoured the town in order to find. The thought of her imprisoned made him crazy with rage.

André wanted to lunge across the room and take the portly delegate in his hands, lift him up, and threaten his life if he didn't bring her to him. But he restrained himself. She was under the king's guard, and even in his fury he couldn't fight a battalion of armed men. This sort of situation had to be fought with pretty words and handfuls of gold—or beaver pelts, which in this settlement was much the same thing. Where was Philippe when he needed him? Only in civilization did battles have to be fought with velvet gloves and silken words. He preferred the laws of the wilderness, where a man could be free with his fists and relied only on his strength and skill with arms to get what he wanted.

"You've been a *coureur de bois* for some time, haven't you, Monsieur Lefebvre?"

André glared at the delegate. "What does that have to do with my wife?"

"More than you think."

"I've been trading furs for a lifetime."

"You were also a soldier."

"I fought the Iroquois in '66, alongside the Carignan-Salière regiment."

"So I've heard." The delegate took his tankard

and walked across the room to the brandy to pour himself more. "I think there may be something we can do that will convince the *Conseil Souverain* to release your wife to you."

"What is it?"

"There's a new settlement across the Saint Lawrence River from Montréal," he began. "It's a small area, heavily forested. You can imagine that few settlers want to build there, with nothing shielding them from the Iroquois but hundreds of miles of wilderness. We may be at peace now, but you never know when those demons are going to strike."

His stomach twisted.

"If you agreed to accept a small *seigneurie* across the river from Montréal, the council may agree to free your wife."

André curled his hands over the back of the chair, his fingers digging into the fine tapestry. His blood ran cold in his veins. He knew what the delegate was suggesting. He would free his wife if he could bind André in chains.

"You are well born enough to warrant a *seigneurie.* The land would be yours. All you would be required to do is find settlers to clear it for a yearly fee of some capons and a copper or two. Of course, you'd also be required to live on it, and build a mill and some sort of defense. Your skills as a soldier will be well used. . . ."

"Why would the king wish to waste my skills plowing the earth like a peasant?" he retorted. "I have other skills. I'll go west for the government. Like Talon sent La Salle west. I can explore farther than even the Jesuits."

"Too many men have left the settlements. Our strength and our virility are drained westward every fall, and drunk into oblivion each spring. We need settlers to clear the land, not fur traders and drunkards.''

"And if I refuse?"

"It is the only option that the council may accept," Lelièvre argued. "I know how much they want a strong man to build on that shore. If you refuse, then your wife will be shipped back to Paris to face punishment."

A drop of hot tallow fell from the chandelier and sizzled on the surface of the rosewood desk.

André imagined himself, sickle in hand, watering the rocky Canadian soil with the sweat of his brow, coaxing maize and peas and beans to grow in the weak sunshine. Then he imagined Genevieve languished in some dark prison, dressed in rags, forced to work long hours for bread and potage.

There were many different kinds of prisons. There were many different kinds of hell.

"Tell your council that I will accept any offer." His throat parched. "But only on one condition: that my wife be freed immediately, without trial."

Dim blue twilight seeped through the cracks of the western wall of the shed. Genevieve sat upon the packed earthen floor in the small room, her head resting against the decaying log wall. Around her swirled the stench of dried manure and rotting hay. Set back in a yard behind a larger stone house, the shed collected the day's heat and concentrated it within its clay-clogged walls. She sighed as another drop of sweat trickled between her breasts.

She had only been in this shed for a matter of hours. It might as well have been a lifetime. Since the morning, she had aged a hundred years.

He knew everything by now. She could imagine his

face as that arrogant official in his neat satins told him the truth. André had not married a woman of the *petite noblesse*. He had married an urchin scooped off the streets of Paris, a common laundress in the notorious Salpêtrière, an imposter in a new land, perhaps a prostitute. He would remember all the times she had shocked him—by killing the goose, by swearing, by acting like anything but an aristocrat. He would argue; she knew he would argue and fight against it. But eventually, he would bow to the truth. She had lied to him, deceived him, and she was nothing but a whore.

Pain speared through her, no duller for having already sliced her heart into bleeding ribbons. Over the long months, she had almost forgotten about the deception. She had woven a history for herself, a mottled tapestry of her early life in Normandy with her mother and what she knew of the lives of the *bijoux* in the Salpêtrière. It was close enough to her youth that it didn't seem like a lie anymore, and as time passed, she and André spoke less and less of the past and more and more of the future. It was the future that mattered, the future they would build together. The past was gone and dead and over.

Or so she had thought. Marie Duplessis had arrived at her door this morning like a corpse risen from the dead. Genevieve wished André had been there, so she could turn to him and tell him the truth—the whole truth—so she could spill out the sordid details of her life and make him understand why she had done what she did. In her heart, she kept telling herself that he loved her for *her*, not for the name and the breeding of Marie Duplessis. In her heart, she grasped desperately on to the hope that he would come and speak to her, that he would seek her out and hear what she had to say, that he would understand.

But a full day had already passed and the only person who had visited her was a maid with dinner. As she watched the rays of the sun lengthen on the packed earthen floor, Genevieve's dreams dwindled and died an agonizing death. She realized that no man could stomach being proven a fool, certainly not a man as proud as André. He would pass off the night on the Lake of the Hurons as a harlot's trick. He would harden his heart. He would discard her like a *pacton* of ruined pelts.

In the course of a single afternoon, she had lost everything.

No.

Genevieve blinked open her eyes. Staring blindly forward through a haze of tears, she ran her fingers against the grain of her velvet skirts and clutched the rounded swell of her abdomen. She dug her fingers into the cloth. She had not lost everything. She still had one piece of André that no one could ever take away from her.

She started as she heard voices outside the shed. It was the voice of the man who stood guard just outside the door, along with a woman's voice— undoubtedly, the servant delivering her supper. Genevieve eased up and wiped the sweat off her brow just as the door opened. A woman entered bearing a tray with a hunk of bread and a steaming bowl of soup. The servant gingerly placed the tray on the floor and pulled back the hood of her cape . . . and once again, Genevieve looked into the eyes of Marie Duplessis.

They faced each other across the room. They had not spoken a word to each other during the trip from the Sly Fox Inn to this house near the Hôtel-Dieu.

Marie had cried piteously into her handkerchief, making Genevieve suspect that she was not a willing party to the betrayal. But she was in no mood to listen to a weeping string of apologies.

There were no tears in Marie's eyes now, only splotchy red trails down her cheeks. Marie lifted a finger to her lips, then turned to peer through a crack in the wall. When she turned back, she untied the string on the cape around her throat and thrust the light garment off her shoulders.

"We don't have much time," she whispered, fumbling with the laces of her bodice. "The guard is standing away from the shed now, but he'll return soon and then he'll be able to hear us."

"What in God's name are you doing?"

"I'm righting an old wrong." She gestured to Genevieve's clothes. "Come . . . you've done this before."

"*Oui*, I certainly have, and that is what has gotten us in all this trouble."

"They forced me to accuse you. I didn't want to do it." Marie peeled open her bodice and tossed it on the pile with her cloak. "François abandoned me. I was alone, with nowhere to go. When I came back to the Salpêtrière, they forced me to confess the whole story. If I had known they would ship me to this godforsaken place, I would have stayed on the streets of Paris forever."

Genevieve met Marie's dry blue gaze and saw the pain in the woman's eyes. There was little left of the innocent girl Genevieve had met in the shadows of the Salpêtrière almost a year ago. Genevieve wondered exactly what happened between Marie and the Musketeer, and how long it had really taken to change that lovestruck young girl into the hurt, aching woman who stood before her.

"Marie . . . we can't do this." Genevieve gestured to her swelling abdomen. "I'm nearly five months pregnant."

"I brought pins to fasten the clothes." Marie slipped her skirts off her hips. "Besides, my cloak will cover you completely. It's twilight, and even if the guard catches a glimpse of your face, he won't know the difference between us. If you want to be with your husband, Genevieve, you'd better start with the laces of your bodice."

"You're wasting your time." Her voice caught in her throat. "My husband doesn't want me."

"In a pig's eye." Marie flushed. "Your husband battled his way through a fort full of soldiers for you. He threatened to rip a man's heart out through his throat. I've never seen such a sight! He was like some sort of wild . . . *beast*."

Genevieve's blood throbbed wildly in her veins.

"He scared the life out of me," Marie continued, crossing the shed and working on Genevieve's laces while the pregnant woman stood numbly in place. "I knew this place would be full of rough, wild—" Marie paused, then concentrated on Genevieve's laces. "I told Monsieur Lelièvre to tell your husband the truth—the real truth—but I'm afraid he has filled him with lies."

"Lies?"

"They're telling everyone that you kidnapped me and stripped me and beat me so I couldn't cry out until you were gone on the ship to Québec. They've painted you like some sort of crazed harridan." Marie tugged the last lace out of the eyelets. "They'll do anything not to admit that I, a Duplessis, willingly ruined myself with a Musketeer. They'll do anything not to besmirch the reputation of the king's girls.

They can't stand the thought that we concocted this entire scheme under the nose of Mother Superior of the Salpêtrière, under the nose of the king himself.''

"Stop, Marie. Stop." Genevieve pushed the girl away. Her bodice gaped open, but she made no attempt to retie it. She realized that André had fought his way in to see Monsieur Lelièvre before he knew the truth. "You don't understand . . . I'm an imposter. Now my husband knows it. I've been here all afternoon and he hasn't visited me. I don't know . . . I don't know if he wants me anymore."

Marie's eyes flickered away. She peered anxiously through the cracks in the shed, searching for the guard. "Your husband didn't look like the kind of man who would give a fig who your parents were."

"André thought he married *you*."

"He didn't break down a door in order to get me back." Marie waved her white hand. "In any case, there's only one way for you to find out for sure. You have nothing to lose and everything to gain if you escape this place."

Hope and fear battled in Genevieve's breast. Did he love her enough to give her the benefit of a doubt? Or did he hate her for her lies? She feared more than anything that she would find hatred, and then there would be no more hope.

"When they discover what we've done," Genevieve murmured, struggling with her waistband, "you'll be punished."

"I've already been punished for my ignorance, for my stupidity." Marie helped Genevieve with her skirts. "The truth is, you will be doing me a favor. If we're successful, they'll ship me back to Paris. I would rather spend a lifetime in the Salpêtrière than one more day in this wretched, uncivilized place."

*   *   *

Genevieve stilled in the shadows of the shop as two drunken men staggered by, singing *La Belle Lisette* off-key and taking turns swigging from a bottle of brandy. It was nighttime in Montréal, and already the houses along Saint Paul Street trembled with the sounds of fighting and singing and swearing and drinking. The houses that weren't converted into dramshops had long bolted their shutters and locked their doors against the madness.

She stood alone, hidden under the eaves of a shop across the street from the Sly Fox Inn. The escape from Monsieur Lelièvre's house had been easy. Swathed in the cloak as if weeping, she had left the shed while Marie pretended to be her, filling the air with some shockingly inventive curses. Genevieve had followed Marie's instructions to the letter, slipping calmly around the house and walking straight to the open gate of the redoubt, which enclosed a cluster of five or six buildings. The escape had gone without a snag, but the flight through the streets of Montréal was not as easy. There were so many drunken men wandering in the alleys that she was forced to escape into a small wooden chapel near the Hôtel-Dieu until dark. Fortunately, a naked Indian had passed by, crazed with brandy, swinging his hatchet wildly, completely clearing the streets. Then she slipped out of the chapel and made her way carefully through the shadows to the inn.

She could tarry no longer. Soon she would be seen huddled against the wall, and besides, she didn't know how long it would take for the switch to be discovered. No matter how much she dreaded the confrontation to come, she had to face it now, or the opportunity would be lost to her forever.

Genevieve lifted her skirts and bolted out of the shadows, bursting into the inn. She scanned the common room, already filled with *voyageurs* drinking their fill of the inn's brandy. When she realized André wasn't there, she raced up the stairs before the men, startled by the sight of a woman, came out of their shock and called after her. For the first time, she wondered if André was even here. Genevieve barreled blindly through the dark hallway. She heard footsteps on the stairs behind her and she prayed André was here.

She didn't bother to knock. Gripping the handle of the door, she pushed it open and stumbled into the room. By the light of a half-dozen candles, she saw two men seated, with several bottles of brandy lying haphazardly on the floor between them.

Tiny whirled as she slammed the door behind her. He spit out a mouthful of brandy. "By the stones of Saint Peter!" With glazed eyes, he looked at the bottle in his hand and then at her, then at the beaver who rushed over to paw the hem of her dress. "What did that merchant put in this stuff?"

André didn't move. His elbows dug into his knees, his head sagged in his hands. His words shot out like bullets. "Tell him to leave the bottle and get out."

"If that's a he," Tiny slurred, "then I'm Saint Genevieve herself."

André lifted his head from his hands.

"Look at her, not at me!" Tiny released a body-shaking hiccup. "You've been drinking this swill, too."

Her eyes met his. A bolt of lightning couldn't have shook her more strongly than the sight of his face, brandy-ravished, tormented, so full of pain that it burned her heart to ashes.

She searched for words, her tongue and her courage failing her. What could she say to the man she had deceived, the man she had pursued until he had fallen in love with her and she with him? *Yes, yes, André. It's all true. I am a commoner, a liar, but I love you. . . .* A hundred different words rushed to her tongue but stalled there, as she searched for a way to tell him, all at once, the fullness of her heart.

He rose to his feet, towering like a giant in the small room. The flickering candles threw strange shadows upon the walls. Even the beaver, sensing the tension, scuttled away from her.

When Andre spoke, his voice was hoarse and ragged.

"Little bird?"

She pressed her hand against her chest, against the laces that strained to keep the edges of Marie's bodice closed over her breasts. Tears stung her eyes. "Oh, André . . ."

Suddenly, she was in his arms, her nose pressed up against the smoke-ripened deerskin of his shirt, his hand buried in her hair, his lips warm and moist on her temple. He smelled of cheap brandy but she didn't care. He slid a hand beneath her cloak and wound it around her waist, pulling her flat against his body. For a moment she pressed against him, speechless, reveling in the feeling of his strong arms around her. Then, like water rushing through a broken beaver dam, the words tumbled out of her mouth, without sense, without order, muffled against his shoulder, the only discernible meaning being that she never meant to hurt him, that she didn't want to lie to him, that she loved him.

"Guess you won't be needing these anymore." Tiny gathered the brandy bottles. They clanked against one another as he staggered past them, toward the door. "Maybe if I finish 'em, they'll conjure up an image like that for me."

He closed the door quietly behind him.

Through her tears, she gazed up at him. "After all this, you still want me?"

"Ah, *Taouistaouisse*." He ran a hand over her forehead and brushed the hair from her face. "How could you doubt it? I love you."

"But I lied to you. I told you I was something I wasn't—"

"I fell in love with the woman who journeyed to Chequamegon Bay with me—whatever her name."

"All day I've waited for you to come and see me," she continued, breathless, not daring to believe. "I was afraid you didn't want me anymore."

"They wouldn't let me see you." His brows lowered in anger. "Even after I sold my soul for your freedom."

"What do you mean?"

"Didn't Lelièvre tell you when he released you?"

"He didn't release me." She leaned back, showing him her clothes. "I escaped."

"Escaped?" André glanced at the black dress that fit so oddly on her figure. "Those are Marie Duplessis's clothes."

"Marie and I switched places again."

"Again? They told me you took her place by force in Paris."

"They lied. Marie warned me they would." She flattened her hands against his chest and looked up at him imploringly. "You must believe me. Marie and I switched places in the Salpêtrière willingly. She ran off with the Musketeer she loved, and I took her place among the king's girls. Unfortunately . . . something happened and she was forced to return to the Salpêtrière."

"And admit to the whole scheme."

"Yes." She dug her fingers into his shirt. "She

hates it here. She brought me supper this evening, and she insisted we switch places again. She thinks that if she helps me escape, they'll ship her back to Paris." Genevieve lifted her hand and lightly traced the blood-encrusted lump on his forehead, just above his temple. "She told me she saw you this afternoon, battling through the fortress to get to Lelièvre—and to me."

His arms tightened around her. "I would have killed the bastard if your fate hadn't been in his hands."

"So instead," she whispered, "you sold your soul for my freedom."

"Yes." His lips brushed hers. "Lelièvre told me that the royal council in Québec would send you back to Paris to face justice. I offered him everything I owned if he would set you free."

"All the furs?" She gripped his shoulders. "The whole winter's haul?"

"Everything. But it wasn't enough for him."

"André . . ."

"He made me another offer." André wound a shimmering claret-colored tress around one finger. "He told me that if I agreed to be the *seigneur* of a tract of land across the Saint Lawrence from Montréal, then he might be able to convince the authorities to release you. The land is in Iroquois country. It would be the first attacked if war broke out between the Iroquois and the French again."

"You did refuse," she insisted. His whiskey-colored gaze wandered over her face. She drew in a deep, ragged breath. "But you could never go out into the wilderness again."

"It was the only way to free you."

Her body shook with a powerful tremor, her eyes locking with his. This was a sacrifice . . . a sacrifice he had never before been willing to make . . . a sacrifice that would cost him dearly. He would be paying for her freedom with his own.

"It will not be so bad." A teasing half-smile shaped his lips. "Now I won't be torn in half every year when I leave for the interior."

A wave of guilt inundated her. Not only was he making the sacrifice, but he was doing it willingly, and he still didn't know the extent of her lies. He didn't know the full truth, not yet. She was not worthy of this sacrifice . . . not until the air was cleared between them. "André, there's so much you don't know about me."

"I will know everything, Genny. . . ."

"There are secrets . . . secrets that even the people of the Salpêtrière didn't know." The doubts assailed her again, for the truth was uglier than the lies he was told. "I'm not what you think. I've stolen. I've poached in royal forests. . . ."

"Stealing to eat is no crime."

"I've picked pockets, and cut purses, and lied to priests and nuns."

"I don't care if you've committed murder."

"My mother was . . . a courtesan."

"You have her passionate nature, then."

"I'm a bastard, André."

"Some people call me a bastard, too."

"I'm serious."

He tilted her chin up. "You are my Genevieve, my wife, the mother of my child. Nothing else matters."

"But . . . but I've done things . . ."

"You did what you had to. It's a wonder you emerged from Paris with any innocence at all. You've survived." His eyes darkened with old memory, and a muscle flexed tight in his cheek. "You've *survived.*

This New World is not a place for the fainthearted, Genny. No man in all of Québec has a finer wife than I."

She closed her eyes, thrilling at the feel of his rough lips upon hers, urging hers open. She tasted the brandy on his tongue. His hands roamed over her back, slipping below the open waistline of her skirt and clutching her to him through layers of linen. Joy filled her heart, and when the kiss ended, she looked up at him, basking in the love in his eyes.

"I would like to linger here," he murmured, his voice choked with desire. "But we've got to hide you before they discover you've escaped. Neither I nor Lelièvre knew if the council would even agree to the terms I've committed myself to." His arms tightened around her. "Now that I have you, they must agree, or we'll disappear into the wilderness and they will lose a new settler as well as a woman wanted by the Crown."

"No."

"It won't come to that, Genevieve. . . ."

"That's not what I meant," she interrupted. "I meant . . . we don't have to take that offer."

Her eyes sparkled. The idea was so simple, so perfect. It was the answer to all her dreams. She could never allow him to till the soil and clear the land when his body and his soul belonged free and unfettered in the wilderness. Part of him would die, and part of her would die along with him. This way, they both could be free.

He kissed her forehead. "We have to. It is the only way you'll be freed."

"I'm free now." She spread her arms, arching slightly away from him, smiling up into his face. "I'm as free as a bird. To the west of this settlement stretches a great, big country. We can fly somewhere where they will never find us. We can fly right back to Chequamegon Bay.''

Shock reverberated through his arms. His hand rounded her back and rested on the swell of her abdomen. "But it'll be dangerous. . . ."

"I'm no fainting aristocrat . . . you know that by now. I've survived worse than what this world can give me."

"I can't do that to you." His voice was hoarse but ribboned with hope. "You deserve a midwife, clean linens, a soft mattress . . ."

"The Indians can help me birth our child. They've done it enough in the wild." She covered his hand with her own. "If we leave now, before I grow any bigger, and if we're slow and careful, then we'll be back on Lake Superior long before autumn."

He shook his head, more with disbelief than with denial, and ran a hand through his shaggy hair. "All we'll have in the wilderness is a temporary hut, a tent of bark, or an open fire. You want more, woman, you deserve more."

"I don't want to live in your father's house. It's full of grief, it's full of pain, and if I live there alone, I'll just fill it with even more grief. Don't you see?" Her breath caught on a sob of joy. "I can't stay, you can't stay; we must escape together. It's the only way we'll both be free."

He searched her face. Hope sparked new color into his amber gaze.

"Let our roof be the open sky or a canopy of summer leaves—I don't care anymore. My home isn't between four walls. It took me a long time, but I understand that now." She slipped her hands around his neck, closed her eyes, and whispered against his lips. "My home, love, is wherever you roam."

Epilogue

Rainy Lake, May 1672

The male beaver chewed industriously on a fresh poplar branch as he basked in the sun near his lodge. Another beaver, the female, waddled along the shore of the shallow lake, with two tiny kits following in her wake. The male beaver started and stretched up on his hind legs, showing the full length of his dumpy body. His brown eyes fixed upon Genevieve, where she sat in the shadow of a small copse of firs.

"He sees us, Christian."

Genevieve glanced down at her breast. Her nine-month-old son was asleep, a trail of milk drying on his cheek. Easing him away from her, she lay him on the thick caribou pelt, making sure that the bright sun dappling the gray fur did not shine on his eyes. She was glad he was sleeping. Soon, she'd have to strap him into an Indian cradleboard and carry him on her back. He hated being confined on the flat, carved board, but it was the best way to carry him whenever she traveled. Today was the day they would leave Rainy Lake in order to set up another post on some other, more distant lake.

Genevieve glanced back at the beaver. He had returned to his work on the poplar branch. Though she hadn't held her pet in her arms for nearly a year, she knew that he still remembered her. If he had sensed any danger, he would have cried out a warning until the female and the kits were safe in the lodge.

Her pet had disappeared into the woods last year, only a few days after she, André, and a small group of men had arrived at this lake after nearly two weeks of travel from Chequamegon Bay. Since her pregnancy was advanced and a village of Cree Indians was nearby, André had decided to settle here for the winter and build a new post. The beaver had threatened to eat through every log they cut, so André never regretted his disappearance, but Genevieve had worried. Only a few months ago did they find him again, when André and two of his *voyageurs* discovered a beaver lodge and a family of beavers in this stream. For the first time, they realized her pet was a male, who had found himself a mate.

It was a testament to how far they had traveled into the wilderness, that a family of beavers could live unmolested within walking distance of a new fur trading post. Genevieve had taken them under her personal protection, spreading a rumor among the local Crees that these beaver were sacred and spoke to her in her dreams. She could only hope that after they left this lake, the Cree would remem-

ber her words and would leave her pet and his family
unmolested.

She supposed it would always be like this. She,
André, and their contingent of *voyageurs* would stay
in a place long enough for her to know the hills and
valleys, long enough for her to understand the new
dialects of the natives, long enough to form a bond
with the land, and then they would move on again,
always westward. Genevieve had come here today to
say her own private goodbyes, not just to her old pet,
but to the land where her son had been born, to the
lake that had given them water and fish, to the land
that had given them berries and corn, and to the
creatures that had given them meat. There was a
sadness in the farewell, but it was mingled with a
sense of hope and excitement.

"I knew I'd find you here."

Genevieve looked up and saw André striding
through the trees. He had shaved his winter beard,
and his teeth gleamed white and even. His tawny gaze
slipped over her hair, then fell lower and clung. She
realized she hadn't laced up her dress after breast-
feeding their son and it gaped open.

She stood up, smiled, and made no move to hide
her body from him. Her gaze fell upon the pouch
at his waist. An idea struck her. "Do you have any
tobacco?"

"Deciding to take up the pipe, *Taouistaouisse*?"

"No . . . this is for something else."

He opened the pouch, pulled out a twist, and cut
off a hefty chunk for her. She curled her fingers over
the leaves, then turned around and took two steps
to the edge of the lake. She held the tobacco to her
breast, then ceremoniously spread the leaves upon
the waters.

When she had finished, he came up behind her and wrapped his arms around her waist. "I'm glad there's no Jesuit to see you do that. He'd think you've turned heathen."

"Perhaps I have. It's been a long time since I've seen a black robe." She hugged his arms to her. "I suppose everyone is waiting for me."

"The men from Chequamegon Bay are anxious to leave. They've been too long without their Indian wives. They're waiting in their canoes to wish you farewell before they return to that post with our furs."

"And your men?"

"They're still packing up the merchandise brought up from Chequamegon Bay." He glanced at the beaver lodge. "Your pet seems to be doing well."

"Yes." She bit her lower lip. "I hope he doesn't return to us as a pelt."

"You've convinced the Crees you're some sort of medicine woman. No other tribe will hunt these grounds."

In silence, they watched the sun glitter on the shallow lake. They listened to the warblers singing in the boughs of the trees, and the nuzzling of squirrels and other rodents in the forest litter. In the distance, she heard the voices of the *voyageurs* as they worked by the wooden stockade. Genevieve glanced at their son, sleeping peacefully in the thick caribou pelt. She signed, breathing in the rich, fragrant air.

"It won't be so bad," he murmured. "The lake the Indians call Winnipeg is said to be full of fish and have fertile ground. . . ."

"I know." She leaned back into his warmth. "That wasn't a sad sigh, it was a contented one."

"You'll miss this place."

"Of course I will. Christian was born here."

"Someday, he might return."

"It's more likely he'll follow his father, blazing trails westward."

"Yes," he laughed. "He'll do that. Maybe he'll find what eludes me."

"The China Sea?"

"Mmm."

"Perhaps he will."

She tightened her grip on his hands. He had taken several trips deep into the interior that winter and had discovered that the "Big Water" the Indians had told him about the winter before was nothing but a large lake. He wasn't disappointed, however, for he had soon found a mighty river that poured into the lake from the west, a river the Indians called Saskatchewan. She knew that this time next year, they would head up that river in search of the sea.

It was an enormous country. Still, she knew it could not be endless. Someday, they would find that sea. Someday, they would run out of land. She could only hope that she and André would be very old and very gray when that happened. She could no longer imagine a world where there were no more trails to blaze.

He slid his hand beneath the open edge of her deerskin dress to cup her breast. Her eyes fluttered open as he teased the peak into attention. His warm lips settled on the sensitive skin behind her ear.

She lifted her hand and buried her fingers in his hair. "The men are waiting for us. . . ."

"There's another ritual to perform before we go." With his free hand, he swept her hair out of his way and gently attacked the nape of her neck. "It's a way of christening a place and making it sacred."

Her laughter dissolved into a throaty moan as he picked her up and lay her against the caribou pelt,

with their son sleeping fitfully nearby. André stripped
her of her deerskin clothing and made long, leisurely
love to her under the open sky.

Much later, Genevieve rose from her husband's
side and dressed. She picked up her babe and held
him against her breast, watching as André brushed
the nettles from his hair and clothing.

"Come, love," he said, holding out his hand. "The
world waits for us."

She took his hand. They walked westward, following
a trail of sunshine.

About the Author

Lisa Ann Verge lives with her family in Upper Montclair, New Jersey. She is the author of six historical romances, including *My Loving Enemy* and *Twice Upon a Time*. She is currently working on her next historical romance, *The Faery Bride*, which will be published in March 1996. Lisa loves hearing from her readers and you may write to her c/o Zebra Books. Please include a self-addressed stamped envelope if you wish a response.

Please turn the page for an
exciting sneak preview of
Lisa Ann Verge's
newest historical romance
THE FAERY BRIDE
to be published by Zebra Books
in March 1996.

Prologue

Wales
The Year of Our Lord 1270

Oh, it was a frightful visitor who came to us that strange Midsummer's Night.

It could have been yesterday, I remember it so well. Twilight had long blackened the crags of my lord's kingdom. The dying gasps of the pagan fires glowed red upon the hillsides. Now, I've been the keeper of this house for enough years to turn my hair full into white, yet never had a visitor come so high in the mountains in the midst of night. And none welcome for these past five years, mind you, with all the changes in the house of Graig. So you can imagine how I nearly leapt out of my skirts when someone banged at the door fit to split the wood.

I knew well enough that all the household was snug inside. They'd scurried back to their hovels from whatever pagan things they do at those fires on Midsummer's Night, like rats to their holes in a storm, not one of them brave enough to risk seeing whatever demons are set loose after the sun sets on this spirit night. And for the best, I was thinking, for I myself was hanging another sprig of St. John's wort over the doorway to the kitchens, to guard against demons and the like.

At first I thought to ignore the banging. No good news comes after dark, you know, and the master . . . well, it's no secret that the master wouldn't take kindly to having his refuge invaded by whatever the likes of man would come knocking at this cursed place in the midst of night. Faith, the master was no fit company for wolves these days—oh, it was not always that way, you know. But now I feared, even not knowing who stood behind that door, for the poor unwitting creature's health. No man deserves the full wrath of this Lord of Graig.

But you see, I'm Irish-born, Welsh-bred, and Celtic to the bone, and I found myself padding through the rushes nonetheless, to pull open the door in welcome.

An Irishman, he said he was. Snarling and snapping at the delay, and me struck dumb with the shock of it all, and wondering how to keep him quiet so as not to disturb the master in his chamber at the other end of the hall. I spoke as kindly as I could and ushered the visitor to the center hearth, offering him a bit of mead and oatcake all the way. Only then did I get a straight look at him. He was a strange spark of a man, too limber and sprightly for the wild night. There was a brightness to him, like to outshine the fire crackling in the hearth the girls work day and night to keep burning. And I found myself lingering until he barked good and loud for the mead I'd promised him.

Then the far door banged open and my heart leapt to my throat, for the master tore out of his chamber breathing fire like the dragon that's said to live amid the caves of Snowdon.

He caught sight of the visitor and I scurried out, not wanting to be burned by the hot edge of his tongue.

And faith, it's true I had no business lurking in the shadows with my ears cocked, me being no more than a servant in the house of Rhys ap Gruffydd, the lord of Graig. But I've earned my meddling, you see, having been with this house long before the present lord took his first squalling breath. I've known the family as if it were my own, I've watched through the good years and now, yes, now in the darkest. So I took little shame in peering around that splintered old wall, telling myself it was my duty to stop the master from tossing the Irishman out into the cold. We're still Welsh, after all, no matter what curse God has put upon this lord and this house. I'll see myself begging in some English village before the Graigs deny hospitality to any whose shadow darkens the door.

Oh, and the two went at it, the master and the Irishman, my master roaring his displeasure and the little man talking back with no mind to the danger to his own hide. Octavius, he said his name was, recently come of Ireland though what he was doing wandering in this place so far from sea or road is a puzzle to all. And he was having none of my master's rudeness—none at all—never did I hear any man talk to my master the way this little tattered fellow did— not even a Welshman, mind you! He even made my master pause a moment with the shame of finding such a harsh welcome in a fellow Celt's house.

Then my lord made to stomp off to that lair of his he lets no one into, when Octavius called out and made a comment on the lights he saw upon yonder lake. Ah, you know the one—the enchanted lake with the fairy isle my master has been trying years to build a castle upon. The Irishman was trying to engage my master in conversation, after all the harsh words that had passed between them! The little man began talking of fairy-rings and dancing lights and all

such things—true enough, not a strange conversation for
a Midsummer's Night, for all the people of Graig had been
talking of the old days and the fairies today—but my master
interrupted the Irishman, as I knew he would. My lord
scoffed as he does at all unChristian imaginings and mocked
the little man, which sent the Irishman to true temper at
last.

"Listen to ye, believing only what you can see," the Irishman spat. "I'd curse you for your ignorance, but for all that
leather upon your face there's no hiding that ye've been
cursed already."

Ah, and didn't that set my blood to freeze! For no one
dared to make mention of it—though all men knew of the
curse upon my master's face. One look at that masked face
set my heart to choking me. I thought my lord was to take
the creature in his two warrior's hands and strangle the life
out of him, and if it weren't for the Welsh blood rushing
thick in his veins he might have done the same. Instead he
spoke quiet like the wind in the trees before a storm—like
to make the hairs stand up on the back of my neck—and
banished the creature into the night.

Before the words were full out of my master's mouth I
made to hurry out and stop such discourtesy, and take the
Irishman aside and give him food and shelter in our kitchens,
humble though they may be. It was no fit night for man nor
hound.

But the Irishman stood his ground by the warmth of the
hearth and smiled, he did, and it was the smile that stopped
me—and the look in his bright black eyes—and my heart
dropped to my stomach, for it was Midsummer's Night, after
all, and Christian though I am, I'll not mock the old ways,
and this creature had come from the air itself.

The Irishman said that he knew a healer unlike any other,
who lived on an island off the west coast of Ireland; a
woman who had healed every ailment she'd touched. A
woman with a touch of fairy blood who could cure my

master's curse with a pass of her hands. A miracle worker, like to be a saint.

I felt the heat of my lord's anger, for hadn't he made a hundred thousand pilgrimages and seen every charlatan and witch from Myddfai to Paris, all to rid himself of this curse?

On the Aran Isles, the Irishman continued, as thick as mud to my master's silent rage. By the name of Aileen Ruadh. Aileen the Red.

Then what happened I never could be sure, for it happened so quickly I wondered if my eyes had deceived me, or if he had just moved so quickly that I'd not noticed the closing of the door. For one moment, the Irishman was there, standing as whole as you or me before the red glow of the hearth fire, and the next moment there was a sparkling around him, and suddenly there was naught there but a wisp of smoke and an echo of laughter that chilled my skin from my scalp to my toes.

After a moment, my master was off to throw open the door and send the wind howling through the house, spewing the bright red embers across the paving stones, and then he was back and glaring up at the smoke-hole while the wind tossed his black hair wild.

I saw a light come into his eyes. I'd seen that light before, long, long ago, before the curse, when the master was young and handsome and still full of blind ambition. It was like before he set off with Llywelyn, the Prince of Wales, to burn the English off Welsh soil for the last blessed time.

And a shiver went through my soul for the likes of Aileen the Red.

Chapter One

The vibrations always came first. They rumbled up against the pads of Aileen's fingertips. A dense heat seeped up with the turbulence, as if she were raising her hands against the stones of a newly-fired kiln in the chill of morning.

Aileen let her eyes drift closed. The chill of the paving stones seeped through the calfskin of her slippers. A sea breeze whirled in through the open door and battered her tunic against her shins. The stinging scent of onion, the crisp sweetness of new-dug turnips, and the tartness of fresh greens wafted up from the table where her mother sat, silent under her ministrations.

As hot as a pressing iron, it was, Aileen thought, as she drifted her hand over the length of her mother's shoulder. So hot it took more than a few gentle strokes of her hands for the wall of heat to give way beneath her fingers. Only then could she probe beyond the turbulence of pain and feel deeper inside, to the high-pitched scream of aching flesh and bone and sinew, to the root of the ache. There, it felt as if she strummed her fingers over her brother Niall's lyre, and the strings gave loose beneath her hand.

"Aye, Ma. . . ." In her mind's eye Aileen envisioned the damage; the stretches of sinew drawn overlong and frayed, stretched too far beyond their capabilities all by the will of a woman who tried to do much more than her age would allow her. "You should have told me about this sooner."

"It's not so bad as that." Her mother shifted on the bench, then gingerly rolled her shoulder through the stiffness. "It only started hurting this morning."

"Next you'll be telling me it wasn't the seaweed-gathering that got you in such a stitch. Ah—" Aileen arched a brow as her mother opened her mouth to protest. "Don't deny it, Ma, it's no use."

The words died on her mother's tongue. Truth be known, Aileen didn't need the tingling of her palms and the skill of her fairy-gift to reveal the source of *this* ache. Wasn't it like Ma to get herself in such a mess? Well past her fortieth year, and still after every gale she heaped her seaweed-basket up well over the rim, then hefted the whole on her back to drag up the steep limestone cliffs of the island of Inishmaan. Not a bit o' sense in her, and she the mother of four sons and three able daughters, healthy enough to do the work for her.

Aye, but there was no use in scolding, and in this place where Aileen's mind wandered during the healing there was little room in her heart for a sour thought. She'd save that for later, when the healing was done.

Aileen brushed a lock of her mother's fair hair off

her neck. "I'll set my hands upon you, Ma. Then we'll have naught to argue about."

She stood up to get a better angle at her mother's shoulder. A bee buzzed in through the open doorway of the hut, circled the small room with its stone walls stained a mellow brown from years of peat fires, then wound its way upon its own path until it tumbled back into the sea air. Once again, Aileen lay her hands upon her mother's shoulder. And all the world drifted away.

Gently and oh, so carefully, Aileen stroked her mother's smooth flesh. Faith, she stroked it no differently than she would stroke the fur of her cat on Sundays, when she sat upon the stoop of the house while all the islanders played games in the field just beyond, if the weather allowed. Open-handed, she stroked and stroked, until something tingling collected on the palm of her hand, and she cast the strange needling aside like so much shedded fur— then stroked again, and again, drifting off to that colorless place until all felt smooth and silky-warm beneath her hand, until the flesh cooled and the screaming ebbed to a rumbling purr.

"Och, lass. . . ."

Aileen blinked as the world rushed in upon her: The muted roar of the waves beyond the cliffs, the shout and laughter of some children down the road, the sting of peat-smoke and the mist of water bubbling too hot. Her mother was gazing up at her, her hand laying upon Aileen's own.

"Lass, lass," her mother repeated, patting her hand. " 'Tis done, the pain is all gone. You've a fine, fair gift, Aileen, you're like to outshine the skill of your own father soon enough."

"Listen to a mother's pride talking."

Aileen let her hands slip off her mother's shoulder. She oriented herself to this shadowed room and the feel of the floor against her feet, to the rush of the breeze in her ears. The islanders often spoke of her gift as a flooding of Heavenly power through her limbs, or a mystical tingling emanating from her spine—or a dozen other sensations that anyone raised half-Christian, half-pagan like herself might attribute to Otherworldly forces. A lot of nonsense, it was. Aye, it was true the gift came to her easily by virtue of her birth into this family where fairy blood still flowed. But surely, it was something any man or woman could learn to do, if they set their mind to it.

But no man or woman ever set their mind to it, didn't she know that well enough. If they did, there would never be any trouble from it all.

A tress of hair hung over Aileen's forehead and tickled the bridge of her nose; she wiped it out of her face. She poked at the fire gone too hot, and shook off the last of the lethargy which always fell upon her after a healing. "No more gathering sea-weed for you this week, Ma. It will take more than a pass of my hands to set that shoulder to right."

"God gave me two shoulders, I'll carry me burden on the other." Her mother cast Aileen a raised brow, a mirror of her daughter's own expression. "Aileen, me first-born, you'd think *you* were the mother the way you do go bossing me about. Mind you remember 'twas I who set to your linens as a babe—"

"There you go again, talking about things passed well over twenty years." Aileen tossed the poker in the basket by the wall and crossed the room to seize her cloak, hanging on a peg by the door. "For the wife of a doctor, a body would think you'd be a far better patient—"

"Where are you going, child?"

"To fetch your daughters." Aileen whirled the wool around her shoulders and set to the ties, casting her mother a strange look for the high pitch of her voice. "We can't have them prancing about in the sunshine, leaving you here with a sore shoulder and a stew to make."

"Let them race about on such a rare sunny day and leave us free of their chatter." Her mother waved a knife at the bench across her. "*You* keep me company."

Aileen let the wool slide off her back. Aye, 'twas more than a sore shoulder that had her mother calling her inside this day. She'd had an eye upon her since Aileen came in from the milking, and a nervous eye at that. And faith, here she was, blushing as if Ma had caught her kissing Sean the son of the fisher again, in the cavern just beyond the southern shore. Blushing, a woman of her age! She cursed the freckled skin that exposed her shame so—and sure, there was no reason for embarrassment: It had been a fine long time since any boy had wanted to curl into that secret cavern with *her*, no doubt of that. Then, she'd been but a girl of thirteen years and as flat-chested and boyishly hipped as all the others upon the island; but as the years passed and the other girls ripened, she'd remained as stringy and shapeless as a bean.

"What is it now, Ma?" Aileen swung the cloak from one finger. "It's been four years since Sean the fisher's son married that girl from the mainland with the long blond hair. I've no more need of hand-holding over that."

"Four years, has it been that long? You all grow up before me eyes like the rye in the fields." Her mother gestured with a knife to a pile of greens. "Set on those cabbages, would you, lass? They're next for

438 Lisa Ann Verge

the stew. And don't be giving me that silver-eyed look of yours, daughter, can't a mother want the company of her oldest child?''

Not when there's a fine bit of work to do on the thatching, and a whole field of seaweed drying on the grass, waiting to be spread over the northern field, and a ship riding off the coast of Inishmaan with boatfuls of exotic things selling right now upon the shore, no doubt.

Aileen frowned. There was never knowing her mother's mind. Her mother *was* restless and uneasy this day, she had been since she'd risen at cock's crow. Perhaps she had a vision. The Second Sight was her mother's gift from the fairies—it showed in the swirling green gaze her mother always hid from outsiders. But it had always been an uncertain magic, its secrets not revealed for the asking, and it often made Ma as uneasy as a cow within scent of a new bull.

Aileen hung the cloak upon a peg and picked up a knife, just as a shadow darkened the room. She glanced up—to see the silhouette of a man looming in the doorway.

"Aye, Ma." Aileen flattened the knife back upon the table. "We've a visitor."

Unexpected visitors were no surprise at the door to this house, but as the man stepped in out of the blinding white light, she froze for a moment. A tall one, he was, and draped in layers of clothes the likes of which she'd only seen upon the backs of the English invaders on the mainland. Bright in shimmering hues of blue, like the primroses which clung to the rocks of Inishmaan in the springtime.

"This," he began in awkward Irish, "doctor's house?"

She didn't answer, not at once. No mainlander, this, for though the mainland Irish was a garbled dialect, she could understand it fine enough. An Englishman, perhaps, but they mostly kept to themselves, the English—and such a finely-dressed one as this would surely send a lackey to do his bidding. There was that ship anchored in Galway Bay. . . . There was no telling where it came from, or who sailed upon it. And any man who asked the mainlanders for a doctor would be told to come here, to the house of Conaire of Inishmaan.

An outsider. Deep down, her insides rumbled in unease. A gift and a curse, it was, Da's skill. It brought too much of the world to her door.

"Need . . . doctor." He motioned east, in the direction of the path that led to the shore. "Man hurt . . ."

The stew popped and splattered a sizzle of broth over the peat. A briny breeze gusted, skidding a few turnip peels across the table, and upending a basket of wool set aside for spinning just beside the door. Aileen glanced at her mother, expecting her to right the tumble of wool, but her mother sat still with her fingers curled around the cutting-knife, a crease of worry deep on her brow.

Then Aileen realized that Ma stared at the stranger as transfixed as herself, without making a move to offer the man hospitality.

"This is the doctor's house," Aileen said swiftly, as she paced to the shadows to pour some honey-mead from a flagon into a cup, and to seize the last oak cake with a bit of linen. What was it about outsiders that caused her insides to twist in unease? They even *smelled* different, without the sea air scouring them clean every day. Above the scent of the stew meat bubbling in the pot over the fire, she smelled him, some sickly-sweet perfume—exotic and unnatural.

"My father is off tending the cows on Connemara,"

she said, holding out the cup and the oatcake. "He won't be back until nightfall."

The man glanced at the offerings, and then took the cup of mead—making a shrugging motion with his other sleeve. It was then that Aileen noticed that the man had only one hand.

A wave of shame washed over her. Aye, but she was being a foolish one, condemning him without knowing his like. He looked honest enough, clear-eyed, open-faced, and how much of a threat to two strong women was a single one-handed man?

"You say," she said slowly, "that there's a man hurt?"

The man nodded over the rim of the cup, which he drained with little effort. He nudged the cup toward the path to the shore. "Man hurt . . . bad."

"Well, then." She reached for her cloak. "You'll have to make do with the doctor's daughter."

The bench scraped against the paving stones. Her mother made a strange gasping sound and clasped hands against her belly. Hefting a bag of herbs and linens on the table, Aileen cast her mother a queer glance. Aileen always took her father's charges when her father was out and about. And this stranger hadn't asked for *her*, as some of the mainlanders brazenly did with a hush in their voice and a shuffle in their gait as if she'd turn them into frogs with the strike of a single glance. The stranger didn't know the Irish very well, and there was a chance he'd heard Da's name and not the whispered tale of Aileen the Red. Moreover, there was a chance a man lay dying upon the shore whilst she grappled with her own suspicions.

As she ruffled through the bag, making sure she had all she might need, she spoke quietly in the thick Inishmaan dialect so the stranger could not understand. "You didn't even offer him honey-mead, Ma, now what's he going to think of us?"

"He's an *outsider*."

"Aye, and what of it?" Aileen swiftly counted the linens. "He's not the first outsider I've set to heal."

The man clattered the cup upon the table and smiled at the two of them as they stared in surprise. He wandered out the door and waited just outside. Aileen returned to her counting, lifting a small linen of herbs and sniffing it before she nodded and tucked it back into the bag.

"You'll be careful, won't you, child?" Her mother leaned over and righted the basket of wool. "Your gift . . . it's fine, but powerful child, so powerful—"

"Don't you think I know it, Ma?" Aileen knew well the price for revealing her gift—she'd learned it the day she'd discovered it, at a *feis* upon the mainland, among too many disbelievers. "I'm not like little Dairine, don't you know, not knowing better than to stay away from the edge of the cliffs."

"Och, don't I know it, no child more practical than you ever came from my womb." Her mother shook her head. "I'm full of foolishness today. Your Da has been away on Connemara for too long, and I grow as skittish as an old woman. Still, you'll be forty summers, lass, before I'll stop worrying about ye. That's the burden and the joy of being a mother. You'll know it someday."

Nay. Aileen dug her fingernails into the strap of her bag of herbs as she hefted it upon her shoulder. There wasn't a man left on the island unmarried over the age of eighteen, and there'd never be a mainlander brave enough to look sideways at the likes of Aileen the Red. *I won't know the joy of being a mother, Ma—I never will.*

"Still hunting for grandchildren, eh?" Aileen paced into the shadows, tugged the flagon of mead off the hook on the wall, and weighed it in her hand. "Look to your other daughters, there'll be no husband for me. I've told you a dozen times, I'm going to build myself a little hut by the lee of the cliffs, like old widow Pegeen, and make my way with my healing like Da. I'll have no man bossing me about and telling me what to do, I'll live me own life, thank you very much."

Aye, that's what she wanted; a peaceful hut in a quiet place, where she could take care of Ma and Da in their old age, with the way her brothers and sisters were talking, always wanting to leave the island. She wanted to stay here, safe, where she could be alone and no one could stare at her and mock her or fear her—or even revere her—for this oddity that set her apart from the world.

"Life does not always take the path we've chosen, Aileen."

"Have you been drinking too much of the new honey-mead, Ma? You're sounding as maudlin as old Seamus in his cups." She tucked the bladder of mead into her bag. "Why should my life be any different? I want it to be so; it shall be so."

"Och, wouldn't it be nice if the world turned upon a girl's whim? What a simple place the world would be, then." Her mother glanced out to the wide expanse of the island, and beyond the mist of the sea, lost for a moment in the horizon beyond the stranger's shoulders. "But there are greater powers, Aileen, with wills of there own, and there's no telling how they'll weave the path of your life."

That set Aileen to stopping and staring, but this time when Ma turned her swirling green eyes upon her, she did it with the softest of smiles quivering on her lips.

"Och, don't go listening too deeply to me, Aileen, I'm all about today. Go." She kissed her daughter's cheek and nudged her toward the portal. "There's someone down there in need of your healing."

"I'll be back," Aileen murmured, whirling one last time to see her mother's pale face with its quivering smile, "in time to help you with the spinning."

Aye, Ma was in a fix today, no doubt about it, as full of teary sentiment as a woman just given birth. Aileen shook her head with the foolishness of it all and set off to follow the stranger's sure and long-legged pace.

'Twas thatching-time, and long ropes of braided hay stretched golden across the fields. Below the sheer cliffs, Galway Bay licked the ledges of rock with tongues of froth, siphoning up thinning whorls of sea mist. The milky vapor hugged the lower part of the island in a sheer white brightness. Aileen filled her lungs with the clean salt-spray as she descended the path toward the shore. It was a rare, fine day. She'd long convinced herself that the Heaven in the clouds the priest spoke of must be very like Inishmaan on the morning after a gale.

And there was another thing to lift her spirits; on one part of the path she caught sight of a crescent mark dug into the mud. The fairies had been here this day, playing ball amid the rocks. When she returned home, she'd tell Dairine about this, and wind a fine yarn of a story around it, to get the wild young lass to settle before going to bed this evening.

The coarse sand sank beneath her *pampooties* as they finally reached the shore. Through the shifting sheets of mist, she caught sight of a single boat dragged up close to the cliff face, and a man pacing beside it.

Her steps faltered. A big man, this, as big as the one who had fetched her from her home. He seemed larger, though, with the sea wind slapping his cloak away from his body as if he felt no cold, and the mists swirling around him as if he were some kind of Otherworldly visitor stepping out from between the veils. He ceased his pacing as he glimpsed them through the mist, then stormed toward them with all the force of a charging bull. 'Twas then that she saw the mask, a leather mask tanned night-black and gleaming with sea-spray, slashing across half of his face, from forehead to jaw, making him look all the more like some inhuman thing.

Her throat closed in the grip of an uncertain fear.

Her guide gave way for the man. The man stopped several paces before her, enough for only a breath of mist to pass between them. Sharp eyes the color of blue winter ice scoured her form, one from the shadows of the mask. She stilled the sudden urge to reach up and tuck a wayward sprig of her red hair back into the braid which snagged down her back. It would do no good; her hair never stayed in its bounds, even in the calmest of weather, and now the sea-breeze tugged it wild about her face. Yet still, he glared, a harsh, lingering look that made her feel as if he burned the clothes from her body and found her lacking.

And what was this? Aye, so she was no beauty, and aye, she didn't look like much of a doctor. She tilted her chin and returned the look in kind. She was well used to not being accepted for what she really was.

And *he*—he was a warrior—there was no doubt about it. She'd recognized the sure gait and the arrogant cast of his broad shoulders, before she'd even noticed the beaten bronze scabbard of the sword hanging from his belt. The mask, too, spoke of a warrior's vanity. She'd seen his kind paint themselves up with blue woad and fancy themselves with chain mail and embroidery before they went off to do their killing. A battle he'd waged, no doubt, and killed enough innocents to satisfy his blood-lust for the morning. Now he brought a wounded man here, one of his own, hoping to patch him together so he could fight another useless fight on another bloody day.

And she wondered why she was mustering so much hate for a man who'd not yet said a single word.

"You are Aileen the Red."

It was a statement, not a question, and he spoke the Irish as purely as any mainlander. A shiver shook her spine but she stifled the chill. Aye, those rumblings of distrust had been right. So he knew her name, and by the look in his eye, he knew the story behind it. She mustered the full of her bile.

"Aye, and what of it?" She jerked her chin toward the one-handed man. "He asked for a doctor. My father couldn't be here—so you'll have to settle for me."

"*You* are the great healer." His lips, firmly formed right up to the corner which nudged the edge of the mask, curled in bitter scorn. "You, a bit of a girl."

That gaze scoured her again, from head to toe, and she cursed the wind which chose that moment to shift direction and flatten her woolen tunic against her body, leaving little to a man's imagination—and a man needed an imagination to see any curves in the lines of her body, to see anything but bones with a bit of flesh on them.

"It's clear *you* are not the wounded man," she

said, returning his gaze flame by flame, "though I'd welcome the man who'd do some damage to your pride."

"You don't look like you'd have the stomach to pluck a bird for dinner."

"But it's not dinner I'm making here, is it?" She peered around him and saw no one else. She set her gaze upon the boat pulled up on the shore. "I'll see to your wounded well enough, for it's either me or no one."

Then I'll see you off this island—we don't welcome killers on Inishmaan. She brushed by him, and it was like brushing by a ridge of limestone. She stilled the urge to massage her own bruised shoulder—she'd not give him the satisfaction. She'd do her healing—masking the true nature of it, as she always did—then she'd return to the warmth of her mother's house, and curse this man and his ilk for their arrogance and their bloodlust and their scorn.

The boat was cocked away from her so she could not see the inside till she seized the rim and peered over. Her pack slid off her shoulder, snagging the collar of her tunic. She clutched it to her arm until her knuckles turned white. Nothing but coils of hemp lingered in the belly of the boat.

A wave crashed upon the rocks near the edge of the cove, vaulting sea-spray over the sand.

She swiveled her heel into the muck. Her one-handed guide was staring at his master with an odd look in his eye. He muttered something in a garbled tongue—a strange language, like Irish, but spoken as if through a mouthful of water. The warrior ignored him and kept his gaze fixed with piercing intensity upon her. His hands curled into fists at his sides.

Fear froze her feet to the sand. A thousand stories

flooded her mind of pirates who seized women from the shores of Connemara, women who were never seen again. She'd heard the tales a hundred thousand times in her youth, and as she grew she scoffed at them as stories meant to keep young ones abed. Even as terror seeped cold into her blood she scolded herself for her foolishness. What would a pirate have with *her*, with all her thin and awkward height, her plain face, her tern's-nest of hair. Perhaps that was why this warrior stood so silent before her, brooding and fierce, eyeing her figure and wondering if he could find a price in some exotic port for such a shapeless, freckled bone of a woman.

What a joke it would be upon Aileen the Red, she thought with cold shame, to be cast back by the pirates in disdain like a rabbit too thin to be worth the work of slaughtering.

Pride rose in her, and she welcomed it to stem the thick seepage of fear. "The tide is coming," she snapped. "Are you to lead me to your wounded, or are we to stand here until this sand is beneath the sea?"

The guide said something again, but the warrior shook his head once, hard. Then he came to her, his boots sure in the sand, his black hair rising above his shoulders by the force of the sea breeze and floating around a face that could have been carved from the stone of Inishmaan.

The scent of him filled her lungs: Leather. Heat. The rim of the boat dug into her thighs. Such eyes as his had never known the meaning of pity.

He reached behind her to heft up a roll of hemp, then seized her in a grip of steel.

"So be it, Aileen the Red. It is you or no one." The first coil of rope scraped her neck. "Say goodbye to Inishmaan."